LADY COME HOME

EIGHTH BOOK IN THE BRIGANDSHAW CHRONICLES

PETER RIMMER

ABOUT PETER RIMMER

~

Peter Rimmer was born in London, England, and grew up in the south of the city where he went to school. After the Second World War, and aged eighteen, he joined the Royal Air Force, reaching the rank of Pilot Officer before he was nineteen. At the end of his National Service, he sailed for Africa to grow tobacco in what was then Rhodesia, now Zimbabwe.

The years went by and Peter found himself in Johannesburg where he established an insurance brokering company. Over 2% of the companies listed on the Johannesburg Stock Exchange were clients of Rimmer Associates. He opened branches in the United States of America, Australia and Hong Kong and travelled extensively between them.

Having lived a reclusive life on his beloved smallholding in Knysna, South Africa, for over 25 years, Peter passed away in July 2018. He has left an enormous legacy of unpublished work for his family to release over the coming years, and not only them but also his readers from around the world will sorely miss him. Peter Rimmer was 81 years old.

ALSO BY PETER RIMMER

~

STANDALONE NOVELS

All Our Yesterdays

Cry of the Fish Eagle

Just the Memory of Love

Vultures in the Wind

~

NOVELLA

Second Beach

~

THE ASIAN SAGAS

Bend with the Wind (Book 1)

Each to His Own (Book 2)

~

THE BRIGANDSHAW CHRONICLES

(The Rise and Fall of the Anglo Saxon Empire)

Echoes from the Past (Book 1)

Elephant Walk (Book 2)

Mad Dogs and Englishmen (Book 3)

To the Manor Born (Book 4)

On the Brink of Tears (Book 5)

Treason If You Lose (Book 6)

Horns of Dilemma (Book 7)

This book is dedicated to Kim Rimmer,
Peter and Kathy Rimmer's baby son who died at birth.

LADY COME HOME

First published in Great Britain in July 2020 by

KAMBA PUBLISHING, United Kingdom

10 9 8 7 6 5 4 3 2 1

Peter Rimmer asserts the moral right to be identified as the author of this work.

PART I

MAY 1950 – "SHIPS THAT PASS IN THE NIGHT"

1

The rattle of the ship's anchor going out woke Livy Johnston, breaking the anguish of her dream. There was light coming through the cabin porthole. Pamela Lavington, across from Livy, had her legs hanging out of her bunk. The legs were thick round the calves, the feet small and podgy.

"What time is it, Pam? Why have the engines stopped?"

"We're in port. Out in the bay of Lourenço Marques. The harbour must be full. You were gnashing your teeth again."

Livy got out of her bunk and looked through the porthole. The outside glass was covered in sea salt. The portholes were bolted shut along B deck – only the expensive cabins on the deck above had portholes that opened.

"I can see a church spire," said Livy, slightly bored. "More like the spire of a cathedral it's so big. The Portuguese have been here for centuries. Vasco da Gama. Read about it before I left London. The Portuguese were trading with Africa long before we got to Rhodesia... Or was it Bartholomew Diaz? Portuguese anyway. This is the capital of Mozambique."

"One more port, Beira, then we're on the train. Can't wait to see my fiancé. Is yours meeting the boat at Beira?"

"Doesn't have any money. He's a learner assistant on a tobacco farm in Macheke. Bottom of the ladder."

"Roger has his own farm."

"You told me, Pam. More than once. Jeremy is meeting me at Salisbury railway station."

"Why are you shivering, Livy?"

"Fear, I suppose. We're almost there. It seemed a good idea in London."

"Now you're awake we can go up to breakfast. We won't be able to go ashore until we sail into harbour. Two days in port to open the hatches and lift out the cargo for Lourenço Marques. I asked one of the officers at dinner last night. Why do the officers change their tables? His name was Michael. I know all of them now. Six weeks on a boat. Tilbury seems ages ago."

"How did you meet your fiancé?"

"I haven't met him yet. He's a friend of my brothers."

"*And* he proposed?"

"Not yet. I just call him my fiancé. There's a terrible shortage of English girls in Rhodesia. Andrew and Colin promised to find me a husband when they left for Rhodesia after the war. They were in the army."

"I've learnt more about who you are in the last two minutes than the whole of the voyage... Who you are inside."

"I don't like to talk about myself. I'm also a little nervous. We've been writing to each other for ages. Roger is a bit older than me. Well, he's thirty-seven. Never had a wife. Now he's got his own farm he wants a family. Of course, he's seen my picture."

After getting back into bed, Livy lay on her back looking at the ceiling. 'Wait till he sees those legs,' she said to herself.

"He has a moustache," said Pamela, interrupting her smile.

"Was he in the war?"

"No, he wasn't. I'm not sure why. Never mind. My brothers are sure he's a good man. A good man. That's all that matters. Good character is more important than good looks."

"Did they tell you that?"

"How long have you known your fiancé?"

"We met for two days while he was in London... At least we screwed each other."

"Livy! You should wash your mouth out with soap and water."

"Whatever for? It's the bright light in my tunnel... Are you by any chance a virgin?"

"Of course I am. All well brought up girls wait until they are married. Why girls are married all in white. They are pure. Pure of mind and pure of heart. That's my motto."

"I lost count."

"What of, Livy?"

"The number of men I've slept with. I'm an artist. Lived in an art community in Chelsea. Free love. It was wonderful."

"I don't know what you're talking about. Please Livy, don't say any more." Pamela got out of bed and walked barefoot to the porthole. "Oh, yes. You're right. What a beautiful church. The Portuguese are Catholic. Will you come ashore with me, Livy? I can't go on my own. We can visit the church. That spire is so tall."

"If you don't mind being in the company of a sinner."

"God forgives all sinners when they repent."

"But I'm not going to repent, Pam. I like my life just as it is."

"You'll have to repent before you are married. Go to confession."

"Oh, Pam. You and I live in different worlds."

"We won't live in worlds anymore. We're going to be the wives of tobacco farmers. Who must keep up appearances. Can't let the side down. There are so few of us in Rhodesia. I'm very proud to be British. We have to show them our British way of life. Our Christian principles... Why are you yawning, Livy?"

"I'm hungry."

"You've stopped shivering."

"So I have."

When Livy got up she pulled on the shorts that hugged the light curves of her bottom. The white, sleeveless shirt hung over bare breasts. She was ready to go down to the dining room. As an afterthought, she slipped into a pair of sandals. Instinctively, Livy looked in the small mirror on the wall. Her skin was tanned a rich brown in the sun. Crispin Dane told her to build up her tan slowly or the tropical sun would burn her skin. Crispin Dane had a cabin to himself with a porthole that opened. Whatever happened with Jeremy Crookshank she would always remember the journey.

TESSA, her Chelsea flatmate, with Jeanne Pétain, James Coghlan and Ben Brown of the Nouvelle Galerie had seen her off at Tilbury Docks on a cold spring morning in April, the railway lines along the pier wet with rain. The *Carnarvon Castle* had sailed out of London at half past eleven in the morning, Livy standing at the rail, waving at her friends down below on the pier. Jeanne owned the gallery that had sold her painting of *Pussy Cat* for four hundred pounds the week before. Livy had painted the cat in a tropical forest she copied from Henri Rousseau to get the feel of it. As they pulled away from the pier, the paper streamers thrown from the ship pulled taut and broke. She knew no one on board. All her friends were down below waving goodbye. None of her family had come to see her off. She was going to write to them when she reached Rhodesia. It was going to be easier to explain afterwards. When the tugs let the ship loose, the ship's engines throbbing under her feet, she had gone down to her cabin. Her trunk had been sent on board earlier after she had gone through customs, her new passport stamped for the first time. She knew the name of her cabinmate from the passenger list.

"Hello, I'm Livy," she said.

"Pamela Lavington. How nice to meet you. Isn't the weather awful? Have you sailed on a boat before?"

"Not even a dinghy."

"Your first trip?"

"Never left England. There's a swimming pool with a bar on the top deck. That's my trunk under the bunk. Do you want to go up for a drink? Have you seen any nice men getting on board?"

"I'm engaged to be married."

"So am I. Sort of. Jeremy bought my ticket. Never look a gift horse in the mouth. My friends think I'm nuts to leave London."

LIVY'S AFFAIR with Crispin Dane began in Las Palmas, their first port of call. She had caught his eye the night before at dinner. It was the first time she wore the dress picked out with Tessa in a small boutique off the

Portobello Road. The back of the dress was slit open right down to her bum.

"You can't spend six weeks on your own, Livy. That one will do the trick. Shipboard romances are the best. They are not intended to last. With that back and no bra you can't fail, darling."

"You think I should misbehave?"

"I know you too well."

"It is rather nice."

"Thanks to Jeanne and the Nouvelle Galerie, you can afford it. Oh to be young on a nice sea voyage."

Crispin was the only one on board apart from the ship's officers to catch her eye. He was older, sophisticated, with naughty eyes. The complete opposite of Jeremy. When she went ashore with Pamela trying her best to make a friend of the other girl in her cabin, he had followed them to the nearest hotel. He was obviously on his own. Whether he had a wife at home was none of Livy's business. They had gone to the bar where Pamela ordered a lemonade. Livy had found out the first night Pamela did not drink alcohol.

"My mother says it leads us into sin," said Pamela, looking at Livy's gin.

"A little gin and a little sin can go a long way."

Livy had ordered a double gin and tonic. The barman spoke enough English to give them their drinks.

"Would you mind if I joined you two? We're off the same boat. Can I buy you your drinks? Where are you getting off? Most of the passengers are going to South Africa."

"Beira," said Livy, leaning slightly forward to drop open the front of her dress. "Then we catch the train to Salisbury."

"Well I never. Where I'm going. I live in Salisbury. I thought you were on some kind of assisted passage to South Africa where they're screaming out for white immigrants. What are you going to do in Rhodesia?"

"Get married," said Pamela, trying to cut Crispin out of the conversation. It was clear to Livy that her cabinmate did not consider it proper to be picked up by men in a bar.

"What a lovely coincidence," she said. "I'd love for you to buy me a drink. It's a double, I'm afraid. Can you afford it?"

"I drink doubles myself. Are you getting married, Miss...? My name is Crispin Dane. I saw you at dinner last night."

"Livy. Short for Olivia. Yes, I suppose I am. It was all in a hurry. Jeremy was flying back to the farm two days after we met in London. I knew his brother Paul, you see. We'll just have to see if it all works out when I get to Rhodesia. Are you married, Crispin?"

"Not anymore."

"Divorced. There's so much of it after the war. Do you know, in London couples are living together? I'm going to suggest something like that at first to Jeremy. Does that sound awful?"

"Living in sin!" said Pamela, turning back to their conversation which she was trying to ignore.

"I'm sorry, Pam. Life has changed since the war. Crispin, this is Pam Lavington. We share a two-berth cabin. Who do you share with?"

"Myself. I'm on A deck."

"Are you rich?"

"So-so... I'm not divorced. My wife died in a car accident a few years ago. Why I went out to Rhodesia."

"I'm sorry... Any children?"

"She was pregnant at the time of the accident. I get a bit lonely. I hope you don't mind me butting in, Miss Lavington. Who are you about to marry? Rhodesia is such a small community most of the whites know each other."

"Roger Crumpshaw. He's a farmer in Marandellas."

"Old Crumpshaw! I had no idea he was getting married. Where did you two meet? He's one of our confirmed bachelors. Well done."

"He's a friend of my brothers. Do you know Andrew and Colin?"

"I'm afraid not. Crumpshaw comes into Salisbury when his tobacco is selling on the floors. Stays at Meikles. He and I have had quite a few evenings together. Old Crumpy drinks doubles with the best of us. Good chap at a party. Well I never. What are you drinking there, Pam?"

"Lemonade."

"Roger will have something to say about that. When in Rome, you know. We all drink too many sundowners. Not much else to do in the bush when the sun goes down. I've been on holiday for three months in England. Well I never. Sly old fox. See what happens when I turn my back... Double Bells, barman. On the rocks. Would you two care to have lunch with me in the hotel? The ship's food is all right but you need a change."

"I'd love to," said Livy.

"When did you last see Roger, Pam?"

"We haven't met. My brothers have arranged my marriage. They say he's a good man."

"That he is. That he is. Well I'll be buggered."

"Please, Mr Dane. I can't abide bad language."

"I'm so sorry. Slipped out."

Livy, giggling, had to turn her face away and look out the window at the sea and the *Carnarvon Castle* moored just off the shore in the bay, the forward crane unloading cargo to a lighter. When she had herself back under control she turned back to the bar. Their eyes met. Livy knew then what was going to happen.

"Don't you want your breakfast, Pam? You've never missed a meal the entire voyage."

"No wonder all the men look at you. I wouldn't dare dress like that."

"You should try. These last six weeks have been quite an education for both of us."

"I'm going to miss you when we get to Beira."

"Why should you? Life works in strange ways. Don't forget Macheke is only a few miles from Marandellas. In Rhodesia, Crispin says that's next door neighbours."

"What are you going to do about Crispin?"

"Nothing. Why should I?"

"I don't understand you, Livy."

"Don't try. I don't understand myself. Life's to be lived. We were both on a ship out at sea. What else were we going to do?"

At breakfast they felt the throb of the ship's engines coming up through their feet. Again Livy felt a jolt of fear mixed with excitement. She told herself she was going into uncharted territory in more ways than one. Would Jeremy be the same person at home? Would Crispin? They all had their friends in Rhodesia. She had no one other than Pamela Lavington she could hope to call a friend. Crispin was a lover.

Lovers were always different. There wouldn't be a Tessa to go to when she got herself into trouble.

"I wonder what they're doing?"

"Who, Livy?"

"My friends in Chelsea. Do you think they've forgotten me?"

"Probably. Once you are out of people's lives, they have other things to think about... Feels like we're about to dock. You can't go ashore looking like that."

"Why ever not?"

"Don't you want to look at the cathedral? Michael says it is a cathedral."

"Bully for Michael. All right then. I'll put on a dress. But I won't wear a bra. Crispin's coming with us. It'll be our last trip ashore together. At Beira it's off to the boat train and up to Salisbury. Takes a whole day climbing up from the coast to the Rhodesian highveld as they call it. Did you know Salisbury is five thousand feet above sea level? Why the climate is so congenial to us Europeans. When you get down into the Zambezi Valley it gets hot. Frank Brigandshaw told me."

"Who is Frank Brigandshaw?"

"Stayed with me and Tessa, sleeping on the couch in the lounge. The couch pulled out into a bed at night. All very convenient. In Chelsea there were a lot of lost souls looking for a bed. Artists coming to London to try their luck. Frank found his own flat soon after. Repaid Tessa by getting two of her paintings sold to Cohen Wells, the big advertising agents. Frank had something to do with them. Did his National Service with Zachariah Cohen, the son of one of the owners. The paintings are still hanging in the Cohen Wells offices. Put my friend Tessa on the map. You never know when a stray is going to repay a kindness. The Buddhists call it karma. The good you get for the good you do. Also works the other way if you are nasty to people."

"Will Crispin mind if I join you?"

"Of course not. He's a friend of Roger Crumpshaw. He expects you to come. Isn't old Crumpy meeting you in Beira?"

"Please don't call him old Crumpy... I've got butterflies in my stomach. Do you think he'll like me? It's all going to be so strange."

"Of course he will. You'll get used to the colonial life. Your brothers are there. Your mother's coming out. One big family. The Brigandshaw family come from Rhodesia. The first Brigandshaw was in Rhodesia before Cecil Rhodes. Before the country was called Southern Rhodesia after Rhodes. I think Frank said he was a big game hunter. Made his fortune shooting elephants for their ivory. Rhodesia is teeming with elephant. Frank and Brian Tobin made a living out of shooting crocodiles in the Zambezi Valley and selling the skins to an Italian shoe maker. Now they're running a public relations firm in London. A bit like me in reverse."

"Do you miss your friends, Livy?"

"I'll make new ones. That's what life is all about. Making new friends. Having an adventure. You can't sit doing the same thing year after year. It's boring... I'm going to have some more toast and marmalade and then the three of us are going ashore."

"Why didn't Crispin change his table in the dining room to sit with us?"

"You don't move away from the captain's table when you're invited, Pam. Whatever would people think?"

Across the dining room, Livy caught Crispin's eye and mouthed 'three of us'.

"Didn't he know, Livy?"

"He does now. You've been a good friend to me."

"When I'm married it'll be different."

"I'll bet it will."

Wherever they arrived on the journey that called at the Ascension Islands and St Helena as well as the South African ports along the coast, Crispin knew just the right place to go. For Livy, it was part of his charm. The sophisticated man of the world. The cathedral of Lourenço Marques, named after a saint whose name Livy had forgotten by the time Crispin found the 'right spot', proved to be an evocative experience of Christianity in the far reaches of Africa that affected her wellbeing far more deeply than she had expected. The great columns towering up towards heaven, the windows rising with them rich in colour in a majesty of art, had her gawping with awe and wonder at so much beauty. Afterwards, the three of them settled down comfortably at a table on the pavement and watched the people of every colour and hue walk by.

"They have the best Portuguese wine here," said Crispin. "LM, as the Rhodesians prefer to call it, is the capital of Mozambique and the

Portuguese like to show it off. With the wine, rather like potato crisps in an English pub, they bring us bowls of prawns and peri-peri chicken livers with little sticks, all on the house. The prawns come freely out of the Indian Ocean, the biggest prawns in the world. A land of plenty. The Portuguese have been here for hundreds of years. They traded for gold with the old Kingdom of Monomotapa we now call Rhodesia. Some say the Zimbabwe ruins came from the time of the Monomotapa kingdom. Others say it was the Arabs. The Portuguese and the Arabs vied with each other for trade with the interior. They traded gold and people. Slaves. Human traffic before the Europeans found out selling slaves to the New World were more lucrative than gold. My three small gold mines in Northern Mashonaland are built around ancient diggings. They didn't have the machinery to get down deep enough to follow the veins of gold. Unlike the Witwatersrand, where Johannesburg was founded, the veins are fickle, petering out more often than not. There is gold all over Rhodesia but in small pockets. I got lucky the first time. The last one isn't so good... But here we are. Pamela, can't I tempt you to a small glass of delicious Portuguese wine to toast our wonderful trip together? To toast your forthcoming marriage to Roger Crumpshaw. I'm sure Roger won't mind you drinking, whatever your mother might have said about the sinful ways of liquor. When in Rome, Pam. Indeed, when in Rome. It's a tradition in Rhodesia to drink. You might even call it the national pastime after tennis and cricket... Just a half glass to try with the prawns... Waiter!"

In surprisingly good Portuguese, to Livy's surprise, Crispin ordered the wine. When the bottle came it was on a tray with three tall glasses. On another tray a second waiter, wearing a red fez on his head, brought the bigger tray of 'snacks'.

"Goodness, Crispin, this looks more like a full meal," said Livy.

"Enjoy yourselves. The bounty of the sea is all around us. Now, Pam, how about a taste of wine for the toast?"

"Oh, all right. You're sure Roger won't mind?"

"I'm quite certain... So a toast," said Crispin, filling up all three glasses. "To a journey we will all look back on happily. Thank you both for making my journey home so pleasant. To our futures. To your health. May the gods always smile on you."

Livy watched Crispin drain his glass almost to the bottom, then throw the last on the floor.

"A libation to the gods, people. Always give the last, in an important glass, to the gods. An ancient Greek tradition... I always imagine Socrates making his libation to the gods. In the good old days before they made him drink the hemlock... How's the wine, Pam?"

"It's delicious."

"That's my girl."

Eating prawns by pulling the shells apart and putting the bits delicately on the table, Livy watched Pam sip at her wine, the sips growing bigger.

"Throw the shells at your feet on the floor," said Crispin. "It's a tradition. They find it easier at the end of the day to sweep them up with a broom off the floor and shovel the debris into a bin. People have been known to eat twelve dozen prawns while drinking beer. The prawns cost the establishment very little. There are so many hawkers trying to sell them... Try the peri-peri chicken livers. They are my favourites. They make you drink wine."

When Crispin filled up her glass, he filled up Pam's without a word of complaint. At the end of her second glass Pam was eating the prawns in her fingers with the rest of them. People at other tables were throwing their shucks on the floor. Pam began to drop hers under the table, the juice from the shellfish sliding down the corners of her mouth. She was smiling at everyone. A second bottle of wine arrived with another wooden bowl full of prawns. The third time Crispin filled Pam's glass Livy gave him a look of warning. Pam ate prawns and sipped her wine, her eyes shining. Then she had a go at the chicken livers, dispensing with the small wooden sticks. Livy thought the wine had the taste of sweet grapes without being cloyingly sweet. Livy was glad she had eaten the extra piece of toast at breakfast. The wine was going to her head. Crispin, watching Pam, was enjoying himself doing 'Old Crumpy' a favour by introducing his fiancée to wine.

"Roger loves a good bottle of wine, Pam."

Pam ignored Crispin's explanation. The peri-peri had stained her lips red, making her face more attractive. Pam did not wear make-up, another product of the devil, according to her mother.

When they took Pam back to the ship they both helped her down to the cabin. Livy hoisted her up into the bunk before going back to Crispin's cabin with its open porthole. They made love for half an hour.

After having fallen asleep they went up on deck for a swim in the pool. The bar was open.

"You want a drink, Livy?"

"Better make it a single, I suppose. I'm still tight from the wine... Another beautiful day..."

"Roger will thank me. Took to wine like a duck to water. Just shows you."

When he went up to the bar, leaving Livy well satiated after their lovemaking sprawled in a deck chair, she heard him order a double gin and tonic and a double Bells. The man had class. She smiled to herself.

"In for a penny, in for a pound," he said, handing her a glass.

When he smiled at her there was a faraway look in his eyes Livy had not seen before.

Later they both went for a swim in the pool, the sea water warm like a balm.

"Care for a game of deck tennis, Livy?"

"Why not?... You think she'll be all right in the cabin?"

"Sleeping like a baby. She can't live on a farm in Rhodesia without having a drink."

Taking her hand, he walked her to the small upper deck with its court marked out. The quoit was hung on the tall post of the net. With the ship in dock no one was playing. Facing him, she watched the quoit come at her over the net, hitting the deck with a thud.

"Told you not to make it a double," she said.

After ten minutes running around they were hot and went down to the deck below for a swim. Livy could still see the spire of the cathedral rising high into the sky.

2

When the *Carnarvon Castle* reached the port of Beira the next day their voyage was over, England far away. Livy went up on deck after finishing her packing, having given the steward her bags and cabin trunk to move from her cabin to where she would find them in the customs shed. She stood looking into the interior rising behind the town of Beira. It was hazy with heat in the great distance where she was going. There were people milling around on the docks, waiting for the passengers to come ashore.

"Can you see him, Pam?" she said.

"Photographs can be deceptive. I'll just wave in case he has recognised me from my photograph."

"He's there all right," said Crispin, joining them. "The chap with the bush hat." Crispin waved. The man down below on the dock in the wide-brimmed bush hat waved back.

"He's recognised me. Good old Crumpy."

"Has he come by car?" asked Pamela.

"Probably not. Most of the road to Rhodesia is strip. Two strips of tar for the tyres. The train's much easier. Too many wild animals along the road at night in the interior."

"What's he doing?" asked Livy.

"Waving his hands. The time-honoured expression of 'where is she?'"

"Point her out, Crispin."

"He's so old," said Pam, ever so quietly, so only Livy could hear as Crispin, looking at Roger, pointed to his right where Livy and Pam were standing looking down from the ship's rail.

The main gangplank was going down. Trunks and suitcases were coming up from the cabins deep in the ship ready to be taken on shore. The hatches were coming off for the cranes to dip into the cargo and pull up what was destined for Beira. Roger took off his hat in excitement and waved it up at them on deck.

"I love you, Pam," came up to them, where they were standing with their hands on the rails.

"Did you hear that, Livy? He loves me. Now it doesn't matter he's a bit old. At least he isn't bald."

Pam waved back frantically as Livy watched. Livy had a bad feeling which she kept to herself. Everyone on board and down on the docks were bustling. Livy found Beira was hotter in the morning than Lourenço Marques. They were nearer the equator, according to Livy's calculations. She looked sideways at Crispin. He was looking at her as well. Both knew it was the end of their affair. She had a warm feeling of having done nothing wrong.

"Can't we go down?" said Pam in her excitement.

"Come on," said Crispin, putting his hat on his head: it seemed to Livy all the men wore hats against the sun.

When they went down, Roger was waiting a little back from the bustle that had gathered round the foot of the gang plank. He was short, Livy thought. Short and powerful. Big hairy arms tanned a rich brown by the sun. He was wearing khaki shorts and a khaki shirt. His eyes were blue. Crispin stood back as the two girls went towards him.

"Pam! This is so wonderful. My dreams come true."

Then, as she feared up on the deck of the ship, Roger Crumpshaw ran forward and gave her a hug. When Crispin had pointed to his right, he had pointed at both of them.

"Hello, Crumpshaw you old fox. Let me introduce you. This here is Pamela Lavington."

Extracting herself from the strong grasp of Roger Crumpshaw, Livy turned round. Pam was crying.

"Of course it is. What am I thinking hugging your girlfriend, Crispin?

How are you, you old bugger? Now make room for the real hug of my life. She's crying with happiness. Just look at her. It's me, Pamela. Your Roger. You're just as Andrew and Colin described you. You're far prettier than your photograph."

"Am I really?... You're not disappointed?"

"How could I be, light of my life?... The train to Salisbury doesn't leave until four o'clock this afternoon. We're all going to lunch at the Grande Hotel. Best food on the coast. We'll get you through customs and immigration in no time. They will put the trunks straight on the train so don't worry about your luggage. How was your trip? How wonderful. Everything is so wonderful."

Watching it all, standing a little back out of the way, Livy had to admire the man.

As they all walked towards the big customs shed, Livy caught up with Pam.

"Your brothers were right, darling," she whispered in her ear. "He's a good man. You'll soon find out how lucky you are."

LIVY SAID goodbye at the Beira railway station. Crispin had said it was better for them to arrive at their destination in separate railway carriages. Pam had gone off with Roger, two strangers destined by circumstances to spend their lives together. To make a family. Livy was truly alone for the first time in her life.

THE JOURNEY through the lowveld of swamps took the train into darkness. There were two old people in her carriage that slept four, two on the bottom, two on the top. Livy gave the two old girls the bottom bunks where it was easier for them to get in and out.

During the day they sat on the bottom, Livy looking out of the window. Before she went into the corridor to find the dining car, a man came with bedding and showed Livy how to let down the top bunk to make her bed. There was a bar in the second-class carriage. Livy ordered herself a drink. Pam and Crispin had been booked in first class when they bought their tickets in London. Livy recognised most of the people from the boat. The two people next to her at the bar were talking

Portuguese. The excitement of her journey was over, reality setting in, a full flight of butterflies in her stomach.

AFTER A GOOD MEAL, compliments of Rhodesia Railways, Livy spread out her bedding on the top bunk and went to bed. She was tired. Too much emotion for one day, the image of Roger's face thinking she was the bride still vivid in her mind. The clacking of the iron wheels on the railway line began to lull her. She heard the two old girls talking as she dozed into sleep. When she woke in the morning, she tried to reassure herself as reality played into her dream. She would be seeing Jeremy.

Livy woke once in the night after the train had climbed further away from the coast into the African bush. In the silence while the train waited for something, Livy heard the roar of a lion. She knew it was a lion because the two women were awake and talking about its roar. Livy had expected a lion to make a different kind of roar. The only roar she heard before was at the local Chelsea cinema in London at the start of an MGM film. When the train again got under way, Livy fell back into sleep.

SUNLIGHT on her face woke Livy in the morning. Leaning up on one elbow she leant down to look through the carriage window. Outside were miles and miles of bushland as far as she could see. There was long brown grass higher than a man's waist with scattered flat-topped trees rising up from it. In groups, herds of wild animals were watching the train go by. The smell of the white trail of the smoke was in Livy's nostrils. She thought the smoke must be trailing straight over her head. The countryside was very beautiful, full of peace. There were no native huts or any sign of people. Outside her train ran the empty bush all the way to a range of blue mountains far off at the horizon. Small white clouds stood motionless in the morning sky which was the colour of duck eggs. Hoping for a cup of tea before she got up, Livy fell back into the comfort of her bunk. When she woke again the carriage door was being slid open.

"Tea or coffee, ladies?" Surprisingly to Livy the steward was an Englishman with a broad north country accent.

"Tea for me," said Livy. "How far are we from Salisbury?"

"We get to Umtali on the Rhodesian side of the border in an hour. Salisbury at lunchtime. It's a lovely day."

"Why did we stop in the night?"

"To fill our bunkers with coal. There's a coal mine. Breakfast is being served in the dining car. By the time you've finished breakfast you'll be in Rhodesia."

THE FIRST LOOK sent Jeremy Crookshank's hormones screaming. Five months had been a long time. She was wearing a tight pair of shorts and a loose shirt without any sleeves. As Livy got off the train her breasts had moved heavily under the white shirt. Even from a distance he could see she was not wearing a bra. When she turned round to help two ladies off the train he could see the cloth of her shorts pulling at the firm bottom he remembered so vividly. Their two nights together had played every night in his head ever since. As Livy waved at him, Jeremy saw an older man look where she was looking. The man looked back at Livy as he stood beside the first-class carriage. The quick exchange of looks between Livy and the man poured cold water over Jeremy's sexual excitement. The man turned away to talk to a man and a girl. The other man was dressed in khaki shorts and shirt like half the men on the platform of the Salisbury Station meeting the boat train from Beira. There were two platforms, one either side of the track. People were hugging each other. The girl had on a dress that looked to Jeremy straight out of the closet of Queen Victoria it was so old fashioned. The long-sleeved dress in dark purple had frills just above the wrists. To Jeremy's surprise, as he stood transfixed, waiting for the surge of jealousy he had felt to calm down, the girl in purple with the wide-brimmed hat waved at Livy. Livy waved back. They all knew each other. Only then did Livy run towards him. Behind her, porters at the end of the train were emptying the guard's van of trunks and suitcases. The smile on Livy's face made Jeremy smile. Without ceremony she planted a wet kiss straight on his mouth. Then they stood back and looked at each other.

"Not bad," said Livy, smiling at him.

"How was your trip?" asked Jeremy as he was meant to do.

"Shared a cabin with the girl in purple."

"Don't I know one of them? Roger Crumpshaw from the club. They only let an assistant in the club because I play cricket."

"She's his fiancée."

"Never seen him with a girl before... Who's the other chap, Livy?"

"Oh, him. That's Crispin Dane. We were all on the ship together. Look, the luggage is coming off the guard's van. How are you, Jeremy? Your brother sends you his regards. He was at Tilbury with the gang to see me off. You remember Tessa?"

"I've got the farm truck, I'm afraid."

"Should be good for the luggage. In my cabin trunk is everything I need to paint including my easel. Are we going straight to Macheke?"

"That's the point, Livy. Flossy Maple would have a fit if I lived with a girl in the cottage to whom I wasn't married."

"Who's Flossy?"

"Bertie Maple's wife. My boss's wife. He owns Ashford Park. They have a thirteen-year-old daughter. They're all a bit prim."

"Where am I staying?"

"I've rented a room for you in the Avenues. Baker Avenue. Mrs Wade is rather sweet. I had to pay her a month's rent in advance."

"After that?"

"I'll hopefully get my bonus. Trouble is, I borrowed most of it to pay for your trip. If it all works out we'll be married and live on the cottage on the farm. As a fully-fledged farm assistant next year, I'll get a much bigger bonus and start saving for my own Crown Land farm. Everything works on this crop. Basic salary and a house to just cover day-to-day living expenses."

"So we've got a month to make up our minds what to do with the rest of our lives."

"Should be enough don't you think? I mean a month, a year, what's the difference?"

"We must both be nuts... Come on. Let's find my trunk. What a lovely tan you have, Jeremy." The tip of Livy's tongue came out and went back again.

"From standing in the lands all day watching the gang. We've finished the reaping. Now I'm in the shed watching them grade the tobacco. We had our first sale today. Why I've got the truck. Bertie Maple is a real sport. Made the sale for the day you arrived. We're all having a late lunch in Meikles Hotel."

"In these clothes! Oh my God."

"You can change into a dress in the ladies' toilet."

"Is his wife with him?"

"I'm afraid so. And the thirteen-year-old daughter. She's a right stuck-up little bitch. She got the afternoon off sport to lunch with her parents. She's boarding at the convent."

"This just gets better, Jeremy."

"Hello, Jeremy," said Roger Crumpshaw, coming across to them. "Are you playing this weekend?"

"I think so."

"I want you to meet my fiancée, Pamela Lavington. I'm taking everyone to Meikles for lunch. Will you join us? How do you two know each other? Livy and Pam shared a cabin."

"If it all works out we're getting married. Met in London."

"Well I'll be buggered."

"Can't join you, old boy. Lunch with the boss."

"And his wife?"

"Afraid so."

"You poor fellow. Are you lucky enough to have little Petronella as well?"

"She's got the afternoon off instead of playing hockey."

"Such a nice chap, Bertie. Half the club feel sorry for him. She had the money you know. His wife's family are stinking rich. It was her money that bought Ashford Park."

"I didn't know."

"Pamela, this is Jeremy Crookshank. Apparently he's engaged to Livy."

"So you're Jeremy," said Pamela, putting out her hand to Jeremy, politely shaking hands.

"See you at the cricket on Saturday, old boy. If I see you in the Meikles dining room ignore me. Can't stand that woman. Isn't my Pamela just so lovely?"

"Yes she is. Nice to meet you, Pamela."

"Crispin!" called Roger. "Don't rush away. We're having lunch."

"Not today, Roger. Goodbye to you all. My chauffeur is waiting for me I'm afraid. Roger, Pam, Livy. Such a good trip."

"Goodbye," said Livy.

There was no doubt to Jeremy. It was the way the man called Crispin looked at Livy. If he had gone to bed with Livy the first night they met at his brother Paul's party, what would she do in six weeks on a boat? The man had a chauffeur. The man was rich. A far cry from an impoverished learner assistant on Bertie Maple's tobacco farm. His mind was in a turmoil as to how he could compete, and something of this unease must have conveyed itself to Livy.

"Ships passing in the night, Jeremy," she told him quietly. "That's all it was. A man like that would never be serious about a girl like me. I want to make our money together if we're going to stay together. Being a rich man's dalliance never ends up happy. Believe me. Ask Jeanne Pétain, That Samuel Chalmers had more money than the king of England."

"And a wife, Livy. Don't forget Samuel's wife... Come on. You'd better show me which one is your trunk so we can load it on the farm truck and take your stuff to Mrs Wade before we go to Meikles for lunch."

"Are you mad with me, Jeremy?"

"We're not married, Livy. Only after we're married will it become my business."

"Does it change things?"

"I don't know."

"Jeanne sold one of my paintings for four hundred pounds."

"Goodness. That is a lot of money."

"The Nouvelle Galerie took forty per cent. So don't worry about me being a financial burden. You'll want to get to know me before we rush into anything we'd regret. It's always better to be honest with each other, don't you think?"

"I suppose so, Livy. It just hurts. I was assuming too much. You're right. Let's play it by ear."

"That one is mine. And those two suitcases."

"Porter!... Thank you. Those three on a trolley. My truck's in the car park."

"Will we have some time before lunch in my new room, Jeremy?"

"I suppose... Why?"

"You'll find out, sweetheart."

With his hormones back on the rampage Jeremy tried to concentrate on collecting her luggage. Then they smiled at each other. All was forgiven.

"Thank you, porter," said Jeremy. "That's the lot."

HALFWAY through the lunch in Meikles dining room the 'spoiled brat' kicked Livy on the shins under the table. Livy had been the centre of attention. The hard-nosed school shoes hurt. The punkahs were going round above the high-ceilinged room. Every table was occupied, the women in their summer dresses, the men in khaki shorts and short-sleeved shirts. Everyone that came in seemed to know Bertie Maple and his stuck-up wife who had talked down to Livy the moment they sat down to lunch. Instead of changing into a dress in the hotel toilet they had driven to Mrs Wade's and unloaded her baggage. There was just time for Livy to change.

"Livy, we have to go to the Farmers Co-op to fill up the truck. The only reason I got the truck was for doing the farm shopping. There's always piles of stuff. I wouldn't have got your trunk in the back if I'd loaded up earlier. It's all waiting. They've put our stuff out in the yard."

"Won't someone steal it?"

"Not in Rhodesia. Anyway, what's anyone going to do with a load of pipes? We're going to pump water from the dam straight to the barns. After curing you have to let steam into the barns or the dried tobacco leaves are too brittle to handle. My job is to lay the pipes."

"Do you know what you are doing?"

"I'll learn. Shadrack the builder will help me. He's done it before. We measured carefully before I ordered the pipes this morning. Mrs Maple doesn't like me using the truck unless it's on farm business. Says it's a waste of money going back with an empty truck. I'll have to go straight to the farm after lunch."

"Aren't we going to see each other again today?"

"I'm afraid not, Livy. Got to rush. Put on some clothes while I talk to Mrs Wade. What do you think of the room? You can cook in Mrs Wade's kitchen. She likes the company. There are two more girls in the house. She doesn't like male boarders anymore."

"Why ever not?"

"She said they get drunk."

"Can't we have ten minutes before I get changed?"

"Mrs Wade would throw us out of the house if she thought we were doing that. No men in the rooms. House rules I'm afraid. She let me come to your room to bring in your trunk with the house boy's help. Now he's gone she'll be waiting for me. She's a bit old fashioned, I'm afraid. All I could find for the price."

"It's a time warp, Jeremy."

"What is?"

"Rhodesia. The rest of the world has changed."

"Better go. See you downstairs. Please hurry. There's a lot of piping to load."

By luck, Livy had put on her high heels with the pointed toes, giving Petronella a kick under the table in return. By the look on the girl's face it hurt. The girl looked surprised, as though no one had hit her back before... The one Livy felt like kicking most was the mother.

"So what did you do in London, Miss Johnston?"

"I'm a painter."

"I never knew women painted houses. So much has changed in England after the war. Land girls and factory workers. Why I so like Rhodesia where the women are in their proper place."

"Where's that, Mrs Maple?"

"In the kitchen of course. Petronella, what is the matter? Why are you grimacing? There's nothing wrong with the food. You didn't have lunch at school before Daddy picked you up?"

"No, Mother."

"I paint pictures, Mrs Maple. Not houses."

"Oh, do you? How nice. Do you paint portraits? I'd so like a portrait of Petronella."

"Only landscapes, I'm afraid. I was thinking of African wildlife," Livy said, having no wish to paint the child.

"Were you now?"

"Do you have game on your farm?"

"A lion ate one of the *mombies* last year," said Bertie Maple. "An old lion too old to hunt. Had to shoot the old chap in the end. Terrifying the blacks in the compound. Set up a trap with what was left of my cow. Came back two nights later. Put his head in the trap and pulled the wire which pulled both triggers on my twelve bore shotgun. Blew a hole in the back of the poor old chap's head. Never thought it would work. When I told them in the club I'd shot a lion none of them believed me. We'd gone to the club for lunch the next day. I'd left the poor old chap where he died on top of the carcase of the *mombie*. We'd all had a few drinks when we came back to Ashford Park to show them my dead lion… There are a few kudu in the thick bush down by the dam in the mornings, Miss Johnston. Plenty of wild pig and small buck. The big game left when we English started this area after the First World War. You have to go to the game reserves or the Zambezi Valley if you want to see the big five. Elephant, lion, buffalo, rhinoceros and leopard. You might see the spore of a leopard on the farm but they mostly come out at night to hunt. We had quite a party after showing them my poor old lion. He was so mangy we couldn't do anything with the skin… Never met an artist before. So you two are getting married?"

"That's the idea," said Jeremy. "I want Livy to get the feel of the place first. Would it be all right for me to take the truck into Salisbury on Saturday morning, Mrs Maple? To pick up Livy to take her to the cricket. We're playing a side from Salisbury. I'll have to take her back in the evening."

"She can get a lift with one of the Salisbury players."

"I suppose she could."

"Have you ever sold one of your paintings, Miss Johnston? So many people paint as a hobby."

"Yes, Mrs Maple. At the Nouvelle Galerie for four hundred pounds to the Honourable Barnaby St Clair." Livy enjoyed the moment of silence as she looked at Mrs Maple.

"My goodness," said Bertie Maple. "That is a lot of money. Wasn't Harry Brigandshaw married to a St Clair, my dear? There was a scandal, I remember. The woman was shot by a maniac at Salisbury Station. Never did get to the bottom of it. Harry married a second time much later."

"Married beneath himself," said Flossy Maple. "The girl's father worked on the railways. Didn't I hear Harry's back in Rhodesia without his wife?"

"He's not well, my dear. I saw Ralph Madgwick, the Elephant Walk manager, this morning on the auction floor. Said Harry's dying of some liver disease. We should pay him a visit, my dear."

"If he hasn't brought that common wife of his, I'd be delighted. Now, Petronella, please eat your food. There are people in this world who are starving."

"Yes, Mother."

By the end of lunch Livy was not sure which one she disliked most, the mother or the daughter. The thought of living close to them on their farm was not appealing.

On the far side of the room Pamela Lavington was being entertained to lunch by Roger Crumpshaw and two other men. Livy guessed the two men were Andrew and Colin Lavington, Pamela's two brothers. They were all having a high old time. The brothers had not come to the station. There was no sign of Crispin Dane. She half expected to see him at lunch with some other woman. There had been no suggestion of them meeting again once they arrived in Salisbury. Their lives together had been on the boat. She didn't even know his address.

Around her they were all talking about the farm, leaving her out of the conversation. Private stories that she knew nothing about. With the thought of soon being left on her own in Mrs Wade's room the reality of what she had done washed over her. At that moment Livy would have given anything to be back in London with her friends. Jeremy was sweet and kept looking at her with sympathetic eyes as Mrs Maple dominated the conversation. The picture in her mind back in England of being the wife of a rich tobacco farmer was different to reality. She had not imagined herself as Mrs Maple. Livy had never met a snob before.

"You'll meet them all in the club on Saturday," Jeremy said so only she could hear, as if it was going to be so much fun to meet the farmers' wives who were Mrs Maple's friends.

She was in a strange land surrounded by strange people. At least Pamela was enjoying herself across the room. All the excitement had drained out of Livy. If she was honest with herself, Livy knew she was miserable. She was lucky to have sold her painting and have the money to get out of the trap she had set for herself. When Pam and Roger got up and left with the brothers she felt even more on her own. If they had seen her they were not saying hello. The brothers were both quite good looking.

When Bertie Maple paid the bill everyone stood up to go. Livy got to her feet not sure what to do.

"I'll drop you back at Mrs Wade's."

"You do that, Jeremy."

They all left the big dining room with the punkahs going round overhead.

"I'm sorry," he said outside when they were alone. "She's difficult."

"A right royal pain in the arse if you ask me. Do you know the little darling kicked my shins under the table? Gave her one back. Hard."

"We've got to hurry. They want me back on the farm by teatime. There's tobacco curing in the barns I have to take out."

"Today!"

"I'm afraid so. Farm work never stops... Will you be all right on your own? I'll get one of the chaps to pick you up on Saturday morning."

"We haven't had time to talk."

"We'll talk at the cricket."

"Will she be there?"

"Not this time."

"Why are you so obsequious to her?"

"She's my employer. The cottage I live in is close to their house. It's easier than arguing. It'll all be fine when I have my own farm."

"When will that be, Jeremy?"

"Four years' time with a bit of luck. Depends on how good the crops are. And the price of tobacco on the floors, I suppose."

"Does that woman decide on your bonus?"

"Probably. Bertie sets it as a percentage of the gross at the start of the season. Bertie's very generous."

"They usually are when it's not their money. So she owns the farm and holds the purse strings."

"I'm afraid so."

"And if we marry I'm living next door to the mother and the spoiled brat."

"She's not that bad when you get to know her. Why did Petronella kick you? What did you do to her?"

"Her father was talking to me. She was being ignored."

"Do you like cricket?"

"Never watched a game in my life."

"You'll like the club. It's fun. I'm not a member yet. They have to get to know you as a guest before the committee approve you. I'm only at the club when I play cricket. You'd better wear a dress."

"Like the rest of them at lunch."

"Floral dresses are the fashion in Rhodesia."

"I'll go and buy one, Jeremy. One just like the rest of them... Between Mrs Wade and Mrs Maple I'm stuffed. Just not the way I intended."

"I'm sorry, Livy. You've got to understand I work for them."

"Oh, I understand."

"This must be so different to Chelsea."

"Are there any other artists in Rhodesia?"

"I don't think so. No one ever mentioned it. One of the wives at the club plays the piano. Not very well, I'm afraid. Sometimes we have a singalong."

"I'll enjoy that."

"I'm sure you will."

"I was being sarcastic, Jeremy."

When Jeremy drove off with a truckload of six-inch pipes they had picked up at the Farmers Co-op, Livy was left outside Mrs Wade's small house in Baker Avenue wondering what she was going to do with herself. The food at lunch had been good. That was something. Then she went inside to her room to unpack her things. There were meant to be two other girls in the house. First impressions were not everything... And the sun was shining.

"When does it rain, Mrs Wade?" she asked downstairs.

"Not until October. This is the dry season. No rain for five months."

"I'm going for a walk. Is it safe?"

"Of course it is. This is Rhodesia."

When Livy stepped out into Baker Avenue she had changed into her shorts and flat shoes. There were trees down both sides of the wide road giving shade to the sidewalk from the African sun. On one side the trees had big red flowers sprinkled among the green leaves. The other side the trees were covered with blue flowers the same colour as the African sky. The road led Livy back into the centre of town. There was a square with tall trees and wooden benches for people to sit on. Many black people were lying on the grass under the trees apparently asleep. A fountain squirted water into the rays of the sun. No one took any notice of her. For the first time in weeks she could not feel movement under her feet from the roll and pitch of the ship. The *Carnarvon Castle* seemed a long way away. Livy looked around her. There was so much public space. She bought some bananas from a black man selling fruit. They were not too heavy to carry home. A shop nearby was selling meat pies. She bought two of them and put them in the paper bag with the bananas. Jeremy had given her five shillings in Rhodesian money. He had wanted to give her more. In the morning, she would find a bank and change one of her traveller's cheques.

After half an hour she walked back the way she had come to find a girl sitting on the porch of Mrs Wade's house.

"You must be the new girl. I'm Carmen Crossley. Where've you been?"

"Buying pies and bananas. Does anyone do anything for entertainment in this town other than lunch in Meikles?"

"You've got to believe it. That's for the tobacco farmers and their wives. The men all talk tobacco. The wives, servants and children. I never go to Meikles. Far too stuffy. You came on the *Carnarvon Castle*? What are you doing tonight? There is always a shortage of girls. We meet at Bretts. It's a sort of bar and nightclub. The men buy us drinks. Will you come with us? I bought a car for ten pounds. Just about gets down the road and back again. Have you ever been in the theatre? Mummy was in the theatre before she married Daddy. You look kind of arty."

"Would you like one of my pies? Livy Johnston. But you know that from Mrs Wade by the sound of it."

"She's very strict when it comes to boys but she's sweet. Candy isn't home from work. Candy and Carmen. She's my best friend. Works for the Standard Bank."

"She can cash my traveller's cheques."

"You have money! Oh, good. I never have any money. Do you have a job to come to?"

"I'm a painter. An artist. The black beret gave me away. We all wear them in Chelsea."

"How exotic."

"I want to paint wildlife while I'm in Rhodesia."

"How long are you staying?"

"I don't know. A month. Maybe a year. Depends on Jeremy."

"Ah. There's a man in your life. So soon."

"We met in London."

"You can take your pick in Salisbury. Dozens of them. I have a new boyfriend every week. When they see those shorts they'll freak. Has Mrs Wade seen your shorts?"

"Not yet. I'd better change if you think she'll chase me out."

"She won't do that. We can eat a meat pie. I'm always starving... That's settled. When Candy gets home we get into our glad rags and I'll drive us all to Bretts. How was the trip?"

"Wonderful. Have you heard of a man called Crispin Dane?"

"Who hasn't? He's rich, charming and single. He was on the boat... Oh, my goodness. You and the Dane. Then who's Jeremy?"

"He's a learner assistant on a tobacco farm in Macheke. Had to go back with the farm truck after lunch in Meikles with his boss and the lovely boss's wife. She was dreadful. I mean really dreadful."

"You'll enjoy Bretts. With luck someone will take us to dinner. They often do that with a new girl. We'll have to stick together, the three of us... Here she comes. Candy! Come and meet the new girl. She's an artist. We're all going down to Bretts when we've changed. You can tell Mrs Wade we don't want supper."

"Does she feed us?"

"Breakfast and supper."

"Jeremy didn't say. He's paid for me for a month while we make up our minds to get married. Hello, Candy. I'm Livy."

"Livy knows Crispin Dane. Met him on the boat."

"Lucky girl. Were you just friends?"

"Not really."

"My word. All my friends would die to marry the Dane. He's so rich."

"Is money so important?"

"It is when you're poor. Only rich people say money isn't important. Are you going to see him again?"

"I don't think so."

"What a pity. I'm going to have some tea before I change. Would you like a cup of tea, Livy?"

"Have a banana."

"There's another meat pie if you want to share with me," said Carmen.

"Are you sure?" said Livy. "I'll have half now and keep the other half for later if we can't get someone to buy us supper at Bretts."

"We're all going to Bretts, Candy."

"Oh good. Today was so boring. Why ever did I end up working in a bank?"

"To pay the rent, darling."

"Did you get a job Carmen?"

"Not today, Candy."

"Did you try?"

"Not today, Candy."

"What did you do?" asked Livy.

"As little as possible. I also worked in a bank. In Ealing. I'm looking for a rich husband. We both are. Why we came to Rhodesia."

"Could your car drive us to Macheke? There's a cricket match on Saturday. The farmers against a side from Salisbury. Twenty-two men. Some of them will be young and single. Jeremy wants me to go but the bitch won't let him take the farm truck."

"We can try. If it packs up we can hitch a lift. Macheke's not that far if you think Rhodesian. They drive a hundred miles here to go to a party."

"How far is it?"

"We'll find out."

After drinking a second cup of tea, Livy went up to her room to change. They were going for sundowners at Bretts. Life wasn't so bad after all. Humming to herself as she changed, Livy looked out of her window. The sun was beginning to set, the colours vivid. She wanted to paint. To open her trunk and pull out her easel. For some time Livy stood at the window thinking how she would paint the African sunset, keeping the colours in her mind. The strange land wasn't so strange anymore. She had found some friends.

"Are you ready, Livy? We want to get a seat at the bar."

"Come in. I'm watching the sun set. I want to paint that picture it's so devastatingly beautiful... It'll take me a sec to change. You look nice, Carmen."

"The war paint. A girl only has her looks for so long. You have to find what you want while they want you... It is pretty. In London you never get to see the sun go right down."

"It's the different colours of blue. So many of them. Reds, orange.

Blood red. The last small clouds bathed in the shards of sunlight. Daggers from the world below. The last thrust of day. This big window is just right for my painting. Lots of light."

"What did you paint in England?"

"Anything that took my fancy. A group of us put together our own gallery in the Portobello Road. One of the girls had a rich benefactor."

"Why didn't she just marry him? Save all the bother."

"He was married... It's nicer to be free. There is more to marriage than a rich husband. I want to be in love and free."

"Don't we all. You have to be practical. You have to make yourself a future that's secure... That sunset's going to be gone in ten minutes. Pitch black it will be. No moon tonight. You'll see the stars. Layers of the stars. They all look different in the African sky. I want to marry a farmer and look up at that sky in peace for the rest of my life... That dress looks nice."

"Can I still wear my beret?"

"Of course. It'll be a talking point at the bar. Men like to have something to say when they first chat you up."

"Do you know them all by now?"

"Some of them. It'll make them come across to talk to us. The new girl in the black beret... You're right. That sky is splashed with blood. Is that an omen?"

"Of what?"

"My friends in England said Rhodesia as we English know it here won't last much longer. That colonialism is wrong. That the blacks would be better off on their own."

"I know nothing of politics."

"Neither do I... Come on then. They have good snacks if we don't get supper bought for us... I like being young."

So did Livy, she thought as she quickly changed.

EVERYTHING WAS SO CLOSE. The car drove well for ten pounds. It had belonged to some old lady who drove it to the shops once a week before she died. The radiator had no water when Carmen first took it to a garage. The mile to the shop had not been far enough to get the car hot.

They went down a long flight of stairs to the basement of a building.

There was a men's clothing shop at ground level next to the sign 'Bretts'. The sign was in bright neon.

The bar was well lit at one end with low tables circled by small stools. Along two walls of the surround was a long bench with red cushions. Through a glass partition at the back Livy could see the tables and dance floor of a nightclub. The drums were standing empty on the bandstand. No one was sitting in the nightclub. In the bar people were sitting in the half-dark on the stools around the low tables, drinking. Waiters in smart white uniforms were waiting to serve them, their black skins in stark contrast to their uniforms. The waiters were all young and smiling. At the high stools along the bar two men were in conversation. The owner said hello to Carmen and Candy as they passed through. There was a big mirror behind the bar counter and in front were rows of bottles. The mirror reflected the bottles making the bar seem much bigger. Before they could sit down two men got up from the darkened tables and sat next to them. Livy thought they had left their drinks on the low round table they were sitting at when she walked through. The young men knew the barman by name. The barman turned to Carmen. Carmen also knew the barman by name. She had said hello to him as they sat down on the stool.

"They're offering you all a drink, Miss Carmen."

"Thank you, Moses. That is very kind of them. My friend here has just arrived from England... Hello, Rudy. Who's your friend?"

"Don't I know you?" said the friend to Livy.

"You should remember my face. We just spent six weeks on the same boat."

"You were Crispin Dane's girlfriend. Where is he?"

"I don't know. But meet Carmen and Candy. Hello Rudy, I'm Livy. Just off the boat. Thanks for offering us a drink."

"We don't let girls buy their own drinks in Rhodesia."

"What a nice custom."

Within minutes three more men had joined them on the other side of the girls to Rudy and Bob. They were being chatted up from both sides. After her fraught lunch with Mrs Maple and her daughter, Livy found the men a pleasant change. Her opinion of Salisbury began to improve. Everyone in the room was young. From the other room, where Livy could no longer see through the glass top of the partition from her

stool, someone hit the drums. The band was tuning up for the
sundowner session, she was told by Carmen. Snacks were put on the bar
in front of them. The snacks looked to Livy as if they had been well made
in the kitchen. Crackers with crisp bacon on top of some of them. Some
had cream cheese and bits of green parsley on top. The girls started
eating the food. The barman called Moses put their drinks in front of
them. Being polite to a stranger, Rudy having asked what she wanted to
drink, Livy had ordered only a single gin and tonic. The barman had
slopped well over the tot glass making Livy smile. She was going to enjoy
Salisbury after all even if poor Bob looked like the back end of a bus,
mostly the reason she had not made friends with him on the *Carnarvon
Castle*. He was also a bore on the boat, talking of nothing else except
himself. It soon turned out Rudy was a friend from his public school in
England. They were both in insurance.

"Cheers, Rudy and Bob," said Livy, never one to look a gift horse in
the mouth. With the remains of Jeremy's five shillings in her pocket after
the pies and bananas, she had no reason to turn up her nose. With his
old friend Rudy, Bob was not so boring. Bob bought the second round.
One of the men on the left bought a third round of drinks. Each time,
Moses remembered the order exactly. By the time they were invited to
dinner the party was merry. Carmen was getting tight and Livy hoped
her new friend would be able to drive them home. More people had
joined them making one big cocktail party and the band was remarkably
good. The piano player smiled at Livy when she sat at their table on the
edge of the dance floor. The piano player was very good looking. Having
made strong eye contact with Livy he went on playing the piano. The
music was jazz but sounded classical.

"Never heard Beethoven played like that before," she said to Carmen.
"Who's the piano player? He's gorgeous."

"Hennie. From Bulawayo. He was a concert pianist before he took to
playing jazz in nightclubs. All the girls love him. More money for him in
jazz. He studied at the Royal College of Music in London."

"Really. Why did he come back?"

"Too much competition. Here he sticks out."

"He's really good."

Later, one of the men ordered a bottle of South African wine. They
all seemed to have money. A piece of steak the size of her plate was put in

front of Livy. Never before had she seen a steak so large. Her knife cut into the beef like butter. A black singer came on the stand next to Hennie. She was young. In London she would have been a sensation. Livy put down her knife and fork to listen. Deliberately the band were playing under the singer. To find a piano player like Hennie and a singer like this in the middle of Africa was a surprise to Livy. One of the men had said the girl's name was Miriam. The rest of the name Livy had not understood, as it was African.

In turn, Livy danced with all the men at their big table. Rudy had put two tables together. There were five young men and three girls. Livy left her wine untouched and ate the steak. There was no point in getting drunk. The music was too good to miss. All the men in turn asked where she was living while they were dancing on the small square in front of the band. There was going to be no lack of company after all. The place had filled up. Only coming so early had given them a table.

At ten o'clock it all stopped and everyone went home. The drink licence stopped at ten o'clock in Rhodesia, Livy was told. No one seemed to mind. The men were all working in the morning.

When they got home to Mrs Wade's they were all laughing. The whole evening had not cost them a penny, except for Carmen's petrol. Carmen patted the car on the bonnet before walking to the small path that lead up to Mrs Wade's front door.

"Don't make any noise or she'll kill us. All look sober if she's still up. What an evening. Welcome to Rhodesia, Livy."

"Who were they?"

"Who knows? They all had a good time. Didn't you know Bob or something?"

"I'd forgotten. Good old Bob. That would have cost five times more in London."

"Cheap booze and cigarettes. Why the boys come to Rhodesia."

"They'll all end up alcoholics drinking like that."

"Who cares? We're young. Take what you can. When it's all over nothing in life matters anymore."

"That's my Carmen," said Candy. "I need my bed."

"Sweet dreams," said Livy.

"I'll wake you in the morning with a cup of tea," said Carmen.

"That would be nice."

"Goodnight," they all said at once as Carmen let them in the front door with her key.

Within five minutes Livy was fast asleep. She dreamed she was singing in a band. Hennie was smiling at her.

When she woke with the sun in the morning she remembered the dream clearly. Outside her big window strange-sounding birds were singing in the trees, the red-flowered trees and the blue-flowered. Before Carmen came in with the tea, Livy had her easel up by the window, a blank canvas on the stand. She had begun to paint the trees in the street outside. Later she would add the sunset. The tea which they drank together was delicious.

"You really paint."

"Sold one in London for four hundred quid."

"Blimey."

"Is he married?"

"Who, Livy?"

"Hennie. The piano player."

"You're wasting your time. He has them lined up waiting for him every night when he stops playing the piano."

"Someone has to be at the front of the queue."

"What about Jeremy?"

"We only knew each other two days. Thanks for bringing the tea. We're going to become friends."

"We are already... Saturday in Macheke. I can't wait. It's the farmers who have the real money. The kind of life I want to lead. If I never see the inside of a bank again I'll be happy. Philemon will be cooking breakfast in ten minutes. You don't have to come down."

"I'm always hungry after drinking the night before... I wonder what all my friends are doing in London?"

"After a while you forget about England. It's a little world of our own here in Rhodesia."

"I didn't ask you last night. How long have you two been here?"

"Three months."

"Goodness."

"See you at breakfast."

"What kind of birds are they?"

"Don't ask me."

3

A few miles from Salisbury, they were out in the bush. The old lady's car backfired on the downhills making the three girls jump. After the third time they got used to it. Soon after, the strip road began, two lines of tar with the dirt road in the middle. Carmen drove slowly, concentrating on the road. They had left Mrs Wade's house directly after breakfast and on the road were singing along above the purr of the engine. It was the first time Carmen had taken her ten-pound car out of Salisbury.

"Where is everybody?" asked Livy. "It was the same looking out of the train. So much space and so few African huts. How many blacks are there in Southern Rhodesia?"

"Don't ask me. Never thought of it. I heard they have to bring labour to the new farms from Nyasaland and Mozambique. With the Crown Land farms opening up there's a shortage of local labour. Look, there are some animals."

"Those are cows, Carmen," said Candy.

"What are they doing there?"

"Someone is farming cattle."

"That bull's enormous. Why are birds sitting on their bottoms? Even when the cows move the birds aren't flying away... There's absolutely no traffic on the road. Have we got enough petrol? Where are we? How far is Macheke? Do you know how to find the cricket club, Livy?"

"It's almost seventy miles from Salisbury. At Macheke we need to ask the way to the club. Jeremy tried to give me directions and gave up."

"Has he got a phone in his cottage?"

"They had to call him from the big house. I spoke to a native. He ran off to find Jeremy wherever he was. Took five minutes. Jeremy hadn't found anyone to give me a lift. Said it will be easier going back. He didn't know any of the phone numbers of the Salisbury team. I think Mrs Maple was listening. She doesn't like him using her phone unless it is absolutely necessary. Which means on farm business. Why are some people downright unhelpful?... Do you think the car will get us there, Carmen?"

"You need a man with his own farm. First thing I ask. 'Are you the manager or do you own the place?'"

"Jeremy's a learner assistant. He said it all sounded better in England. But he doesn't mind. Five years of hard work learning how to farm and he'll be on his own. I'm going to tell him to find a new job if the bitch won't offer him a good bonus... Look. There are some more animals. Those aren't cows. What are they?"

"Some kind of buck," said Candy. "When we get to the next filling station I need a pee. Three cups of tea at breakfast. What speed are we doing?"

"Forty miles an hour," said Carmen taking her eye off the road and sending the car off the strips into the gravel. "Whoops. These roads are tricky... Now we're back on the strips again. Can someone light me a cigarette?"

"Have you ever watched cricket?" asked Livy.

"Of course not. I watch the men. The men in the pavilion. There must be a bar. That's the place to be when they're out on the field."

A car tried to pass them, hooting from behind.

"He wants me to get off the strip. One wheel on and one wheel off... Here we go. Have a look at them as they pass. There are four men. Probably going to the cricket match. Maybe you should wave... They're about to pass us. Wave, everyone!"

When the dust settled and the car was back on the strips, Livy relaxed. The four men had waved back. They were all young.

"You're quite a good driver, Carmen. I'm impressed."

"At least there's someone on the road if this old jalopy packs up."

"Think positive, darling," said Livy. "Everything's going to be fine. They were wearing blazers. Must be cricket. The one nearly broke his neck craning round to look back when they went past. Oh isn't life so nice? Lots and lots of gorgeous men. What more can three girls want?"

"Why are you getting married, Livy?"

"He paid my passage. There's lots of time. I'm just getting the feel of the place. When are we going back to Bretts?"

"Too often, they get used to you. Don't buy you dinner."

"You've done all this before."

JEREMY CROOKSHANK WAS HAVING a bad day. When he went out to open the batting at eleven o'clock there was no sign of Livy. She had said on the phone the car was old. He imagined her stuck on the road. It was all his fault, starting with his suggesting she came out to Rhodesia when what he had to offer was so far in the future. Everything was falling apart. Only when he managed to phone Roger Crumpshaw to say he could not get to the ground had anyone done anything to help. The Maples had gone into town taking the keys to the truck with them. Jeremy had thought of driving a tractor to the ground. The likelihood of the keys going missing by mistake seemed small. Mrs Maple most likely had them in her handbag. He had never thought of asking Bertie for the keys before they drove off in the Mercedes on their way to town. Petronella was playing hockey for a school side, a far more important game. Roger himself had arrived at the farm to pick him up. Pamela Lavington had had a good look through his cottage. She was staying with her brothers who owned a farm close to Roger Crumpshaw. Pamela was not very impressed. She was going to be at the cricket, which would be nice for Livy had he found her a lift that worked.

"Roger would have gone into Salisbury to fetch her," Pamela had said after looking through his small cottage. "Wouldn't you, darling?"

"Of course I would, my pet."

"There's a girl she's staying with at Mrs Wade's who has a rattletrap. With luck she thinks it will get them to Macheke. Three of them are coming. So good of you to come, Roger."

"What would we do without the star batsman, old boy? Did you lose the keys to the truck? It's standing outside the barns."

"They must have mistakenly taken the keys to town. Wasn't on the hook in the kitchen when I looked after they left. Can't think what made me look so early this morning... This time I didn't ask to use their phone."

"A bugger being an assistant."

"Really, Roger."

"Sorry, my pet. Come on. We're going to be late."

"Are you opening with me?"

"Of course I am. We're going to score lots of runs in front of our girls."

Halfway to the crease, Roger stopped and looked back at the clubhouse. There was a long veranda in front of the building looking out on the cricket ground. Next to the cricket field was a nine-hole golf course. There was no sign of Livy or another car arriving. Mostly people came at lunchtime to watch the cricket.

"She's still not there," he said to Roger.

"She'd have phoned. You did give her the number of the club?"

"I forgot. She only has the Maple's number."

"Not much good to her with you playing cricket."

"I'm never going to concentrate on the bowling."

"You'd better, Jeremy. Or you'll have to walk back to Ashford Park... Just kidding. She'll arrive. Stop worrying."

"It's all my fault."

"You're facing the first ball, old cock. Isn't she lovely?"

"Who?"

"Pamela, of course. Just what I was hoping for and we'd never met. Have to watch the drinking and bad language but that doesn't matter. She wants ten kids... Good luck, old boy. Concentrate on the cricket and everything else will come right."

"You think so?"

"You just have to believe in yourself."

Trying to put himself in the zone as his coach at school had called it, Jeremy asked the umpire for middle and leg. With his guard taken, he looked around the field. Then he settled in for the first ball and everything outside the zone vanished from his mind.

. . .

BY THE TIME Candy was having her pee, Jeremy had scored his first runs. The girls had bought three bottles of Coca-Cola at the petrol station. The man who owned the garage said the backfiring down the hills was the timing and that they had nothing to worry about.

"You could hear his balls cracking," said Carmen when they got back in the car.

"Did you understand his instructions to the Macheke Country Club? Must be the place. Man was impressed. Why do men look at your boobs like that? Makes no sense. Tits are only useful to men when they are babies."

"Freud says it's the mother complex in men. That men want to fuck their mothers. The tits remind them."

"How disgusting. Like fancying your father. Agh. No one I ever knew fancied their dads in that way. Freud must be a pervert. Is he still alive?"

"Never heard of him," said Candy. "Twenty minutes to the turn on the road. When do they serve lunch at a cricket match?"

"Why are you two always hungry?" said Livy. "When you get older it will make you fat."

"We'll be married by then. It won't matter. Once you've had a couple of kids you get fat anyway. Some men like fat girls. They like to wallow in it... I know a man in London who liked to wallow in fat girls. Not bad looking either."

The turn came quicker than they expected. Chatting made the time go quickly for Livy. Two well-signposted turns took them into the driveway of the club with the game being played out on the field. There were cars parked next to the clubhouse. Carmen cut the engine of her car with satisfaction. When they got out she patted the bonnet. There was a line of trees up to the buildings with tennis courts on one side. Had it not been for the hot African sun Livy thought she could have been in England. The chock of the bat on the ball, followed by polite clapping, echoed across the field. Big white movable sightscreens were at either end of the field. Livy watched the bowler run in to bowl as she looked around for Jeremy. No one had come out of the clubhouse. She had hoped Jeremy would have been watching for them. On the field the ball was hit hard, coming straight in their direction towards the boundary. Livy watched it hurtle into the long grass as it left the well-cut grass of the field. Clapping broke out from the side of the clubhouse looking out onto the cricket field. The man in the middle was moving his bat like a lunatic.

"Didn't think they were allowed to get so excited at cricket," said Carmen.

"It's Jeremy," said Livy. Livy stood on tiptoe and waved back at him. "He's seen me... We'd better go up and wait for him on the veranda. He just scored a four."

They all watched the fielder pick up the ball and throw it halfway to the bowler. The next fielder threw it on. The bowler walked back to his mark. The next ball skittled Jeremy Crookshank's stumps. The bowler put his hands on his hips and watched Jeremy walk away from the pitch.

When he reached Livy, carrying his bat and gloves and wearing his thick white pads, he was grinning at her all over his face.

"Once I saw you, I lost my concentration."

"Did you get many runs? Hello, Jeremy. Meet Carmen and Candy. The jalopy got here. What do you think of it?" she said, pointing. "Ten quid."

Without ceremony, Jeremy kissed her hard on the mouth.

"They can't see us from the pavilion... Hello, girls. Come on. Twenty-two runs is good enough to keep me in the team. Roger's out there still batting. Pam's on the veranda with the rest of the wives and girlfriends. She and Roger are as thick as thieves. What have you been doing with yourself in Salisbury without me?"

"Not very much," lied Livy. "Are there any single men in your team?"

"You have me, Livy!"

"Carmen and Candy, idiot. Why they came. They wouldn't just want to drive old Livy all this way... How did you get here?"

"Roger had to pick me up for the cricket. The keys weren't left for me."

"What a bitch. Get another job, Jeremy. This one isn't working."

"Come on. I want to get my pads off and introduce you to everyone. They've heard nothing but Livy since I came back from England. You look wonderful."

"Thank you, Jeremy."

"Thank you, Carmen, for bringing her. So you all stay with Mrs Wade? My word. Three gorgeous girls in one house."

Formally, Jeremy put his hand out to Candy and Carmen and shook their hands. Then they all walked up under the shade of the trees to where another man wearing pads was walking out onto the field. To Livy, it was all so very English.

"They give us a buffet lunch in the hall where they hold the meetings. There's going to be a federation of the three British colonies in Central Africa. If it isn't tobacco or cricket it's politics. Go and find a deck chair with the other women while I get off the pads."

"Well played, Crookshank. What happened to that last ball?"

"Not a good shot, I'm afraid, sir... This is Livy Johnston I've been talking about."

"Jolly good."

The man turned away to talk to someone else. Livy felt something was wrong. She raised her eyebrows to Jeremy.

"You have to be a member to invite guests. That was the club chairman."

"Aren't *you* a member?"

"Oh goodness me, no. You have to be an owner or a manager. They let me in on cricket days to score some runs. The others won't mind. He's just a stickler for the rules. I'll ask Roger to sign you all in."

"Stuck-up pig."

"Please, Livy. I live here. Rules are rules. You'll see. Break the rules and everything falls down... Here comes Pamela."

"Livy, darling! We're getting married next week in the Salisbury cathedral. Isn't it wonderful? You'll come, of course. The reception is at Meikles. Andrew's giving me away. Mother's flying out. Oh, I'm so excited."

"These are my friends Carmen and Candy. We're lodgers in the same house. Isn't it all a bit quick?"

"He's batting so well don't you think?... What happened to that last ball, Jeremy?"

"I saw Livy when I hit the four. Wasn't watching the next ball."

"Naughty you. Roger's just batting so well. He's going to get his fifty. Livy, you'd better join me. Has a member signed you in?"

"Not yet."

"The *Carnarvon Castle* seems so far away... I'm going to change all the curtains. Bring in some new furniture. He lives so like a bachelor. That's all going to change... Look! Roger's scored another boundary."

Livy watched her erstwhile cabinmate clap furiously. The club chairman was still looking at them. It was the perfect welcome, she thought, if you had a sick sense of humour. Nothing she had imagined in England was quite like the Macheke Club. The man had spoken with a plum in his mouth. Pamela's way of speech was more affected than it had been on the boat. The girl seemed in her element. Livy felt anything but. Jeremy was looking at the rest of the farmers and their wives. She thought he knew what was going through her mind: that living among this lot was not her cup of tea. She was the assistant's girlfriend. She was being snubbed. Not that it mattered to Livy. It was the look of pain on Jeremy's face that mattered. His dream shattering right in front of his eyes.

"Are you allowed to buy us a drink at the bar, Jeremy?" she asked sweetly.

"I can try."

"Put it on Roger's card," said Pamela, a little too condescending for Livy's liking. "I'll ask Ignatius. He's the black barman. Come on. I want to tell you all about my wedding. Go and take your pads off, Jeremy. I'll look after Livy."

"And Carmen and Candy?"

"Of course. Hello, I'm Pamela."

"Are there any single men?" asked Candy looking around.

"I have no idea. I'm engaged."

They all followed Pamela.

"His bark's worse than his bite," said Jeremy.

"I hope so," said Livy, staring at the chairman's back while the man politely clapped another run.

WHEN THE GAME stopped for lunch Livy had drunk two double gin and tonics on Roger Crumpshaw's account and was feeling better. The man who had craned his neck to look back at them in the car came into the bar. With him were three friends. They were all dressed in their cricket whites. All four had wide grins on their faces. The game for Livy and her friends was on again.

"Got you with that one, Crookshank," said the man who had craned his neck. "Hello! Weren't you three in the car we overtook on the road? Can I buy you lot a drink?"

"Do you drink when you're playing cricket?" asked Carmen.

Livy wanted to laugh. The girl was being coy. Candy was flirting with her eyes.

"How do you know them, Crookshank?"

"I met Livy in England."

"Oh, good. You can formally introduce us. It's so hot out in the field the beer evaporates through the pores of the skin before it gets to the brain."

"Is that true?" said Candy, trying to look innocent.

"Makes a good excuse."

Formally, Jeremy introduced them to the four men from the Salisbury team. Only one of them wore a wedding ring. All four it turned out were farmers from Salisbury South, a farming district close to the capital. There was a club and cricket ground in the area where they farmed. Livy watched as Carmen, ignoring the one with the wedding ring, found out from each of the young men if they owned their own farms.

"Are you going back today?" asked one of the men.

"After the cricket."

"Why don't we travel in convoy?"

"That would be nice."

"Come on," said Pamela. "We're going into lunch... Oh, Roger, darling. Can you sign Livy and her friends into the club? We've had a few drinkies I'm afraid."

Livy followed behind Pamela. The girl was slightly tight. So much for her cabinmate not drinking. Crispin Dane had done her a favour in Lourenço Marques by introducing her to wine. A girl needed a drink or two in the Macheke Country Club.

"You took to it like a duck to water, Pam," she said, smiling.

"What, Livy?"

"Drinking. Now you've joined my club."

"You see it's Roger. He rather likes to drink. Isn't it all so exciting? We've had to get special permission from the archbishop to have our marriage banns read on time. Normally it's three weeks. Saturday. A week from today. Will you be my bridesmaid, Livy?"

"Maybe not, Pam. You see Jeremy doesn't own his own farm. Won't that make a difference?... Haven't your brothers friends to help you? Where are they by the way?"

"They're coming later. It's all work on the farm. They get up with the sun and stop work when the sun goes down. I have an idea. Why don't you all stay over tonight on the farm? One of my brothers can take Jeremy back to Ashford Park. A good natter. That's what we need together. There's so much to tell you about the wedding."

"Better wait for your brothers to meet Carmen and Candy."

"They'll love them."

"All right," said Livy, thinking of her friends. "We'll have a party."

There was no doubt about it, the girl was more pleasant after a couple of drinks. They had their own car if anything went wrong. The three of them from Mrs Wade's house were not beholden to anyone. Not even to poor Jeremy. If it didn't work out, all she had to do was give him back his hundred pounds and go back to her friends in London, wiser for the experience. She would sell her painting of an African sunset in Jeanne Pétain's Nouvelle Galerie. Pay for her trip both ways. The painting would make a fine splash of colour in rainy old England... The chairman of the club was talking to Roger Crumpshaw and looking at her at the same time. Livy waved at the old goat who promptly turned his back on her. She even thought he had gone redder in the face. When it came to pecking orders in society, artists like herself didn't give a damn what other people thought of them. Just because the man had a farm and money it didn't make him any better than anyone else. With the gins still making her feel brave, Livy marched up to the buffet table, took a large plate off the stack at the end and began to pile it up with food. On either side Candy and Carmen were doing the same thing.

"Grub looks good," said Carmen.

"Doesn't it?"

"So where are these brothers?"

"All in good time, young lady."

"That old bugger was staring at you. Dirty old man. I said you should have worn a bra."

"No you didn't, Carmen... What's in this sauce?"

"Stick in your fork and try it."

"Don't you think that might be going too far?"

"Probably. Who cares? Tomorrow's another day."

BY THE TIME the Salisbury South side went back on the field, Jeremy knew he was out of his depth. He was broke. Plain and simple. He had no money to compete. There were so many young men with cars under the trees, shiny new cars. Farms they owned or farms they managed on fat bonuses they received when the crop was sold. Big houses full of furniture. Something to show to a girl. It would take him years to know what he was doing, let alone make enough from his bonuses to buy a car that wouldn't break down on the farm roads, let alone pay a deposit on his own Crown Land farm. It was one thing to look at a field of tobacco and know which leaves were ripe enough to reap. To Jeremy, in his first year, the colour of the tobacco leaves all looked the same. In the grading shed he had no idea which grade of leaf was which. He stood and watched the gang all day, hoping they knew what they was doing. He was a white bossboy all the way from England. Bertie Maple never told him anything about the crop that increased his knowledge of farming. He was told to stand in the lands or in the grading shed making sure the rest of them worked. However was he going to learn? Curing a barn of tobacco was an art in itself. Knowing when to put more wood in the fires to raise the temperature inside the barns. Too quick and the leaves dried out while the stems stayed green, dropping the price of that tobacco on the auction floors by half. Growing flue-cured tobacco to get the right quality of dried leaf was an art requiring knowledge. As he watched Livy flirt with the men, he had neither. How could he possibly expect her to invest her life in him when he himself had no idea where he was going? She could waste the best five years of her looks with him and end up with nothing. So many of the others, single, had it all already. Some of them went to England every year taking their wives and children once the tobacco had gone out of the sheds, giving them three months' holiday before the start of the next growing season. He was a fool in England not to see what he was up against. Of course she wrote back with glowing excitement. He was all she had to get to Rhodesia and the grand life he wrote about that was going to be hers. To make it all worse, he had yet to receive his bonus from the Maples to pay back his friends the hundred pounds he had borrowed. If the disappearing truck keys were any indication, he was in for a shock. The bonus part of his employment had only been a promise if the Ashford Park crop was good. He had taken their word. He was a fool. Now he was trying to drag Livy into his mess.

"Are you going to stay with us tonight Jeremy?"

"I don't think so, Pam. Roger promised to drive me back to the farm right after the game. There's a barn of tobacco to take out for the grading tomorrow."

"You can't work on Sunday."

"Bertie wants to get as much tobacco as possible to the floors while the prices are still good. The last sale was the best we've had. He pays the gang a Sunday bonus so they don't mind."

"And you?" asked Livy.

"I'm the assistant. When they grade the tobacco it's my job to be in the grading shed. Or I won't get my bonus. I still owe the hundred pounds I borrowed for your boat fare."

"Oh look!" said Pamela. "Roger's scored a four. That brings up his fifty. He's so clever. Clap, everyone. Roger's got his fifty."

They were never on their own to talk to each other. Jeremy had written more to Livy in his letters about himself and what he wanted from his life than he had said to anyone. Including his mother and his father before his father was killed in the war trying to evacuate a last boatload of British troops from the Dunkirk beaches in the *Seagull*. Would he have ever have come to Rhodesia if his father had lived and the money hadn't run out in England? Livy had told him so much about herself when she answered his letters. Were they writing letters to each other or writing letters to themselves? He had fallen for who she said she was in her letters. His driving need for sex after his one and only encounter had been part of it. Sexually, he had never known anyone else. Losing his virginity in London, on his trip back to England paid for by his brother to see their mother on the Isle of Wight, had taken less than a minute. Later in the night she had shown him what to do, the lovemaking indelibly imprinted on his mind. Had they both fooled themselves as much as each other by carrying on instead of leaving their brief affair as a memory? Whatever it was, she expected more from him now. So much of the excitement at her coming to Rhodesia had come down to a fight with the Macheke club chairman about giving her a drink. All that way from England to end up with a problem over a gin and tonic. A problem of no keys on a hook to drive ten miles to see the girl who had come six thousand miles to see him in the middle of Africa. All his dreams of the last five months were in tatters. He was a fool to have expected so much when all he had to give in return was a dream that relied on the likes of the Maples to come true. He had built the future of owning his own farm on other people's promises. He would have been better to get himself a job in London after he came out of the navy. Like his brother, Paul, in an insurance company as a clerk. Paul had done all right for himself in England once he saw an opportunity out of insurance. He was a fool. A bigger fool if he thought in his heart of hearts that the new Federation of Rhodesia and Nyasaland was going to succeed. There were so few whites in Africa making the economy work, and so many blacks with their own dreams and aspirations. To Jeremy in the cold light of his discontent it was simple. The two cultures, black and white, were poles apart.

Jeremy watched Pamela go off to congratulate Roger on his fifty runs. Fifty stupid runs in cricket everyone thought so important. After getting his half-century Roger had made a cow shot, hurtling the ball up into the air. The man who had his eye on Livy during lunch had caught the ball easily. They had seen each other on the road. The man had his own farm. Carmen and Candy were talking, keeping him away from any meaningful conversation with Livy. When Roger joined them with Pamela on his arm they looked so happy together.

"Can you give me a lift back when the game's over, Roger? Jolly good show."

"Aren't you staying with Pam's brothers tonight?"

"Mrs Maple would never forgive me not clearing out the barn tonight or first thing tomorrow."

"I'll ask one of the chaps to give you a lift. We're going to declare. We're going out on the field in a couple of minutes. With a bit of luck we can win this one. Are you coming to the wedding on Saturday?"

"I'll try harder to get the truck."

"I've got a better idea. We'll invite the Maples to the wedding. They can bring their daughter. Petronella will love a big wedding in the cathedral."

"I'm sure she will, old boy."

"Are you going to bowl?"

"I will if the captain asks me. I opened the batting and bowling at school."

"Good thing I picked you up this morning. What happened when you got out, by the way?"

"I saw Livy."

All they were interested in him for was the cricket. Livy gave him a look of sympathy. Her smile made him smile. If his bonus came through as promised maybe he'd be better to go back to England with Livy. Unless she found another man who was rich. They could take a boat up the east coast, through the Suez Canal. There were Italian ships that went up the coast. Someone had done a train trip from Venice to England. It had taken six weeks. For five pounds. There was always a way round in life. He would find a chance to talk to Livy at the wedding on Saturday. If the Maples would give him a lift.

"When are you buying some furniture for your cottage, Jeremy?" asked Pam.

"There's a bed and two chairs."

"Livy will want more than that."

"When I get my bonus. I'm only a learner assistant."

"I'm sure the cottage will be fine," said Livy. "If I ever get a chance to look at it."

Then they all laughed. The girls were enjoying themselves, which was something.

"I've got to go out and field. I'll see you later, Livy."

Another fleeting look. It was all so frustrating.

"Crookshank! We're going out on the field."

"Coming, old chap."

4

*P*embringham Estate was just what Livy had had in mind. The long sweep up to the manicured lawns through an avenue of flowering trees, the same blue-flowered trees outside her window at Mrs Wade's. A bungalow-style ranch house of extraordinary proportions with a long thatched roof. Servants running around everywhere. Pedigree dogs of three different breeds. Flowerbeds ablaze with colour. A rose garden the size of Hampton Court. They were being driven in Roger Crumpshaw's car having left the jalopy at the club to be picked up later. The boys from the other team were forgotten.

"You never said your brothers were this rich, Pam."

"I wanted to surprise you."

"Oh my goodness," said Carmen from the back seat of the car. "Just look at it. Looks more like an English country estate."

"Our family on our mother's side were once rich. Landowning squires in Pembrokeshire. They had everything except a title to pass down the generations. Andrew and Colin wanted the family estate to flourish again."

"All out of tobacco!"

"They came out to Rhodesia before the war. When Andrew was nineteen and Colin seventeen. They left the farm to join the British Army at the start of the war. There wasn't much here then. A thatched house built from poles they had cut out of the bush as they cleared the land to plant tobacco. The big job at first was to turn the bush into farmland. Isn't that right, Roger? I'm much younger than my brothers, of course. They've been asking Mother to join them out here for years. Now Father's dead it doesn't matter leaving England. She's so happy I'm marrying Roger. We're going to be one big family again. Isn't it wonderful? After the war, with the Americans being so beastly and making us British pay for their tobacco in dollars, Rhodesia became a goldmine. High prices for tobacco paid for in sterling and low colonial taxes. It is rather nice don't you think, Livy?"

"Why aren't either of them married?"

"They don't meet girls in Rhodesia. They've gone over to England twice since the war. They met nice girls but the girls always wanted to stay in England. There's a swimming pool and tennis court. The garden covers ten acres of flowers and rose garden. If you think this is nice, wait until you see Roger's farm. Yours is just as nice, isn't it, darling?"

"I think so, my pet."

"I can't wait to be married and have my own beautiful home. Just the furnishings are going to change, aren't they, Roger?"

"Whatever you want, my darling."

The brothers had gone on ahead before the cricket finished to get the party ready. Livy had to smile. Candy's eyes were popping out of her head. Carmen and Candy had met the brothers briefly when they spent an hour at the cricket in the afternoon. Neither of them were particularly exciting to look at – two balding men with short legs approaching middle age. They were better looking sitting down at a distance as they had been in the dining room of Meikles Hotel. Livy could see it was what they had that mattered to Candy and Carmen. When Andrew and Colin greeted them as they all got out of the car, her friends were full of smiles. To all three of them the brothers looked different with the background of the house behind them. Like a painting, the background was important.

"Did you win, Roger?" said Colin.

To Livy he seemed more interested in the cricket than three pretty girls. She tried her best smile on Andrew standing next to his brother, pushing her naked breast against the cloth of her shirt, making the right nipple stand out. Nothing happened. He looked at Livy briefly before turning back to Roger.

"Crookshank skittled out their tail end. It was all over half an hour after you went home."

"Jolly good. That is good news. I always like to beat those chaps from Salisbury."

"Andrew and Colin are the club's tennis doubles champions. Andrew won the singles last year. Always ends with the brothers playing each other in the final. No one else in the club can beat them."

"That does sound fun," said Livy, not meaning a word.

"Come on," said Pam. "Let me show you the house. The men will want to go off and look at the tobacco."

"Ask Sampson for anything you want," said Andrew. "He's organised your rooms. Pam, you don't have to do anything."

"Isn't Rhodesia wonderful?"

"Yes it is," said Livy, wishing Jeremy was with her. "Do you think Jeremy got a lift home, Pam?"

"It was a long way to walk. Someone will have given him a lift. Probably one of those Salisbury South cricketers. Ashford Park is a bit on their way. Come on. I'll show you inside."

Wondering if Jeremy would make enough money for such a home, Livy followed Pam. She could see the men's backs walking away towards a cluster of buildings beyond the formal garden. There was smoke coming out of the top of the tallest buildings. Livy could smell the woodsmoke.

"Those are the curing barns," said Pam, following the direction of her look. "The boys have got something called spot on the tobacco. They want Roger to have a look. Everyone asks Roger his opinion."

"Do they now?"

"Oh, yes. He was grower of the year, last year."

"What does that mean, Pam?"

"He had the best tobacco on the auction floors."

"You're learning quickly."

"Men like it when you listen to what they say. Without quality tobacco where would we be? It's all in the detail. Doing each job a little better than the rest of them. That's what made my Roger grower of the year. And rich. It's so nice to have lots and lots of money. I can't wait to show my mother the house. Roger made all the arrangements for her to fly out to the wedding."

"That's very kind of him."

"He says nothing is too good for his mother-in-law."

"Doesn't Roger have any family?"

"There's a father he doesn't speak about. His mother is dead. He was an only child. We're going to have ten children."

"I wish you luck."

"Don't you want kids, Livy?"

"I don't think I could cope with ten of them."

"When are you getting married?"

"We haven't spoken about it. We haven't actually spoken. There have always been people around."

"You can talk all you want at my wedding."

"I hope so."

"I am getting married all in white."

"A true virgin, Pam. I'm impressed. No wonder the archbishop was happy to marry you so soon. It is the bishop marrying you on Saturday?"

"Of course. It's his cathedral."

Livy, trying not to imagine the wedding night of a virgin with all its surprises, found the inside of the Lavington brothers' house a surprise. There were original paintings on most of the walls. Good ones. None of them recognisable as collector's pieces but all well done. The boys had good taste. She had judged them too soon.

"Who painted the pictures?"

"Don't ask me."

"I like them. They're good... Who plays the grand piano?"

"Colin. He's very good. Mainly classical. I prefer musicals myself to concerts. In the off-season they have a lot of time to themselves."

"Where did they get the paintings?"

"You can ask them when they come back from the sheds. Do you like my brothers' house, girls?"

"It's fantastic," answered Carmen and Candy in unison.

"They were going to have a formal dinner party in the dining room. But of course you didn't bring your evening clothes to the cricket. We're going to have a *braai* outside. That's a barbeque. Lots of chops and steaks on the fire. Rather informal, I'm afraid."

Livy, walking off to look at each of the paintings, left them to their conversation. Life had so many twists and turns. If the one brother

played a grand piano just maybe the other one painted or wrote poetry...
Poor Jeremy, she thought. She hoped he had got back to his cottage with
the bed and two chairs. She would have liked him to be with her, looking
at the paintings. She had travelled so far to see him. And on the money
he had borrowed from his friends. The men at the club appeared so
grand. They had been rude to Jeremy the assistant. Again, a picture of
her flat in Chelsea flowed into her mind. It made her homesick for her
friends. Where she was now felt so strange, as if her body was walking
through the lounge but her mind was still in England.

"Would you like a drink, Livy?" called Pam when Livy came back
from her tour of the paintings.

"Yes. I rather think I would."

"We can all have a good natter. In Rhodesia the men talk to the men.
About farming. Roger always likes to talk about the farm."

"Don't you talk to him when you're on your own?"

"Only about the wedding... Gin and tonic, Livy?"

"Thank you."

"Sampson puts everything out so nicely."

"Can we look at where we're sleeping tonight?"

"Does it matter? You don't have suitcases."

"What are you drinking, Pam?"

"I thought I'd have a glass of wine. Have you seen Crispin Dane while
you were in Salisbury?"

"He doesn't know where I am."

"He's rich too, Livy. You should think of that. Girls, what are you
going to drink? If you want to see your rooms I can show you. They're
down the corridor. Three rooms next to each other. There are so many
bedrooms in this house. Whenever my brothers throw a party the guests
stay overnight. They all drink so much. There are wild animals on the
road at night. We often have weekend guests. Why the house is so big.
You have to entertain each other in Rhodesia."

"Are there any more bachelors in the area?" asked Candy, looking at
the door.

"Oh, lots of them."

"Here they come."

Like two homing pigeons, Livy thought, both Carmen and Candy
turned their attention to the door as the men came into the room.

"What a lovely piano," said Carmen. "Colin, you play the piano. I wish I could play too. It's so clever. Can we have a tune?"

"I prefer classical... Roger thinks we put too much heat in the barn which is causing the spots. We've got to cure the leaves much slower to avoid those spots... Now, I really need a drink. Is my sister looking after you girls? We can go and sit on the *stoep*."

"What's the *stoep*?" asked Candy, trying to get into the conversation.

"The veranda. It's Afrikaans, a sort of Dutch they speak in South Africa. There's a mosquito mesh against the moths along the open side of the *stoep*. We can watch the sun set behind the hills."

"I like your paintings," said Livy. "Who's the collector?"

"We both are," said Andrew. "Do you know anything about paintings?"

"Just a little."

"They make the rooms come alive. A wall without a painting is a dead wall."

"Where'd you find them?"

"We bought them all in England. From a Bond Street art gallery on our last visit. Do you want to have a look?"

"I've looked at them. All my friends in England are painters."

"I'd much prefer to have been an artist," said Colin. "Do you like Chelsea?"

"I lived in Chelsea. Sometimes we can't have everything we want in life. You can either have money or be an artist. Very few artists make money and most of them for the wrong reason. Controversy and fame are often more important than good art when it comes to selling a painting."

"Let's all have a party," interrupted Pamela. "When is Sampson going to light the fire for the *braai*?"

It was going to be a long weekend, thought Livy, as the men went back to talking tobacco, taking their drinks out onto the *stoep*.

The sunset was spectacular when she joined them. The hills in the distance were a soft mauve. Livy wished she'd brought her oil paints and her brushes with the easel and a canvas... She could have painted while the men talked farming and Pam told the girls every possible detail of her wedding. It was journey's end. As far as she was going. Finally, she had arrived at a farm in Rhodesia though not the one with Jeremy. Like so many times before in her life, the journey had been better than the ending.

Letting the others carry on talking, Livy went back into the lounge to have another look at the paintings in the fading light. When she couldn't see properly anymore she passed the drinks trolley with its small paraffin lamp now burning. Sampson must have lit the light. Picking up the gin bottle she slopped a good measure into her empty glass, filling it up with ice and tonic water.

She went back to the veranda to listen to the conversation and watch Carmen and Candy doing their best to flirt with the brothers Lavington. The drink was helping all of them. What was left of the sun was blood red. A violent colour on the horizon. Away from the sunset the stars were coming out in the darkening sky. The crickets were singing, screeching in her ears. Far away she could hear the sound of drums coming, she thought, from some native village. She liked the sound.

When the last colour went out of the sky it was pitch dark. She went outside, opening the mesh door that kept out the moths and mosquitos, careful to close it behind her. No one had noticed. Then she looked up at the sky. There were three layers of stars. She had never seen so many stars so deep in the universe. The drums were louder. Night birds she had never heard were calling. It was all so forbidding. Nothing familiar. She wanted to go home. Back to England. Back to Chelsea and her friends. Back to where she belonged.

She went back to the veranda. Mosquitoes had begun to bite her bare flesh. The others were still talking of farming and the wedding. Sampson had lit the fire at the end of the veranda against the wall where there was a fireplace built for cooking. The wood was burning brightly. A shiver went through her body despite the heat. No one took any notice of her as she sat down in a chair. Poor Jeremy. No wonder he wanted a wife so badly. So far from England all on his own.

After a few drinks the brothers Lavington began to lose their inhibitions. The conversation turned away from tobacco. Pamela was left talking to Roger about her wedding. Sampson and another servant had set up a table next to what Andrew called the *braai*. The coals were getting ready to cook the meat. The long table was covered in bowls of salads. Then to Livy's surprise, Colin began to do the cooking, the servants back in the house or wherever they went. Black men whose faces she could not see in the dark. There were paraffin lamps strung along the veranda. Nothing moved the flames. Not a breath of wind from the night.

Moths that had come inside when she opened the mesh door began to incinerate themselves in the flames of the lamps. Their world shrank to the light from the lamps, the flames of the fire dying out leaving the red-hot coals.

Carmen and Candy began doing their best to chat up the brothers Lavington. Livy felt out of the game. There had to be some kind of code of honour even for assistants. Pamela, Livy thought, must have told her brothers about Jeremy. Told them why she had come all the way to Africa. No one mentioned his name.

Standing back from the rest, partly in shadow, Livy listened to the sounds of Africa on the other side of the wire mesh that let in the warm night air but not the mosquitoes. No one had mentioned malaria. Jeremy had not had time to tell her what to do. There was some preventative medicine that had to be taken before going into the malaria parts of the country. Livy put the thought out of her mind. With enough gin in her blood she hoped there would not be a problem.

A bird hooted in the trees that flanked the formal garden. The drums were louder. The hoot sounded like an owl. She was going to ask one of the men but they were all talking. Roger, now a little drunk, had not taken his eyes from Pamela. She looked prettier in the half-light. The half-bald heads of the brothers were not so visible. She thought about what they had done. The jalopy was all on its own outside the club. Livy didn't have so much as a toothbrush to clean her teeth.

The fat from the lamb chops sizzled and flared on the hot coals. The meat was being burned to a cinder. To give herself something to do, Livy forked some potato salad onto a plate. Then some lettuce. Then poured salad dressing over the lettuce.

Andrew put a burned chop on her plate, his arm touching her shirt and the bare breast underneath. Then he looked at her with so much lust she pulled away. The light from the nearest lamp had reflected in his eyes, making them look cruel. Livy hoped it was a trick of the light. Or her imagination. Later, she would suggest the girls all sleep in the same room. Telling herself all three were gentlemen, she began eating her food.

The owl hooted again. The crickets, if anything, were getting louder outside. The drums too. Andrew was now concentrating his efforts on Candy, filling up her glass. Livy felt responsible. It was her idea to bring them out to Macheke. More than anything she wanted Jeremy. For protection. If she did not know Jeremy so well, she knew his brother Paul. She had seduced Jeremy in London, not the other way round. She was in a strange world she did not understand. Pamela had changed from the boat. She was now one of them. The drink and the flickering half-light were getting to her.

Wine was opened and handed round. The wine made her relax. She had gone from being tight to getting drunk. Carmen went off first, not long after they had their food. She had gone with Colin. Neither of them came back. Candy went soon after with Andrew.

"Can you show me which one is my room, Pam? I've drunk too much I'm afraid."

"Of course I can... Don't go away, Roger darling."

When Livy got in the room having said goodnight to Pam, she locked the door and went to bed. Her room was in the middle. She could hear both of them. The sounds were anything but erotic to Livy.

Later, she fell asleep and slept all night.

The sun coming into the bedroom in the morning woke her up. She had forgotten to draw the curtains.

When she got up she went to the swimming pool. There was nobody around. It was still hot in the tropical morning. Not caring what she did to her clothes she dived head first into the water to make herself clean.

At breakfast, Andrew and Colin were their old reticent selves. The girls looked happy. Roger had gone back to his farm and Pamela was still in bed. It was as though nothing had happened.

After breakfast, Colin played them all the piano. He was as good as Jeremy's brother Paul. Her fear had gone.

When they went to the club to pick up the jalopy, she was happy again. Ignatius said Jeremy had found a lift home. With Carmen driving they all went back to Mrs Wade's. It was nice at the end of the journey to get back to her room. The sun was setting through her window. For half an hour, Livy stood in front of her easel to paint the sunset again. This time she was only going to paint the sky in all its blood-red colour.

PART II

JUNE 1950 – "YOU'RE ONLY YOUNG ONCE"

On the Saturday morning, Jeremy Crookshank was driven into Salisbury in the Maple's Jaguar. Florence Maple was driving. Jeremy was sitting alone in the back. They were to pick up Petronella from her school, the convent, and go straight to Salisbury Cathedral. No one said a word to him. Livy was meeting him at the church. Except for a brief word on the phone under the eye of Mrs Maple, they had not spoken since the cricket. The chap from the Salisbury South side had dropped him at the gate to Ashford Park, not wishing to go any further. Jeremy had walked up the driveway to his cottage where he had changed and gone down to the barns. The Maples were back from Salisbury. They gave him the keys to the truck to shine the lights on the barn to take out the tobacco in the dark. No one had asked him how he got to the cricket. Mrs Maple never asked him anything personal when he was on the farm... Roger Crumpshaw had asked them to take him to the wedding.

They arrived half an hour before the ceremony to pick up Petronella. To Jeremy, the wedding was the same as every other wedding he had been to. Pamela was in white with a veil. Roger looked anything but comfortable.

Livy was already in her pew when they arrived. They smiled at each other. With her were the two girls from Mrs Wade's house with the Lavington brothers. The Lavington brothers were in morning dress. As ushers they both had white carnations in their buttonholes. Jeremy was surprised to see them sitting with the girls.

After the wedding, a pompous affair conducted by the archbishop of Central Africa, they all drove to the reception at Meikles Hotel. Jeremy found he was seated next to Livy with the Maples at the same table. She gave him a smile. He wanted to kiss her but didn't with Mrs Maple watching, dressed in smart clothes with a picture hat that was so big it got in the way. Since picking her up in school, Petronella had not said a word to him.

The upstairs room at Meikles was crowded with people neither of them knew. On arrival at the reception, Jeremy had shaken hands with Roger Crumpshaw who was waiting at the door with his bride.

Next to their table sat Colin and Andrew Lavington with the two girls.

"How was the party last Saturday?" said Jeremy to Livy, looking at the girls.

"As good as you see. The brothers have quite a place. Carmen and Candy were impressed."

"So I can imagine looking at them now."

"We had a *braai*, and drank too much wine."

"A habit in Rhodesia. Nice of Roger to seat us at the same table."

"We are together, Jeremy... What a lovely wedding, Mrs Maple. I am looking forward to visiting your farm. When Jeremy gets his bonus we're going to buy a banger to get us around. It's so difficult in Salisbury without a car. There are no Tubes or buses like there are in London."

"What bonus, Miss Johnston? Learner assistants don't get a bonus. Assistants receive a bonus. Next season, Jeremy. You didn't expect a bonus this season did you? You can't yet speak the native language. The first year we are giving you more than you are giving us. I thought my husband made that quite clear when you were employed. A perfectly common practice to give the learner assistant a house and a small salary for food. You must understand."

"I borrowed against the bonus to buy Livy's ticket."

"Then they'll have to wait until next year... Petronella, my dear. What have you been doing at school this week? Wasn't the bride pretty? I so love a wedding. A pity we will have to be going home straight after this beautiful reception. Roger has done so well. Quite rich, I should think."

"Jeremy's not going back today, Mrs Maple."

"We're grading tomorrow, old chap," said Bertie Maple.

"Jeremy isn't, Mr Maple. If he doesn't get a bonus there isn't much point, is there?"

"What's it got to do with you, young lady?" snapped Mrs Maple.

"One hundred pounds, to be exact. The price of my boat ticket which Jeremy borrowed from his friends. Jeremy was expecting a bonus this year."

"It's vulgar to talk of money at the dinner table."

"You started this conversation."

"Really. This is too much."

"I couldn't have put it better," said Livy.

"He doesn't have any money."

"But I have money, Mrs Maple. Just before leaving London I sold a painting for four hundred pounds. After lunch, Jeremy is coming home with me to Mrs Wade's."

"She'll never allow it."

"Probably not. Then we'll find him another room with the help of my friends."

"Bertie! Take me home. I've heard enough of this. Petronella! Come with me. Please give our apologies to the Crumpshaws. When I tell them they'll understand. That's a broken contract young man, do you understand?"

"Yes it is," said Livy. "But not broken by Jeremy. What ever happened to an Englishman's word being his bond?"

"Really, Bertie. Now we are being insulted."

With a flourish, hat and all, the Maples got up and left, watched by Jeremy and Livy. Jeremy laughed. A good solid belly laugh.

"Do you have much left on the farm?" asked Livy.

"Not really. We'll pick it up somehow... What made you do that, Livy?"

"Someone had to do it. You see, lover, I came all this way to save you. What a bitch... Look. We have two bottles of wine on the table. Pick them up, Jeremy. We're going to join the girls."

"I feel so much better."

"So do I. Later we'll talk. Probably tomorrow. Tonight we sneak you into Mrs Wade's."

"What about her?"

"She's away for the weekend. Rather convenient, don't you think?" Livy was smiling sweetly.

"I've lost my bonus."

"You never had it."

NOT SURE WHETHER she had done him a favour but feeling good, Livy went across to the brother Lavingtons' table. Jeremy had picked up the two bottles of wine.

"What was all that about?" asked Colin, his hand on Carmen's knee for all to see.

"I'm out of a job," said Jeremy. "And a house for that matter. What you see is all I got. I feel marvellous. Mrs Maple didn't want to pay me the bonus Bertie promised me before I left England."

"There's a lot of that I'm afraid. Young lads from England being taken advantage of. Didn't you get the job from an introduction by Harry Brigandshaw? Now there's an honest man. He's back in the country. Something wrong with his liver. On the grapevine I heard he's seeing a witchdoctor. The tribal healer. They use herbs and ground roots they find in the bush. Not all hocus-pocus. Like some of the ancient Chinese remedies. Wasn't he a friend of your father's? Elephant Walk is a lot nearer than Macheke. Why don't you go and see him? Poor old Bertie. He does just what she tells him. It was her money. Come and sit down. We can bring up two more chairs. Sis had quite a wedding don't you think?"

"We don't have a car."

"The jalopy got to Macheke," said Carmen.

"Would you?" asked Livy.

"Lucky Mrs Wade's away for the weekend!"

"I thought so too."

The band struck up as two more chairs were squeezed into the table. Beside the bandstand someone brought in a stuffed lion to give the wedding the look of Africa. There were two official photographers going round taking pictures with flash lights. The poor lion had glass eyes that stared at Livy seeing nothing. Livy would have preferred to paint the animal in the wild. There were other stuffed animals around the room. Anyone in England seeing the photographs of the wedding would know they were taken in Africa.

Once they were comfortably seated she took Jeremy's hand under the table. He squeezed it and they smiled at each other. She would make it all up to him later.

When they went on the dance floor they danced up close. They were both relaxed. There was no need to talk anymore. They were enjoying themselves. When the newlyweds came round to each of the tables, Pamela asked what had happened to the Maples. Colin told Roger. Roger looked at Livy with a surprised look on his face. No one mentioned the Maples again. Roger and Pamela went on to the next table to receive more congratulations.

Pamela's mother sat down at their table with her sons while the bride and groom did the rounds. Mrs Lavington was a small woman with round glasses and a fringe. Livy could see both the boys in their mother but not Pamela. The old woman looked tired from her flight out from England. She seemed bewildered by it all. When an old man came across to her table and asked her to dance, Livy had to smile to herself. The old girl had a chance in Rhodesia of getting married again. The eyes behind the round glasses had brightened up no end.

Later, the bride threw her bouquet as required. She was wearing her going away outfit and she had told Livy they were going to Mauritius for their honeymoon. Livy smiled her best smile at Pamela, hoping in her mind the night would bring her joy. If she was going to have ten kids it was best to get started.

She only danced with Jeremy all through the reception. When it was over they walked away from the hotel holding hands. They didn't want to stay with the others who were going out to dinner. The brothers Lavington were staying the night at Meikles in two of the hotel's rooms.

They walked through Cecil Square, meandering along. A pair of doves were chasing each other in the trees, their tails fanned out. June was apparently the breeding season for doves in Rhodesia, Jeremy told her.

In her room she showed him the two paintings she had done of the sunsets. The last one was very violent in red.

"They're beautiful, Livy. I'm not just saying that to please you. No wonder you sold the one in England for four hundred pounds... What do you want to do?"

"Right now, make love. I came a long way for you."

"Are you really for me, Livy?"

"We'll just have to find out. Why talk now? You're out of it. We'll get your clothes. I like the idea of visiting Harry Brigandshaw. I heard a lot of good things about him in England."

Slowly, carefully, Livy took his face in both her hands. Then she kissed him. For the rest of the night they were going to make love. Nothing else mattered. It was primal, like the blood-red painting on the easel by the window with the light of day fading out behind it as the whole world shrank down to themselves.

THE NEXT DAY Jeremy's life was back in focus. He was broke, without a job but did not care. They had slept all night in a single bed both comfortable with each other. Carmen brought them a cup of tea.

"What happened?" asked Livy.

"First you get them interested. Too much and they get bored. We both came home after dinner with Colin and Andrew. You have to think, Livy... How's the unemployed today?"

"Could I borrow your car, Carmen? If I don't get my gear out of the cottage today she'll change the lock on the door. I'm a good mechanic. My father was an aeronautical engineer so if anything breaks I'll be able to fix it."

"The timing's out."

"I'll adjust the points if that's what's wrong. Have a good look at it on the farm in the workshop before we return. Then I'm going to phone my brother in England and ask him for money to go home."

"You're going back to England?"

"What else can we do?...Thanks for the tea. I'll be as quick as I can with the car."

"The boys are picking us up for lunch. We owe Livy for introducing us to the brothers Lavington. Of course you can have the car. It got there once. It can do it again. You might have to push start it. The battery is nearly flat. Do you want breakfast now?"

"We went to bed early."

"I'll bet you did."

TWO HOURS LATER, Jeremy and Livy drove on to Ashford Park and straight to his cottage. There was no one working in the grading shed. The gang had been given the day off by the look of it. There was no sign of the Maples. Jeremy used his key to let himself in, standing back from the door to let Livy pass into what until yesterday had been his home.

"Pam wasn't wrong about the furniture. Not even curtains on the windows."

"A bachelor doesn't mind. Ten minutes to pack. I hate confrontations. Better to go before they find out I'm back."

"Won't they have heard the car?"

"Probably. They'll realise what I'm doing and leave me alone."

"Doesn't he owe you a month's salary?"

"The salary came mostly in food and groceries. They deducted the price of vegetables they sold me from the farm. Butter, eggs and milk the same."

"How lovely. Don't people have a conscience?"

"It was what I found. What could I do? I thought a good bonus would make up for the lack of salary. I ate okay. Without a car, there wasn't anywhere to go to spend money. I used a shotgun to shoot guinea fowl for the pot. They roost in the trees in the evening. The cartridges came off the farm. The shoot boy used the gun at night to keep the wild pigs out of the maize."

"Hurry up. I want to get out of here." Livy was looking out of the window while Jeremy packed. "Your ex-employer's coming, Jeremy."

"Which one?"

"Bertie Maple."

"He can't stop me picking up my own gear."

With his back to the one door in the cottage, Jeremy went on packing. Most of what he had was still in the cases he had brought from England.

There was one small wardrobe. The place was a mess. He could hear footsteps outside followed by a knock on his door.

"Is that you, Jeremy?"

"Yes, sir. I'm just packing up my things."

"May I come in?"

"Of course."

Bertie Maple came in, not looking pleased with himself.

"This is for you, Jeremy. Just don't tell my wife. I hadn't told Florence I'd agreed to give you a bonus."

Jeremy took the envelope and looked inside.

"Three hundred pounds," said Bertie Maple. "Enough to pay your debt and get you both back to England."

"That's far more than I expected, sir."

"We were going to pay the gang tomorrow. The money was in the safe. I'll go to the bank and get some more in the morning. You were right, Miss Johnston. A gentleman's word is his bond and I'm sorry it ended like this. If you require a reference for another farm they only have to ring me. My wife is a little conservative with money. If you stay in Rhodesia to farm, likely I'll see you again on the floors."

"Thank you, sir."

"We all have our crosses to bear."

Without another word they were left alone to finish the packing.

When they left the cottage, Jeremy took the car to the workshop to use the farm tools to change the timing.

Ten minutes after Jeremy drove away from Ashford Park for the last time. There was no fluffing coming down the hills. The engine sounded good.

"Life's full of surprises," said Livy. "Why did he marry the bitch?"

"She had the money."

"What are you going to do, Jeremy?"

"Celebrate. Think. Try and make up my mind. We can go home up the east coast. See something of Rhodesia first. I can use a little of the money to buy a banger. I want to visit Elephant Walk when I have my own transport. Harry Brigandshaw flew a seaplane to Switzerland with my father. They were friends. I always like talking about my father with someone who knew him. Then we can make up our minds."

"I can paint on the trip in the bush."

"This car just needed timing. Goes like a bird."

A safe journey brought them back to Mrs Wade's. Mrs Wade had returned from visiting her daughter on the farm. Her car was back in the driveway.

"Like so many others, the daughter came out first to Rhodesia," said Livy. "Mrs Wade sold the family house in Surrey and bought this house in Baker Avenue. There is a son farming in Marandellas. The only money Mrs Wade has is in the house, which is why she takes in paying guests. That and the fact she was lonely, I expect, on her own... Leave your stuff in the car and come and meet Mrs Wade, she will know of a house that lets rooms to young men. There are a lot of young men out from England looking for opportunities. Skills are short in Rhodesia. The blacks don't have any skills in mechanics or plumbing or engineering of any kind. If we have no luck today there's a boarding house up Second Street. Maybe that's better. A room and three meals... Who are the three friends you have to give back the money, Jeremy?"

"Friends don't lend you that kind of money I'm afraid. That bit was a fib. Neither do the banks unless you have collateral, something to put up against the loan as security. I borrowed your fare from Paul. Not being able to pay back my brother would have been the worst day of my life. He brought me over last Christmas to see Mum. It was all his idea to find me a girlfriend. I'm too gullible. I believe what people tell me. I should have asked for a contract in writing but it seemed so rude at the time. I had no idea the farm was owned by his wife. Why didn't he tell her he had promised me a bonus at the end of the season?"

"They tell the wives what they want to hear to avoid arguments. He might have given you a bonus behind her back. Or maybe not. Skated over it. Avoided the issue when it was time to pay your bonus. Conveniently forget. People are like that."

"I'm too naive... The boarding house sounds fine to me now I have some money. The most I had hoped for was a hundred and fifty quid."

"Conscience money. The bit about the word of a gentleman got to him."

"Was that intentional?"

"Of course it was. You should have seen Jeanne Pétain working on Samuel Chalmers to put up the money for the Nouvelle Galerie. Learnt a few tricks from our Jeanne."

"As long as you don't play them on me."

"Carmen and Candy must still be with the brothers Lavington or they would have come out by now. After saying hello to Mrs Wade we can drive the car to Terraskane, the lodging. Full of young people. Food isn't much good by all accounts but everyone likes the place. You can pay by the week or the month. Paying by the month comes out cheaper."

"My brother Paul met Jeanne in America. They both worked for Harry Brigandshaw in New York selling Americans English antiques after the war when the British aristocracy began to go broke. Paul was rather keen on her, I think. She was asked to the party he threw for me when I met you, Livy. I don't think she came. There were so many people. Once I saw you, I wasn't looking at the other girls. Paul now works for Harry in London. They market a brand of cigarettes. Seems ages ago."

"What a beautiful evening."

"Yes it is. In more ways than one. Here comes Mrs Wade. I met her first when I paid your first month's rent. Scraped that bit up from my salary."

"You didn't say it included breakfast and dinner."

"Didn't ask her."

THE CONTRAST STRUCK JEREMY MOST. One day he was on his own on a farm in the middle of nowhere, the next he was eating breakfast in a small dining room with people. He had given Terraskane a week's rent to first get his bearings. Livy still had three weeks' rent paid to Mrs Wade in advance. In a more liberal-minded world he would have moved into her bedroom, if Mrs Wade had allowed it. With neither having an income, every penny had to be watched while they made up their minds.

Livy had gone back to painting in her room while Jeremy looked around. His first job was to buy a second-hand car without being sold a pup by some glib salesman. He found five open stands selling second-hand cars in the first two hours of walking around the Pioneer Street end of Salisbury. All had been cleaned and polished, including the engines. When the cars started it was a different story. Jeremy bought the *Rhodesia Herald* and looked for the smalls and second-hand cars. He had walked half the morning, finding a seat at a table outside the men's bar to the left of Meikles Hotel, away from the hotel's main entrance. To savour his feeling of liberation, Jeremy ordered himself a beer. He was rested, mentally and physically, Livy never far from his thoughts. When he found what he was looking for in the paper, he sat back to look at the people walking the street going about their business. When the beer was savoured and drunk he went into the main part of the hotel to look for a phone.

"Could you bring the car to Meikles Hotel? I've just arrived in Salisbury. I can pay you cash. How do we register the car in my name? I'll be at a table looking out on the street next to the bar."

The car when it came, driven by a young man, not much older than Jeremy, was a Morris Minor, built in England. With the young man in the passenger seat they went for a drive.

"That's fine," said Jeremy back at the hotel. "I'll take it. How does twenty pounds sound?"

"It was twenty-five in the paper."

"All right. Twenty-five if you bring it back here registered in my name. I don't know my way around Salisbury. I was on a farm in Macheke. How long will it take?"

"Give me five quid now, the rest when I return. Take me an hour at the most. They don't bugger around in Rhodesia. How long you been out?"

"Nearly a year."

"Your bonus, I suppose."

"Something like that."

"I'm going home for a wedding. I'll be back some time. Nice doing business with you, Jeremy Crookshank. She'll get you around for twenty-five quid."

"I hope so."

"You going to stay here?"

"Why not? Nice spot. I don't have anything to do without the car."

"We can have a beer when I come back. Where do you want to go?"

"To a farm in Mazoe. Arguably, the first farm in Rhodesia. Before Rhodes hoisted the Union Jack in the name of Queen Victoria. Elephant Walk. Ever heard of it?"

"Who hasn't heard of the Brigandshaws? Someone said he's back in the country. Harry Brigandshaw. Quite a legend in these parts. Twenty-three kills as a fighter pilot in the First World War."

"Friend of my father. They flew together."

"Only know him by reputation."

"When's the wedding?"

"Next week. I'm flying. You buying the car helps me a lot."

"Good deals are made that way. Both parties equally satisfied."

"She needs new tyres."

"I can see that."

"Cars don't rust in Rhodesia... You'll either be here or in the bar?"

The man drove off whistling. An identical car of the same year had been on the third second-hand car lot selling for fifty pounds. Livy would be happy. They had transport if the man came back. Jeremy thought he would. The man wanted the rest of his money to take to England. The British and Rhodesian pounds were on a par, easily exchangeable as part of the sterling block.

Going inside, Jeremy bought himself a beer at the bar and looked around. From a day of disaster, life was suddenly just going right.

"You look happy," said the only other man at the bar.

"I am. Oh, yes, I am."

There was a girl waiting and money in the bank where he had put it in the Standard Bank opposite the hotel earlier in the morning. What more could a man want, he asked himself.

"Can I buy you a drink?"

"Let me buy you one. I'm waiting for my new car. Well, not new in that way. New to me. Everything is new to me today. My name's Jeremy."

"Crispin Dane. You're Jeremy Crookshank, Livy's fiancé. Livy and I met on the boat. I had my first beer in this bar when I came to Rhodesia. It's my lucky bar. Where everything started. I met a gold prospector. An old timer. We're partners now. Both of us rich. He knew where to find the old diggings of the Monomotapa. I had the money to mine the gold deep. You're very lucky, Jeremy."

"Got fired yesterday."

"I was talking about Livy."

"I know you were. Are you a threat, Mr Dane?"

"No, Jeremy. I'm not. Life has strange ways of coming around in circles. I saw you meet the train."

"I saw you looking at her. I thought I recognised you when I came in the bar."

"It's over. Believe me."

"I hope so... She's painting again."

"I'm glad. Why did you offer me a drink?"

"I like to know what I'm up against."

"You're a clever man. That's the first rule of business if you want to win."

he next day after a good breakfast – Jeremy's in the dining room at Terraskane, Livy's at Mrs Wade's – they hit the road. The man who had sold him the car had given him the directions. Civil servants were a lot quicker in Rhodesia. The man had come back to the bar with the car newly registered in under an hour. After the one beer, Crispin Dane had gone on his way.

"That one is easy. You go out on the Mazoe Road until you reach the dam. It was built by Harry Brigandshaw to irrigate his citrus. When you see the orange trees, and there are miles of them along the river, you're on Elephant Walk. The sign post to the farm house is on the right before you get to the Mazoe Hotel. Can't miss it. Get lost, anyone will give you directions. Have you got an appointment?"

"Not really. My brother Paul runs the Brigandshaw companies in London. I just want to see if he is all right. He's not been well."

"Carry on from Terraskane and follow the sign to Mazoe."

"Have a nice wedding in England."

They picked up the Mazoe signs without any difficulty. Livy was dressed a little more demurely than usual. He did not tell her he had met Crispin Dane and had a drink with him. What was in her past was best left in the past. He did not want to know what they had been doing on the boat for six weeks.

They were greeted by a pack of dogs on Elephant Walk. They were all Rhodesian Ridgebacks. Lion dogs. Used and trained by the pioneers to hunt lions, Jeremy had been told. The first ten miles of the road had been fully tarred. For the rest, Jeremy had battled to keep the small car on the strips. Off the strips was a drop that had to be taken when cars passed them from the opposite direction. Farmers going hell for leather into town. Dust flying up so both cars went off the strips at the last moment to minimise the lengths of the clouds of dust. Both playing chicken right up to the last minute.

A black man told them where to find Harry Brigandshaw at the big house. There were five houses of different sizes in the compound with lawns going down to the Mazoe River.

"What a beautiful farm," said Livy. "It's all so established. The brothers Lavington farm is rather more ostentatious. This one welcomes you as a friend."

They found the man they had come to see under a tree sitting in a deck chair. They had only to follow the dogs. All five dogs sat down round his chair and watched them.

"Jeremy Crookshank! Wonderful to see you. Who's the lovely lady? Weren't you meant to be working on Tuesday? Mrs M's a bit of a stickler I seem to remember. Welcome to Elephant Walk. I won't get up from the deck chair. Once I'm down in one of these I like to stay."

"I got fired."

"If you ring that small bell on the table over there someone will come and we can ask them to bring us a pot of tea."

"This is Livy Johnston. She's come all the way from England to see me."

"Lucky man. There are more chairs on the *stoep*. I remember sitting under this msasa tree when I was a child. Before the First World War. My goodness. Time flies. Where have all the years gone? I prefer being in the shade of a tree than sitting under a man-made roof."

"How are you feeling, sir?"

"Much better since I got home. I went to see the *sangoma*. He knew me from when I was a boy. He's rather old but wise. He gave me some *muti* to take every day. No idea what's in it. Lives in a cave in the hills over there... Picked up bugs in the Congo when I was staying with the Tutsis. He threw the bones to make an impression and then asked me lots of very intelligent questions. All in Shona. An African traditional healer for an African disease. I'm beginning to feel better... My mother has gone to Salisbury with my sister Madge. Ralph Madgwick, the farm manager, is out in the lands. We still grow tobacco. The oranges are a separate division. His wife Rebecca is in their house over there. She's the daughter of Sir Jacob Rosenzweig the banker. Old friend of mine. I'm gabbling, I'm afraid. What a sight for sore eyes. The son of an old friend and a beautiful woman. I miss my children in England. Anywhere, here I am. The doctors in London thought I'd be dead by now... Wouldn't she pay you your bonus?" There was a twinkle in the old man's tired eyes that said he knew what happened to Jeremy.

"How did you know, sir?"

"Word travels in Rhodesia. The drums. Well, not quite. It was quite a display at the wedding. I was phoned the next day. I hoped you would come and see me."

"I'm not here for help. Bertie Maple paid me three hundred pounds."

"Finally a gentleman's word is his bond... He won't tell her of course... Goodson, can you bring us a large pot of tea? I don't know how you get from the kitchen so fast when you hear that bell. First bring us some chairs. You'll have to move the dogs out of the shade. There will be two more for lunch. Please tell cook... Now, where were we? You see, I got that little scene at the wedding word for word. She's not very popular, I'm afraid. The whole of Salisbury is laughing. Quite a woman you have, Jeremy. Quite a woman. What are you going to do?"

"I've bought an old car to show Livy some of Rhodesia. I want to take her into the bush. She wants to paint the animals. Sold one of her paintings in England for four hundred pounds."

"What kind of car?"

"A Morris Minor."

"Won't get you in the bush. You'd better borrow the Land Rover. Four-wheel drive. Three spare tyres. There's camping equipment somewhere in the sheds. We'll ask Ralph Madgwick when he comes in from the lands. Better you go with someone in a second vehicle. If you break down in the bush on your own you have to walk in the wilds in the sun. Not good. I took horses when I went in the bush on a long trip... Brings back so many memories. I've had a wonderful life. So many wonderful people... Take Livy into the Zambezi Valley. You won't see a footprint of man. You go in past Makuti and cross the widest part of the valley to the river. They're going to dam the Kariwa gorge further upriver from the Lusito Sugar Estate. Which is my point. Ralph knows the young Italian who's employed among other things to keep the elephant out of the sugar cane. They're irrigating five thousand acres along the river. Lusito Sugars. Big English sugar company. The man's also an engineer, his main job for Lusito Sugars. In charge of the pump station for the irrigation system. Visited Ralph to help us with our own irrigation now we've built the dam... He's your man. One of the best shots in Rhodesia, so they say. Mario Tuchi. He is the man to take you in the bush. Bit of a ladies' man. Do you have any girlfriends, Livy? Take another girl with you and visit Mario. He'll kiss you both as well as the girl. Very Italian. Two or three days are enough. A week's better. Thank you, Goodson... Dogs! Get out of the way! The Madgwick children are in boarding school. Three of them. Place livens up a bit when they're at home. Madge's kids are all married and long gone... Maybe you'd like a beer?"

"Tea's just fine," said Livy. "I've heard so much about you, Mr Brigandshaw. I'm a friend of your son, Frank."

"We made friends in the end... He's not actually my son. His father was once my brother-in-law. The Honourable Barnaby St Clair."

"I sold him my painting."

"They say we all know each other through someone in the end. Frank's doing well. When the tea comes you can tell me all about Frank. For the last few years he wasn't talking to me or his mother... Why is life always so complicated? I'd been here on the farm. They'd been lovers long before I met Tina. Childhood friends. The baron's son and the rail worker's daughter. People. We always complicate our lives. She's seeing him now. My wife, I mean. I asked Barnaby to look after her when I came home to Rhodesia. Tina hates Africa. And our children are in England. Most of them. Kim's still roaming around the world trying to find something to do with his life. Who knows, he may visit Rhodesia."

"Can we really borrow a Land Rover?" said Jeremy.

"Of course you can... Your brother Paul phones every week. The business in London and America is doing well... So there we are. Young Jeremy Crookshank. Didn't you have a barney with Frank when you were kids? Your family were staying with us at Hastings Court for Christmas.

Before the war... You must so miss your father. How's your mother?... Oh, good. Here comes the tea. What would we all do without a cup of tea?"

"You have a beautiful home. It's all so peaceful. The dogs have gone to sleep."

"They'll wake when the Egyptian geese show up. The birds honk at the dogs from the safety of the trees... What are you going to do, Jeremy? Maybe you should go back to England. Young Josiah Makoni was here on vacation from Fort Hare University when I got back. I'm paying for his education. His father and I go back a long way to our childhoods. How I learnt my Shona. Princess is so proud of her son. She's Tembo's youngest wife. There are four of them, poor fellow. I find one quite a handful. Josiah and I sat under this same tree for a long talk. Telling me all about Fort Hare. It's the black-only university in South Africa. His eyes shone when he talked about African nationalism. He's caught up with the crowd espousing African nationalism and communism as the panacea of their people's ills. Says if India got independence from Britain, why can't South Africa and Rhodesia? Not that South Africa's a true colony anymore. The Boer Nationalists have their own ideas down south. Fort Hare's a hotbed of intrigue, according to Josiah. He was full of a past student who's also a Shona like Josiah. Robert something. I didn't catch the chap's last name. Wants to chase us British out of Southern Rhodesia. Take back the land. Make the country communist like Russia. If I understand what the boy was saying, there's trouble down the road. The British Empire is collapsing. The Americans won't mind. They want to get into traditional British markets once the Union Jack is hauled down. Who knows how long it will all take? Years I should think. The average chap doesn't think about politics until someone stirs him up and gives him a cause. People like this Robert usually stir up expectations for their own ends. People are so gullible. I have no idea which is best for everybody. Most of the time, nationalists like Hitler lead us all into war. Politics. I keep right out of it. They all have an answer that never quite works in practice. Revolution is exciting for a young mind. Josiah has changed since I sent him to Fort Hare. He doesn't think I'm his friend anymore by the way he looked at me."

"So you think a farm of my own won't be such a good idea?"

"Not if someone takes it away from you when you've done all the hard work. And make no mistake, the hardest work is thinking. Anyone can do the work when they are told what to do. You have to think to make a business work properly. The work has to be constructive for everyone. When it comes down to it, a farm's a business like any other. You have to grow a crop at a profit. A farm is no good to anyone unless it is farmed properly... Take a trip in the bush with Mario Tuchi and think about it. A good idea today can sometimes be a bad one tomorrow. After two wars, the British are tired. They won't want to fight for the colonies anymore. America is the power now. They fought the British for independence back in the eighteenth century. It's the Russians they worry about. They'll do anything in Africa to stop the communists gaining control. The two big powers are going to be played off against each other. We colonials are likely to be the football they will both be kicking... So old Bertie paid you your bonus. Good for him... Thank you, Goodson... Livy, would you be kind enough to pour the tea? No sugar for me. After the war and all the rationing I stopped taking sugar."

THE OLD LADY joined them after they drank the tea. She had driven back from Salisbury with a driver. She was younger than Livy expected. Looking at her and the old man in the deck chair they could have been husband and wife. Jeremy had gone quiet. The picture of Ashford Park and Pembringham Estate no longer looked so bright to her. Livy wondered if all of them were not living with their heads in the sand in colonial Africa.

"I was seventeen when I had Harry."

"I'm so sorry, Mrs Brigandshaw. I hope I wasn't staring."

"Harry looks younger with a functioning liver. So you want to live in Rhodesia both of you? Has Harry been talking about young Josiah's visit? You look pensive, young man. You'd better tell me who you are. How you came to know my son."

"My father flew the Short Sunderland flying boat with Mr Brigandshaw. On a trip to Switzerland before the war. My father drowned in his boat off Dunkirk."

"I'm sorry."

"I visited Hastings Court with my family the last Christmas before the Battle of Britain."

"How nice for you. I grew up at Hastings Court. My father was the last English baronet. The current baronet is an American who doesn't use the title of course. By then my father was living here at Elephant Walk. I took his body home to be buried in the family mausoleum alongside his ancestors. So you know the ancestral home of the Mandervilles? Everything comes to an end, young man. Life itself comes to an end. The secret is to enjoy what you have at the time as much as possible. Goodson tells me you are joining us for lunch... Now young lady, what is your story?"

"There isn't one at the moment."

"There is always a story."

"She's a painter," said Jeremy coming out of his stew. "A very good painter."

"Ah. You love her. We always say such nice things about the people we love."

"You're in luck, Jeremy," said Harry Brigandshaw, sitting up in his chair. "Ralph Madgwick has come back for lunch. That's his truck. He usually has his lunch sent to him in the lands or the workshop. You'd better go and ask him for the Land Rover. Why not ask him over for lunch with Rebecca? They both like new faces. Rebecca will enjoy meeting an artist. Is there enough lunch, Mother?"

"There's always enough bread, cheese and cold meat. Homemade pickles. Ralph loves my pickles... Thank you, Goodson. Two more plates for lunch and two more chairs when you bring the table. We'll eat under the tree if the dogs will get out of the way."

Jeremy had got up and given Mrs Brigandshaw his seat. She watched him go off with Goodson to get another chair. Livy smiled at the thought of the simple lunch. There was so much difference between Elephant Walk and the other two farms. Livy smiled at the old lady. She liked her. There was an inborn graciousness in the old girl, something Livy had not seen for a long time. One of the last of her kind.

Ralph Madgwick when he came was a man close to fifty, his skin richly tanned by the African sun. He had a nice smile. His wife looked Semitic, probably Jewish with the name of Rebecca. Livy had never seen two people so clearly in tune with each other. Ralph was English with a public school accent that hadn't gone away farming in Rhodesia. They both talked of their kids. There were three of them, Livy learnt. Faith,

Jacob and Becky. They were all teenagers by the sound of it, away at boarding school in Salisbury.

They all ate their lunch under the tree. The dogs had gone off to bark at the geese down the bottom of the long lawn by the river. Afterwards, Harry Brigandshaw and his mother went back into the house. Ralph Madgwick had helped the old man to get up from the deck chair. He couldn't get up on his own. The dogs trotted back to see what was going on. A tractor started up from the sheds, the top of the barns clearly visible above the trees that dotted the lawn. Around each tree was a circular flowerbed bursting with colour. The diverse colours made Livy want to paint. The dogs began chasing each other around the trees. Dogs, an old man contented at the end of his life surrounded by the young colours of flowers under the soft green of the trees. A painting of hope.

"The dogs are destroying the flowers," said Ralph Madgwick. "Why don't we all take a walk down to the river before I go back to work? We've finished the work in the lands. The gang are finished for the day. They get up at sunrise to work in the cool of the early mornings. Their wives have lunch for them in the compound. Only at the height of the reaping season do they work all day. My afternoons are spent in the workshop fixing the machinery. There's always something broken. Too time-consuming and expensive to send a tractor into Salisbury. Can't afford to have even one tractor out of commission for longer than necessary. If I get stuck I bring out a mechanic. We have everything in the workshop including a lathe to make spare parts. A farm like this is an island to itself. You never stop work on a farm... I have an idea. Why don't you both stay the night with us and drive back with the Land Rover in the morning? Harry gets tired very quickly. So does his mother. Madge Oosthuizen runs the house for them. Her son Tinus works with your brother Paul for Oosthuizen Brigandshaw. But I'm sure you know that. He's based in New York. Paula and Doris, Madge's other two kids, are married. Once the children are married you don't see much of them. Madge should be back soon. She took the truck yesterday. Her mother went in this morning with a driver to have coffee in Meikles with her. The old lady doesn't like to do the shopping anymore. Leaves it to Madge. Only time Mrs Brigandshaw gets off the farm. Madge will likely join us for a drink. She likes young company."

"Doesn't she have a husband?"

"Barend was shot by Braithwaite on Salisbury Station before Tembo shot Braithwaite. The same man who shot Harry's first wife Lucinda. Lucinda is buried on the farm with their unborn child. They'd let him out of the asylum in England. The war over the trenches had twisted his mind. It's all rather a long story, I'm afraid, one no one talks about. Madge has been on her own ever since. No one talks about it... No, they don't talk about it... I'll give Mario Tuchi a ring. They all like a bit of new blood for company on the sugar estate. Harry's right. Never go into the bush without someone who knows what he is doing... The Zambezi Valley. Now there's a place to be. Primal Africa untouched by human hand. The kingdom of the animals where the lion is the real king and not us humans. In the valley the lion is on top of the food chain. You'll need to take anti-malaria pills and luckily the tsetse fly aren't too bad this time of the year... You do have a gun, Jeremy?"

"Not anymore. I used the farm gun on Ashford Park. I've left them, I'm afraid."

"Sounds like Mrs Maple. Didn't they want to pay you your bonus?"

"Something like that. You must have heard the wedding story from Mrs Brigandshaw."

"I'll lend you a .375 and a fishing rod. The Zambezi bream are the best freshwater fish in the world. Beats salmon or trout any day. The rivers close to the banks are full of them. Out in the stream are tiger fish. Great fish but you can't eat them. Full of small bones... So, Livy. How are you liking Africa?"

"I'm not sure at the moment. Jeremy was going to stay and get his own farm. Mr Brigandshaw says the future isn't quite so certain."

"There are problems everywhere. Aren't there, Rebecca? Sometimes it's nice to get away from people and their prejudices. We found that. Here we have no problems. In England a Jew marrying a Gentile had all sorts of problems. There are problems everywhere. Most of them man-made. You just have to take your pick which one you prefer to avoid... You'll like Mario Tuchi. Everyone does."

THEY LEFT Elephant Walk after lunch the next day. During the night Livy had had to behave herself in her separate room. They had said goodbye to Harry Brigandshaw and his mother. The sister was visiting the clinic she ran for the black labourers. The Land Rover had a winch in the front and six empty petrol cans in a long bracket at the back to give the vehicle a longer range, and a roof rack for all the equipment. The Morris Minor was left in one of the sheds for when Jeremy brought back the Land Rover. Ralph Madgwick had phoned Mario Tuchi the previous night. The call had come through on the party line at supper two hours after it was booked. There were seven other farms on the party line, Ralph had explained. In the countryside, everyone shared the same telephone lines, only picking up the phone when it rang with their rings. Ralph's ring was two longs and a short. When Ralph told Mario she was bringing her friend Carmen, the open invitation to the Lusito Sugar Estate was made. Anytime the next week. They just had to ask for him when they reached the estate. Jeremy had spoken briefly to Mario to make the personal contact, saying the man had a pronounced Italian accent. Jeremy said he was charming. They would spend the first night they arrived in his bungalow on the estate, then drive down the valley and camp by the river. Livy thought how easy it all was with the right contacts. They drove all the way back to Salisbury with her hand resting lightly on his knee.

"Oh my goodness," said Carmen when they arrived at Mrs Wade's. "Has the old car not turned into a swan? What's the gun for, Jeremy? Fishing rods? Camping equipment?"

"We're going to camp on the banks of the Zambezi River, Carmen. You want to come? There's a charming, single Italian by the name of Mario at the other end. Jeremy told him about you. Unless, of course, the brothers Lavington have a monopoly on your time?"

"No man has a monopoly without a wedding ring. Not even them. When are we going?"

"Tomorrow," said Jeremy. "I want to drive up in daylight to see where I'm going."

"Can't I come?" asked Candy through her window of Mrs Wade's house. "The bank owes me some leave. If there's one charming Italian maybe there's two."

"What are you both going to say to Andrew and Colin?" asked Livy.

"Nothing like a little competition to concentrate a man's mind... What have you done with the Morris Minor?"

"It's in the shed on Elephant Walk. Borrowed this one for our trip into the bush."

MRS WADE MADE them up a picnic basket before they left, Candy having phoned the manager at the bank and received his permission to go on the trip. The basket was stuffed full of hard-boiled eggs, bread rolls and Mrs Wade's liver pâté alongside a large bowl of trifle. There was fruit in a separate brown bag, two flasks of hot tea, and all the plates and cups needed for camping.

"You're so kind to us, Mrs Wade."

"If I don't have to feed you for a couple of days it's the least I can do."

They took the north road. Within an hour they had lost sight of civilisation. The road was strips before the strips gave out to gravel.

"We're as prepared as we can be," said Jeremy. "For now until the sugar estate we're on our own. How does it feel, girls?" No one answered him.

Three hours from Salisbury they stopped for tea.

"Typical," said Livy. "Tea in the middle of nowhere. We English must have a screw loose somewhere. Anyone want a boiled egg?"

They had found a single tree by the side of the road to give them shade. Then they drove on deeper into the bush. There were small settlements on the way with English names. Jeremy filled up with petrol at one of them.

"How far is Chirundu?"

"Right on the road."

With a hand of bananas bought from a vendor on the side of the road they drove out again. Not one car had passed them coming the other way. Jeremy had found being told 'you can't miss it' was usually not the case. The other person giving the directions knew where they were going. It was his idea and his responsibility to get them where they were heading. He only half-concentrated on the singing in the back of the car. In his mind, his whole future had come to a dead end. All the dreams he had spoken of to Paul in London were no longer going to be real. The big chance had gone. Or better, he told himself, the big chance had never been there. The Maples had wanted a man to stand over the gang for the price of living in a house with three sticks of furniture. A man who had been brought up to do what he was told. The big bonuses and Crown Land farm was a smokescreen for good, English labour so Bertie Maple could linger over his breakfast in the house knowing the job in hand was being watched by a responsible man. There wasn't an easy way forward in his life without any money. Without any prospect of making his fortune, his life was going to be bleak. He would get a job in London and work for someone else for the rest of his life, paying off the mortgage on a semi-detached house at the end of thirty years. It just wasn't going to be any fun. Livy back in London would quickly find herself a man with far better prospects. All he could hope for now was a holiday in the bush and a journey on a boat back to the drudgery now waiting for him in England. All he would have in the future was a distant memory of happiness.

"There it is!" said Candy from the back of the car. "You've gone past it, Jeremy. Whatever would you do without us girls in the car?"

"I saw it too late to turn," lied Jeremy, who had been way too lost in his own self-pity to see the small sign by the side of the dirt road.

Turning the vehicle round, Jeremy retraced the last hundred yards and turned down the small side road with its wooden sign reading 'Lusito Sugar Estate'.

"They can't get too many visitors with a sign like that," said Candy.

For five minutes they followed the track through the bush.

"What's all that green up ahead?" said Candy.

"Sugar cane I should think. Irrigated sugar cane. The rest of the bush is as dry as a bone."

"There are buildings up ahead," said Livy. "That sign says 'Clubhouse'. Why don't we look for Mario there?...That lush green sugar cane. Just shows what you can do with water."

"And good British engineering. Lusito Sugars who own the estate are British."

"Paradise blooming in the desert. What won't I do for a cold beer?"

"You drink gin and tonic."

"Not today. I'm parched. All those miles of suspense... We're here. Well done, lover."

Driving up to the building, Jeremy parked the car and looked around. The place was an oasis. From so much nothing there was suddenly plenty. Outside the clubhouse cars were parked in a row. Jeremy counted twenty of them.

"Must be sundowner time. Come on. If I go in there with three pretty girls they'll never throw me out. They must all work for the sugar estate. Jack said there was a small village. You can't make something like this bloom in the bush without skilled people."

"Maybe they'll offer you a job," said Livy.

"What for? I have no skills."

When they walked in everyone at the bar turned round to look at them. There were a few women but mostly men. Jeremy watched a smartly dressed man come towards them.

"Mario Tuchi. You must be Jeremy. Welcome to the Lusito Sugar Estate."

LIVY PAINTED ALL DAY. She had got up with the dawn the morning after they arrived at the river. The riverine trees were much taller with some of their roots taking up water from the river. There was a hillock under the trees looking downriver where she put up her easel. In the river was a small island covered in trees. On a sandbank in front of the island two fully grown crocodiles watched her while they basked in the sun. Neither of them blinked. The canvas was the biggest she had brought with her packed on the roof rack of the Land Rover. While she was setting herself up to paint in the rising dawn, animals came down to drink at the water on both sides of the river. Through the day, Mario explained what kind of animals she was looking at.

When they swam in the shallows of the river in the heat of the day, Jeremy and Mario stood on the bank either side of the girls, first firing their rifles into the water. Livy's crocodiles slid into the water at the sound of the guns. The girls swam in their knickers and bras, Livy without a bra. She did not care. The day was too hot. Mario was so confident in what he was doing, she was not afraid. There were just the five of them down at the river, twenty or so miles from the sugar estate. The rest of the men had to work. As the chief electrical engineer on the estate, Mario had given himself permission to camp with them at the river.

They had hung mosquito nets from the trees to sleep under with a big fire burning all night in front of them. The two men had taken it in turns during the night to feed the fire with wood. Mario said the fire kept the lions and hyenas at bay. Both he and Jeremy had slept with their guns loaded next to them. Livy had heard the lions in the night far back in the bush away from the river. Only in the morning had the tawny lions come down to the river to drink and hunt. The females had made the impala kill leaving the male to eat first.

The previous night, before they went to bed under their mosquito nets, both the girls had made a play for Mario. He was one of the most handsome men Livy had ever seen. Jeremy had slept alongside her under the same mosquito net. They had made love twice in the night, each time Jeremy feeding the fire when they had finished. He had waited ten minutes holding her hand before getting out from under the net. All the time sounds came from the bush. All the time there was the high-pitched screech of cicadas above them in the trees.

Her painting was of the day but she thought of the night. Of the river, the island, the crocodiles. The tawny lion she was going to paint in later when the background was finished. He was the most beautiful of animals. The detail of the crocodiles with their big eyes would come later.

Each time she got back to painting from her swims, the crocodiles were back on the sandbank. Looking at her. Not blinking. They had swum downriver away from the sound of the guns. For breakfast they had all eaten Mrs Wade's liver pâté and the trifle. Livy had never eaten trifle for breakfast. With breakfast they drank Rhodesian coffee that had grown in the Vumba. Livy had never had a better breakfast. Whatever happened with Jeremy she would never forget him. Why the painting was so important. She wanted to remember every detail forever. No one was going to be allowed to buy her painting unless back in England she was desperate for money.

Quietly, into each other's ears, they had talked in the night, the flickering flames showing her his eyes. He loved her. She could see it in the soft look of his eyes. Without a job and the real prospect of getting his own farm, he wanted to go back to England with her on the boat through the Suez Canal. Taking her moments as they came, she had agreed with him. It was after that they made love the second time, a gentler, sweeter lovemaking.

All day he watched her painting when he was not with Mario and the girls.

The men went fishing for bream which they ate for lunch, whole fish cooked over the coals of the fire still warm from the night. When the ash was taken off, the coals were red hot underneath. All through lunch the crocodiles watched.

Livy went back to her painting on her hillock in the shade of the trees. A fish eagle in a tree behind her watched the river, not moving for hours. Going down once in a swoop, the talons planing the big fish over the water back to the shore. The fish was too heavy for the bird to fly up in the sky. Livy began to paint the big bird into her painting. There was going to be so much life, everything she saw through the day.

When she stopped painting to watch the sun go down with the light fading, the men came back with a small buck they had shot away from the camp. Mario skinned the animal. There were two fires now, one for protection, the other for cooking the buck. Mario had cut a piece of strong wood from a tree, sharpened the end and skewered the carcase. With forked poles at either side of the cooking fire the men spit-roasted the small buck. Mario said he only shot what he was going to eat. He said he loved the animals in the bush. In a sack they had put bottles of beer in the river. The night like the day she was going to remember. Forever. With or without the big painting still on the easel unfinished waiting for her and the dawn of the next day.

When the light went right out of the sky, leaving three layers of stars above in the heavens, the flames from the fire to keep them from being the prey played up in the trees. Livy could see Jeremy watching her over the light of the fire. Each of them was drinking a beer straight out of the bottle. The beer was cool from having been in the water.

Two hours into the night, the men began carving the meat with their hunting knives. The same knives they had used to prepare the carcase before it was spitted over the coals. Mario had basted the venison with a mixture of crushed oranges and lemons mixed with vinegar and sugar.

After the first carving the flesh underneath was raw. Mario basted again. The meat Livy ate was crunchy with burnt sugar on the top where the meat had been seared by the fire.

The dark bush around them was a symphony of sound. Sometimes Livy could hear the plop of fish from the river. The stars were reflected in the surface of the slowly moving water. There was no moon. The rains in Angola that would swell the river were far away, she was told. All of them made Mario talk, telling them what was happening around them in the dark. The man knew so much about the bush. When he moved in the shadowed light of the fire down to the river and the cool sack of beers, Livy thought he moved like a panther. He always took his gun and stood outside the light of the flames for a moment to look out at the darkened bush to acclimatise his eyes to the dark. Looking for danger. Without Mario to protect them, the girls said they would have been frightened all alone in the African bush. With Mario it was peace and contentment, both girls' eyes hungry for more than protection.

That night, one of the girls climbed out from under her mosquito net and went to Mario. To Livy it was all too natural. They were animals like the rest of them. Part of nature. Part of the process of life. Again through the black of the night, Livy could hear the lions. Back behind her hillock, Livy could hear something big moving in the dark of the night. She snuggled closer to Jeremy. He was sound asleep, his rifle hard on her hand when she stretched her arm across the small of his back.

That night she got up to feed the fire. The men had brought back a pile of brushwood during the day. Only when the fire was burning did Livy feel comfortable enough to fall back into sleep.

THEY WERE at the river three days. Livy had finished her painting. Everyone told her the painting was good. When they left the river to drive back in the Land Rover the crocodiles were still on the sandbank in front of the island. They still had not blinked. The fish eagle was back in the tree. The lions had not come back to the river to kill. Like Mario, they only killed when they were hungry.

Both Candy and Carmen had said they were in love with Mario. Both of them had slept with him in the dark of the nights. They said it felt natural sharing the same man. No one wanted to go back to Salisbury. They were back at the sugar estate when Mario said he had to go back to his job. One of the generators down by the river had broken down. As they left the sugar estate they saw Mario go off to look at the broken generator. The generator fed the power to the pumps to irrigate the sugar cane. Both girls were looking back at him through the small back window of the Land Rover.

On top of the Land Rover, tied down on the roof rack, was Livy's painting of the river. She put her hand on Jeremy's knee. She was content.

here was traffic on the dirt road to Elephant Walk. Cars in both directions. The idea had been to pick up the Morris Minor and get Candy back to Mrs Wade's in time for her to get ready for work the next morning.

There were cars parked at random from the barns to the family compound. They were all silent in the Land Rover as Jeremy parked in front of Ralph Madgwick's house. No one came out to greet them when they got out of the car. All of them stretched their legs from cramping up on the long journey from the Zambezi Valley. The first person Jeremy saw was his brother Paul.

"What on earth are you doing here, Paul?" he said, smiling all over his face. "I've got your hundred quid for Livy's boat fare."

"Harry Brigandshaw is dead. He died three days ago. His family have flown out from England. All except Kim. We can't get hold of him. Somewhere in the Himalayas on his walkabout."

"Why all the cars?"

"People, Jeremy. Come to pay their respects. Harry was something of a legend in these parts. The funeral is tomorrow at eleven o'clock in the Salisbury Cathedral."

"He lent me the Land Rover. We were chatting under that tree in front of his house four days ago. We've all been in the Zambezi Valley with a friend of Harry Brigandshaw's. Livy, you remember my brother Paul?... I've lost my job I'm afraid."

"Hello, Livy. How are you two making out?"

"Pretty good," said Livy with a smile, never having known Harry Brigandshaw other than as an old man in a deck chair drinking tea under a tree.

"We've got to get back into town. We drove straight through Salisbury to bring back the Land Rover and pick up my old Morris Minor I bought for twenty-five quid. We'd better get out of the way. How long are you staying in Rhodesia?"

"Can't leave the business for longer than necessary. Harry would understand. His nephew, Tinus Oosthuizen, has flown out from New York with his wife Genevieve. They've left the kids in New York."

"The actress?" said Carmen.

"The same. Vic Bell was on the same flight from London with William Smythe and Horatio Wakefield. Vic was Harry's adjutant in France during the first war. Came with his wife, Sarah. She and Harry shared an underground shelter during the Second World War. When Harry was in Intelligence at the Air Ministry. He had so many friends. Helped so many people. Beth can't believe how kind people are being to the family."

"Is Frank here?" asked Livy.

"Yes. Frank is here. He and Harry made up their differences about his birth before Harry left to come back to Elephant Walk... Harry is going to be buried next to his first wife Lucinda and their unborn child. The request is in Harry's will. His wife Tina came over the day after us with Barnaby St Clair and his brothers, Lord St Clair, Genevieve's father, and the writer, Robert St Clair. Robert and Harry were up at Oxford together. How Harry got to know the St Clairs I suppose, and married the sister. They are all flying back after the funeral. Most of Harry's old friends are staying in Meikles Hotel. There'll be a wake in the hotel function room after the funeral. Half of Salisbury are expected at the service. Beth and I are staying with Harry's mother and his sister Madge. You'd better come and thank them for the Land Rover."

"Of course. Where's Ralph Madgwick?"

"In Salisbury. He's arranging everything for tomorrow."

"I'm sorry. This is Carmen and her friend Candy. They live in Salisbury in the same house as Livy."

"How do you do?"

"Shouldn't we stay in the car? We don't know the family."

"Whatever for? Everyone arriving at Elephant Walk gets a cup of tea or a drink. Usually a meal and a bed for the night. It's a tradition begun by Harry's father who started the farm in the last century. Before Rhodesia became Rhodesia. Harry would expect you to have a cup of tea. He's in his old bedroom. They're moving his body to Salisbury tomorrow for the funeral. Why there are so many people paying their last respects on the farm. Ralph said it was lucky it isn't the summer. Not so hot for the lying-in-state so to speak. To some people in this country, Harry Brigandshaw was royalty. What a man. Few men have been loved so much... Now he's dead. Tina is tormented why she let him come back to Rhodesia on his own. Poor woman. She's beside herself."

"Who's going to inherit the farm?" asked Jeremy.

"Dorian doesn't want it. Tinus might have inherited but they live in New York where they have most of their friends. His grandfather, after whom he's named, was Sebastian Brigandshaw's partner when the farm was first put together. Dorian's writing a book about his grandfather. The rest of the estate in England and America will go to the kids, I suppose."

"You'll be marrying a very rich girl, my brother."

"I hadn't thought of that. Katherine, Harry's secretary, wanted to come out to the funeral. I said she had to stay in London to look after the business. We have enough on our plate running the business not to think of who's going to own the shares... How are you, Jeremy?"

"How's Mother?"

"She's well as can be expected living in the house all on her own... Mrs Brigandshaw. I believe you have met my brother, Jeremy?"

"I'm so sorry, Mrs Brigandshaw."

"A mother should never live long enough to bury her own son. This is the third one of mine to die before me. George was killed in the First World War, he was Harry's younger brother, and then there was dear little James who was only a baby... Come and see my son, young man. He looks so peaceful... I've lived too long. Much too long. There have been three terrible wars in my lifetime. My husband's partner was hanged by us British during the Boer War as a traitor. He came from the Cape, a

British Colony. Said he was British. What nonsense. He was a Boer through and through. Why do we make such a mess of our lives?"

"Your son didn't, Mrs Brigandshaw."

"No, Harry didn't. He hated war. It was the war that got Lucinda killed. That man Braithwaite had killed so many Germans he didn't know right from wrong anymore... It's all a muddle to an old lady... Would you all like a cup of tea?"

LOOKING at a dead body was not Livy's best end to the trip. The man's eyes were closed. The last time she had seen him he was alive saying the future of Rhodesia was not all that Jeremy had cracked it up to be in his letters to her over the months. That their dream of a farm was a false dream that would not have a happy ending.

Jeremy had hold of her hand as they peered into the open coffin. She had never before seen a dead person. It gave her the shivers. Likely the last deed of the dead man had done her a favour. She would never find out, most likely. There was always some kind of future. Her father had said the First World War was the war to end all wars. Which it hadn't. None of them ever did. Life would go on in Rhodesia, whatever people did to each other.

They filed out of the room that Livy thought must have been the man's bedroom as a small boy. There was a picture in a glass frame of the Teddy Bears' Picnic over the end of the bed. Livy wondered if it was the last of everything that Harry Brigandshaw saw. Mrs Brigandshaw had said, while they were inspecting the body not knowing what to say, that her son died in the room.

They drank their tea quickly and left the old lady's house. The Morris Minor was still in the shed. Livy had rolled up the canvas of the river and put it in a cardboard tube. The easel was more difficult to get in the small car. There was no roof rack on the Morris. They left the one side window open, the legs of her easel sticking out, the front resting on Carmen's knees. They had given back the gun and the rest of the equipment.

Jeremy dropped all three of them at Mrs Wade's. They were all tired, physically and emotionally.

"Will you come with me to the funeral, Livy?"

"I suppose so. I hate funerals."

"Don't we all? We can talk to Paul at the wake. I want to give him back his hundred pounds... Death is quick. We were talking to him earlier in the week. Apart from his mother and sister, we were the last people he saw. We can't argue now with his prognosis of Rhodesia."

"Do you think he was right?"

"Probably. We only think what we want to think. The big farm and the swimming pool. A brood of happy children. Staying in love for the rest of our lives... Never happens that way. Without British protection we few English in Africa will be on our own. Are the British going to give up the empire? Of course they are. India was the biggest part of the empire and India has gone."

"Then we'd better go home. Make the best of England."

"It's always better to have a dream when we are young. Even if it doesn't quite work out. That was the most beautiful four days of my life down by the river."

"Mine too... Sleep tight, my love. Dream of me, Jeremy."

"I will... Good night, girls. Can you carry that easel? If I hurry they'll still be serving supper when I get back to Terraskane."

Livy waved to the car as Jeremy drove off. They walked up the short drive. Mrs Wade was waiting for them at the front door. The poor old girl got lonely on her own, Livy supposed... One week it was a wedding reception at Meikles Hotel. Tomorrow was a wake. Life at the start and the end.

She was thinking of the dead man in the coffin as she went up to her room with her painting of the river tucked in its tube under her arm. In the bedroom she took it out of the long container to have another look.

"Best you've done, old girl. Even if I say so myself."

Then she went down to Mrs Wade's small dining room to tell her all about their trip into the bush. About the two crocodiles. The tawny lion. The fish eagle on its perch in the tree. The flow of the Zambezi River. Nature at its best.

'There has to be a God to make so much beauty,' she said to herself.

JEREMY AND LIVY sat at the back of the church. It was more the size of a church than a cathedral. Frank had smiled at Livy as he walked into the building. The man next to him was clearly his father, the woman on the other side his mother. They were all dressed in black mourning. Behind them walked Dorian and Beth with Jeremy's brother Paul. They all half-smiled at him in a way that said the day was not for smiling. They were uncomfortable. Livy thought Dorian must have been given compassionate leave from the army to go to his father's funeral. The army was like that with death. Behind the family were three black people, an old man and a much younger beautiful black woman. Livy would like to have painted the woman. With them was a confident young man in a good suit, his eyes confronting the white congregation as he strode down the aisle. Livy thought he looked like the woman's son. She was smiling at him. She had a beautiful walk, her head high, her back straight. A proud woman.

"Who are they?" she whispered to Jeremy.

The organ was playing the funeral music. Below the crucified figure of Christ on his cross, at the front of the church in the chancel was the closed coffin of Harry Brigandshaw on a low stand. Frank walked up to it and placed a single red rose on the lid of the coffin, bowed his head and walked back to sit in the family pew. Livy's seat on the wooden bench was at the end, on the aisle, so she could see everything happening in the church. There were many flowers on the coffin. The cathedral was packed. At the back, behind them, latecomers were having to stand. A man over to her right was in uniform with a triangular hat with a feather under his arm.

"Who is he?" she whispered again. "Where have they all come from? Not everyone could have known Harry Brigandshaw personally."

"Some dignitary. Just look at all the people. Half of Salisbury is here."

Vic Bell read the eulogy. Ralph Madgwick had had a programme printed for the service. It told Livy who he was and which hymn to sing when the time came. The man broke down during his speech. They had been friends a long time, he said, recovering his voice. He finished the eulogy looking at the coffin. The dead man had done so much with his life. The man listed Harry Brigandshaw's accomplishments. He was crying as he spoke. Livy could see the tears down his face. She tried to remember the face so she could paint what she saw. When it was over they walked with the rest of them to Meikles Hotel. It was not far away – on the other side of Cecil Square, she was told.

"Who would call a square Cecil?" She was glad to be away from the coffin and the thought of a dead man lying under the closed lid. The end so final. The old man crying.

"After Rhodes. His first name was Cecil."

"Poor man."

"I could be wrong. The Earl of Salisbury's surname was probably Cecil. Cecil Square in Salisbury."

"You're showing off."

Paul met them at the door of the function room. Inside people were drinking. There were smiles and laughter. The mood had changed from the church.

"Who was the black woman in the church, Paul?"

"Princess. Tembo's number four wife. Tembo and Harry go back a long way to their childhood. A true friendship. The boy is Josiah, their son. Spent two days in a bus coming up from South Africa to be at the funeral. Harry was his mentor and sent him to Fort Hare University down south. Blacks only. Harry's paying the tuition. Probably came back to make sure the money will continue to put him through university."

"Will it?"

"Harry had written a codicil to his will, according to Ralph. Provided the boy passes his degree within four years of going to Fort Hare. He's a proud youngster. He is inside now with his parents standing on their own."

When Livy went inside and was given a drink she caught the eye of the young black man. Livy was looking at the boy's mother, remembering her face to paint later. The boy's eyes looked straight into her. Challenging her to disagree with his right to be in the room. A black man among so many whites, all but Livy ignoring him. As if he were not in the room... Livy looked around at everyone partaking of the food and drinks. To them, the black man did not exist. Livy shivered. Someone had walked over her grave. She took Jeremy's hand and gave it a squeeze.

"What was that for?" he said happily.

"I'm glad we're going back to England. We don't belong here. None of us do... I'm going to paint that black woman from memory... Have you asked your brother to look for a job for you?"

"Not yet. So we're going?"

"Yes, Jeremy. On the next boat up the east coast. It will be summer in

Europe when we get to Venice. We'll criss-cross the Continent. You never know when you'll have the chance again in life. We've got money and time. What more can you want to see the world?... When are they getting married?"

"Who?"

"Beth and Paul."

"I have no idea."

"And Dorian? There was a story in London before I left that young Dorian had got a nice young girl up the pole. My flatmate Tessa told me. What a world. You never know what is going to happen next." She looked up into his eyes.

"Are *you* pregnant, Livy?"

"I have no idea."

"But you are being careful?"

"Of course I am. We were going to get married. Have a big farm in Africa with a swimming pool for the kids. Why ever would I not be careful?"

"Be serious, Livy. What about Crispin Dane?"

"He's over there if you want to know. With Roger Crumpshaw. They all knew of Harry Brigandshaw... Relax, Jeremy. I'm not pregnant. But as for that nice young girl Nancy. Very promiscuous by all accounts. She's the one Dorian got up the pole. Don't you love me? Don't you want me to have your children? Come on. Better go and talk to Pamela. Strange how last time in this room we were here for a wedding reception."

"What about Crispin?"

"What about him?"

Enjoying her tease, Livy walked across to the girl who had shared her cabin on the *Carnarvon Castle*.

"Aren't you meant to be on your honeymoon?"

"Roger wants to see all the tobacco out of the grading shed onto the auction floor before we go. Then it's off to the Mediterranean for a cruise... Everyone is here, Livy. We had to come. Mr and Mrs Maple and their charming daughter are over there. They knew Mr Brigandshaw from the old days when he lived in Rhodesia. Don't you both want to go over and say hello?"

"You must be kidding after what I said to her at your wedding."

"Are you staying in Rhodesia?"

"Probably not."

"Wise after ruining poor Jeremy's career. Things like that get around in a small community you know. Florence Maple is a pillar of our society. Put it down to your artistic temperament. Did she know you are an artist?"

"I'd put it down to common decency, Pam. You can't promise a bonus and go back on your word."

"She didn't give her word as I now understand it. The money wasn't his to give. First year assistants don't get a bonus in Rhodesia."

Deciding not to dump Bertie Maple in the manure for his generosity, Livy dropped the subject. Her friend was now quite the lady of the manor. All it took was a wedding ring.

"How was the trip, Livy? Tessa sends her love. Seems only yesterday I was sleeping on the pull-out couch in your lounge without a proper job."

"Frank! You remember Jeremy?"

"Of course I do. I set him up at the party for Paul. One good turn deserves another. Back then, somewhere to sleep was rather important to me... He was a good man. Paul made me go and see him at Hastings Court before he came back to Rhodesia. We made up. It wasn't his fault he wasn't my real father. Thank you again, Paul. I am eternally in your debt... So, when are you flying back? Strange to be at his funeral with both my parents when for years they told me Harry Brigandshaw was my father."

"Have you seen the will, Frank?" asked Paul.

"Of course not. It's none of my business."

"It is. He's left his estate in five equal parts. To Dorian, Kim, Beth and you, Frank. With the fifth share going to his nephew, Tinus."

"What about my mother?"

"She has an income for life."

"And Hastings Court?"

"You are all free to do what you like."

"How do you know all this, Paul?"

"I'm a trustee of his estate. Along with Tinus and the family solicitor. Ralph Madgwick gave me the will. The estate is left in trust until the youngest of you turns fifty, which is Kim. In the meantime you will receive an income equal to a fifth of one per cent of the estate's value every year. The government will get their chunk. Death duty on the British estate will be prohibitive. Not the American."

"And Elephant Walk?"

"His sister Madge has life occupancy along with his mother. Should the farm be insufficient for their needs the estate will make up the shortfall."

"In a way you are now the boss. I'll be buggered."

"Harry inherited his money. He wants the generations to come to have the same privilege of security and education he enjoyed. That's the simple reading of the will. There are education clauses for grandchildren. A bequest to his father-in-law. To Josiah Makoni over there with his parents all looking somewhat uncomfortable. He said he loved you, Frank, the same as your brothers and sisters."

"When are you two getting married?"

"When the family have had time to mourn. How's your public relations business coming along?"

"Couldn't be better."

"Harry was proud of you making it all on your own."

"We've both come a long way since I punched you on your nose that Christmas at Hastings Court before the Battle of Britain. What was the fight about, Paul?"

"I have no idea."

"Neither have I."

"How's your mother coping?"

"Mother's enjoying the drama. My poor mother. We're all flying out on the same plane tomorrow."

"I know. I booked the flights."

Livy watched the family interplay. Frank went off to be with his mother and biological father leaving Livy wondering if anyone knew who they were.

"Why don't you and Paul have a long chat, Jeremy?" Livy said in his ear. "I'm going to walk back to Mrs Wade's. It's better you two talk on your own. I thought I'd call at the Manica Travel agency on the way and check sailings up the east coast. Do you want me to make a booking?"

"Can we book a double cabin?"

"Won't they look at our passports? Maybe one of us can have a single cabin. The other can have the cheapest berth on the boat as it won't be used very much. I'm going to say goodbye to old Mrs Brigandshaw and the sister, Madge. I don't know the widow. What a life. She looks quite radiant with Frank's father. He really does look like Frank. You know he bought my painting? How the world goes round. Maybe Frank can give you a job. Why don't you ask him?"

Giving Jeremy a soft kiss on the side of his cheek, Livy left the room. Outside in the street the sun was still shining. It was always shining in Rhodesia. With a spring in her step she walked down Second Street on her way to Union Avenue and the travel agency. She was going home. To her friends. To England.

"WE'VE JUST GOT MARRIED," she told the shipping clerk half an hour later. "Haven't had time to change my British passport to my married name. We were married in Rhodesia."

"That'll be fine, Mrs Crookshank. A double cabin with a porthole that opens on a deck of the *Esquilino*. Lloyd Triestino Line. Very Italian. You'll love the food from Venice. Two train tickets which you can use to go anywhere in Europe for two months provided you don't retrace your steps."

"When do you want us to pay?"

"The ship sails in a month from the Port of Beira. Once you pay me I can issue the tickets. Say a week, Mrs Crookshank? How lovely to be married."

With a smirk on her face Livy left the shipping office. The open porthole amused her. Reminded her of Crispin Dane. At the wake he had ignored her completely.

When she reached Mrs Wade's, Jeremy was waiting for her.

"A double berth. Three hundred quid between the two of us."

"You're really something, Livy."

"Said my passport is still in my maiden name... I want to paint until the boat sails... Did you get a job in London?"

"One bridge at a time... So that's final. I'm going home."

"Let's just enjoy ourselves while we have a bit of money. Let life take care of itself. We're young. It's wonderful to be young. Most people don't realise they've got what they want until it's all over... Carmen. How is it going, girl?"

"Next weekend with the brothers Lavington."

"Enjoy it all while you can."

"They want to take us back to England with them. When all the tobacco is out of the grading shed."

"It can only get better. Why don't we all go to Bretts tonight? Listen to Hennie play the piano."

PART III

JULY TO AUGUST 1950 – "CONVERSATIONS WITH LIVY"

*A*n invisible door had been slammed in Jeremy Crookshank's face. So far as the farm owners were concerned he was persona non grata. They had laughed behind Florence Maple's back at her indignant exit from the Pamela and Roger Crumpshaw wedding reception but it had not helped Jeremy. He had broken the rules. He had confronted his employer in public. No one wanted an assistant with such bad manners. If he had done it to the Maples of Ashford Park he could do it to them. It was one thing to enjoy Florence Maple being shown up as a skinflint, another to become involved themselves. Day after day the same thoughts played through Jeremy's mind.

With Harry Brigandshaw dead, there was no one for him to turn to. Even if he wanted to serve his apprenticeship to learn how to grow tobacco, no one came forward to offer him a job. He was out in the cold. No one said anything. Livy had shot his bolt. A person of good breeding never challenged the integrity of a lady and her gentleman in public. So far as the Rhodesian tobacco growers were concerned, Jeremy Crookshank no longer existed.

"They say sometimes your worst enemy does you your biggest favour, Jeremy," said Livy. "Forget about them. You're out of the club."

"I was never a member of the Macheke Club. They just let me play cricket."

"You know what I mean. It's a small community. However generous they like to appear, people are usually mean with their money. You can separate a fool from his money. No one can say Flossy Maple is a fool however much they dislike her nose stuck up in the air. We're on our way home. We're out of it."

"What am I going to do, Livy?"

"First, enjoy the trip. Then you'll think of something. When black rule comes to Rhodesia we'll be safe in good old England. They won't like the Flossy Maples any more than you do, just you see. You'll have the last laugh when they all have to run back to England with their tails between their legs, without their farms and their money. No more living like a feudal baron. People look pretty ordinary stripped of their wealth."

"You're making me feel better. Wouldn't that be terrible, to build a farm and a life in Rhodesia only to lose it at the end? She brought all her family money from England to set up Bertie on the farm. It's all sunk in Rhodesian land."

They walked on down the pier.

"Oh just look at her. She's all white. What a beautiful boat."

"You don't think they'll want to see our marriage certificate before they let us share the cabin?"

"They're Italian, not stuffy old British."

Taking Jeremy's hand, Livy went off to look for their luggage. In the cabin trunk she had bought in England, carefully stored, were the new paintings.

AN HOUR later they went on board the MV *Esquilino* without a hitch. No one questioned them sharing the cabin. It was all a big Italian welcome.

The ship sailed at noon. Jeremy had counted less than twenty passengers getting on board with them at the Port of Beira.

Downstairs in their cabin, Livy opened their port hole high above the ocean, putting out her head to smell the sea. When she turned back to him she was smiling.

"Lock the door, lover. I want to christen this place. Make it ours."

"Don't you think we should wait until the ship's out of port?"

"Whatever for? It's just the two of us. Isn't that what you always wanted? So far as the rest of them know, I'm your wife."

. . .

PLAYING MARRIED WAS A HOOT. Jeremy had bought her a cheap wedding band that looked as if it was made of gold. With luck the gold plate would not wear off while they were still on the boat. The engagement ring was a piece of crystal set in a white metal band that hopefully looked like platinum. Livy was careful not to hit the stone on anything hard. Crystal, Carmen told her, had a bad habit of shattering into small pieces when knocked on something hard. They had bought both pieces from an African vendor selling them in the street when they went to pay for their tickets, each paying half of the three hundred pounds of their fares. They wanted their money to last them as long as possible while they travelled through the Continent by train. What was left of Livy's two hundred and forty pounds, the amount Barnaby St Clair had paid for her painting after deducting the Nouvelle Galerie's forty per cent commission, was put in a joint account kitty, along with the remnants of Jeremy's three hundred pound bonus given by Bertie Maple without his wife being told.

After the rail tickets and paying back Paul his one hundred pounds they had nearly one hundred and fifty pounds to spend on the boat, see them around Europe and leave them with enough funds to live frugally in London until they found a way to make money. The heavy luggage was booked from their last port of Trieste direct to the shipping agent in London by rail. Wherever possible they would travel at night and sleep in the train to save the price of hotels.

It was all a game to be played right up to the hilt, Livy told herself as the boat steamed up the Mozambique channel their first afternoon at sea. After a good lunch, Livy had taken her easel and paints and found a place to work on an upper deck. There was a canvas awning for shade. Jeremy had followed her to sit in a deck chair while she worked. When Livy was happy, her mind free of distracting thoughts, she liked to paint. In her mind's eye she could see the Zambezi Valley as clearly as when she was standing under her riverine trees on the bank of the river. With her mind concentrated on the picture in her mind, she began to paint, oblivious of where she was.

All afternoon she painted, Jeremy reading a book. They were alone and undisturbed. On the canvas the river came back to life again, a log floating down, clogged with debris, a buck, feet splayed, head down to the water drinking in the dawn, the last stars reflected in the surface of the river. The trees on the far bank grew under her hand, at first sketched and then in more detail. There was the faint image of birds in the trees. One of them gave the impression of singing.

One of the crew looked over her shoulder not breaking her concentration, going away soft-footed on rubber soles to get on with his work of sweeping the deck. The breeze from the sea was soft and cooling, the throb of the ship's engines felt through her feet.

When they went down for dinner she was deeply satisfied with her day's work, her body satiated with pleasure. Jeremy was carrying her easel and paints as they went down to A deck to leave her things and change.

"Do you know how good you are, Livy?"

"I just paint. Enough reward for me. To bring it back again and make it all live on the canvas. It's so satisfying. Not even making love is so satisfying as getting it down in a painting... I'm hungry. I love Italian boats. All the meals go with free wine on the table. Something Italian for lunch, a glass of wine, a snooze next to my love. What more can a girl want? Always live in the present, Jeremy. Too many people live for the future, dissatisfied with what they've got. Life is only right now. This moment... Come on, lover. Aren't you hungry?"

"Starving... I wish I could paint. Or play the piano like Paul. He has a grand piano in the London flat. Classical and jazz. He would have liked to hear Hennie at Bretts."

"You could write it all down. What you've seen in Africa. You can paint it with words while I paint it with colours."

"Do you think I could?"

"Why not try? All you need is a pen and paper. We can work side by side in London when we find somewhere to stay."

"Are we going to live together?"

"Now, Jeremy. Only think of now... Do you think they'll let me go without a bra at dinner?"

"They're Italian."

A BAND WAS PLAYING when they went in to dinner. A man was singing in

Italian a song Jeremy had heard many times on the radio in his cottage at
Ashford Park. It was a lonely song by Mario Lanza. Jeremy was wearing
the new beige suit he had bought in Salisbury with Livy. The light colour
made him feel self-conscious. All the other suits he had worn were dark
and tailored in London.

The dining room was almost full. They had sat at the bar next to the
deck where Livy had done her afternoon painting. There were three
small bars in tourist class. Across the barrier which separated them they
could see the bar of the first-class passengers, the passengers all in their
finery, most of them old. There was one young boy who kept looking at
Livy and Jeremy.

With two stiff drinks inside of them they looked around, not sure
where to sit. At lunchtime the room had been half empty, leaving them a
table to themselves which no one questioned.

"Do you have your place at table? I am the assistant purser."

"We just sat down at lunchtime."

"Lunch is informal. Now I must give you your place at table. Your
name, please?"

"Jeremy Crookshank and Livy Johnston."

"I have places for Mr and Mrs Crookshank. They came on board this
morning according to the list."

"That's us," said Jeremy. "We just got married."

"All a bit new is it? Please come with me. Lieutenant Colucci, the
ship's chief engineer, is at your table. He will introduce you to the other
guests. The rest of your table came on board at Cape Town. Please have a
good trip with Lloyd Triestino, Mr and Mrs Crookshank."

"Does he speak English?"

"Of course. All the officers speak English... You are the only married
couple at the table. I hope you don't mind. We try to put all the young
people together."

"Did I have to wear a tie?"

"Not if you did not want to, Mr Crookshank... I will show you your
table. The steward's name is Luigi. Not so good English."

With Livy following behind the assistant purser, Jeremy took up the
rear. No one looked up from their food as they passed the tables.
Couples were dancing on the floor in front of the band. Jeremy was still
conscious of the throbbing of the ship's engines coming up through the

deck into the soles of his feet. They were steaming into the night, but inside the lights were bright. People were talking and eating. For a moment Jeremy saw in his mind's eye the seas around them, their ship one small light in the wilderness.

The lieutenant stood up to introduce them round the table. The purser had gone off back to his desk and his list of passenger seating. They smiled at their fellow passengers and sat down. Jeremy never remembered names at first. The lieutenant poured them glasses of wine. It was uncomfortable being sat among strangers. The drinks at the bar were not working on Jeremy. It was difficult for him to enjoy himself with nothing at the end of his journey. He had no future after the boat. Livy had her painting. He had nothing. On his way out to Africa there had been the excitement of expectation. Of everything new. Of a glorious future rushing around in the back of his mind. It was never good to go backwards, Jeremy told himself. To a drab England where clerical jobs were so badly paid he would be lucky to afford a bedsitter in a rundown part of London. To enjoy himself among strangers without anything in his future was going to be difficult if not downright impossible, despite what Livy said about always enjoying the now.

"That's a lovely engagement ring, Mrs Crookshank. You're very lucky to have a rich husband. My name is Angela Lipton. I'm a nurse. Going home, I'm afraid. My mother is sick. I've been living in Cape Town."

"Don't believe everything you see, Angela... Call me Livy. This is Jeremy."

"What do you do, Livy?"

"I'm a painter. Portraits. Landscapes. There are quite a few of us in Chelsea. Came out on holiday and going home."

"So nice to have so much money to travel. What does your husband do?"

"Oh, he inherited his money. Jeremy doesn't have to work. Do you, darling?"

"How lucky. I always wanted to be a lady of leisure. Where are you living in England?"

"We haven't decided yet. You know, footloose and fancy-free."

"What were your family in, Jeremy?"

"Aircraft," said Jeremy, thinking off the top of his head. "My father designed the first commercial flying boat."

"How exciting. I'm sure we'll get to know all about each other by the time we reach Trieste. Are you taking the train to Venice?"

"Of course we are," said Livy. "Wouldn't miss Venice, now would we?"

"Are you going to be painting during the voyage?"

"I was painting all afternoon on the upper deck."

"May I perhaps look at your painting?" said the lieutenant. "Our captain is a great lover of the arts. I will tell him we have a painter on board, Mrs Crookshank. With your permission."

"Please call me Livy."

"So nice to have money and the time to fulfil your art," said Angela, looking harder at the ring on Livy's finger until Livy pulled her hand under the table.

"Would you like to dance, darling?" said Jeremy.

"I just love this Italian music... Come on."

When they reached the small piece of deck where the others were dancing, Livy was giggling.

"Where'd you find the bit about aircraft, lover? That was quick on your feet. You know we've got to keep this up for another three weeks?"

"Dad was chief designer of the Short Sunderland before he drowned off Dunkirk in the *Seagull*. He just didn't make money as an employee. Always get some of the facts right when telling a lie. It's easier to remember."

"You look good in that suit. The light colours shows off your tan."

"That engineer is flirting with you."

"Of course he is. He's Italian."

"What happens if they find out?"

"Who cares? They can't dump us in the ocean... On the second look she didn't think it was a diamond... My, how easy it is to lie."

"When you look at it there's not much difference between a quartz crystal and a diamond."

"They're not impressed with the beauty of the ring, only the money that bought it."

"I wonder what the rest of them do?"

"We'll find out, you can be sure. People like to talk about themselves. We'll have their entire life stories by the time we get off at Trieste."

They went to bed early, both of them tired from the rail journey. Sleeping on a train had always been difficult for Jeremy, especially with all the worry about his non-existent future churning around in his head. They fell asleep before they made love.

LIVY WOKE in the dawn with a start, not knowing where she was. She was alone in a strange bed. Only then did she see Jeremy asleep in his bunk. He looked so young without the tension she had seen in his face of late. The confident farmer of the future she had first met in London at his brother Paul's party had gone.

Stretching luxuriously, Livy got out of bed. She had left the porthole open to the sea when they went to bed soon after eating their dinner. Jeremy had not been in the mood for small talk with strangers. She looked out at the calm sea and back at the wake of the big ocean liner. The ocean was empty, a strange smell overlaying the salt of the sea. The smell was warm, a little menacing in its unknown. She had never smelt that smell before.

When she looked round Jeremy was awake and smiling. The previous day's tension had gone out of his eyes.

"Come over here and smell the sea. There's a strange smell that isn't from the boat or the water."

"Good morning, Livy."

"Good morning, lover... Come on, lazybones. Get out of bed."

"I'm naked."

"Good."

When he put his arms round her naked body from behind he felt good. He nuzzled the back of her neck, making her want to purr.

"Put your head out... What is it?"

"The smell of Africa. You can't see the continent but it's just over the horizon. All that vast, brooding, mostly empty land. That's the smell of Africa."

"Are you sure?"

"What else can it be? Dry and musty... Why are you shivering?"

"I prefer the smells of England. I know what they are... I'm getting dressed and going up on deck to paint. I want that smell in my painting."

"You can't paint a smell."

"Oh yes you can... Before the day is too hot."

"You'll miss breakfast."

"Bring me some buttered toast in a paper napkin... I'm going to take off the crystal ring. Say I put it in the ship's safe with our passports and money. Tell our Angela it's too valuable to have on my finger all the time. All last night she was trying to get a good look at it."

Turning, Livy kissed him into excitement, pushing him back on his bunk. Then they made love, lying in his bunk until the cabin steward knocked on the door. The steward brought them tea on a round silver tray. On the tray with the pot of tea and two cups was a plate of biscuits, all of them chocolate.

"I could get used to this," said Livy.

"So could I."

THE SAME DECKHAND was leaning on the handle of his broom. He had his back to Livy looking out to sea. There was no one else on the same upper deck, or across the barriers in first class. The small bar they had been in the previous night was closed, the shutter drawn down from the ceiling to metal clips on the deck. Quietly, Livy began to put up her easel. The man heard her and began to sweep the clean floor. When he turned to come back she smiled at him. The man smiled in return. They understood each other with the smile. He stopped his sweeping and went back to looking out to sea. The man was skiving off work, away from the prying eyes of his superiors.

The canvas was the largest Livy had brought on the boat to give her the most room to play. Thinking of smells, she began to paint in her lily. Mario Tuchi had found the red flower and shown it to her while they were still at the river. She had sketched the delicate flower to use later.

"It's a flame lily, Livy. The emblem of Rhodesia. Our national flower. It is so beautiful."

"Do you like flowers, Mario?"

"I like anything beautiful."

"So do I. I will sketch now and use it later."

"You are so lucky, Livy."

"Why?"

"To be able to paint and keep this beauty alive forever."

Content with her memory of Mario Tuchi, Livy began to paint the flower in the colours of red and yellow she remembered as she recalled their conversation. The small flower would draw the eye to the bottom edge of the canvas giving the eye a sweep of the Zambezi River. Absorbed and happy, she forgot the man leaning on his broom. Slowly, carefully the flower began to bloom in her painting. The time went on its way without Livy noticing anything but her work.

A noise of frantic sweeping brought her out of her conversation, out of the Zambezi Valley. When she turned, a man in uniform wearing a peaked cap was standing behind her, watching her paint.

"Please go on, Mrs Crookshank. I didn't want to disturb you. The flower is so beautiful."

"How do you know my name?"

"Lieutenant Colucci. I am captain of the ship. An amateur painter but not very good."

The man with the broom had swept his way off the upper deck, away from his captain.

"I have been watching you for half an hour." The captain's eyes followed the path of the now absent sweeper. "You have much talent. Sorry now. I will leave in peace. Do you have any finished work on board?"

"Only the canvases I painted in Rhodesia."

"Could we arrange to show them? In first class. Some of my passengers are rich. Two in particular I have spoken with are patrons of the arts. One is Italian, the other an American. The American has the most money. He travels much on boats. A little bored I would say. It would please him to look at your paintings. If he buys one I expect it will please you, Mrs Crookshank. Did you miss your breakfast?"

"Jeremy is bringing some buttered toast."

"Your husband. To be a painter and in love. So much joy. Oh yes. So much joy."

"Isn't there joy in sailing the oceans?"

"Sometimes. Not all my passengers are talented painters. So, a little exhibition? Tomorrow afternoon?"

"Of course. Every painter wants to sell her paintings. All except one. That I must have forever."

"Bring it. Everything has its price."

"We shall see."

"If you sell you can paint it again."

As silently as the captain had arrived he went, leaving Livy alone. She hoped the deckhand would not find himself in trouble. Within a minute she had forgotten where she was again, her mind back in the Zambezi Valley.

Only when Jeremy brought her the toast wrapped in a paper napkin did she come back to the reality of the ship.

"I love your flower."

"So did the captain. He wants to give me an exhibition in the first class."

"The chief engineer spoke to him?"

"He was watching me paint without me feeling his presence. I'm starving. What did you have for breakfast?"

"Bacon and eggs."

"You always have bacon and eggs... Can't I have a kiss? No one is watching... There's a rich American on board."

"Bully for him."

"What's the matter, Jeremy?"

"You have something to do. I have nothing."

"You'll find a job... So you like my flame lily?"

Livy could feel the tension back in Jeremy. Maybe, she thought, the exhibition was not such a good idea after all.

"I'll let you get on. I'm going to jog round the deck a few times and think. What I want is a way to make money when we reach England. Some kind of a business. I can't live on thin air. You have to make money in this world."

"You can go on the dole. All those lovely benefits of socialism. Do you know the government now hands out free spectacles? Mr Attlee's new National Health Service. You don't have to work in England if you don't want to anymore."

"What about a man's pride?"

"Who cares, if the government is paying your bills? Work's all right like this if you love what you are doing. Then it isn't work. Find something to do you enjoy. It's a whole new world, this social democracy. You just see what they do to the estate of Harry Brigandshaw. The estate of a man that rich will pay the government ninety per cent of his wealth in death duty. Read it somewhere. Your Paul's fiancée won't have much money when the Labour Government have finished. Why should she? She didn't work for it."

"There's big money for Beth in America. They believe in private enterprise. Encourage people to make money. And don't rob them afterwards."

"You know what I'm saying. Why should she enjoy the fruits of inheritance and you can't enjoy taking money from the government? What's the difference? When you find something that is fun to do and makes money, you can start paying our taxes to a grateful society."

"I wouldn't feel comfortable bumming off the taxpayers."

"What goes around comes around. Just don't worry. Everything's going to be fine. Everything has changed for the better in England. Socialism takes time. You'll see."

"I hope so."

"Go for your jog. It'll make you feel better. Come back when you're ready to go for lunch."

"You make it all sound so simple."

"Life's a lot more simple than you think."

When Livy looked round from her painting Jeremy had gone. There was nothing she could do for him. He had to work out his own life himself. The paper napkin with the toast was on top of the wooden box where she kept her tubes of coloured paints. She put down her long brush with her palette, wiped her hands on the dust coat she wore when she was painting and picked up the toast. The butter was still runny from the heat of the day. She ate hungrily, thinking of nothing but her food.

Smiling, Livy went back to her canvas. She began to paint a small frog into the other bottom corner of the picture, opposite her flame lily. On the frog's forehead Livy painted a bright crimson triangle. Mario had shown her the frog in the reeds by the big river. He had not known the name of the frog. Three times she looked at the sketch she had made of the frog by the river before it was finished. Then she looked up. The young man in first class she had seen the previous day was watching. They smiled at each other and the man went away.

When Jeremy came back they went down to lunch.

"What happened to your lovely ring?" asked Angela when they sat down at the table.

"I put it in the safe. I don't like it on my hand while I paint. I was worried I'd put it down somewhere and forget where it was."

"Very wise for something so valuable."

"The captain came by where I was working," she said to the engineer, giving him a smile.

"He likes to keep all his passengers happy. On a passenger ship there is more to the job of captain than sailing the boat. Head office likes the passengers to have a good experience. Some of them grow bored on a long voyage despite the calls at port when they can go ashore."

"He offered me the chance to exhibit my paintings. Do I put a price on them?"

"Why not?"

"How rich is the American?"

"Oh, he is very rich. Don't forget, the very rich only like expensive art. The bigger the price, the better the art. Everything in a rich man's life is about money."

"A thousand pounds."

"To him that is nothing."

"I don't really want to sell that painting. It will put him off."

"But you don't need money, Livy," said Angela, smiling sweetly.

"You can always spend more money, Angela. The more he pays, the more it appeals to my ego. We all have our payments in life. Do you know, every artist underneath thinks he's no good. We have big mouths and big inferiority complexes."

She knows, thought Livy. The bitch knows. She's playing me. Then she looked at Jeremy. He was fiddling with his fork, turning it over and over on the table. Under the table she put her hand on his bare knee, just below his shorts. They would have to find him something to do when they reached London or poor Jeremy would go crazy watching her paint. But what, she asked herself. The Royal Navy and growing tobacco. Not exactly skills needed in London. When she tucked into the plate of pasta that Luigi the steward put in front of her, the food was delicious. The chief engineer had poured her a glass of Chianti.

"Cheers," she said, raising her glass to the engineer and then to the rest of the table. "Pasta and red wine. What more could a girl want? I don't know which is better, the wine or the spaghetti."

She had left her easel and wooden paint box in a corner of the upper deck, her painting still propped on the easel. She hoped they would be all right. She didn't think they had much value to anyone else other than a painter.

After two glasses of good red wine and three courses she went back up on deck. All her stuff was still in the corner. The deckhand was nowhere to be seen. Feeling good from the wine and food, Livy began to paint.

'YOU NEED AN IDEA,' Jeremy kept telling himself. An idea that people wanted. The only trouble was, nothing came to his mind however much he racked his brains. Frustrated and lonely despite Livy, he walked round the deck stopping each time at the first-class barrier. The rich and the poor. It was always the same.

A slight wind was coming up when he went back to Livy still painting her picture of the Zambezi River. There was now a frog in the corner with a red head.

The bar steward was letting up the metal grid that wound up into the ceiling above the small bar. Livy's canvas was moving every now and again with the wind. Jeremy sat on the end barstool. She had not yet seen him. Every time a gust of wind moved her canvas propped up on the easel, she stopped painting. The smell of Africa had gone, the wind blowing onto the shore. So often on the Maple's farm a wind came up an hour before sunset, sinking back with the sun.

He watched her. Livy's contentment merely added to his own frustration. A young man he had not seen before sat at the other end of the six-barstool bar. The barman was looking at him expectantly. They were just sitting, he and the young man, watching the girl painting.

Finally, Livy put down her brush in frustration. The wind was just too much, rattling the easel. She put the painting on the floor, propped up against the wall out of the wind.

"Hello, Jeremy. How long have you been watching?... Aren't you from first class?" she said, looking at the young man. "We're not allowed over the barrier. My name's Livy. What's yours? This is Jeremy. I've seen you watching me from the first-class section of the ship."

"Cecil. They're all old fogies in first class. No young people. Can I have a proper look at your painting? I'm travelling back to Kenya with my mother and father. We have a large coffee plantation among other things. I'm going on to England. We had a holiday together in Cape Town. My father is the Duke of Tewkesbury. I suppose I'll be Duke one day if Mr Attlee doesn't dissolve the House of Lords."

"What do you do yourself?" asked Jeremy.

"Nothing. I flunked getting into university. Didn't want to go. What's the point? My life's mapped out for me. Inheriting money is one big bore. Rather like travelling first class... Better get back."

"Don't you want to look?" said Livy.

"I'd better not let my mother see me."

"Just a quick look. I'll hold it up on the easel."

"Thank you. You're very kind. Maybe I could join you both after dinner when my parents have gone to bed?"

"We can both commiserate at having nothing to do," said Jeremy.

"I have a learning problem. Couldn't read until I was thirteen. My maths is fine. The rest is terrible... This is awfully good, Livy. We have frogs in Kenya with red triangles on their heads. Did you actually see one? They are very rare. I used to know the Latin name but I've forgotten. Better go before I get into trouble."

"How old are you, Cecil?"

"I'm eighteen. I just turned eighteen."

Instead of climbing over the barrier the boy went off to the steps that led down to the lower deck. Jeremy thought there had to be an entrance from tourist class to make his return more dignified.

"I can sympathise with boredom," said Jeremy. "At least he's got family money if they're all travelling first class... You want a drink?"

"What are bars for? I'll have a glass of lemonade. Too early to start on the booze. You either have too much or too little in this life."

"He must have a title."

"His father is still alive."

"As the eldest son of a duke he'll be a marquis or something... You meet all sorts on boats. Poor fellow. A man has to work or go nuts. Can you imagine a title and all that money with nothing to do with the rest of your life? That's not an inheritance I would want. That's a curse. Generation after generation looking after someone else's money.

"That can be work."

"They have bankers to look after that sort of stuff... Give me a beer and a lemonade," Jeremy said to the barman, "I don't know the names of your Italian beers."

"Did you know Rebecca Madgwick on Elephant Walk is the daughter of Sir Jacob Rosenzweig, of Rosenzweig's Bank in America?"

"What's she doing as the wife of a farm manager?"

"He's Jewish. Wouldn't have liked his daughter marrying a gentile. The Jews are fussy about those kind of things. Must have cut her off. It's one of the largest banking families in the world. England, Germany, France and now America."

"How do you know these things?"

"I listen when I'm not meant to be listening. James Coghlan throws parties for the rich to meet young artists. All older men. Most of them married. They're after the young girls as much as the art. James is a sculptor. A bad one, though I never say so. But he knows how to sell. You'll meet him in London. Jeanne Pétain met Samuel Chalmers at one of his soirées. How she got the money and connections to start the Nouvelle Galerie. He wanted to get into her pants. I heard Samuel talking about Sir Jacob Rosenzweig and the Rosenzweig banking empire. He was showing off to someone."

"How did you find out Rebecca was his daughter?"

"We got talking at the funeral. Asked her where she came from in England. Just making polite conversation. You were talking to your brother. She told me the family had lived in London. That her father was now an American. I was curious. I thought she was Jewish by the look of her. Jews rarely divorce or separate. I asked her what he did in America. 'Runs the Rosenzweig Bank. Haven't seen each other in years. Never seen his grandchildren.' Then she clammed up. I felt a bit awkward. As if I'd opened a Pandora's box. Then Ralph chipped in. Apparently the father and Harry Brigandshaw were friends. He'd tried to bring father and daughter together again. It's a strange old world."

"Those two truly love each other. You can see the way they constantly interact with each other as though they are one person. Not just for show. That must be wonderful. To have three almost grown-up kids and still love each other. How much can that be worth in this crazy life?"

"Everything... That boy brought it back to my mind. What I'm saying is, money isn't everything."

"Nothing when you've got it, Livy. Everything when you haven't... Do you think I could make sandwiches, pack them in cellophane and hawk them round London's offices on a tray? Anything beats sitting at a desk working for somebody else."

"The sandwich man. Brilliant. Change mine to a gin and tonic. Let's celebrate."

"I haven't done anything yet."

"Oh yes you have. You've started thinking. Positively... How am I going to frame my canvases for the captain's exhibition?"

"If I could find some wood, I'm good with my hands. They must have a carpentry store on board. Somewhere in the bowels of the ship. Things get broken on a voyage. A big ship like this would need a maintenance man. I can frame your pictures well enough for them to be seen... The wind's starting to go down again. With the wind blowing on shore you couldn't smell that smell of Africa. Did you notice? With the wind dropping the musky smell is coming back again... I'll enjoy framing your paintings. Give me something to do."

2

*W*hat seemed simple over an Italian beer and a gin and tonic took Jeremy two days to complete. By then they were steaming into Dar es Salaam harbour in the British Territory of Tanganyika. With the help of a member of the crew who only spoke Italian he had removed wooden slats from packing cases in the storeroom that served the galley for the tourist dining room. The wood was rough but thick enough to make a frame when joined over the edges of Livy's paintings. There were small nail holes in the wood that had to be covered up with putty after the slats of wood were planed smooth enough to paint and not show a rough surface. His first attempts broke the slats of wood as he took them off the packing case. Inside the crate, underneath heavy brown paper tarred black on the inside, were pots and pans packed in straw. It was a labour of love that Jeremy enjoyed. Only when the last painting was finished, the one of Princess looking proud and beautiful, did Jeremy bring them up to the cabin.

"You're not only a good lover, lover, you're a bloody genius. What's the smell this time? It's coming from the other direction to the smell of musk. The wind has changed again."

"Zanzibar is off the starboard side of the ship. The island of cloves. It's the only industry. What we're smelling are the cloves drying out in the sun. Zanzibar supplies Britain with most of its cloves... If I had had some nice bevelled strips of seasoned wood I would have stained the frames, not painted them. A good frame sets off a painting. On first glance no one will see these are made of cheap wood. Good enough to show people on the ship. We can put them up the day after tomorrow when the ship leaves harbour for Mombasa in the British colony of Kenya. Young Cecil has been giving me a rundown on British East Africa. Tanganyika was a German colony before the First World War. They lost it to us at the end of the war. The South African army fought the Germans in East Africa during the war. One of those side wars overshadowed by what was happening in France... We have an invitation from the Duke and Duchess of Tewkesbury. She's Australian believe it or not. Daughter of a rare rich Australian in the automotive industry. Had a lecture on that too. They are going across to Zanzibar with the British Resident and we're invited. It's rather quaint. Old Arab town. Very picturesque, according to Cecil. Bring your sketchbook was my instruction. A day's outing in a Royal Navy frigate that's in port for a two-week visit. Cecil didn't know which ship. I asked him."

"We have come up in the world. Should I wear my engagement ring?"

"Better not, Livy. Those types would know a real diamond when they see one."

"What are his parents like?"

"I have no idea. The invitation came from Cecil. Just one thing. We have to call his mother, 'Your Grace'. She likes it. His father doesn't give a damn."

WHEN THE TENDER CAME ALONGSIDE, Livy and Jeremy were standing next to each other at the rail of the ship, the town of Dar es Salaam in front of them. Moored next to them was a warship painted grey.

"HMS *Lamerton*," said Jeremy. As he spoke, Livy noticed a slight twist to the side of his face.

"How do you know? There's no name on the bow."

"I served on her for the last eighteen months of my Short Service Commission. If you wanted to do your National Service in the navy you had to sign on for three years, not the usual two. It was two years in the army or the air force. They took very few in the navy. My father had taught me to sail as a small boy on the *Seagull*. The same sailboat he went down in off Dunkirk. I was in the Brighton College naval cadets. Paul had won a music scholarship to Brighton College before me. How I got in to boarding school."

Livy watched him staring at the ship as if his mind was a long way away. There was still so much she did not know about him. The ship's guns had a menacing look about them – a predator in the midst of an old town on the shores of the Indian Ocean. She could see no one on board, just the guns pointing from their turrets. With a shiver, Livy turned to go down below. They were to be allowed on shore in the morning, the *Esquilino* sailing for Mombasa the following day.

"That's how we conquered a large part of the world," said Jeremy. "The navy. First the merchant ships and then the navy to protect them and their travel routes. All we had was trade. The ports and the people with which to trade. An island set in a silver sea. Shakespeare made it sound romantic. That ship's the reality. Bugger around with what we are up to and we'll blow you out of the water. Or blow your coastal town to pieces. Along the shores of the world and up the rivers. The French and Dutch tried to fight the English as they expanded their own trading empires. The Royal Navy stopped them. It's all about trade and making money. Selling Manchester textiles and British machinery. The trade comes first and then the arguments. Always been the same throughout man's history. Every nation trying to get a trading advantage, trying to get on top. The poor sods who fought the battles like Trafalgar were mostly press-ganged into the navy."

When they went in to dinner the chief engineer asked about the paintings.

"They are all in our cabin ready to be exhibited. The captain can send someone for them any time he likes."

THE LOUNGE of the Royal Hotel reminded both of them of Meikles Hotel in Salisbury. The same colonial style. The same punkahs going round and round overhead stirring the humid air. It was hot in Dar es Salaam.

Both of them remembered to call the Duchess of Tewkesbury 'Your Grace'. They shook hands with the duke. He had got up from his chair at the low round table when Cecil brought them across. He was a small man with a bald head. His eyes were what made him different. They looked straight into Jeremy, like gimlets.

"So, my son says you are leaving Africa, Jeremy. You don't mind my calling you Jeremy? I hear you knew Harry Brigandshaw. Never met him, I'm afraid. Everyone knew of him in Africa, of course. All us whites anyway. And his father Sebastian. Famous white hunter with F C Selous and William Hartley. Those were the days. No politics then. Permission to hunt from the local chief and no one bothered you except the wild animals. So Harry Brigandshaw told you to go home? Wise man. Why I am insisting Cecil go back to England and make a life for himself. In Kenya they are taking oaths to kill the white settlers. They don't want us anymore, now we have built our farms with our capital and knowledge. I came out in 1921. To grow coffee and tea for the British market. Once we were established in Kenya we needed a colonial government to run the place. Built them roads and railways. Put in the telephone. Built Nairobi. Created the structure for a viable country... What are you going to have to drink, Mrs Crookshank? The Resident will be joining us in half an hour when we go on board the *Lamerton*. Get to know you first. Cecil has talked about you and your painting. Wonderful talent... Now, where was I?... Mau Mau. The outlaws in the Aberdare Forest taking their oaths to kill us. We'll fight them at first, I suppose. You always try and defend your own property. Some of our house servants have secretly joined the Mau Mau so we are told. It's the Russians. Anyone with a grievance in the capitalist world is being given money and training by the communists to stir up trouble. They tried blockading West Berlin last year. Cutting off the roads and railways that went through East Germany. The airlift of the Royal Air Force and the Americans stopped the Russians swallowing the whole of Berlin. But the writing is on the wall. They want to spread communism around the world. A Russian empire bigger than the British. They are now sweeping into Africa. I don't think we have the will to hang on to the empire. India's gone. Harry Brigandshaw was right, Jeremy. Go home. England will stay the same. I don't see England going communist any more than it went fascist. It's all about power. We British are losing our grip... All good things come to an end. Now, tell me what you are going to do with yourself back in England?"

Glad it was not her problem, Livy looked out of the window into the street. The black people all wore white robes down to their ankles. The blacks were all outside. In the lounge drinking tea and coffee at the tables it was only white people.

Livy was glad to be going home. To the safety of good old England. She only half-listened to the conversation. When the British Resident arrived they all got up. Outside the hotel was a Rolls-Royce car with a white chauffeur. The Union Jack was flying from the bonnet of the car. The car doors were opened for them by the obsequious chauffeur. They all got inside.

At the docks they were piped on board HMS *Lamerton*, Livy watching Jeremy out of the corner of her eye.

"Morning, Wilson."

"Good God, it's Crookshank. What are you doing here?"

"On a swan to Zanzibar, old boy. You've got to know the right people."

"Do you miss the navy?"

"Not really. I was never cut out to be a professional sailor. Better go. This is my wife, Livy."

"My word, you are a lucky chap. What have you been doing with yourself?" The man called Wilson kept looking at her as he spoke to Jeremy, his eyes popping. Livy thought the navy did not see too many young white girls in their travels. She found his stare mildly amusing.

"Not very much as it turned out."

When Livy looked back, the gangplank was up, the thick ropes to the bollards on shore being cast off, the feel of the engines pulsing up through her feet. Then they left the dock and headed out to sea. The man called Wilson was still looking at her. To Livy's surprise he came to attention and saluted her smartly, turned briskly and marched off back to his duty.

"We came on board together the same day," said Jeremy, watching the man's back. "He signed on for another two years."

"Are you really happy to be out of the navy?"

"I have to be, Livy. As I'm happy to have left Rhodesia. You can't look back with regrets. Life doesn't work that way. Come on, I'll show you round."

They had been left behind. The Resident and the important guests were taking up the captain's attention. Nearer, the guns were even more menacing. Livy put her hand up and felt a part of the turret. The steel was cool to the touch.

As they steamed closer to the island of Zanzibar the smell of drying cloves grew stronger. The ship ploughed through the still water sending back a long wake. Livy felt the wind in her hair.

"To be here with a girl on this ship is so strange," said Jeremy.

"You introduced me to your friend Wilson as your wife."

"What else could I do? Their graces think we are husband and wife. Can't rock the ship, can we?"

"Certainly not this one. It's so powerful after the *Esquilino*... What was that all about Mau Mau?"

"Never heard of them. Probably will."

"I'm glad we're going home."

"So am I."

With her sketch book held in her hand, Livy watched the shore of the island coming closer. She had no mind to sketch the ship.

THE OLD ARAB town of Zanzibar was a painter's paradise for Livy. So many shades of brown. Small, etched windows with ornate bars to the street. Women in veils, dark and mysterious. The thought of lush gardens behind high walls. Eyes watching her but never seen. The smells. So many rich smells of spice mingling with the scent of flowers. A slow pace in the heat. Sandalled feet. The calls to prayer. Looking up at the tall tower next to the mosque from where the priest was calling the faithful to prayer... Sketching. Fast and furious. Oblivious of Jeremy or the rest of them gone she knew not where, or cared as she sketched, her hand desperate to capture what she saw.

"Livy! Are you there? We've got to go back on board the ship."

"How long have I been sketching?"

"Two hours."

"Felt more like ten minutes. This place excites me... Where are they?"

"The Resident had some business. Why he came. Bringing the duke was to see his old friend while he worked. They were at school together."

"What was this place before we Europeans took over?"

"Arab trading port, by the look of it. The dhows came down all the way from Arabia, hugging the coast I was told. All the way back to the time of Christ."

"All these lovely buildings."

"An old civilisation, the Persian Empire... We all have our chance. Now it's going to be the Russians... Have you got what you want?"

"I never have quite what I want, Jeremy... Where's Cecil?"

"Over there under a tree. I think he's bored again. I'll show him over the boat when we get back on board."

"Time goes so quickly. This trip will be over before I can blink. All I'll have are these sketches and the memory in my mind. We'll be gone but everything will stay the same... Do you think they have harems anymore?"

"The British Resident would frown on harems."

"He wouldn't know. Who's going to tell him? I want to go through one of these doors, have a look inside. What is that lovely smell coming over the top of the wall?"

"Jasmine. At night the smell is stronger. Mrs Maple planted jasmine bushes all round her garden. I could smell them at night from the cottage when the wind was right."

"Do they play music at night?"

"I'm sure they do... Cecil, old chap. We'd better be getting back to the ship."

"They must think we're odd," said Livy, looking at an old man who had not even looked at her.

"We are, Livy. We are. You in particular. Most of the men have never seen the face of a woman other than their family and friends. That priest up there would have had something to say if the old men had stared at you."

"Zanzibar. Such an exotic name. Where did it come from?"

"Somewhere out of history."

"You think it means something?"

"Come along, Mrs Crookshank."

"Why is everything good in life so short? We're always chasing off."

"You won't have so much to chase once we get back to England."

"I suppose not. Give me your hand, lover."

. . .

THE PAINTINGS WENT into first class but not the painter. Never break the rules. It made Livy smile. All those lovely barriers. The rich from the not so rich. To make people feel superior, she supposed. All those nice little compartments where they could be among their own kind, secure in familiarity.

"How many classes are there in society?"

"What are you talking about?"

"For something better to do the rich and bored in first class are going to look at my paintings with their noses in the air. People who think they should know something about the arts after all their expensive educations will pass judgement on my work yet they don't want to meet me as I came from tourist class. In Zanzibar two days ago it was the colonials in the Royal Hotel and the people whose island it was out in the street. Never the twain to meet. When did you ever meet the working class in England, Jeremy? There weren't any at school with you, of that I'm certain. We all like to feel superior to someone. Makes us happy. Bloody ridiculous if you ask me."

"If they give you the thousand pounds for your painting of the river you won't mind so much."

"I want to keep that painting. No one will shell out a thousand quid for an unknown artist. They want a name on their wall to boast about. To hell with what it looks like. And they think they know so much about art. Bullshit. It's only about being one up on their friends. I thought we'd get a free glass of wine or two for the exhibit. Nothing. All your hard work and mine for nothing."

"Someone's looking at them, Livy. That must mean something... What are we going to do in Mombasa?"

"I suppose so... Walk around. Look at the poor natives. We really are a snooty lot we British."

"Too late to change us now. How we were born. Can't change your country any more than your parents. Or your outlook on life, if what you say about the class system is true. If you ask me it's all about people wanting to mix with their own kind."

"We could go to America?" said Livy.

"They have just as many barriers between people. Just a different kind. In America it's all about money and calling everyone Chuck. As if being on first-name terms makes them all equal. Reverse snobbery, if you ask me. 'I'm so bloody rich but I still call you Chuck.' That kind of thing. Like the do-gooders who aren't doing as much good as they would like you to think."

"We're a weird species."

"Say that again. It's all about survival according to Darwin. The more money you've got, the better chance your kids have of surviving and passing on your genes. All quite primal. Pretty basic really... When we get to the Suez Canal we can take the train to Cairo while the ship discharges cargo and sails slowly through the canal. From Cairo we can take a trip to the pyramids. I've always wanted to ride a camel."

"They are nasty animals."

"How do you know?"

"What's Cecil going to do with his life?"

"He doesn't know any more than I do."

"You're going to make sandwiches and flog them at lunchtime round the city... Could you get back in the navy if you wanted to?"

"I don't think so."

"Why is life always so difficult? Cows get born and live their lives in a field. Why can't we be the same?"

"Cows get eaten, Livy."

"Not the milk cows."

"They all get eaten in the end."

"And we all die. What's the difference?"

"Why are we having this conversation?"

"I have no idea... It's deck quoits or a drink."

"Too hot to run around."

"That's my boy. Let's be decadent while we have the opportunity... Do you think they'll like my paintings?"

"Of course they will."

"You can only be sure when they pay for them, you know. People tell you what they think you want to hear. They have to put their money where their mouths are if you want to be sure."

"We're back to money."

"Always about money. You're right. The only measure that we all understand."

. . .

Jeremy had made a small crate of the paintings the day before they reached the Port of Suez. No one had bought one. A deckhand had delivered them back to their cabin without any ceremony. Neither of them spoke of the rejection when they first found them back in the cabin, only later, when they were all crated ready for the luggage train at Trieste to go on unaccompanied to England.

"When the Honourable Barnaby St Clair bought my first painting he did it on the spur of the moment. The way he looked at me when I took the painting to his house in Piccadilly with James Coghlan he seemed more interested in me than the painting. There was a cat in his house just like mine, the one I had put in the painting surrounded by tropical foliage I had lifted from a Rousseau jungle scene. It's all about luck getting a start to a name that sells paintings. At least I didn't sell the river. I'm glad. We'll just be flat broke in London as we planned. Now you've framed them so nicely they can go straight into the Nouvelle Galerie when we get home."

"You're putting on a brave face."

"You have to. You can't take rejection personally as an artist or you'd never do any work. Look at Van Gogh. All that prolific work and he only sold one painting while he was alive. And his brother ran an art gallery. Family and friends never think you are any good until they are told by someone else."

"I think they are good."

"You are my lover. When a man wants a woman's body, anything she does is good. It's a bit like women sucking up to rich men when they want to marry them."

"You can't accuse me of being rich so why do you bother with me?"

"You're good in the sack, Jeremy. Oh yes, you are good in the sack. At our age the rest doesn't matter. Only when men stop looking at me the way they do will I worry about money. The trick is to marry a rich bugger just before they put you on the shelf. Or a poor man who is going to do well in his life. Like you."

"You got out of that one."

"Oh, Jeremy. Let's just enjoy ourselves. To hell with the paintings. We're going to Egypt tomorrow. The land of the Pharaohs. We're going to ride camels. Make love in a Cairo hotel with all those lovely smells of the far away Arabian desert wafting through our window. Then it's on to

Europe and Venice. Ballads sung to us by a gorgeous Italian while we sit together holding hands in the back of a gondola."

THEY HAD NOT SEEN Cecil since his parents got off the boat at Mombasa to go back to their farm in Happy Valley where the white farmers had carved out their homes in the highlands of Kenya. Twice since he first heard it from the Duke of Tewkesbury, Jeremy had heard the name Mau Mau. Once in a bar in Mombasa, when he and Livy had gone ashore, and again from a young man who had just joined the boat. He and Jeremy were the same age, with similar backgrounds, both going back to England with their tails between their legs.

"It's far worse than the authorities are letting on," Martin Wells had said the first night out of Mombasa. "They never let on until the problem takes over. Don't want to upset the apple cart. Britain has a lot of money invested in Kenya. The commies have got at the Kikuyu, one of the local tribes. A few of them have missionary educations. Just smell a political opportunity for themselves if they can kick out us British. They don't give a damn about communism. They smell power. If you tell the ignorant they are hard done by and are under-privileged, you get them on your side by just giving them a pile of promises. Promises are wonderful weapons of politics. Everyone promises everyone the moon when they want something. When they get what they want they forget the promises. There are seeds of dissent against colonialism being spread throughout Africa. The British government, especially the Labour Party, are not going to put up a fight. Why should they? Their constituents are in Britain. Anyway, administering an angry empire instead of one that is grateful costs money. More money than we make in trade, according to some in London. To hell with the colonials. They are expendable. Had their time in the sun. Let them have their comeuppance."

"Where did you hear all this?" asked Jeremy.

"Why I'm going home while I'm young. All everyone talks about in the club. The only one that will put up a fight is South Africa. The Boers don't have anywhere to run to. They've legislated separate development. In Afrikaans it's called apartheid. Stopping the races mixing. A bit like King Canute trying to stop the waves coming into shore if you ask me."

"So keeping the races living separately won't work?"

"Of course not. Don't so much as think about going back to Rhodesia. Mau Mau. They are going to cut our throats while we're lying asleep in our beds... Do you two want another drink?"

"You paint a bleak picture for Africa... Thank you. I'll have another beer."

"Might as well enjoy cheap booze a little longer. In England you can't afford to drink or smoke."

"Don't you believe it," said Livy. "There's always a way."

"How long have you two been married?"

The name Mau Mau kept ringing in Jeremy's head even as they sailed away from Mogadishu in Somaliland two days later. The ship had stopped in the roads to offload cargo onto lighters and to take on fresh produce. No one was allowed to go ashore. The man was right. There was more going on in Africa than met the public eye. It made Jeremy's gloomy feelings that much worse.

THE TENSION WAS BUILDING up inside Jeremy when he and Livy went in to dinner. He would not be able to avoid the issue for very much longer. Only one thing was certain as they steamed ever closer to Europe. There was no going back to Africa. Ever.

His mind on his own problems, Jeremy did not pick up the smirk on Angela Lipton's face before it was too late.

"Did you sell all your paintings, Livy?" she said sarcastically.

"You must know damn well I didn't. Who told you?"

"Oh, didn't you sell any?"

For the rest of dinner the two girls glared across the table at each other. Jeremy thought Angela was jealous, herself not being married.

"There's a new man on board, Angela. I asked him to join our table. There's still one chair vacant. I asked the chief engineer to change his place setting on the roster. You'll like him. He's young. Going home. Got on at Mombasa."

"Oh that is sweet of you... Where is he?"

"Right behind you... Martin Wells," said Jeremy standing up. "I would like you to meet Angela Lipton. Got on at Cape Town. If we shuffle the seating you two can sit next to each other."

Before Martin could sit down Jeremy felt Livy's claws sink in his knee, her fingernails pushing the cloth of his trousers. Leaning close, he whispered in her ear, "Better than you throwing a glass of wine in the bitch's face."

The small pain in his knee stopped, followed by a stroke which went up inside his leg. They were both smiling, watching Angela turn her attention to Martin. She was all over him.

The next morning at breakfast Angela Lipton had a satisfied look on her face. Martin Wells gave Jeremy a boastful look. Jeremy decided he did not like Martin Wells.

"Why don't we all go through to Cairo together on the train, Jeremy?" said Martin. "Angela said she's so looking forward to seeing the Cairo museums. She wants to take the trip out into the desert to see the pyramids. I said I'd take her. Lots of fun together. What do you say, Livy?"

"I'm going to ride a camel. Wouldn't you like to ride a camel, Angela?"

"Yes I would. What fun. It's always better to go anywhere with friends."

Jeremy wanted to laugh. The girl had completely changed. From a disagreeable sourpuss the girl was enjoying herself.

"All she needed," said Jeremy when they went up on deck to watch their ship sail into the Port of Suez.

"Do you think they are sleeping with each other so soon?"

"Of course they are. They both look like cats who have got into the cream. The boastful part of Martin Wells was best kept to himself. One of the unwritten rules of male conduct was never to tell people when they had slept with a girl."

"She's less antagonistic. Why are some people just plain disagreeable?"

For Livy it was all commercial. Everyone looking down at something to sell or something to buy. Angela was more interested in the postcards from the Egyptian museum to impress her friends back in Cape Town and England. When Livy tried to sketch the antiques on display she was shoved along by Martin and Angela. It was the opposite of the Zambezi

Valley where they had stayed put in one place, a place she would always be able to feel and remember.

From the Port of Suez it had been so organised, never time to feel the history of a civilisation that built the pyramids. As for the tourists that flocked alongside them, Livy doubted if many had any idea of what they were looking at. Buy the postcard. Always buy the postcard so that later the only reality of the visit to Egypt was in a badly printed photograph.

The camel ride when it came was another opportunity for a photograph to stick in an album to boast about later.

They spent one night in Cairo in a room next to Martin and Angela. From table companions, Martin and Angela moved quickly to sharing a room.

"They are perfectly suited, those two, and that's all that matters. What are we going to do tomorrow? Will you promise me when we get to Trieste we go to Venice on our own?"

"What's the matter, Livy?"

"I'm frustrated when I'm not painting. Or sketching. I'm no good at being a tourist."

They left Trieste on the train with two small suitcases. The cabin trunks and the crate of paintings had gone on to London unaccompanied. Angela Lipton and Martin Wells had barely said goodbye to them, more interested in each other. In the rush to get off the ship and go through Italian immigration and customs they had not seen Cecil. Livy had looked back at the big white ship that had been her home. All those familiar faces she would never see again.

For three weeks they took the trains around Europe as they meandered across the Continent towards Calais. Livy thought she would remember eating pasta in small Italian restaurants. The rest was a blur of buildings and countryside all flowing together. After Cairo there had been nothing she wanted to paint. Italian and French countryside was not a lot different to England. Painting the snow-capped mountains of Switzerland had been done so many times before. Everyone in England knew what Rome looked like. There was nothing new for Livy like the African bush with its strange animals and birds. She could still smell the wild sage in her nostrils when she thought of the big river flowing slowly through the bush.

3

They came across to Dover on the ferry. The white cliffs. A man from customs on the boat was looking for a man from Africa smuggling diamonds. The customs man had quizzed Jeremy in the bar after he heard Jeremy was back from Rhodesia.

They were back on English soil, looking at each other not knowing quite what to say. Jeremy had to catch a train to Portsmouth where a boat would take him across the Solent to his mother on the Isle of Wight. In London he was going to stay with his brother Paul. The parting was a kiss on the lips without any passion. People all around them on the platform. Jeremy put his suitcase in the carriage and got up inside the compartment. Before he could turn round, the train jerked forward, throwing him back onto the hidden seat. By the time he got the window open the train was halfway down the platform. They both waved. Livy began to cry, the tears pouring down her face. It was all over. She was no longer Mrs Crookshank.

Feeling lonely, Livy carried her small suitcase to platform seven where she was to catch the train up to London. The journey from England to Africa and back again had taken a lifetime. A part of her life that would always stay in her mind. When she was old she would see herself young with Jeremy. Remember the sunsets and the Zambezi Valley. Her happiness.

. . .

WHEN SHE GOT to London and Tessa's Chelsea flat, no one was at home. Her suitcase had become heavy. Sitting on it outside the front door of her friend's flat she had a good cry. The cry made her feel better. She waited an hour for Tessa to come home.

"Livy! What are you doing back in England? How long have you been sitting on your suitcase?... What happened to Jeremy?"

"He's gone to the Isle of Wight to see his mother."

"Didn't it work out between the two of you?"

"Rhodesia didn't work. I got him fired from his job on the farm."

"Is this all you came back with? Come inside. I have a new flatmate. You can sleep on the pull-out couch."

"The trunk went ahead... With my paintings of Africa. Jeremy put them into frames on the boat."

"You go inside and unpack. I'll go to the off-licence for a bottle of gin. Then we can talk."

"Nothing changes in Chelsea."

"Why should it? You'll like Abigail. She's fun."

"Can she paint?"

"She's into abstracts which I don't understand... Now don't go away. Take me five minutes."

"I've got nowhere to go, Tess."

She watched Tessa Handson go off down the corridor. She was home. Going inside the two-roomed flat she felt much better. Everything was familiar. Pussycat, the pussycat she had painted and sold for four hundred pounds with the help of her plagiarising of Henri Rousseau, was sitting in the big bay window. The cat took no notice of her as usual.

"Don't you love me Pussycat, you cold old thing?"

On the easel in the bay window was an abstract painting. Livy stood in front of it, trying to understand, lost in her thoughts.

"Hello. I'm Abigail. Who are you?"

"I'm Livy."

"You're meant to be in the wilds of Africa... Where's Tessa?"

"Gone to buy a bottle of gin. I'll be sleeping on the couch for a couple of nights."

"Stay as long as you like... What do you think of it?"

"Does the cat ignore you as well?"

"Always... Have you been crying?"

"Just a little. For six weeks I was Mrs Crookshank. Now I'm plain Livy."

"You got married and divorced?"

"It's a long story. Better we wait for the gin."

"Feel like a sandwich?... Now what's the matter?"

"Sandwiches. They make me think of Jeremy." She was crying out loud, blubbing like a child. The girl put an arm around her shoulder, sensibly not saying a word.

"I'm sorry," said Livy. "Other people's problems always seem so trivial."

A WEEK LATER, with still no word from Jeremy, Livy picked up her cabin trunk and the small crate of her paintings from Waterloo Station. The porter helped her put the trunk on the open platform next to the taxi driver. The paintings went inside.

"Where to, luv?"

"Chelsea to drop the trunk. Then to the Portobello Road. The Nouvelle Galerie. You know where that is?"

"Course I do. That's my job. You an artist like, wearing a French beret?"

"Yes. The crate's full of my paintings. I've been to Africa."

"All those lions and tigers. Frighten me they would."

"They don't have tigers in Africa. Only leopards and lions."

Half an hour later, after paying the cab driver, Livy was down to four pounds. Jeanne Pétain was waiting for her. Ben Brown helped unpack the crate, putting the paintings one by one on the wall of the gallery.

"Who framed them, Livy? Not very good wood."

"Packing case wood off the ship."

"Looks like it. Never mind. It's the paintings that count. They are wonderful. Just look at them, Ben. I'll let James Coghlan price them. We'll have an African night. Send out invitations."

"I need the money, Jeanne."

"Don't we all? Have you started painting in the flat?"

"All I do is paint. All I want to do is paint."

"Any word from Jeremy?"

"Not yet. It was just an affair. Affairs end and everyone moves on. Anyway, with neither of us having any money there isn't much chance of us getting married. The point of getting married is to have kids. Right now we can't support ourselves. His mother was lonely. Said he'd stay awhile... They look nice in the gallery. Different."

"Are you going to stay on the couch?"

"Nowhere else to go."

"So much for dreams."

"We have to dream. All of us. Without dreams life is without purpose. Reality is boring most of the time."

IF NOTHING ELSE, Livy told herself, the painting was going well. The three of them painted side by side with their backs to the big bay window where the light was good. When Jeremy did phone at the end of August it was to say he was going back to Rhodesia. Like Livy he was flat broke. He had run out of practical ideas for making a living in England. Roger Crumpshaw had offered him a job as an assistant on Ingwe Estate and sent him the money to buy a plane ticket from London to Salisbury. Pamela was pregnant. There was a cottage near the main house. Mrs Florence Maple had been exchanged for Mrs Pamela Crumpshaw. Jeremy said he had had no alternative but to accept the offer. He hoped Rhodesia and the new Central African Federation would be the success Roger assured him it was going to be. That Mau Mau would not spread down Africa. He was in London with his brother Paul ready to be driven to the airport when he phoned, thinking it better for them not to meet in case he changed his mind.

"A man has to go where he can make a living, Livy. I can't be just a clerk for the rest of my life. Or sell trays of sandwiches round the offices of London. I must have some kind of a future in my life... We can write."

"I don't think so, Jeremy. We tried that last time."

"I love you, Livy."

"No you don't. You love what we had together on our trip. An affair to remember. Let's keep it like that."

"Roger has promised me a bonus at the end of next season. They're preparing the seed beds on the farm when I get back. Now he's married he needs an assistant on the farm. Pamela likes to gallivant a bit and takes him off the farm."

"Bertie promised you a bonus."

"Roger is different."

"Pamela isn't. She'll have her nose in the air the same as Flossy Maple. She fancies being lady of the manor. Why she married Roger if you ask me. We shared a cabin. Good luck in the cottage."

"She's our friend."

"She was. Now she's the boss's wife."

"Have you got any money?"

"I'm fine. Tessa is looking after me. You tootle along to the airport. I'm sure Harry Brigandshaw and the Duke of Tewkesbury were wrong. Africa will do just fine. When you visit the Zambezi Valley again stand at the side of the river and think of me, Jeremy. They can take away our money but they can't take away our memories. Something like that."

"Will you be all right?"

"Of course I will. It was just a holiday."

"Was it, Livy?"

"That's what it has to be. For both of us. Could you imagine me living in a cottage down the path from Mrs Pamela Crumpshaw? I'd get you fired in a day."

"Can we talk again when I have my own farm?"

"In five years! Who knows? Nothing is ever written in stone."

"I've got to go. Paul is getting agitated. He has his own problems with so much death duty that has to be paid on Harry Brigandshaw's estate. They are having to sell Hastings Court. May have to sell the company Paul works for. There wasn't as much money as people thought. Helped make up my mind. A job's a job. No one ever really knows what's going to happen in the future... Goodbye, Livy."

"Goodbye, lover. I'll miss you."

"So will I, my God, so will I."

She was going to tell him about the African exhibition at the Nouvelle Galerie that was happening that night. James Coghlan had put a price on each of her paintings. The phone went dead and she began to cry. He had gone. She had lost him.

"What's the matter, Livy?" asked Abigail when Livy tried to go back to her painting.

"Jeremy's gone back to Rhodesia. Now. On the plane."

"You'll find someone else."

"You never find that first love again... Life's a bitch."

THAT EVENING at nine o'clock in the Portobello Road Gallery, Livy sold the smaller painting of the Zambezi River for twelve hundred pounds. At half past nine she sold a painting of the African sunset she had painted in the window of Mrs Wade's house in Baker Avenue. A third went before the exhibition closed. Three buyers wanted the one with the crocodiles she had done by the river. Her big Zambezi River painting. The painting that was not for sale.

The following day Livy found herself a studio flat down the road from Tessa and Abigail. The painting of her river went up on the wall. She felt empty. Drained of excitement. Someone was missing. Jeremy was missing. She couldn't even tell him about the sales of the pictures still in their frames he had made for her on board the MV *Esquilino*.

That afternoon, in perfect sunshine, Livy walked the north bank of the Thames. There was a barge going upriver. The man on the barge waved. There was a dog this time on the barge. She was back where she started.

"Oh, to hell with it," she said. "I'll get myself a cat."

PART IV

OCTOBER 1952 – "THE PRODIGAL SON"

*K*im Brigandshaw came home from his travels two years and four months after the death of his father. His shoulders were broad from tossing sheep on their backs in the shearing shed of a three-hundred-square-mile property in Western Australia six hundred miles north of Perth. His legs were strong from riding horses outside Milo, a small town in the state of Kansas. There was a scar down the right side of his face caused by a knife wound he had received in a bar in Singapore from a man trying to sell him opium. He had told the man to shove the opium up his arse. The man, who had said he was an Englishman, had tried to punch him in the face before pulling a knife. By then Kim had heard his father was dead so there was little point in going home. He was older but not much wiser as he walked down Regent Street looking in the windows of shops. So far as he knew, none of the family were aware he was back in England. When a pretty girl stared at him he put a hand up to his scarred face.

"Plastic surgery, old boy," he murmured to himself. "That poor girl looked terrified."

On the corner of a side street a man was selling the *Evening Standard*. The headline was about Mau Mau killing another white farmer in Kenya. Kim skipped to the sports page to see if there was anyone playing county cricket at Lord's or The Oval. Kim had not watched a game of cricket since leaving the Royal Air Force at the end of his two-year National Service, when he was twenty, before he took off on his travels to see the world, never once asking his family for money.

On his back was a sheepskin jacket he had had made in Australia. He was wearing high leather boots he had bought in Milo. Having read what he wanted, Kim put the paper in the big inside pocket of his sheepskin jacket. Maybe it was the smelly old jacket that had frightened the girl, not the slice down the side of his face. He had left his backpack at Victoria Station to give him time to look around London, thinking what to do. There was no cricket at Lord's or The Oval, Middlesex or Surrey. He had some money from his last job outside Milo on a ranch where he worked with horses, a skill they had taught him on the sheep property in Western Australia. Kim had enough money in his pocket to last him a while, until he made up his mind what to do.

From Liverpool, right off the ship, Kim had phoned his family at Hastings Court. The number had been disconnected. He had not been good at keeping in touch with his family for fear of being told to come home. To get a job. A proper job. To live like a man who had been given an expensive boarding school education. A man who had been eighteen when he received his commission in the air force. The last thing he had wanted was to hear his mother telling him again to grow up and face life's responsibilities. Only once had he phoned his family on his travels. In America without a job, he had phoned his cousin Tinus in New York. Walking down into Piccadilly, Kim remembered their conversation.

"You do what you want, cousin. Don't let them make you do what they want. Are you short of money?"

"I have enough... Did Dad suffer, Tinus?"

"I went out to Rhodesia for the funeral... It was quick. Your father was a great man. Let me know if you want anything. There are big problems in England with your father's estate. Death duty has wiped out most of the money. Your siblings are squabbling. They are trying to sell Hastings Court. No one has the money to run an old English country estate anymore. The rates and taxes are too high."

"Is Mother all right?"

"She's in London. In a flat near Barnaby St Clair."

"Really?"

"Most of the income that's left from the British and American estate is going to your mother. The capital was left to Harry's children: you, Beth, Dorian and Frank. And me. We each inherit a fifth of the estate with a stipulation your mother lives comfortably. She's expensive, Kim. Paul Crookshank, myself and the family solicitor are executors of the estate."

"What's happened to Elephant Walk in Rhodesia?"

"Doesn't make much of a profit. What there is goes to your grandmother and your Aunt Madge for their upkeep. Much like your mother."

"So the family is broke! What a laugh. That'll piss off Dorian. He fancied being the rich man's son, writing books while not having to make a living."

"When are you going back to England?"

"When I'm ready. You think these friends of yours will give me a job in Milo?"

"You can only ask them. Look after yourself. Come and visit us if you get to New York."

"Thanks, Tinus. I appreciate your help."

"What are family for if they can't help?"

"Is your wife still acting?"

"Not with the kids. Maybe when they're older she'll go back into films."

"Saw her *Robin Hood* film twice in Australia."

"That's so old."

"In the outback of Australia any film is a good one. However old. She sure was a beautiful woman."

"Still is... Take care."

"You too, cousin."

Turning on his heel at Piccadilly Tube station, Kim walked down into the Underground. He would surprise his sister. Knock on her door. See the surprise on her face.

Catching the train to South Kensington, Kim sat back and looked at the other passengers. On a Sunday morning the Tube was mostly empty. The middle-aged man opposite gave Kim a look of disapproval. Kim's hair was down his back. Long wavy light brown hair more like a girl. The man had a short back and sides and wore a bowler hat on the top of his head. There was an umbrella standing up in between his legs. When the man's eyes reached the cowboy boots he looked away in distaste. When he looked back, Kim gave him a smile that twisted his scar. The man got up and walked to the back of the train.

'That was the scar,' he told himself. 'What a prick.'

At South Kensington, Kim left the train without looking at the man who was now reading his paper. At Beth's flat Kim rang the doorbell.

"May I speak to Beth Brigandshaw?" Kim said politely to a stranger.

"She doesn't live here anymore. Anyway, she's now Mrs Crookshank. Mrs Paul Crookshank. When she got married, she and the other girl with the baby moved. My wife and I took over the lease."

"Do you know her address?"

"I do as a matter of fact. Who are you may I ask?"

"I'm her brother Kim."

"Do you know that coat smells, young man?"

"Not the coat, I'm afraid. It's me. You're not the first person in England to wrinkle his nose. I was on a cattle boat to Liverpool from America."

"If you don't mind me saying, it's rather unusual hearing English spoken so well from a man in those clothes. Have you been away long?... I'll get that address for you."

When the man gave him Paul Crookshank's address in Hammersmith, Kim shook the man's hand.

"England must be strange to you."

"More than anyone here could understand... Have a nice day."

"But it's raining when I looked out the window."

"It's an American expression... Good old England. I'm obliged to you."

BETH CROOKSHANK OPENED the door to the smell of wet dog. She was eight months pregnant and her back ached. Her feet were bare and swollen as she took in the sight of her brother, her eyes weary. Moving forward she put her arms round her brother's waist and her head on his shoulder.

"Where've you been, Kim?"

"All over I suppose."

"Why didn't you come home when you heard Dad died?"

"What was the point? I only heard he was dead two months after the funeral. He had gone to Rhodesia without Mother. I didn't want to get into a family argument. How is our mother?"

"Living in luxury in a flat off Park Lane. With a paid companion and a Pekingese dog. She likes to say she has lunch with Barnaby St Clair once a month. He feels sorry for her. After paying for Mother the family doesn't have any money."

The piano playing in the lounge stopped.

"Who's there?" said Paul coming out of the lounge.

"Kim."

"I'll be blowed... What on earth's that smell?"

"Me and my fur coat," said Kim, shaking Paul's hand.

"Come in. Come in. It's cold and Beth can't fit in her shoes. Something to do with water retention from the baby."

"Congratulations... I had the coat run up on a sheep property in Australia by one of the other hands... I came over from America on a cattle boat to get a free passage looking after the animals. Worked on a cattle ranch in America so I knew what I was doing. Doesn't pay to have some of the cows die on the way over. You get to know the animals are sick by looking at them."

"When did you last have a bath?"

"*Is* it that bad? You can never smell yourself."

"Where are you staying?"

"My haversack is at the station. The boat landed at Liverpool... Where's Dorian now he's out of the army? What's he doing?"

Beth had closed the front door. They were all still standing in the corridor.

"How did you find me here? You didn't write, Kim. No one knew where you were for months on end."

"Who's the girl with the baby? The new tenant gave me your address."

"Nancy. Dorian's the father but he runs away from his responsibilities. They have a little girl called Wendy. Dorian's living in a room in Cornwall writing his books. Says he hasn't any money so what can he do... Don't they cut hair on cattle ranches in America? You'd better have your hair cut before you see Mother."

"How did she take Dad dying?"

"Have you had anything to eat?"

"Not today. So you two are married... What happened to Frank?"

"Believe it or not, he's the only one of us with any money. Has his own PR business. Our half-brother Frank is an artist at bullshit."

"So it's official. Has Barnaby St Clair acknowledged him as his son?"

"Too many questions, Kim. Follow me into the kitchen while I start supper... Tell us what you've been up to. Mother's happy with her companion. You could say she and Dad split up when he went to Rhodesia. He was buried on the farm next to his first wife and their unborn child."

"Who's living at home?"

"We had to sell Hastings Court for a pittance to pay death duty. The new property tax was prohibitive. Welcome back to socialist England. They don't like people inheriting money. All that family history down the drain, right back to William the Conqueror. Everyone is meant to be the same. If you have any money they take it from you to give to the underprivileged. They want everyone down to the same level so no one can be jealous. All the same. A bit like your cattle, I suppose... The Brigandshaw business is just hanging on with Paul running it in England. Tinus in America spends most of his time looking after his wife's money. Barnaby St Clair helped her invest some of her film money in London bomb sites after the war. They're rich. We're poor. The antiques market collapsed when the sellers in England wanted too much money and the Americans wouldn't pay... I'm going to make macaroni cheese. Do you like macaroni cheese?... There's no point in moaning. We're all the same family with or without Hastings Court. It's just sad all that history came to an end. Governments make the rules. They can tax what they like if they have a majority in parliament. Then it's legal to take a family's home away from them, I suppose. Even if you owned it for hundreds of years. What are you going to do with yourself? There isn't any money in sheep or cows in England even had we still owned the few acres round Hastings Court... You could go and farm in Rhodesia. They are looking for a new manager. Old Sir Jacob Rosenzweig died in America leaving Rebecca and her brothers a large fortune. The Madgwicks have gone with the kids to live in America. Aunt Madge is trying to run Elephant Walk on her own."

"What about Dorian?"

"He lives in a world of his own. Literally. His world of fiction."

"What does he live off?"

"The five pounds a month from the estate and whatever else he can earn. We kids and Tinus each get five pounds a month after the trustees processed Dad's estate."

"There's some back money for you, Kim," said Paul. "I'm one of the trustees. Enough to buy you a haircut and some clothes... Sorry. Just kidding... How about a beer? We're not that broke under Labour. You got a free health service like everyone else. It isn't all bad... When are you going to see your mother?"

"So it's all changed for the Brigandshaw family?"

"Afraid so. Everything has changed in England since the war... You can move into the spare bedroom until you decide what to do."

"Thanks, Paul... What a world. You never know what's going to happen next... When's the baby due?"

"Next month," said Beth. "Before you sit down in my lounge you are going to take a bath and wash that hair. Paul will lend you some clothes."

"What do you want me to do with the sheepskin?"

"Put it in the bathroom closet and shut the door. Tomorrow I will take it to the dry cleaner."

"Genuine sheepskin. Skinned the sheep myself. Don't let them run off with it... My word. What a lovely painting," said Kim, looking at the painting on the wall inside the lounge. "Saw a sunset like that in the outback of Australia. Just look at those colours. Whoever did that can paint. What did you pay for it, Paul?"

"Nothing. It was a gift. From Livy Johnston. I loaned my brother Jeremy a hundred pounds so Livy could go out to him in Rhodesia. She sold the other one like that for five hundred quid to a collector who knows more about painting than me."

"I'd better go and have that bath. Any chance of a beer while I'm soaking?"

"What did you do to your face?" asked Paul.

"Bar fight in Singapore."

"When you've bathed and had supper you'd better start at the beginning. All those experiences. All I've ever done is work and play music. I envy you. Now I'm a staid old married man about to become a father."

"I envy you, Paul. That's the strange part of life. We often think the other chap's got the answer. The Buddhist monk. The sheep farmer. A man who can play the piano and live a happily married life... That painting's good. Really good. Who is this Livy?"

"You'll meet her. Keeps in touch. She and Jeremy still write at Christmas and birthdays. This year he moves up to a manager of his own section of Ingwe Estate. He'll have his own farm in a couple of years' time. Jeremy is doing well."

"Are they getting married?"

"Livy's convinced herself Africa has no future for the white man. She's probably right. A few old colonials trying to hang on too long. The blacks are cutting the white man's throats in Kenya. Trouble is, Jeremy has nothing to come back to. I can't do anything for him. I have enough trouble keeping the company alive. The big cigarette companies don't like upstart competition. Ridgeback barely breaks even. What with the increase in tax on cigarettes, we're having a hard time keeping our heads above water. You need a fortune to throw at advertising which we don't have anymore... I'll go and get you a beer. Lots to catch up on. Welcome home, Kim."

"Did Dorian finish his book on Grandfather Brigandshaw?" said Kim, going into the bathroom.

"Keeps rewriting it. Too much theory of writing from Oxford and not enough inspiration, so he says. The characters won't talk to him... There's plenty of hot water. Take as much as you like. You'd better close the door even though she is your sister. I'll see if I can't find a bottle of wine at the back of the cupboard. The prodigal son returns. Can't afford to keep a wine cellar these days. We get by. A treat tastes much better when you can't afford it so often. There's still rationing. Seven years after the war. All those lives and national treasure down the drain fighting the Germans. Self-destruction if you ask me. Did neither nation any good. Or the Japanese."

"The Americans won the wars, Paul. And the peace. They were the ones to benefit. They're going to dominate the world by controlling the money. Not that I know much about it. What they say in America. The States are booming. All those assembly lines. Money controls the world. Without money you're nothing but a pawn in someone else's hands.

Friend of mine in Milo said that. Maybe I'll go back to America when I've had my bath."

KIM COULD HEAR them talking softly in the kitchen as he soaked in the luxury of his bath. With the bathroom door closed he could not hear what they were saying. There was no sign of his beer. All the thoughts of being rich when he got back to England had evaporated. His brother-in-law was short of money by the sound of it. No chance of an expensive private education for the kid on its way. The war had changed everything. Trying to think what he was now going to do with himself, Kim studied the big toe on his right foot that was sticking out of the water. The toe was black, trodden on by a steer on the boat coming over. When the new nail had grown underneath, the old one would fall off. The toe had been painful when trodden on by the steer. Going up on deck he had sat by the ship's rail and meditated on the universe to obliterate the pain, his mind far away from his body. Three months in a Buddhist monastery in Bhutan had taught him how to remove his mind from the inconveniences of his body. A letter of introduction he had carried to the King of Bhutan from the King's English tutor had let him into the kingdom. They barely talked in the monastery. Kim had worked hard in the garden to pay for his keep. He had never been happier in his life. There were no human arguments. The countryside and mountains around were beautiful, the food plain but plentiful. He had slept on a hard floor right through the nights neither cold nor warm. It was all in the mind, they had told him.

When the water grew cold Kim turned on the tap. He washed his long hair with his sister's shampoo. It made the water around him dirty. He washed the hair twice to be certain it was clean. Then he cleaned the dirt from under his nails, trying not to realise he was back in England with decisions to be made he could no longer avoid.

The knock on the bathroom door brought him back to his predicament. The clothes came in with a glass of beer. Paul left him alone while he dressed.

With a broad smile on his face, Kim emerged carrying his empty glass. The beer had not touched the sides going down his throat. The supper was being served on a small dining room table in the lounge. Kim looked again at the painting of the sunset as he passed. On the table were three wine glasses and a bottle of wine with its cork taken out and lying across the neck of the bottle. Paul gave Kim the cork. It smelled of lovely old red wine. Kim wrinkled his nose with pleasure.

"That's better," said Beth. "You men all need a woman in your life or you live like animals."

Kim was still wearing his leather boots, his dirty clothes left in a basket next to the bath. His sister was right. A man needed a woman. But not for the reasons she had in mind. There had only been one woman in his travels, a girl in Singapore. The slash down his face had been as much to do with the girl as the drugs. The man had been after his Chinese girl. Neither of them had been able to speak each other's language but it did not matter. When he closed his eyes he could still see her face. It was the most beautiful face. After the slash down his cheek he had never seen her again. They had to stitch his face to stop the bleeding. When he came back from seeing the English doctor she was gone. Kim knew the memory of her face would always stay in his mind. Forever. She was just that beautiful.

"What's your next step?" asked Paul.

"I never know. Part of the excitement. Where is there to go? What is there to do? Get a job and settle down? I don't think so. Once you start rolling I don't think you stop."

"Don't you have any ambition?" asked Beth.

"Maybe in the future. Not just yet. I'll go and see Frank and Dorian while I'm in England. Get my usual lecture from Mother. She'll never forgive me for going away for so long... This is just wonderful seeing you both again... It's difficult without Dad. To be here in England without him won't register on my mind. He was always there when I needed him."

"When we all needed him," said Beth.

Kim took up his glass that Paul had filled from the bottle of pre-war French wine.

"I give you a toast. To our father. May his soul rest in peace."

THREE DAYS later Kim went to visit his mother. The sheepskin coat was soft and clean without a trace of a smell. He had tied up his long hair at the back to hang down in a pigtail. With a jaunty step he walked up Hay Street thinking of his sister. Not since they were small children had she mothered him so much. She was going to make a wonderful mother for her child, her life fulfilled in motherhood. The thought of his sister's happiness made Kim smile. Despite their shortage of money she was not going to work after the baby was born. The new trend of both parents working was not to be for the Crookshanks. Not for his sister Beth. She wanted a family, not a discordant group of people who by an accident of birth had to live in the same house.

"You can't do two jobs at once, Kim. That way both of them suffer. You become a lousy mother. All this feminism is going to destroy the family. The children will suffer most without a stable, loving upbringing. You have to nurture in peace, not in a permanent state of turmoil. When you get married and have children don't let your wife work. You may not have so much money to spend but you'll have a lot more happiness. Our mother may have been fickle when it came to the Honourable Barnaby St Clair but she looked after us children. Even if she did drive me mad at times. I love her unconditionally whatever she did... Go and see her, Kim. Whatever the nonsense, there will be real joy in her heart when she sees you. She always said you were her favourite. The last of the litter."

"She never told me that."

"Of course not. You'd have taken advantage. The only mistake our mother made was loving Barnaby St Clair since they were kids. You can't do anything about that sort of thing. It's nature. Don't get mad at her. If her father had been out of the right drawer and not a railway worker only Frank would have been born. A different Frank. The four of us Brigandshaws would not have existed. Life's one big game of chance."

"Anthony's monument and the graves of our ancestors went with Hastings Court."

"He died fighting for England."

"Such a waste of a life. I hate war. The Buddhists taught me that and a lot more... Thanks for cleaning my jacket. The fur inside is all white and fluffy."

"Did you eat the sheep?"

"I'm afraid so. I'll surprise mother. Buy her a bunch of flowers in Hyde Park. There were always people selling flowers next to Hyde Park."

2

---

*T*he door of the Hay Street flat in its smart neighbourhood was opened by a middle-aged woman.

"You must be Kim. You're expected. Your mother is in the lounge."

"About time," said his mother, glaring at him from the sofa. On her lap was a dog with a flat face that bared its teeth at Kim.

"I bought you some flowers."

"Don't look so surprised. Beth phoned me the moment you arrived. When you were in the bath... You missed your father's funeral. Everyone was there."

"I didn't know, Mother."

"Kiss me on the cheek. I don't want my lipstick smudged. I am going out to lunch. Where did you get that awful jacket?"

"In Australia... How are you?"

"As well as can be expected. My children have abandoned me. I never hear from Dorian from one month to the next. He's somewhere in Cornwall. Beth's married. Once the girls are married all their attention goes to the husband. She's pregnant, you know."

"That's rather obvious... She still loves you. She said so."

"Nonsense. She just wants money now she isn't going to work when it's born. She should put the child in a crèche and go back to work. In the end I hated being cooped up in that great big house. Thank goodness we sold it. I suppose you want a cup of tea. Or something stronger? Come and sit down next to me. So long as I hold Chin-Chin's collar she won't bite. Very protective is Chin-Chin. You've met Miss Sayers. She's my companion. We get on very well don't we, Mabel?"

"Yes, Tina. Very well. We are most happy."

"My father is sick. You'd better go and see him before he dies... Children. I sometimes wonder why I went to all that bother."

Instead of kissing his mother on the cheek, Kim bent down to the sofa and picked her up, the dog yapping in between them as he gave her a hug.

"What was that for? Poor Chin-Chin."

"You're my mother. I'm pleased to see you. Whatever you think, we all love you. Are you very sad without Dad?"

"Of course I am. What have you done to your face?"

"It's a long story."

"Sit down next to me on the sofa."

"Miss Sayers, could you take Chin-Chin? Before the pair of us have a fight. I'm used to bigger animals that don't sit on laps."

"Don't be rude about Chin-Chin," said his mother. "I sometimes think Chin-Chin is the only person who loves me."

"Chin-Chin is a dog, Mother. Or I think it is."

"Mabel, take the dog and give it some of that nice piece of steak. And make some tea."

Wearily Kim sat back on the sofa. In more than two years his mother had not changed. To his surprise she put her hand out to where his left hand was lying on the sofa. She squeezed his hand, the gesture worth more to Kim than any words.

When the tea came the dog had been left in the kitchen behind the closed door.

FRANK WAS next on Kim's list, the day after visiting his mother. Beth had given him the address in Fleet Street where Frank had his offices. Looking for 'Frank Brigandshaw and Partners' on the board downstairs, Kim came up blank. Then he saw it: 'Frank St Clair and Partners'. His brother had changed his name.

Upstairs there was a big reception room with a young girl behind the counter. The girl screamed sex appeal. She had big breasts and a provocative smile that took him in all in one piece. There were three people sitting in chairs waiting for what Kim assumed were their appointments. Staff were coming in and out. The whole place was a-buzz.

"And who might you be?" asked the girl with the large breasts that Kim could not take his eyes off.

"I was hoping to see Frank Brigandshaw. Am I in the right place?"

"Sure. What do you want with Frank?"

"Do I need an appointment?"

"Sure do."

"Then maybe you can make one for me." Kim was grinning at the girl, playing her game. "Tell him his younger brother would consider it a privilege if he could have five minutes of his time."

"Kim's here," yelled the girl through an open door to the side of her reception desk. The other three looked up at him from their seats. All three had the look of envy on their faces as if they had been waiting a long time for something they were most likely not going to get.

"You've met Milly, I see," said Frank coming out of his office. "Milly Worthington meet Kim Brigandshaw. Milly's been with me since I started. Come on in. Nice coat. Where'd you get it?"

"Australia." Kim was still looking at Milly as he followed his brother. There were three more open doors leading off reception with people inside getting on with their work. Milly gave him a last smile and picked up the phone. There was a switchboard with keys on her desk, one of which Milly plugged in. Another man came into reception from outside and was waved to a seat next to the others. Milly, it seemed, could do three things at once. Still feeling the rush of excitement in his loins, Kim waited for Frank to sit down behind his desk.

"Have you changed your name?"

"You could at least say hello before asking questions."

"Sorry, old boy. How are you?"

"Rather good as a matter of fact."

"Is the name legal? Did the Honourable finally do the honourable thing and adopt you or something?"

"Deed poll. Didn't ask my father."

"He was never a father to you. Don't you have a conscience about the man who brought you up as his own instead of kicking you and our mother into the street?"

"Of course I do, Kim. We made peace before he died. Whatever they did to each other doesn't change who I really am. So here we are. Frank St Clair... The world's changed. People don't care how you were born. If you think about it, does it really matter as long as you are alive and healthy? That I am, brother Kim."

"Saw Mother yesterday."

"That bloody dog needs strangling. What can a man do? It's her life."

"Do you see your father?"

"Not much... I went to your father's funeral in Rhodesia. Tried to track you down. You'd disappeared somewhere in the Himalayas."

"Bhutan. In a monastery. They have no communication from the outside. It's a rather nice way to live. You don't pick up the world's problems and play them through your head. You live day after day in a serene world of your own. Content."

"Did you find yourself?"

"Bits of me. Now I'm back, most of them have gone."

"What do you think of Milly? Gorgeous isn't she? Clients come to visit me to see Milly. Saves me a lot of time."

"Is she your girlfriend, Frank?"

"Of course not. Business and pleasure never mix. You should remember that. Are you looking for a job? What those chaps outside are doing. PR is all about the gift of the gab. Don't need formal qualifications. The new world they started in America is all about selling. You have to sell everything. Nothing sells on its own however good the product. Beth and Paul call it bullshit. I call it marketing... Who sliced you down the face?"

"A man in a bar in Singapore."

"What did he look like after you finished with him?"

"He passed out on the floor."

"You always had a good right at school. So? What are you going to do now?"

"Insist my brother take me to lunch. Apart from Mother and Chin-Chin you're the only one in the family with any money. What on earth happened to all that Brigandshaw money?"

"Dad was too honest. He was a farmer. The tax man. Mother's extravagance. Take your pick."

"You called him Dad."

"Good habits are hard to change. I envy you, Kim."

"Why?"

"He was really your father. Finding out at the age of ten the man you thought was your father wasn't, makes you sad and lonely. Especially when no one would tell you what had happened. Call it shattered innocence at an early age... Where do you want to go?"

"Lead the way."

"Milly. Hold the fort. I rather think I won't be coming back today."

"What about your appointments?"

"Tell them the truth on the phone when you call them. My brother's back from his travels. They'll understand."

The look the girl called Milly gave Frank made Kim stop looking at her breasts to look up at her face. It was a look of complete surprise.

"Just kidding," said Frank. "Back in under an hour... Are you chaps being looked after? If you get through the first interview I'll see you in my office... Well, this is a nice surprise, Kim."

Instead of being taken to a fancy restaurant as Kim had expected, Frank walked from his office building to the Lyons Corner House across the street where they sat at high stools round a high table just big enough for two plates.

"The only time I waste money in restaurants is when I want to get into the pants of a good-looking girl. Then I'll spend the money. Often three or four times until I get what I want."

"Then what happens?"

"Depends how long it takes to get enough of her. I don't ever drink alcohol at lunchtime. They usually send up my lunch. Sometimes I take a walk to get some air from the office. Making a success of a business is hard work. You either make money through speculation like my real father or you work fourteen hours every day. I prefer working for my money. More satisfaction. Now, what are you having?"

"A cream bun and a glass of milk."

"They do good bangers and mash."

Kim smiled at his brother.

"Bangers and mash for two, darling," Frank said to the waitress in her miniature apron.

"Coming up, Frank."

"They know you here. How many of the girls have you wined and dined?"

"None of them. They are not that expensive. They're grateful to be taken to the pictures... So, Kim. Start at the beginning. Fill me in on your travels. Only keep an eye on the clock. You've got half an hour."

Kim watched his brother take off his watch, put it on the table in front of him before looking up at Kim with a smile. Behind the eyes his brother looked tired.

"Milly would never forgive me if I missed an appointment."

"How do I get to know Milly?"

"You don't."

When Frank picked up his watch half an hour later and stood up, Kim was still in mid-sentence. The lunch was over. Frank paid the bill. Kim followed him out.

"See you around, brother."

Leaving him standing on the pavement with his mouth open, as there was so much more to say, Kim watched Frank run across the road towards his office dodging the London traffic. Kim waited but Frank did not turn around before disappearing into the building through the slowly revolving door.

"I'll be buggered. He's forgotten me already."

"Did you say something, young man?"

"Sorry, madam."

"I should think so too. My goodness. What did you do to your face?"

With the rest of the afternoon to himself and with nothing to do, Kim hailed a passing taxi. The driver scudded his way through the traffic to stop at the pavement twenty yards down the road. Kim ran for it.

"The Nouvelle Galerie in the Portobello Road if you know where it is."

"Course I do."

Slamming down the 'For Hire' sign that started the meter, the cabbie drove back into traffic. Beth had said there were more paintings by the artist who had given Paul *African Sunset*. On a whim, Kim thought he would like to look at them. Apart from the taxi ride, the afternoon would cost him nothing. Later in the day he was going to take Beth and Paul out to dinner. He owed them a dinner to thank them for putting him up.

Outside the gallery a man was sketching out on the pavement. There was a barrow next to him selling what looked like antique jewellery. Kim paid off the taxi.

"That's very good," he said in passing, nodding at the drawing.

There were a few people in the gallery. Kim started to wander around. It was his kind of place. Most of the people looked like they were artists. One of them was wearing a French beret. Briefly she watched him. Some of the paintings were modern and incomprehensible. Kim found a painting by the *African Sunset* artist without any difficulty. Below the big painting of a river was a small sign that said the painting was not for sale. There was a lion in the painting. A big bird with a fish in its claws planing the heavy fish over the water towards the near bank. A crocodile with staring eyes on the edge of an island in the river. The whole body of the reptile was ready to attack. In the bottom corner in contrast was a small frog with a red mark on its back. In the opposite corner was a red flower that looked like some kind of a lily to Kim. There were many trees in the painting next to the water. The river had the look of flowing water, debris floating in midstream. Just above the red lily, Kim recognised the girl's signature. Next to the painting was a painting of a beautiful African woman. Next to the woman was another of a man standing in the pulpit of a church looking at the congregation. The man was crying as he spoke. Kim recognised the man.

"That's Dad's adjutant from the Royal Flying Corps," he said out loud with surprise. When Kim looked closer he began to recognise some of the faces in the congregation. One was the face of his mother. Another the face of Frank. The title *The Funeral* was on the frame of the painting. Only then did Kim know what he was looking at. He was looking at his own father's funeral, the one he had not known about until it was too late. The karma had come back to him. All the good thoughts he had poured out mourning his father. Vividly, his call in the Buddhist monastery came back to him. The death of his father had completed its circle. Through Livy Johnston's painting he was at his father's funeral. Then the tears began to flow down the scar in his face.

"I have never seen anyone react so strongly to Livy's painting."

Kim turned to find a young woman standing next to him looking at the painting. She was wearing a smock splattered with different coloured paints.

"When I'm excited paint gets off the palette into my clothes. This smock is pretty old."

"The man inside the coffin is my father. I only heard about his death two months after. I don't often cry in public... I was in a monastery in the Kingdom of Bhutan trying to find the meaning to life. I'd gone away after finishing my National Service in the Royal Air Force. Non-flying commission. Dad wouldn't teach me to fly like Anthony. Anthony was shot down over Berlin in 1944. He would have turned twenty-one the following week. Anthony was the eldest of us kids."

"You must be Kim Brigandshaw. Livy was at the funeral in Rhodesia with Jeremy Crookshank. Livy and I shared a flat before she went after Jeremy. Didn't work. She came home. He went back to Rhodesia. An affair to remember. What she says."

"Do you know where she lives?"

"In a studio down the road from me and Abigail in Chelsea. When Livy came back from Africa, Abigail had moved in. Livy sold some of her African paintings and found her own place. No one bought *The Funeral* or *Princess*. People are prejudiced against funerals and black faces hanging on their walls. Personally I think she's exquisitely beautiful."

"So do I... Can you give me Livy's address? I'm staying with Paul and Beth. Taking them out to dinner for looking after me the last few days. She might like to join us and tell me who else was at my father's funeral. The family don't like talking about the funeral or Dad dying. I've only just returned to England."

"Where are you eating?"

"A small Indian restaurant near Paul and Beth in Hammersmith. I am rather partial to oriental cooking... All those spices."

"We can phone her from the gallery. Jeanne won't mind. That's Jeanne in the beret. My name is Tessa Handson... Have you seen Frank?"

"Had lunch with him."

"He did the PR that launched this gallery. He's good. His friend Zachariah Cohen bought my first painting. Hangs in the entrance to Cohen Wells Advertising agents. They're really big... What are you going to do about that face? This new National Health Service Labour introduced might do it for nothing. Plastic surgery has come on in leaps and bounds since the war. So many pilots burned in flaming aircraft. You'll have to prove it's for medical reasons and not vanity. Worth a try. Such a pity. Makes you look a bit frightening from this side... Come and meet Jeanne. Then we'll phone Livy... Now I've met all the brothers."

"I'm taking the train to Cornwall tomorrow to see Dorian."

"What do you do, Kim?"

"Nothing. That's the trouble. Nothing much to excite me in England if I'm to be stuck behind a desk in an office... This painting is so real. Why won't she sell *The Big River*?"

"Reminds her of Jeremy. When she was happy. You see, she won't go and live in Africa. They cut white girls' throats in Kenya. To Livy, Africa is all the same. One big place that doesn't like us white people. So she stays in England on her own."

"You can't have everything in life."

"Then there's her painting. You can't sell paintings stuck in the middle of Africa when no one gets to hear of you. You have to sell your paintings. Promote them yourself by being seen around. You need to know people like Zach and Frank. They would have forgotten Livy Johnston on a farm in Rhodesia by now. All those lovely paintings and no one to look at them. What a waste."

"Why doesn't he come home?"

"Like you, can't abide the idea of being stuck behind a desk... You want some coffee? We make our own. Instant coffee I'm afraid."

"Thank you, Tessa."

Before Kim could stop her the girl took a handkerchief out of her pocket and wiped the tears from his face. Kim took it as a gesture of sympathy.

The man who had been drawing the face out on the pavement had come inside. Being sensitive to other people's body language, Kim took the man and the girl in the beret to be lovers. The man outside next to the barrow was looking in through the window as if he was expecting something.

"This is Jeanne Pétain who owns the gallery. Ben Brown the artist. Once upon a time in America Jeanne went out with Paul. How she came to England. In another life Jeanne was an artist in the interior decorating business. Painted on canvas what the customer was going to get before they bought it. Didn't you, darling? Now she paints what she likes. That's one of hers over there on the wall. I'm surprised that one hasn't sold, Jeanne. This is Kim Brigandshaw. He wants to ring Livy."

"There's an option on the painting. I think this time I asked too much money. You have to price them just right. Ben's made himself another quid out on the pavement."

"What does the chap outside want?" Kim asked Jeanne.

"His cup of coffee. Ben and Stan are good friends. The jewellery is fake, of course. Welcome to the Portobello Road, Kim Brigandshaw. So, the prodigal son finally returned. Have you seen Frank? The phone is over there on the desk. Livy's number is under Johnston in the little black book."

"Will she be at home?"

"Probably. She's either painting in her studio or outside sketching. Livy's our bestselling painter. They all love her stuff."

"Not the funeral or the black girl?"

"That black girl lives on your family farm in Rhodesia. Tembo has four wives. Princess is the youngest. Your father put her son through university in South Africa. He's over here now. Came to look at Livy's painting of his mother."

"What's Josiah doing in England? Never met him but I know why Dad put him through college. He's bright. Tembo and my father grew up together on the farm. There was much more to that relationship than Dad being the boss. When Dad went missing in his aircraft in the Congo, Tembo went looking for him... The disease my father picked up in the Congo finally killed him. Where is Josiah? Why didn't Frank or Beth mention him?"

"Better ask them. Politics brought him to England. Told me all about it. They want Rhodesia to have independence like India. All the colonies in Africa are going to want their independence, according to Josiah Makoni. The Fabian Society have given him a grant to the London School of Economics. To get him a degree in Politics, Philosophy and Economics. Bright young man. Very charming. Spoke highly of your father. The Fabian Society have their socialist claws into everything. They believe in the slow process of socialism by democratic means. Educating a young man like Josiah is one of their ways of doing it."

"Do you have his address?"

"No. You'll have to ask the university. He has digs somewhere around here where it's cheap. In Victorian days Holland Park was the place to live. Not anymore. Some call it genteel poverty. All the houses need painting. So, are you staying for a cup of coffee? What brought you to the gallery?"

"Livy's painting in Paul's flat. I can't paint or play the piano but I love beautiful paintings and classical music. No one taught me to paint or play an instrument, I'm afraid. We were all more concerned about the war."

"You can always become an art critic, I suppose. They make more money than the artists. They can make or break a new artist. This is Ben Brown. We still live next door to each other. You should come to one of James Coghlan's parties where all us artists gather. With that coat and the long hair you'll fit in like a glove. What happened to your face?"

"Everyone asks me that... I'd love a cup of coffee."

"Maybe I should call Livy first," said Tessa. "Kim wants to take her to supper. He's going to have plastic surgery on his face... Ben, you'd better take Stan his cup of coffee. He's getting agitated outside. It's cold. He's stamping his feet and blowing breath into his hands. How you draw in that temperature is beyond me."

"You have a lovely gallery, Jeanne," said Kim looking around at everything.

"Thank you kindly, good sir," said Jeanne, giving him a mock curtsy.

"Who told Josiah there was a painting of his mother in your gallery?"

"I have no idea."

THE GIRLS HAD PUT CONDENSED milk in their coffee. The man outside sat down on the bench below the long open lid of his barrow, his woollen gloved hands round his mug of coffee. He was smiling. When a customer looked at his merchandise he put the mug on the bench and stood up. His entire attitude changed. The cockney salesman with all its sales talk took control. Kim watched with fascination.

"He's good," he said to Ben, who had come back inside after giving Stan his coffee.

"One of the best. The barrow boys are all up and down the Portobello Road. There's one that sells tinned carrots with the labels ripped off. Tells his customers some of the cans are peaches. The more cans they take the better their luck. Never sold a can of peaches so long as I've been here though they only find out it's carrots when they get home. Best salesman in the world, the London cockney. Mostly misguided as there isn't much money in fake antiques. Stan out there likes the game as much as the money... Look at him. He's sold one. We'll have a beer in the pub when I help him push his barrow home this evening. The cockneys like each other's company. What it's all about. Selling a good product at the right price would not be so much fun."

It was a whole new world for Kim, inside and outside the gallery. Tessa had a smile on her face as she put down the phone over on Jeanne's desk.

"Livy's coming over," she called. "Has a new painting to show Jeanne. How's your coffee?"

"Sweet. How long will she be?"

Half an hour later, a girl came into the gallery. Under her arm was a canvas encased in brown paper. Kim thought she looked in her mid-twenties. Sexy rather than beautiful.

"You must be Kim," she said. "There's some of Frank in you. A lot of Dorian. So, you're a Buddhist?"

"Not exactly."

"If you think it any good, hang it, Jeanne," she said, handing over the painting. "They framed it this morning. *Swans on the River*. So, Kim, what brought you to the Nouvelle Galerie?"

"Your painting of *African Sunset* in Paul Crookshank's lounge. Then I saw *The Funeral*. You're very good. I like the one of the river best. We're all going to dinner tonight. Can you come?"

"I don't think so. Too much of Jeremy comes back to me... I saw your father just before he died. On Elephant Walk. Tessa said on the phone you want to talk about him. Did you know he told Jeremy not to stay in Africa? So here I am on my own with that painting over there of the Zambezi River to remind me about a time when I was oh so happy. Have you ever been really happy, Kim?"

"Would you like dinner with me when I come back from Cornwall after seeing Dorian?"

"Why not? Tessa warned me on the phone about the scar down your face. Can I paint you before you get it fixed? Makes you look so interesting. A man with a past."

"Would I have to sit for long?"

"As long as you like. I can pencil sketch and paint later or do it straight onto the canvas in oils."

"How much do you want?"

"Nothing, Kim. Without your family I would never have met Jeremy."

"Then go out to him."

"There's been a lot of water under the bridge since we split. I wouldn't fit in Rhodesia. Not the colonial type... Can I have some coffee, Jeanne?... What do you do for a living, Kim?"

"Nothing at the moment. I might go to Rhodesia. Never been. My mother took us to Cape Town during the war to get away from the bombing. Never went north. Only Frank went to Rhodesia before we all came home to Hastings Court at the end of the war. Now the old house has been sold. No skills and no money to speak of. That's me. We have a farm in Rhodesia with no one running it. Why I want to talk to Dorian. What other option do I have?"

"You sound like Jeremy."

"You know we met as kids? Both of us have a good boarding school education. Both commissioned after we were drafted into the services. In the old days we would have joined the Colonial Service to help administer the colonies. Not much point in that anymore."

"So you agree with your father?"

"Probably. India was the first to go. The alternative is joining an insurance company like Paul did at first. Or a bank. I don't want to be a clerk, Livy. Paul got out of it with the bright idea of selling British antiques to the Americans."

"It's wonderful, darling. What price do you think?" said Jeanne, holding out Livy's new painting.

"Six hundred pounds."

"That's more than I'd get in a year clerking," said Kim, feeling sad. "You've got talent. All I've got is a scar down my face."

To Livy, looking at her painting of Harry Brigandshaw, it was all so long ago. The old man giving his eulogy thinking of his own life with the man he was talking about. Missing him as the tears poured unashamedly down his face. The best part of his own life dead with the man in the coffin. Livy knew she had captured that feeling of irreversible loss in the man's eyes. She never remembered his name, only his mood now frozen for eternity in her painting. A better title for her painting would have been *An End of a Life*. For both of them. He was lucky, whoever he was, to have had so much in his life to remember. To be sad about. The man had to have had so much to have lost so much.

Happy with her painting, if a little sad, she looked at the painting of Princess hanging between *The Funeral* and *The Big River*. The woman was exquisitely beautiful.

Keeping *The Big River* for last she turned her eyes to the big painting and let the Zambezi Valley come back into her life. Though Jeremy and Mario Tuchi were not in her painting they were the eyes of what she saw. With Carmen and Candy they had all been so damned happy.

"It's a pity you can't bottle happiness and keep it forever," she said to Kim. "Your father lent us a Land Rover and all our camping equipment. When we took it back to the farm he was dead... So much in one man's life. He was lucky. You are lucky, Kim, to have had such a father. He was a good man to everyone."

The man next to her was tall with broad shoulders. Not an ounce of fat on his body. The hair long down his back like a girl's except there was nothing girlish about him. He was young. Younger than herself. Too young for Livy. All her men since coming back from Rhodesia were in their thirties and forties. More like Crispin Dane than Jeremy Crookshank. She had never painted Jeremy. She had what she wanted of him in her memory, not to be shared with the rest of them. The memory would always be there and never broken by familiarity and argument. In her memory they would always be happy. It was better that way.

Kim Brigandshaw was smiling at her, the kind of look she was used to from men. The look of sexual anticipation.

"I'd better go if I'm to take Beth and Paul out to dinner. With my sister you have to get ready to go out to dinner. Part of the ritual. Women like to dress up. Makes them feel good. You sure you can't...?"

"No, Kim. Not today. How about a walk downriver when you come back? Pick a good day."

"Am I too young?"

"Probably."

"It's not the age but what we've been through. I've seen a lot in the last two years. Makes it more difficult to sit in an office and take orders from men who have known nothing more than a life in suburbia. I don't want to waste my life. Rhodesia may not have a future. I'm sure my father was right to tell you to come home. Paul told me... Maybe I don't want to see my life mapped out for me towards a comfortable old age. There would be physical comfort but no memories. And who's to say I won't be run over by a bus crossing the street one day? Or killed by some maniac with a knife in a bar?... We'll have a long walk and talk some more. I love your paintings. Did you know the woman's son is in England? There will always be a part of Elephant Walk in us. What Dad told me. Part of our history. Who we are. If any of you find out where Josiah Makoni lives, let me know. He came to look at the painting of his mother... We were well educated by my father. Now isn't that strange?... Is there any meaning to life, Livy Johnston? I asked that of the monks in Bhutan in the brief time we were permitted to talk in the monastery. None of them could give me an answer. Only one spoke a little academic English. I asked him to ask the others. Lack of communication or they all knew the truth? I think life is for the moment. Not yesterday or tomorrow... I'll give Paul your regards. Have you heard from Jeremy?"

"A poem on my birthday."

"That's nice... I hope you sell your new painting."

"So do I."

Livy, feeling sad, watched him leave the gallery saying goodbye to the girls and Ben on the way. He was a link to Jeremy. Why she did not want to go out to dinner... At the door, Kim turned and waved to her. He was a good-looking boy.

"Why is life so complicated, Tessa?"

"That's when it's fun... Do you like him?"

"Too young for me."

"They're never too young... Are you coming to James Coghlan's promotion party tonight?"

"Of course."

"Why didn't you invite him?"

Livy ignored the question. Tessa was always trying to fix her up with a man.

"What do you think of my new painting? Is it any good? Is it finished?... Am I being a fool not to go back to Rhodesia? That boy's going, whatever his father said. If it all collapses in Africa we can always come back to England."

"Don't ask me, Livy. It's your life. You can always meet someone in England. You're young. Good-looking. Talented. That way with a nice man in England you'll have the best of both worlds. You don't have to chase off halfway round the world. In the end men are all the same. We make too much of them when we're young. When the sex is good. After that they grow paunches and lose interest. Familiarity breeds contempt, so they say. I suppose we will all find out someday."

"You're a cynic."

"Not really, Livy. I've just found they are usually not quite what I want in the end. They change. You were the one to say never shatter a good memory. Leave it as it is. He's there. You're here. You're making him out to be more than he is by building it all up in your mind. Put the feelings in your paintings. Where they belong."

LIVY'S NOSTALGIA lifted after the second cup of coffee. There was no point crying over spilt milk she told herself time and again. The chances were, now he was a manager of his own section with a house away from Mrs Pamela Crumpshaw, Jeremy would have found himself a new girlfriend whatever he wrote in a poem and his letter on her birthday. Their affair was in his past. An old friend to write to no longer a lover... She was selling her paintings in England. Making a name for herself. She would not have done that on a farm in the middle of the African bush however well she was painting. She knew in her heart she could never get everything. There were always swings and roundabouts. Better to count her blessings and concentrate on finding herself a husband in England instead of finding fault at the first opportunity. No one was perfect. Certainly not herself. She had to compromise.

At six o'clock when the caterers arrived to make ready for James Coghlan's party, the real reason for her coming to the gallery and not a sentimental walk in the past, she had put Rhodesia and her trip to Africa out of her mind. She was in the present. Most of the Chelsea artists were coming whether they had something to exhibit or not. They were as much the bait for the customers as the art. The temptation for rich men to come and look at the paintings and the rest of the works of art. Put a rich man next to a pretty girl, feed him a glass or three of wine and *voilà*, as Jeanne Pétain liked to say. Or as Frank Brigandshaw put it, 'good marketing and public relations'. The girls were the baited hook, the gallery the place to sample the life of bohemia, away from their dull wives and demanding children. It was the way for them to sample another world without it being too obvious what they were really up to. 'Patrons of the Arts, darling.'

At seven o'clock Livy had her first glass of wine to get herself in the mood to circulate. Between Frank St Clair, as he now liked to call himself, and James Coghlan, invitations had gone out for the cheese and wine party to one hundred potential customers. There was always a chance of a nice young single man finding his way to the gallery. A girl had to think positive.

James had brought his latest sculpture made from metal picked up on the scrap heap and welded together. Today's effort was in squares and triangles stuck on a polished block of mahogany. For some reason beyond Livy's comprehension it was titled *The Resurrection*. James was dressed in an arty cape, purple on the inside like the cloak of a magician. He had lately taken to using a long cigarette holder which he affected to hold up so the cigarette was at the level of his shoulder. The cigarette was Turkish with a foul smell when he puffed on it, James as much the art as his sculpture.

Frank St Clair arrived with his latest girl. A man with a flute had been positioned to play right behind James Coghlan's *The Resurrection*. The flute was a pan flute and blended well with the occasion. London was finally rising from the bombing, money beginning to be made by an assortment of nouveau riche. For many of them, buying a painting would bring them up in the world.

Smiling, Livy went in to play. To do her part. To start the selling. Pretty waitresses supplied by the caterers were offering glasses of French wine on trays. The evening was going to plan. Livy looked around to find a mark before starting to work the room.

"Hello. I'm Livy Johnston. Do you like that painting? It's rather marvellous don't you think?"

3

His brother Dorian was waiting on the platform when Kim Brigandshaw's train pulled in to Penzance Station the following day. With his sister eight months pregnant, the evening in the Indian restaurant had been short, letting Kim get up early after a good night's sleep to catch the train. He had changed trains once in Exeter before completing his journey.

His brother was all smiles. They had not set eyes on each other for over two years.

"Hello, old chap. Have you grown or something? You didn't seem that tall when you went away. Do you mind riding on the back of a motorcycle? Before they sold off everything at Hastings Court I swiped Dad's old BSA 1925 vintage and it still goes like a bomb. Just shows how well they built motorbikes before the war."

"How's the book going, Dorian?"

"I'm writing the odd article on the back of my Oxford degree in English Literature. They always put BA after my name. Makes their magazine seem more important to the public. All that education in English and I'm no good at writing fiction. Every sentence is perfect but the book on Grandfather Brigandshaw won't come alive."

"Why don't you write it as a biography?"

"Doesn't have the size of market. People want stories in which to lose themselves. Get away from their mundane lives. The people around them. Relieve the boredom. That sort of thing... What have you been up to, Kim?"

"Moving around. You're the first in the family not to pick on my scar."

"Oh, I saw it all right. Moment you stepped off the train. I'll describe it in a character in the book. You see, I can only write what I see in front of me. Chaps like Hemingway see their stories in their heads. They become their characters. All rather frustrating. The articles pay Mrs Fenton's rent. We're broke, Kim. After keeping our dear mother in luxury, we are broke. All that wealth down the drain. Anyway, it gives me an incentive to do some work. I'm not sure inheriting a fortune would have been all it's cracked up to be. There would be no challenge to do anything, just play around. Rather boring don't you think? Put that pack on your back and we'll go for a ride. How's Beth? How's Frank? Don't get to hear too much stuck down here in Cornwall. What are you going to do for a job, brother Kim?"

"Mother sends her love," said Kim, ignoring the question for which he had no real answer.

"That's something... Poor Mother. I don't think she's ever been happy. How awful to go through life and never be truly happy."

"What are you going to do about Wendy?"

"So they told you. What can I do? It was a one-night stand."

"Then how do you know she's your daughter?"

"Nancy liked to put herself about a bit but she kept a meticulous diary of her sexual activity. My name sticks out at the right time like a sore thumb. Her parents have a bit of money. I was hoping she would marry and have her husband adopt the kid."

"But if what you say is right, she's your kid, Dorian. Your own flesh and blood."

"It's a bit of a bugger. Anyway, I don't need any lectures. It's my problem not yours."

"Have you seen her?"

"Not yet... How about a beer and a bite to eat in the pub?... Have you got any money?"

"Consider supper on me, Dad."

They both laughed and walked off to find the motorcycle in the parking lot behind the station. With Dorian straddling the bike Kim got on the back.

"Hang on round my waist, young brother. Don't want you falling off."

"Whoopee!... This is fun. Reminds me of Dad."

THEY BOTH HAD mackerel cooked under the grill. It was Kim's favourite fish when it came straight out of the sea. The two pints of bitter on the small table were more for companionship rather than the alcohol. They had ridden the old motorcycle up the heads until it was almost dark.

There were not many people in the pub. The holiday season was over. Dorian knew the owners but did not introduce Kim. Kim thought it was either the long hair flowing over his shoulders or the scar down his face. They talked trivia until they had both finished their fish.

"What happened to Mrs Craddock?" said Kim. "Her only home was Hastings Court. I was going to ask Beth."

"Didn't they tell you? Dad left her a few thousand pounds in his will. She's living with her widowed sister outside Swansea. All the long-standing staff received legacies that were paid out by the trustees of Dad's estate before anything else. I think he knew Mum was going to sell Hastings Court and move up to London. She was a good old stick, Mrs Craddock. Whenever I was hungry I went down to her kitchen. She'll be all right with her sister."

"Did you know Josiah Makoni is in England?"

"No I didn't. I met him on Elephant Walk when I went to see Grandma Brigandshaw to research my book. Dad paid for him to go to Fort Hare University in South Africa. What's he doing in England?"

"Taking a postgraduate degree at LSE. The Fabians are paying for it. Paving the way for democracy in Rhodesia. That should be fun... I'm going to see him when I find out where he lives. Has digs in Holland Park, I'm told."

"The communists will get at him if they haven't already done so at Fort Hare. Part of the Russian plan to spread their empire. It's easier to conquer the world with a good idea than an army. Costs a lot less. The Russians are clever. My tutor warned me to be careful at Oxford. If you can indoctrinate the leaders of tomorrow when they are young then they will do the dirty work for you in the future. Without the white man in

Rhodesia there wouldn't be an economy. Rural life with a few cows and goats was feasible when Grandfather Brigandshaw got to Rhodesia before Rhodes. There were less than half a million natives in the entire country between the Limpopo and the Zambezi back then. Now there are over two million. You need tractors and modern farming for those kinds of numbers. And they are multiplying with modern medicine provided by the Rhodesian government. My goodness they are. Granny Brigandshaw says only one in five of the children survived to adulthood when she arrived with Grandfather. Some of the girls start having families at the age of twelve. Tembo has four wives. Work it out. They'll multiply themselves to extinction without modern, urban economy. The villagers in the tribal trust lands grow two bags of maize to the acre if they are lucky. On Elephant Walk with Dad's irrigation out of the new Mazoe dam we're getting forty bags to the acre. Every year. Even in the years of drought. Someone should point that out to the likes of Josiah before they do anything silly. I had a few chats with him about life at university so he knew what to expect at Fort Hare. A nice, intelligent man. His mother was so proud of him. Things are never as simple as people like them to look. He must be careful not to find himself being manipulated by the Russians putting ideas of grandeur in his head that in a practical world just won't work."

"I didn't know you had met him."

"A little knowledge is a dangerous thing. An old cliché that has created trouble throughout history. It's always easy to look at one part of the story and not think forward to all its repercussions. They were fine living the way they did before we got to Africa, in small communities on the banks of the rivers. Now everything has changed."

"I'm thinking of going out to run Elephant Walk if you don't want to go. With the Madgwicks in America, Aunt Madge can't run it on her own. Even with the help of Tembo. They're both getting old. Why I want to have a chat with Josiah, seeing he's in England."

"Don't be stupid, Kim. The British Empire is finished. Find something to do in England. Or go and talk to Cousin Tinus in New York. Just don't go to Africa. Dad was right to warn Jeremy Crookshank against staying in the country. There are too few whites... Do you want another beer?"

"Why not?"

"Go and see Josiah. Find out what he's thinking. My guess is he'll frighten the holy shit out of you. This new Federation they're planning won't work. They imagine importing half a million Europeans with all their skills. The likes of Josiah Makoni are being told they can run their own country sometime in the future without the help of us British. Maybe they can. Good luck to them. Just don't you put your head in the lion's mouth... Me going to Rhodesia? The thought never entered my head. You've been away a couple of years. A lot happened in England under Labour. They didn't want an empire, Kim. They thought it a liability and they are probably right. We should get out of Africa fast as we did from India before we get ourselves into trouble. Cost Britain lives and treasure. Treasure we don't have any more after fighting two world wars. Do you know we lost twenty thousand men on the first day at the Somme? We've bled ourselves of the best. The French and the Germans, having half-destroyed each other, are now talking to each other about some kind of European community linked together by trade. To stop us periodically scratching out each other's eyes. Let Africa sink back into Conrad's *Heart of Darkness*. They don't want us and we can't afford to police an empire anymore. Europe's the future. Mark my words. The devastation of the last two wars might just have taught us all a lesson in this part of the world. For how long we learn the lesson is another matter. People have too short memories."

"What about Russia?"

"Communism won't work. People are too greedy. To do any work they need an incentive. For themselves. At first socialism and communism look fine. Politicians love giving away other people's money. It's when there isn't any more money to give away the trouble starts. Of course there has to be some kind of balance. Enough incentive for the competent to make money so there's enough left over to look after the less fortunate. In the years before the wars the church provided charity. Looked after the poor. The power of religion is losing its grip as people become more educated about how the world really began. But who knows? Religion is a tricky subject. Always has my gut churning when I deny what I was taught as a child. We all want to believe in God. It makes me feel protected. Now we have a declining church on one side and the rise of an atheist communism on the other. We'll most likely blow ourselves into oblivion now we have the atomic bomb to throw at each other. There hasn't been a weapon in history that hasn't been used with impunity."

"You think we'll destroy the world?"

"Probably. If history is anything to go by."

"You've been here on your own too long, Dorian. Don't you have a girl?"

"I can't afford to take myself out to dinner let alone an attractive girl."

"Finish the book."

"I'm trying."

"So it's really all about making money and hoping the Russians won't drop a bomb on our heads?"

"Something like that. Stay put while I go up to the bar. This one's on me. Good to see you, Kim. It really is. Good to talk to someone. When I come back with the drinks I want to hear all about your stay with the Buddhists."

TWO DAYS later Kim caught the train back to London, his future as uncertain as when he arrived. Both of them were in limbo.

He had slept on the floor of Dorian's room. Kim had given Mrs Fenton half a crown. At night when it was cold on the floor he had made his mind leave his body, the way they had taught him in the monastery. Then he had not felt so cold.

There was still only one practical option for him and that was Rhodesia. If the world was going to explode it didn't make any difference where he was living.

London was overcast and grey when he got off the train. There was a cold drizzle making the thought of the African sun that much more appealing. Beth and Paul were at work when he let himself into their flat with the key Beth had had made for him before leaving. He was at a loose end with nothing to do. There was no point in phoning Livy for a walk downriver when it was raining.

Picking up the telephone book, he found the number of the London School of Economics and gave them a ring. The girl put him through to the personnel department.

"You have a student by the name of Josiah Makoni. Do you have the address where he lives? His father works for us in Rhodesia."

With the address written down, Kim pondered what to do... He thought of worrying Frank in his office, then put the idea quickly out of his head. Frank would think he was fishing for a job. Looking for a favour. Growing up together, Kim had found it better never to ask Frank for a favour. The price was always too high. Frank asked favours, never gave them... He couldn't go back to Australia or America. He had kicked his heels enough in both countries, passing his time, enjoying himself but getting nowhere... He missed the advice of his father. After Dorian there was no one else to turn to. Certainly not his mother.

He went downstairs and bought himself the *Daily Telegraph*. With heavy heart, Kim began to look in the paper for a job. There were two of them he might have applied for, after getting himself a short back and sides. One was in a bank, the other a city firm of insurance brokers. His RAF commission would help with both of them... Then he felt the scar down his face and walked to the window to look down into the street. A man was walking along on the other side of the road, his collar pulled up to his ears, a picture of apathy. The man kicked an empty packet of cigarettes, having bent down to find the packet was empty. Kim guessed the man was out of a job like himself, looking for a smoke.

Half an hour later when the sun came out, Kim walked from the block of flats into the street. He could see the same empty packet of cigarettes lying on the opposite pavement. Kim crossed the road and picked it up, dropping it in the bin next to the lamp post.

Feeling better with a stride in his step, Kim walked to the Tube station to take the train to Chelsea. Livy had been to Rhodesia. In a roundabout way they both had the same problem. Both of them had been told by his father not to make their lives in Rhodesia. She was an artist who worked at home. With luck he would find her in. With the sun now out they could walk downriver. She had invited him. If it rained again he could look at her paintings. And talk. It was what he wanted. Someone to talk to. The fact she was also an attractive girl was not the reason for his visit. Or so he told himself as he walked down the street from the Tube station on his way to her studio. He was feeling better. Much better.

There was no one at home when he rang and rang the doorbell. It just wasn't going to be his day. On the way back to his sister's flat in Hammersmith, Kim felt the piece of paper in his pocket on which he had written Josiah Makoni's address. Scrunching it up he dropped the paper in a dustbin at the top of the stairs before walking down into the Underground. What was the point? What was he going to say? 'I'm Kim Brigandshaw. My father paid for your education. I'm thinking of going to live on Elephant Walk and came to ask if you think I would have a future in Africa.' What could the young man say to such a question?

Back at the flat, Kim phoned the firm of insurance brokers and made an appointment for the following Monday. It was the first appointment the man on the phone would give him. For the last time he looked in the mirror at his hair.

Kim found a small men's hairdresser three blocks from the flat. He went inside. A man in a white dust coat looked at him with surprise.

"Do I need an estimate? Short back and sides if you please."

"Are you sure? Take a long time to grow it back again."

"Of course I'm not. Just do it. While I close my eyes."

"Never cut a bloke's hair that long before."

It was over, Kim told himself. His life was over.

PART V

MAY TO AUGUST 1953 – "AS YOUTH GOES BY"

1

*L*ivy Johnston finished her painting of Hastings Court on the last Saturday in May. It was her first commission. Money up front before she put paint to canvas. The new owner of Hastings Court, the Honourable Barnaby St Clair, wanted a painting of his country house to hang in the lounge of his Piccadilly townhouse to remind him of the irony of life. The man who had bought her first painting had called at her studio with Frank Brigandshaw now calling himself Frank St Clair. The two of them were in high old spirits. From being the bastard in the Brigandshaw family Frank was now heir to the Brigandshaw family estate that had been in the maternal side of the family for centuries. There was no chance of either of them inheriting Purbeck Manor in Dorset, the seat of the St Clairs. Lord St Clair was alive and well. Then there was nephew Richard, the heir to the barony and Purbeck Manor, son of Barnaby's older brother Robert.

"My mother couldn't find a buyer for the place," Frank had told Livy at one of James Coghlan's promotional parties where Livy was helping to sell the paintings. The Honourable did her a favour. Or so he said. Since he bought the place a year ago the value had risen by twenty per cent. "Of course I don't tell my mother. Not that she cares. She wanted to get out of the countryside to live in London. The other children and Cousin Tinus are the losers. Quite a hoot, really. After all the nonsense I'm going to be Lord of the Manor in a manner of speaking. What goes round comes around and all that nonsense. He wants you to paint the place. Well, I suggested it. I'll drive you down in my new MG next week. Business is good. For every loser there's a winner. I don't think Dorian and Kim are amused. Poor chap's working in the City. Hates it. Dorian's still in Cornwall, getting nowhere with his book. Paul just won't listen to me when it comes to Ridgeback cigarettes. He's got to borrow from the banks or British America Tobacco will cut his brand out of the market. The old Brigandshaw company in London is really struggling. Tinus is doing all right in New York where he controls the business through his five per cent shareholding. Paul never had a proper business training. It shows."

"Why me, Frank?"

"Because when we feel inclined we are lovers."

"You make me sound like a whore."

"Really, Livy... Mind you, what the rest of you get up to at the Nouvelle Galerie isn't far short. Wear something nice. We'll spend the weekend together at Hastings Court. Show you around where I grew up. The bit of luck is Mrs Craddock. Her widowed sister died in Swansea. She's back in the kitchen despite her legacy from my legal father. It was her home. I'm happy. So is she. God works in strange ways, don't you think?"

LIVY FELT GOOD. She always felt good after a day's painting when the painting worked. Crenellated battlements. The big, old cedar trees. Bright flowers of spring in the well-tended beds. She had caught the history of the place, complacent in its certainty, outlasting so many generations of men. Livy looked at her painting from every angle. Yes, it was finished... One of her secrets was knowing when to stop.

Taking off her paint-streaked smock, she ran herself a hot bath. The studio was one big room with a double bed in the corner, just in case. Off to the sides were a kitchen with a table and a bathroom with a big tub. With her clothes strewn on the floor, Livy climbed into the bath and soaked. The hot water drained out the tension from hours of painting. All the time in the studio standing at her easel she had to see the old house in her mind's eye.

When the water in the bath cooled she turned on the hot tap. She was happy. After putting down her brush she had phoned Frank to come and take it away. Her commissions went through the Nouvelle Galerie. James Coghlan made sure she was paid. James took the unpleasant work out of painting. Frank took the complications out of making love…

When he came round they made love on the big bed in the corner, opposite the large canvas of the old house still up on her easel.

"What do you think, Frank?"

"You're a good fuck, Livy."

"The painting, not me."

Satiated, they both lay back in the big bed looking at her painting.

"Did you hear from Jeremy for your birthday?" asked Frank. "Glass of wine?"

"Are you jealous?"

"I've never been jealous in my life. Paul says next year Jeremy's buying his own farm in a new block a hundred or so miles north of the capital Salisbury. He's grown the best crop of his life on the section he manages for Crumpshaw."

"I'm glad for him. So he gets his bonus with Roger?"

"The more Jeremy makes, the more Roger puts in the bank. You have to encourage people to make you money."

"This year he didn't write for Christmas. Rather sad. All I have to remind me is that painting of the Zambezi River."

"Red or white?"

"The dreaded red. Let's celebrate."

"You want to go out?"

"What for? There's a case of red. Cheap plonk but it makes me drunk just the same. My friends don't like fancy wines. They drink to get drunk. Not to impress people with their knowledge of wine. The bouquet. All that rubbish."

"So I won't get dressed… For the first ten years of living in that house I thought Harry Brigandshaw was my father."

"Does it help knowing you are going to own the place one day?"

"Mother says she'll never visit."

"Do they see each other?"

"Who?"

"Your parents."

"Sometimes for lunch. The Honourable never married. I'm all he's got."

"You're quite something to have, Frank."

"I hate sarcasm... I'm hungry. We're going out. Put your clothes on. Hurry."

"Yes, master... You know, Frank, I'm just so bloody glad I'm not married to you."

"Cheap wine gives me a hangover."

"You really are a bastard, Frank."

GOING out to dinner after having sex was an anti-climax for Livy. What they had in common was a need for sex, not polite conversation. The sex got rid of Livy's physical frustration and let her paint in peace. On the way, they had taken the painting to his father's Piccadilly townhouse where it was admired and hung on the wall like some trophy. What Barnaby wanted two homes for when he was all on his own was beyond Livy's comprehension. The man had more money than sense. The Honourable could only sleep in one bed at a time. Barnaby St Clair was not the first person Livy had met who accumulated unnecessary possessions. She knew a girl with fifty pairs of shoes, all paid for by a rich father. Most were never worn. Livy hated new shoes until she had worn them in and made them feel comfortable. Frank's new MG sports car fell into the same category. In London it was far easier to catch a bus or a Tube. The Tube was always quicker in the rush hour than a car... It was all show. Trying to make other people envious. Showing off.

"What's the matter, Livy? Don't you like your food?"

"Why do people accumulate more wealth than they can possibly use? Did he buy it to impress you or show your mother he was still the boy from the big house? A childhood game they played as children?"

"When you get a business running properly the money just comes. You can't stop it. I like the game of making money. So does my father. We're both good at it. All about winning. Would that painting have been as good if it wasn't sold?"

"Provided I have money for rent and food, I don't care. I like the process of painting. It makes me happy. If I don't paint for a week I'm miserable. Creating something you think is beautiful is a joy. That old house was smiling out at me. Well-satisfied with its self-knowledge. With everything it knew of what had gone on between its walls since the time of Henry the Eighth. A house can smile like a human face, happy in itself. All that knowledge kept to itself. A house like that needs a family with lots of children or it will die and lose its soul."

"You think I should find a wife and have a dozen children? Are you suggesting something to me, Livy?"

"I wouldn't marry you in a fit, Frank Brigandshaw."

"It's Frank St Clair."

"Or him, either."

"Then why are we here?"

"You service me, Frank."

"Isn't that a bit basic?"

"Not at all. It's truthful. We all admit to requiring food and drink to service. We don't admit to needing sex. Primal instinct. Civilisation has tried to tell us we must hide our lust. That sex is a dirty word not to be used in polite society. It's as important to human wellbeing as breathing air... Can you pour me another glass of your expensive wine?"

"I don't understand you, Livy."

"There's nothing to understand. Here I am. You get what you see. I'd have been just as happy with a bottle of plonk in the studio. You don't have to pay me, Frank. You don't even have to get me commissions like the one we just delivered to your father. What I paint I sell. My needs are small. All I want is to be comfortable. Well-fed and warm. Too many possessions are an encumbrance. They need looking after. More trouble than they are worth. I like to keep life simple. Then I enjoy myself. What you and I mean to each other, Frank, is quite simple. We both get good sex when we need it. We satisfy our lust. Get it out of the way."

KICKING her heels the next day with nothing on her easel to paint, Livy went for a long walk in the sunshine. Along the way she called at the Nouvelle Galerie. After a stretch of painting Livy liked to talk to the girls. Ben Brown was outside on the pavement talking to Stan. The Portobello Road was full of people doing their Saturday shopping. Saturdays were good days to shop from the vegetable barrows. With the market closed on Sundays the owners of the barrows that lined the street wanted to sell off the remains of their week's produce. Only a few of the passers-by glanced at the fake antique jewellery on Stan's barrow. Both Ben and Stan were holding mugs of coffee. With her wicker basket of fruit and vegetables Livy went to go inside.

"You look chirpy, Livy."

"Had a good night."

Inside the Nouvelle Galerie a young black man was looking at her paintings, standing quietly in front of the *Princess*. The man looked sad. The last time Livy had seen the man was at the funeral of Harry Brigandshaw. At the funeral he had been with both his parents. All three of them at the wake had looked like fish out of water, drawing Livy's attention, making her want to paint the beautiful woman.

"You must be Josiah Makoni."

"When I get so homesick that it hurts, I come here to look at my mother."

"I watched her at the funeral. Made some quick sketches when your mother wasn't looking. I have a memory for faces... Do you want a cup of coffee?"

"Don't worry about me. You caught her enigmatic smile. I miss my family. Miss my country. England is so different to Africa... No one bought your painting of my mother."

"No, or *The Funeral*. *The Big River* is not for sale."

"When I stand in front of that painting of the river it takes my spirit back to Africa."

"Me too. I was only there a month."

"Did you drink the water of the Zambezi?"

"Yes. We camped on the bank for three days."

"Then you will go back to Africa," he said, turning to her with a smile, his own face lit up. "It's a legend among us blacks. If you drink the water of the Zambezi it always draws you back. However long you are away... I only live down the road in Holland Park. The Fabian Society gave me a bursary to the London School of Economics. They pay the rent of my room. Something for food. Nothing else. I get lonely. Not many of my people in London... What happened to the young white farmer you were with?"

"Did you see him?"

"Of course, Miss Livy. You were staring at us a long time. We didn't feel comfortable. The only blacks in the room. Boss Harry meant a lot to my father. And to me. He gave me the chance to be properly educated... When are you going back to Rhodesia?"

"I'm not... Come on. I'll introduce you to the rest of the girls. You're always welcome to coffee in the Nouvelle Galerie. I'll make that a rule with Jeanne. It must be terrible to live so far away from family and friends. Have you made many friends in England?"

"There are those who like to patronise us blacks. They encourage our cause of independence. They are communists mostly with their own agendas. The same ideas I heard at Fort Hare. They think we will be the future leaders of our country with their help."

"Harry Brigandshaw told me Africa was no longer a place for the white man... Come and have that cup of coffee. I don't understand the big world. Don't want to. I paint... She's a beautiful woman, your mother."

"Why hasn't anyone bought the painting?"

"I don't know, Josiah. Maybe because it's different. People like the familiar in their own houses. A picture that makes them feel comfortable."

"We all like to feel comfortable in our own homes. That's the trouble with Rhodesia. It isn't our home anymore. The British want to live as they lived in England. Think we want to live their way as well. Why they teach us English."

"Don't you want to live in a house with electric light and running water?"

"Maybe. Later. It's hard to give up tradition. To change who you are. Africa had had no contact with your civilisation until a hundred years ago. The Boers in the south a little longer. We were happy as we were. Now many of us are changing our ways. It's difficult. May I say, you're a very good painter, Miss Livy."

"Call me Livy."

"That's difficult."

"When we have our next exhibition I'm going to ask Jeanne Pétain, the owner of the gallery, to send you an invitation. Lots of wine and lots of cheese. Get you out of your room for an evening. Living in England must be difficult... Do you like England?"

"Some of it."

"You think the Fabians have an ulterior motive in bringing you to London?"

"I'm sure of it. There's a price for everything according to my philosophy tutor."

"What are you going to do with your degree when you go home?"

"Go into politics. What else is there? All the jobs are reserved for the British."

"Are you a communist?"

"Not yet."

"At least you're honest. Come and meet some friends. Some real friends, Josiah, without an ulterior motive. Artists are different. They are not after something except maybe the chance to paint in peace."

Trying to make the man, so far from home, feel comfortable was more difficult than Livy had expected. His English was grammatically correct, his accent more difficult to understand. Livy had the impression Josiah was thinking in his own language, translating in his head and only then speaking out loud. Watching his face, the expressions did not coincide with his words. A man's expressions often said more to Livy than the words. There was a barrier between them, as if the African in Josiah was a long way away from the English in Livy, their cultures which gave them their thoughts a long distance apart... All those long centuries of isolation had left them unable to comprehend each other.

After politely drinking his coffee and listening to what everyone said, none of which Livy supposed had any common ground with Josiah or any mutual interest, he left to walk back to his room. He had written his name and address on a piece of paper for Jeanne. He looked sad, giving a last glance over his shoulder to the painting of his mother on the gallery wall. Livy watched him through the glass of the window being swallowed up by the crowd of people walking up and down the pavement, a solitary black figure, incongruous and ignored, in a sea of Londoners going about their morning business.

"He's like a fish out of water," said Ben, standing next to Livy. "Must be hard having little to talk about with the rest of us. Nothing to say to us. That's the loneliest man I ever saw. What made him come over to England?"

"Harry Brigandshaw sent him to school thinking he was doing the boy a favour. Why do we always think what we have is best for everyone?

Jeremy is going to be as lost in Rhodesia one day as that man is lost in England."

"They have to catch up with the rest of the world, Livy."

"How sad... Look at London out there. All scurrying along as if their lives depend on it. Like so many ants. All that concrete and brick. Cars running up and down the road. Everyone looking inward. You've never been in the Zambezi Valley, Ben. There it is life surrounded by nature, not all this man-made stuff. No wonder he's lonely. If you ask me, they can teach us a thing or two."

"Did you finish the painting?"

"And delivered it to the Honourable Barnaby St Clair."

"I'll tell James."

THREE DAYS later Livy was given the cheque to pass on to the Nouvelle Galerie at a dinner party in the Piccadilly home of the Honourable Barnaby St Clair. His brother Robert and Robert's American wife Freya were in London and their son Richard who worked in America. It was something of a family reunion with Frank and Livy invited to make up the party. Smithers, who had first worked for Lord St Clair in London, before Merlin buried himself in the country at Purbeck Manor, was in his element. He had done all the cooking himself and looked proud of it to Livy, as if impressing the Honourable's guests made him happy. To a large extent Livy supposed he was part of the family after so many years of service to the St Clairs. Early on in the evening Livy gave Frank a questioning look as to why she had been invited. Only after the meal did she find out why.

"I'm going to be presumptuous, Livy, and offer you some advice," said the host, putting down his knife and fork and wiping his mouth with his linen serviette. They had all eaten thin slices of anchovy toast as a savoury to clean their palates from the sweet taste of Smithers's sherry trifle before enjoying the last of the wine.

"That cheque I gave you is a large sum of money to some people. Don't get me wrong, your painting is worth every penny. I wasn't doing you any favours. In a few years' time your painting will be on auction at Christie's for ten times that amount of money. It's the speculators in this world who make the money, rarely the people who do the work. I'm a speculator.

Always have been. Why I am now rich. But I wasn't always rich, Livy Johnston. Ask my brother Robert. When I left the army at the end of the First World War, where I had been in Palestine, I was stony broke. But that's another story best left to my novelist brother whose new book has come out at number seven on the *Daily Mail*'s bestseller list. Well done Robert, for the umpteenth time. Our mother and father would both be proud of you if they were still alive. May our mother and father rest in peace... What I'm worried about is what happens to my money when the Nouvelle Galerie give you your part of the cheque. For some people without financial knowledge it is easier to make the money than hold on to it. With the exception of Genevieve, my niece whom I acted as financial consultant for when she was making her films, artists of all stripes have a bad habit of ending up separated, one way or another, from their hard-earned money. When they need it most they are broke. The right way to have money is to keep at it as a safety net. To give a man or woman independence. Some call it lifelong security. Words like inflation and investment mean nothing to an artist who has not been buffeted by the unpredictable world of commerce. You said you were going to put the money in the bank with the rest of the money from your sales. That money was not important to you. That your studio flat was all you needed to paint. The problem is that what the bank gives you as interest and what they charge when they lend it out are two widely different figures. Your deposited money makes the bank money, not you. Inflation wipes out your interest. It's the difference between those two rates of interest where the security of your money lies. What you must do is invest with a long-term view in the shares of businesses that won't lose their real value over the years. Of course, some companies will do better than others. Some will go bust. What you must now do with your money is invest like Genevieve in a well-managed portfolio that will hold its true value. I offer you my services. Without actresses like Genevieve and artists like yourself it would be a poorer world."

Frank looked from his father to Livy before he spoke.

"For a moment I thought you were going to talk about something else," he said to his father.

"I know you did. What you and Livy get up to is none of my business. Anyway, who am I to preach? I just don't want to see your money go down the drain. If you don't want my help, just ask your bank manager to put your cash in mutual funds. Preferably more than one fund to spread your risk. You can leave some in cash but invest the rest... Now, after boring my guests, who would like a liqueur in the lounge? What a lovely evening. Smithers has done us proud. Stealing Smithers from Merlin was the smartest move of my life."

"If I may say, sir, it was the thought of burying myself in the countryside. I am a Londoner. Where I belong... Coffee will be served in the lounge."

"Do I have to make an appointment?" said Livy, smiling.

"Of course."

"Must I bring Frank?"

"Whatever for?"

Not sure whether the Honourable was airing his knowledge for the sake of the young girl who had been giving him sheep's eyes through dinner, Livy settled back to listen to their conversation. The talk of money had gone clean over her head. Inflation was something she did to her bicycle tyres when she was a girl trying to ride her bike to school and Tommy Taylor had let them down to make her late. Richard, the heir to the Purbeck Manor estate and the title, had been watching her all evening. She thought him the same age as Kim Brigandshaw, a couple of years younger than Frank. The looks at dinner had made Frank annoyed. When Frank had mentioned the painting and his father now owning Hastings Court, Richard had shown no interest other than to glance at the painting and give her a smile. The man had a strange quirk. When he spoke to his American mother he did so with an American accent. The rest of the time he spoke like the rest of them. There was a brother called Chuck.

Putting the concern about her money in the back of her mind to be looked at later by someone in the bank, Livy enjoyed the small glass of liqueur that went with her coffee. The drink tasted of peppermint. It was sweet... They were talking about their family which had nothing to do with her. The grandmother had recently died of old age. The housekeeper by the name of Mrs Mason had died soon after. None of it meant anything to Livy.

Without being conscious of what she was doing she bounced her crossed right leg off her knee. There was nothing worse than being talked over. They seemed a nice enough family. The trouble was they weren't hers.

When Frank got up to go she was glad. She shook hands with everyone and put on her coat. The MG was parked downstairs.

"What's the matter, Frank?" she said in the car.

"Richard. I don't like him. He always looks down on me."

"He was doing that to me, darling, but for another reason... Goodness me. You are jealous."

"Nonsense... I have a heavy day tomorrow. Do you mind if I drop you at your studio and go straight home? Oh, and do what my father says if you want to hang on to your money. Go and see him."

"Can I trust him, Frank?"

"If you're insinuating he'll make a pass at you, you're out of your mind. We do have certain principles. Other people's wives. Or our children's girlfriends."

"Your mother was a married woman."

"But she wasn't my girlfriend. Give that cheque to James. Get your part of the deal. Bank the money and go see my father. Your money well-invested will give you financial independence."

"That would be nice. Thank you, Frank. It's just I don't understand money."

"Neither did Genevieve. Now she's worth more than her father."

Only later, alone in her double bed, did Livy see the irony. If Frank's father had not gone to another man's wife, Frank would not have been given his life. It made her chuckle. Good old Frank completely missed the point. Then she thought why not? Free professional advice. What was good for the famous Genevieve was good enough for her.

The next day Livy gave Barnaby a ring and made her appointment.

2

A week after Livy had her appointment Kim Brigandshaw resigned his job. Whichever way he looked at it there were years of boring drudgery ahead with nothing certain at the end. He was an employee. Always would be. Always arse-creeping to some department head, hoping one day if he smarmed them right they would give him the job of a senior broker at Lloyd's of London.

With his resignation on Bingley's desk, Kim walked out of the office building and crossed King William Street. It was the first time he had left the office during the day without permission. For an hour Kim walked the streets of London. Only then did he make up his mind.

"At least the sun will be shining."

By the time he reached Frank's office in Fleet Street he was happy as a lark. All the clouds had lifted.

"What are you doing here, Kim? Come for a job?"

"A chat really, Frank. I've decided. I'm going to Rhodesia, whatever they say about the future of colonialism."

"What about your job?"

"I've resigned."

"About time... Let's go and have lunch... Do you want to borrow some money? There's nothing worse than a dead-end job. Good for you, brother. Do you have to go back to the office after lunch?"

"If I don't they won't give me my last pay cheque. They're that stingy. The bastard just smiled at me when I handed him my resignation. Me throwing in the towel gave him pleasure. I never want to sit behind a desk again for the rest of my life."

"What are you doing tonight?"

"Nothing as usual. I don't have the money to do anything. You need money to enjoy yourself in London."

"They have a cheese and wine party at the Nouvelle Galerie. Come and meet the girls. They won't recognise you without the scar and the long hair. That operation worked. Lucky chap. Why did you avoid me for so long?"

"Because I don't have any money. And I don't like being a bum."

"Does Mother know?"

"She won't care. She's more interested in that damn dog."

"She's lonely."

"Try living in one room with a gas heater that guzzles money. Most weekends in the winter I stayed in bed reading. Couldn't afford to feed the gas fire with shillings. I hate being poor. Do you think our Aunt Madge will give me a job on Elephant Walk?"

"I don't see why not... By the way, she's not my aunt... I'll tell you what. Why don't I ring your office and tell them you've been called away to see your mother? What's his name?"

"Bingley."

"Bingley it is... Milly," shouted Frank to Milly Worthington through the open door of his office, "Get me a Mr Bingley on the line at Kim's office. When you get him tell him I'm busy and ask him to wait. When he's waited a couple of minutes put him through."

"What is all that about?" asked Kim.

"Pissing him off. I have a rule in this office. Never use Milly to get someone on the phone."

"I've got him, Frank," said Milly five minutes later.

"Tell him to hang on."

"Mr St Clair will be with you in a minute, Mr Bingley. Please hold on."

Through the open door at Frank's office Kim could see Milly Worthington with the big bust enjoying herself.

Sitting in silence, smiling at Kim, Frank waited.

"Hello, Bingley. St Clair. Kim Brigandshaw's half-brother. We have to go and see our mother, I'm afraid. He won't be in for the rest of the afternoon... Resigned has he? I didn't know... I'll tell him, Bingley."

When Frank put the phone down he was grinning.

"It gets better, Kim. Says you don't have to go back to the office. They'll send you your last cheque in the post. Really pissed him off. How I hate little men."

"What if he doesn't?"

"He'll send it. That kind of twerp goes by the rules. Come on. Time for a quick lunch. At seven o'clock I'll meet you at the Nouvelle Galerie. Relax, Kim. You're a free man... What were they paying you?"

"Five hundred a year."

"Good God. Whatever made you take the job in the first place?"

"They were going to train me in insurance. Put me through all the departments. In October I was going into the Fire Department."

"*All* on five hundred quid a year?"

"You got it. At the end my salary would have risen to nine hundred."

"What my dad paid Livy for one painting. Come on. I'm hungry. Say goodbye to the lovely Milly."

AFTER A GOOD LUNCH and feeling like a man who had just been let out of gaol, Kim took another long walk. This time to the office of the Union Castle Shipping Line in Regent Street where he booked his passage to Africa. The accumulated five pounds a month from his father's estate paid for his berth on the ship. He was to disembark in Cape Town and take the train up to Salisbury.

Feeling the side of his face where the scar had been, Kim gave a more sober thought to his predicament. Apart from a few trips they had made to Cape Town to see them during their years of exile during the war, he barely knew his Aunt Madge or his grandmother Brigandshaw. Thinking it better to surprise them rather than write, Kim thought through the rest of his options. Not the least, he hoped, his surname would help him in Rhodesia. Then there was Jeremy Crookshank, Paul's brother, about to embark on a farm on his own.

By the time he walked home to his cheap rented room in Holland Park and had a bath it was time to take a slow walk to the Portobello

Road and the Nouvelle Galerie. It was six o'clock, an hour before Frank was due with Livy.

The same man was selling his fake antique jewellery from the barrow outside the gallery. Kim smiled at the man having forgotten his name. Tessa saw him first. She was talking to a black man as Kim walked in.

"Frank said you were coming. He wanted you to meet Josiah Makoni."

"Well, this is a nice surprise," said Kim putting out his hand.

For a long moment the man hesitated. Then they shook hands.

"What happened to the hair and the scar?" asked Tessa.

"The scar was removed by a plastic surgeon. He said there was a chance the seared tissue would turn cancerous later on in my life. At least I got something out of British socialism... Can I get another glass of wine, Josiah?"

For half an hour Kim tried to talk to Josiah about Rhodesia. The man was surprisingly reticent, his demeanour uncomfortable. Kim's questions were answered but never expanded, a one-sided conversation both of them found awkward. Apart from Josiah knowing Kim's father, they had nothing, it seemed, to talk about.

"I have to go and study. Learning a second language is difficult."

"Good luck, Josiah. Maybe one day we'll meet in Rhodesia. I'm going out next month."

"For a holiday?"

"To work, I hope."

"Please tell my mother I'm all right."

"Why shouldn't you be?"

"England is difficult for a black man."

"I didn't know. Everyone is the same to me."

"I hope so, Mr Brigandshaw."

Putting his empty glass of wine on the table, Josiah left, not looking back. Kim had a premonition of something wrong. He shivered, as if someone had walked over his grave. The skin graft on the right side of his face began throbbing.

"What's the matter, Kim?" asked Tessa.

"I don't know. It was what he didn't say that worries me. He wasn't exactly friendly. When I told him I was going to work in Rhodesia he put down his glass and walked out."

"You're reading too much into it. He doesn't know you. Students have to study. Come and talk to Abigail. My word, the gallery is full tonight."

"I'll catch up with you later."

Kim drank his wine as he walked round the gallery. His feelings of disquiet would not go away. It was the way Josiah had looked at him that had created his unease. The man had something to say and wasn't saying it. As though he knew something that was not going to help Kim one bit.

A WEEK later Kim plucked up the courage to go and see his mother. Miss Sayers answered his knock. Miss Sayers always looked a little frightened to Kim, like a rabbit out of the safety of its warren.

His mother was ensconced on the sofa in the lounge with the Pekingese dog on her lap. Kim looked at the dog's big round eyes popping out of its flat-nosed head.

"To what do we owe the pleasure at this time of day? Why aren't you at work?"

"I resigned, Mother. I'm going to Rhodesia."

"You'll never succeed in life by chopping and changing."

"It was a dead-end job."

"They all will be to you, Kim, with that attitude. You can't expect success to come overnight. Anthony would never have chopped and changed. He would have stuck to one thing and made a success of his life. You are going to be a failure."

"Anthony is dead, Mother."

"More's the pity. What Dorian thinks he is doing buried in the backwoods of Cornwall is beyond me. All that expensive education at Oxford and now look what he's doing. He took a First in English Literature. He should be teaching English in a prestigious public school, Eton or Harrow. I would be proud of a son of mine who became headmaster of Harrow. What in the name of heaven are you going to do in Rhodesia?"

"Farming. On Elephant Walk if they'll have me."

"Don't be ridiculous, Kim. You've never grown a carrot. Takes years to learn farming with very little salary for the first two years. Your butterfly mind will never concentrate long enough. Paul was telling me what a struggle his brother Jeremy was having. Now there's a boy that stuck to his lathe. You've got to stay the course to get anywhere in this life. You'll amount to nothing, Kim Brigandshaw. All that gallivanting around the world. What did you gain from it other than a scar down your face? You'll be thirty before you know it with nothing to show. A rolling stone never gathers moss. You've got to pull yourself together. Now come and sit down. I'm sure if you ask them they'll give you your job back again. Whatever would your father have said? You're twenty-four and no career."

"I could never earn a good living in insurance."

"Then why did you go into it in the first place?"

"There wasn't anything else, Mother. There isn't any money left in the family for us kids."

"You won't get anything from me if that's what you're after. You can have anything you want in this life when you earn it yourself... Mabel, please take Chin-Chin and put him in the kitchen. He's baring his teeth. Then you can make us some tea. Even the dog doesn't approve of your behaviour, Kim... If it wasn't for Frank doing so well I'd think there was something wrong with all my children. If you ask me, you and Dorian just don't like work. Has he finished that book? Of course he hasn't. Like you, he never finishes what he starts."

"He finished Oxford. I did all right in the air force. I got a commission."

"What have either of you done since? You must both grow up and face reality. No nice young girl will want to marry you. Why Beth married that Paul I have no idea. Since the baby was born she hasn't had a job and they are short of money. Without your father, Brigandshaw Limited has struggled with Paul. Did you know he likes to play his clarinet in a jazz band! He's going to be another failure. You have to work hard like Frank. That child of theirs will never get a proper education."

"Yes, Mother."

"And don't 'yes mother' me. You need another haircut."

"I'm growing it."

"There you are again. Running away from responsibility. You have to fit in to get anywhere in this world. People who want to get on in life don't grow their hair down to their shoulders. Why is your cheek twitching?... Where are you going?"

"Tell Mabel I don't want any tea, Mother."

"Please yourself."

OUTSIDE HIS MOTHER'S closed door Kim stood quietly. The tips of his fingers were painful as they had been as a child when his mother hurt his feelings.

Not sure whether she meant well or took pleasure in knocking him, Kim walked out of the building. Why did his mother's opinion always matter so much to him? Ever since he could remember. Mostly she was right. Another of his mother's pet sayings came back to him: 'Sometimes you have to be cruel to be kind'.

Crossing Park Lane into Hyde Park, Kim walked among the green-leafed trees. The pigeons were calling. Ten minutes later the hurt in his fingers had gone with the twitch in his face. A girl had smiled at him. The world was still a pleasant place.

"Oh, to hell with it. If I don't like Rhodesia I can go someplace else."

Then he strode out down the path happy in the knowledge he would never again in his life have to set eyes on Mr Bingley.

3

The day in August when Kim arrived on Elephant Walk to be greeted warmly by his Grandmother Brigandshaw, Livy was driving north out of London in her brand-new Volkswagen Kombi. In the back was a mattress and a gas cooker along with everything she needed to paint. The mattress was on a low wooden bed built into the back of the van by Ben Brown and his cockney friend Stan. The weather was perfect, the summer having finally arrived. She was going to travel up to the Lake District and paint, paint, paint, sleeping at night in her van by the edge of the water, the noise of London no longer sounding in her head.

"You can't go alone," Jeanne Pétain had told her.

"Why ever not? Where I'll be going there'll be nobody around. Peace and quiet, Jeanne. All to myself. I'm going to hug myself with solitude. Up with the dawn. Swim in the lake. Tea made on my gas cooker. The smell of bacon and eggs wafting up into a pure sky without the trace of smog."

"You'll get bored on your own."

"I've never been bored with my own company. If some gorgeous young man wants to take me for a sail on his boat I won't complain. There will be pubs. Places to meet people when I've worked all day. That's the joy of living in the back of the van. Total freedom. Go and stay where I feel. No clocks to be watched. Meals when I'm hungry. The sound of the birds and the wind in the pine trees. After Cumbria I'm going to drive up to Scotland. They say you can put a car on the ferry across to the Isle of Skye. Paint all the crumbling castles. Free as a bird. What more can a girl want? My money has been invested. Not a care in the world. If I like where I am I'll stay until the end of the summer. Life on the banks on the Zambezi River all over again."

"Do you ever hear from him?"

"Not a word. You can never look back in life. You have to go forward. There's always something more exciting just down the road."

As the car drove slowly up the lanes of England, day after day, stopping when anything caught her eye, Livy found herself supremely happy. As a precaution she had spent her last night in London with Frank, satiating herself against her sexual frustrations... Good old Frank. So useful when she needed him. So easy to lose when she'd had enough of his nonsense. The perfect relationship. They both used each other when they wanted... She had been too long in London. The countryside was so beautiful, and all was well in her life that had once seemed so tentative, before her paintings began to sell.

ON THE SIXTH day of her journey Livy parked by a lake. To the right, over the water, an old house stood between trees. There was what looked at the distance like ivy growing up the face of the house. In the still of the evening, sunlight caught the top row of the windows giving them life. Around Livy water lapped over the small pebbles along the shore, making them shine.

Foraging for dry wood as they had done by the Zambezi River, she built up a pile. The fire was to cook her food. There were no wild predators in England. She built a fireplace out of big stones found high up on the shore and started the fire. The smoke rose straight up in the air. On the lake a water bird took off into the setting sun, thrashing the still water with its wings. From the Kombi Livy took out one of her bottles of wine. Ben Brown and the girls at the Nouvelle Galerie had put two cases of wine in the car as a present. They were both mixed cases of different wines. James Coghlan had presented her with a corkscrew, the handle in the shape of a snake's head, the tail of the snake the metal of the screw. Pulling the cork from a bottle of red wine, Livy put it with a glass on the folding table that Ben had made and travelled in a bracket opposite her bed. Two folding chairs came with the table.

With the fire going Livy sat down facing the sinking sun through the trees on the far side of the lake. Behind the lake in the distance were mountains the colour of heather. Livy poured herself a glass and smiled. Two lights had come on in the house now darkened by shadow in the trees. She wondered if they could see her fire. Whether she was camped on their property. In the gloaming there was not one sight or sound of man other than those two lights in the trees. Earlier, Livy had prepared a green salad to go with her chops. The chops were pork and lamb and sizzled over the fire on the grill she placed across her stones. She could smell the fat burning in the coals. Livy drank her wine. It tasted so good. She was smiling with happiness all to herself. A dog fox barked from somewhere behind her, the sound sweet in the night air. For a moment Livy thought of Jeremy. And Mario Tuchi, Carmen and Candy. In a strange reminiscence she could smell the wild African sage, the sense of smell in her mind. She hoped he too was enjoying his life... The coals from her fire were dying down, cooking the meat ever so slowly. She drank a second glass. The wine was from Spain, it said so on the bottle. One of the lights in the house went out. Faintly, through the trees and across the still of the water, the surface of the lake reflecting the last colours of the sun, Livy could hear the strains of classical music. The sound was beautiful to her ears, as if it were in tune with the lake. Before it was too dark Livy lighted her hurricane lamp. When the chops were cooked she poured her prepared salad dressing over the greens in the small wooden bowl and ate by the light of the lamp. The dog fox barked again, from farther away.

When Livy climbed into the back of the Kombi to go to bed she had drunk half her bottle of wine. With the cork in she had left the bottle on the table. The sound of the music seemed nearer, resonating in the metal of the sides of her car. It was the last she remembered.

Livy woke once in the night to a splash from the lake and then it was morning. The birds were singing. At first Livy thought it was the classical music.

Getting out of bed and out of the Kombi she set up a canvas on her easel facing the water and began to paint what she saw of the rising sun from the lake. There was not a ripple on the water.

Later, her hands tired from holding up her palette in one hand and brush in the other, she stopped and lit the fire to boil her kettle. The smoke rose to the height of the trees.

When the kettle boiled where it sat over the fire she made a pot of tea and put it on the table. The glass and wine bottle were still standing where she had left them. With a woollen cosy over the teapot, letting the tea draw, Livy took off her clothes and went for a swim. The water was cold and pure. After a good rub with her towel she put on clean clothes and sat at her table. The tea when poured was rich and perfect.

All day long Livy painted, changing her canvas to suit each time of the day, four paintings of the lake in its changing colours. There were boats out on the lake. She could see two people down by the house in front of their trees.

In the evening she finished the wine having washed her glass in the lake.

"What else can a girl want?" she said, watching her piece of steak on the fire.

There was no music that evening from the house across the lake. Tired, happy and slightly tiddly, Livy went to bed in the back of her Kombi, instantly falling asleep.

She slept through the night, woken by the dawn chorus of birds. There was a low mist on the lake which she painted into her morning canvas.

The cough came from behind her, breaking Livy's concentration. The mist had risen from the lake. A sailboat was making little progress, the wind but a breath, far out on the water.

"I'm sorry. We saw your fire the past two nights from the house. Your painting is going to be very beautiful."

"Oh my goodness. I thought I was alone. Am I on your property?"

Next to the man, sitting on its haunches was an old dog.

"Yes, as a matter of fact. The beauty of your painting is worth the remission. My name is Claud Gainsborough."

"Are you related to the painter?"

"We always like to say so. I'm not really sure. My family have lived by the lake for two hundred years. Don't get much chance to be here these days. I'm in the City. The days of gentlemen not having to be in trade are long over. My mother saw you first. Said you were a painter. Why we left you alone. She has a pair of binoculars to watch the birds. Are you a professional painter?"

"Do my paintings sell? Yes. Have you heard of the Nouvelle Galerie on the Portobello Road?"

"I'm afraid not. In London I have to work rather hard."

"Does your mother live alone?"

"She prefers it that way. The family money just lasted my mother and father. Her family were in coal. Why he married her I suppose. Doesn't really matter. Father's been dead these five years. He loved the lake. Don't we all? We haven't been introduced."

"I'm so sorry. My name is Livy Johnston. I live in my studio in Chelsea... Would you like a cup of tea? I hope you don't mind the fire. A trick I learnt in Africa. Everything tastes so much better over a wood fire. Even the tea. The kettle boils surprisingly quickly."

"I'd love a cup of tea."

"I put the fire out with the water at night. In case the wind came up. They have bushfires in Africa... Have you been to Africa, Mr Gainsborough?"

"Claud, please. I'm only a few years older than you, Livy. The balding pate makes me look ten years older they say. Runs in the family. What can you do?... That's very good Spanish wine."

"They say it's wrong to drink on your own."

"Maybe tonight if the weather holds I could join you round the fire? Mother said she could see you were enjoying yourself. Sent me to find out what you were painting."

"Understanding mother."

"She always likes other people to be happy."

"She must be happy herself."

"I have never known her not to be... After tea, could we go for a walk? No. You don't like being interrupted."

"A walk will be nice. You can tell me all the names of the birds. Did you hear the fox bark in the night?"

"I've seen him many times over the years. And the vixen. They get to know you by sight. You never see them until they stop being afraid."

"It's dried milk, I'm afraid."

"I don't take sugar. During the war we couldn't get sugar. Probably good for us. What seemed at the time was such an imposition probably wasn't. Too much sugar they now say is bad for you... Am I gabbling? Not used to talking to girls unless they've been formally introduced. Mother says I'm shy."

"It's nice to talk after so many days on the road. Come and sit down. I'll get the other chair out of the Kombi."

"You're very organised."

"Thank you."

The dog followed her. Claud stayed where he was, looking out over the lake. Livy found the bone of last night's T-bone steak in the plastic rubbish bag she hung on the door inside the Kombi and gave it to the dog. It was a small bone from a small steak. The dog dropped the bone and looked at her. The dog's whiskers were grey. She thought the dog was smiling at her. Rummaging in the plastic bag, she came up with a bone from the lamp chop and gave it to the dog. The dog dropped the bone and smiled at her.

"My father taught him never to accept food from strangers."

"What's his name?"

"Queen Boadicea. Pedigree as long as your arm. She answers to Bo."

Claud bent down and picked up the bones and gave them to the dog. The dog sat back on its haunches and crunched the T-bone, gnawing out of the side of her face.

"They say border collies are the most intelligent of the dogs. They say a pig is more intelligent than a dog. Who knows? Give me the chair. Old as she is, she'd walk with me all day. Put up a rabbit and she'll run. Nine years old. Not bad for a dog. Do you like dogs?"

"I've always had cats in London. Easier to keep in a flat. The first painting I sold was of a cat. I borrowed foliage from a Rousseau print to make it look tropical. I was about to go out to Africa."

"You're lucky. I hate working in an office. During winter, unless I leave the office at lunchtime I never see the light of day for months on end. Artificial light. What can you do? I make a living, which at the end of the day is what it's all about. The life of a gentleman farmer doesn't pay the modern bills if you want a family."

"You're not married?"

"I'd like to be. I'd like to have kids. My ancestors had a good life here. Good food. A good fire at night. Swims in the summer."

"Did you see me?"

"I'm afraid so. Mother passed me the binoculars without saying a word. I put them down straight away of course."

"I'll bet you did... Bo? Do you want the last bone? There's a pork bone still in the bag... I looked around. Swimming naked gives me the feeling of complete freedom. Primal. How it was before all our civilising made us keep our clothes on to swim in a lake. Wonderful to live free... When do you go back to London?"

"Tomorrow. I'm an employee. Do what I'm told... Why don't you come and have dinner tonight with me and mother? How long are you staying?"

"Until I've finished the four canvases, unless the landowner chases me off."

"Mother won't do that. You'll like her. She'd like a little company. You could paint the old house. We think it's rather interesting. Have you ever painted a house?"

"Oh, yes."

"The kettle's boiling."

"So it is."

"Mother was in the theatre before she met Dad. Her father in coal didn't approve, of course: never put your daughter on the stage, Mrs Hetherington! During the Great War. Dad was home on leave from France. She'd like to meet a fellow artist."

"So your mother sent you?"

"Something like that."

"Before or after you looked through the binoculars?"

"Just after, I think. Come on, Bo. You can bring your bones, old girl. She has such friendly eyes, don't you think?"

"What about the tea?"

"I was trying to change the subject."

Livy grinned up at him. The man was tall. Then she leaned over the boiling kettle on her fire, picked it up and poured into her brown teapot.

"Takes a couple of minutes to draw... Come on, Bo. A quick walk and back for our tea."

The dog barked at her with excitement. Next time she gave Bo a bone she would likely not drop it in front of her. Out on the lake the solitary sailboat was lying motionless, its sails hanging. There was not a breath of wind on the water. A pheasant called from a thicket on the top of the small hill, taking off into flight then gliding down the hill into the grass. The dog had stopped, one front foot up, standing motionless. The pheasant had disappeared.

"She knows when she's beaten," said Claud.

They walked side by side along the shore of the lake, away from the old house in the trees. Livy wondered if the old woman was watching them through her binoculars. Just in case, she turned and gave the old house a wave.

"What was that for?"

"Your mother."

A WEEK LATER, the four canvases finished to her satisfaction, Livy went back on the road, driving north for the Scottish border. In politeness she had called on the old lady her last day by the lake to thank her for being allowed to camp on her land. The stones had been put back where she found them, the wood ash scattered in the grass. The tyre marks would soon disappear. The old lady had given her a cup of tea but had not invited her to dinner. They talked of Claud. The woman was only interested in Livy as it affected Claud.

"Does he have your number in London?"

"We went for a walk with the dog before coming to dinner."

"He knows you exhibit at the Nouvelle Galerie in the Portobello Road. I'm sure he will find you. He's so shy. How much do you charge for your paintings?"

"The last one went for nine hundred pounds. Can I give you one of my paintings of the lake?"

"My goodness, no. You must sell it in your gallery. Artists have to be paid like the rest of them. People forget that. Think they are doing you a big favour by coming to see your show or hanging your painting on their wall. The butcher never gives away his meat, does he? Now off you go and work, Livy. Watching you paint is pleasure enough. You don't want to sit and talk to a boring old lady. I'm happy with my books and my memories. When you marry, make sure it's to be happy. So often young girls marry a man for his money or his position in life. Not for his love. Marriage lasts a long time. Be sure you get on with each other. Bill and I never had a cross word in all those years."

"Did you have other children?"

"Just the one. Just Claud. After that there was something wrong with me. Now all I want is grandchildren... Run along and paint. Why don't I give you Claud's phone number in London? You could invite him to one of your exhibitions. As a favour to me. You must know lots of other young girls who are artists."

"Lots of them."

"Good. We understand each other. Stay by the lake for as long as you care... Another cup of tea?"

AT THE END OF AUGUST, without a canvas to paint, Livy turned the Kombi round and headed south from Scotland. She had used her last canvas painting a ruined castle close to the ferry that had taken her on a day trip across to the Isle of Skye. She was in a hurry to get home. Brief encounters with people left her wanting the company of friends.

It took Livy two days to reach the flat of Frank Brigandshaw where she spent the night. She had left the finished canvases in the racks locked in the back of the Kombi. By morning they had both used each other to full satisfaction. Frank went off to work while Livy drove to the Nouvelle Galerie to unload her canvases and show the girls what she had done, both her mind and body relaxed. They had the perfect relationship, no doubt about it.

Ben and Stan helped her unload the van.

"It's a Volkswagen car with a van attached to it, Stan."

"Looks like a van to me."

They were all happy to see each other.

Inside, Jeanne looked at the paintings one by one.

"The girl has been busy... You had a visitor while you were away. We didn't know when you were coming back."

"I told Claud's mother I'd give him a ring or send him an invitation to one of our exhibitions."

"His name wasn't Claud. He must have gone back by now. Stood an hour without moving in front of *The Big River*."

"Who was it, Jeanne?"

"Jeremy Crookshank. Over to see his mother and brother. Paul asked me to phone him the moment you were back."

"What did Jeremy want?"

"You, I rather think, Livy. We drank a bottle of wine together before I closed the gallery. All he talked about was you. And the new Crown Land farm he was being allocated in the Centenary. A new block named for the centenary of Cecil Rhodes's birth. Six thousand acres, I think he said. One hundred miles from Salisbury on the way past Elephant Walk."

"Did he see Frank?"

"Frank had drinks with him and Paul, I believe."

"The bastard."

"How much do you want for these?"

"That's your job. I just paint them... Are they any good, Jeanne?"

"Not bad. You're good at sunrises and sunsets. What a beautiful lake. I'll give Tessa and Abigail a ring to come and have a look. James is coming at five with a new sculpture."

"I have another name for the invitation list."

Livy handed Jeanne the address she had written down from Mrs Gainsborough.

"Any relation?"

"He doesn't think so. I camped on his mother's land by the lake. That's their home you can see in the distance between the trees. He's looking for a wife. Maybe one of the girls."

"Has he got any money?"

"They own a big tract of land in Cumberland."

HALF AN HOUR after Tessa came in to look at what she had done, Jeremy Crookshank walked in the door. His tan was richer than Livy remembered. He was a good-looking man, grinning all over his face.

"Jeremy! How did you know I was here?"

"Not the welcome I hoped for, Livy. Tessa gave Paul a ring. I'm staying with them for the last week of my leave. The last I spent in the Isle of Wight with Mother. Where have you been? No one knew where to get hold of you when I flew into London... It's almost lunchtime. Can we go out somewhere? I want to talk to you. It's all so exciting. Roger Crumpshaw is a ripper. Really good chap. Pays the bonus exactly as he said he would down to the last penny. After every sale I get my two per cent straight into my bank account... So what have you been doing? You disappeared."

"Painting holiday. You want to have a look?"

"Don't I get a hug?"

"Of course you do. It's just the gallery is full of people. You can't believe how successful Jeanne has made the place."

"With the help of Frank Brigandshaw, so I hear from Paul. When did you get back to London?"

"Last night. I have a camper."

"I rang your studio. I've rung it twice a day since I got back to England."

"I stayed with a friend."

"Male or female?"

"You don't want to know."

"We haven't seen each other for three years. That's a long time. Everything changes, Livy. I just hoped I might still stand a chance. I get my own farm next year. Virgin bush. Live in a tent while I build six barns. Stump out thirty acres and plant tobacco. The barns should be finished by the time the first leaves ripen in the lands."

"You want some coffee?"

"You don't want lunch?"

"There's a shop that makes sandwiches. They come in with a tray every lunchtime."

"They stole my idea."

"Lots of people take round lunches in London. They're calling them take-aways. Everyone is so busy they don't have time to go out for lunch unless it's on business... Come and have a look."

"You didn't sell *The Big River*."

"No, Jeremy. I want to keep that one. I'll give you one I've done of Cumberland. To take back to your new home."

"Hang it on a tent? Why not? I've done crazier things in Rhodesia."

"Why don't you first build yourself a house?"

"Don't have time. The barns first. They're two storeys high with tiers of poles going up inside where we hang the ripe leaves of tobacco across sticks. There's a big fire at the bottom we feed with the wood we stump out of the lands. Then the grading shed. Bulk shed. Workshop. Only then will I have the time and money to build myself a house. After two seasons, maybe. If the crop's good and the prices stay up on the floors. We sell by auction. Bale of tobacco at a time. Depends how keen the overseas buyers are to have our tobacco. The Americans are buying as well as the British. The money at the moment is in growing the tobacco. Paul says they are stopping Ridgeback cigarettes. Too much competition from Big Tobacco. All that advertising. Everything in consumer products is about advertising. Distribution and advertising. Paul's in a bit of a jam. I've told him to come out to Rhodesia and join me. A lot's changed in three years."

"Is he coming? They've just had a baby."

"Keeps me up all night... He may. Sometimes we don't have an alternative in life... Coffee would be nice. You look so well. Paul was saying you've sold lots of paintings."

"When do you go back?"

"Let's not talk about that now. What are you doing here this evening?"

"Oh, Jeremy. Are we going to start all over again? You there, me here. I'm an artist. There would be no market for me in Rhodesia stuck out in the bush."

"There would be me."

"Give me that hug."

They sat outside on the bench Ben Brown had placed in front of the gallery window to drink their cups of coffee, both of them silent. Stan was doing his best to con a tourist into buying his fake antique jewellery. They watched, smiling. When the couple went off with their new prized possession Stan gave Livy a wink.

"He's good," said Jeremy.

"It's more the game that amuses Stan. When Ben hasn't got a client to sketch he sits here and watches Stan do his act."

"I need a wife, Livy."

"What will you do if I won't come?"

"Return next year in the tobacco off-season and look for someone else. You're my first choice. Most people don't get their first choice when it comes to marriage. Or anything important, really. Career. Where to live. Who to have as a friend. They say in the end it doesn't matter. That we are all much the same. That we have to live with ourselves in the end, the rest a passing parade. The grand passion turns to the more practical things of life, like earning a living. Surviving. Living as comfortably as possible. We can never choose our kids. They just arrive and stay. It's all pretty much accidental."

"You've been alone in the bush too long."

"Maybe... Thinking life through gives me a certain sense of comfort. I want you, Livy, but if I don't get you I'll find someone else. Who's to know what we'll all think about it forty years from now? Then it will all be different except for one thing. Individually, we'll be exactly the same person. Wiser, hopefully. Probably not. It's the game of life."

"Have you told Paul you want to marry me?"

"Of course."

"Is this a proposal out here on the bench?"

"If the answer is going to be no there isn't much point. I've never been good at rejection... You can paint in Rhodesia. I don't understand you."

"It would be so lonely on a farm stuck in the back of beyond. My friends here make me want to paint. We're all doing it together. Encouraging each other. I'm making a name for myself doing what I love best. With a brood of kids and a house to keep, I'd just be a wife and mother."

"Isn't that what you want?"

"I don't know, Jeremy. Right now with you sitting here I may be making the worst mistake of my life. But who knows? You just said yourself you can't read the future. All I know is if I don't paint, I'm miserable. Do you want a miserable wife? The kids, whoever they are, are going to have a miserable mother. I want to be happy. Only painting makes me truly happy. Maybe I'm selfish but it's the truth. You'll find another girl, lover."

"But she won't be you... Thanks for the coffee. I've got to go. There's lots to do."

"Like finding a wife."

"Not this trip, Livy. I've been waiting for you. I'll go on waiting until next year when I go onto my own farm... If you've been living in the back of a camper a tent won't seem so bad."

"Let me go and get the painting of my *Cumberland Sunrise*. That way we'll always have something to look at to remind us of each other. My *Big River,* your *Cumberland Sunrise*. And paintings, once they are done, never change. That's the beauty of them. Art lasts longer than human life. You sit there. You'll have to make a frame but you're good at that. I'll roll and put it in a tube so you can carry it back on the plane... Why are you crying, Jeremy?"

"Because I'm an old fool. Right now I've never felt worse in my life. Please go and get it. For a few moments I want to be alone. Our lives together could have been so beautiful. Now I'm not sure how mine will be."

"I'll just sign it 'Livy'."

"You do that."

THE BIGGEST SURPRISE came at five o'clock when Livy went back to her studio. The phone was ringing before she put the key in the door. When she answered, it was Frank Brigandshaw and not Jeremy. After one of their sessions it was usually a week before either of them needed to contact the other.

Livy had eaten her sandwiches with Tessa sitting out on the bench in the sun. Ben had found himself a five-bob customer and was busy on a sketch. The subject was an old man in a bowler hat, unusual for the Portobello Road. Having shared a flat together, Livy and Tessa had the good habit of talking to each other.

"Are you sure saying no is the right answer, Livy? By next year when he comes back you'll be twenty-eight. Time to start a family or you'll be on the shelf. Our looks don't last forever. Neither of us are the young, freewheeling girls without a thought for the future we used to be when you and I shared the flat. Thirty comes and then forty before you know what has happened. Men are only interested in us when we're young. By the time we're thirty we need to have nailed one down, given him some kids and secured our future. After thirty the pickings get slim. If a man isn't married by the time he's thirty there's something wrong with him. The girls have had a look at him and run away. Or he's divorced. Second-hand goods... Be careful, Livy. Rhodesia may not turn out to be all you want it to be. That's the chance you take. At least you'll be Mrs Crookshank. He's not the kind of man to run away from anything when it gets tough. A country or a marriage. Just my opinion. Take it or leave it. It's your life. As an old friend I'm saying be careful. If there were women all over the place in Rhodesia as there are in London, he'd have been snapped up. Especially now he's got money and going to have his own estate. You'll be Livy, Lady of the Manor, not Livy the painter who's gone out of fashion."

"Who says I'm going out of fashion?"

"We all do. It may not last but we all go out of favour one way or another. I haven't sold a painting in ages. Cohen Wells don't show me anymore on the walls of their office. Zach has found someone else who caught his eye. It's a warning to all of us. We go in and out of favour. Artists only get famous when they're dead. Then their paintings are worth something materially."

"I like painting."

"Then do it on a farm in Rhodesia."

"With kids running around? He needs someone to help him run the farm as much as he needs a wife. To look after the families of the workers. Run a clinic. Start a primary school. He's talked about it. There's work for the wife to do on a farm. Painting will become a memory. Now I'm on a roll I don't want to leave London and give up the one thing that gives me real satisfaction."

"You've got a year to think about it... Jeanne will be all right. She's turned her painting into a business. It doesn't matter to her who'll be selling in ten years' time. She'll still get her cut. She doesn't have to get married."

For a moment, Livy was caught off guard when she heard it was Frank on the phone. Then the sometime cynic in her made her smile.

"What do you want, Frank? I thought it was Jeremy."

"I thought you might. Why don't we take in a show tonight? Go for supper afterwards."

"Are you asking me out?"

"Well, I thought it would be nice. I'm finishing work in a couple of hours. Time for you to tart yourself up. I'll drive round and pick you up at seven. Where've you been all day?"

"At the Nouvelle Galerie... Seven o'clock. What are we going to see?"

"You pick. If the show's full I'll buy tickets from a scalper outside the theatre."

"Expensive, Frank."

"Who cares? Business is good. You deserve a night out after all that camping in the wild."

"Is that the truth, Frank? Or is the thought of Jeremy in London bugging you?"

"Seven o'clock."

"I'll be ready... They liked the new paintings."

"I'm glad... Milly! You can show him in... Got to go."

Smiling to herself, Livy sat down and looked around her studio. Everything looked just the same... It was nice to be home.

"There's nothing like a bit of competition," she said to the pigeon cooing on the rooftop outside the one big window.

Going into her small bathroom she ran the bath... Frank had invited her to go to the theatre. What was going to happen?

She poured herself a gin with a dash of French vermouth and sipped the drink as she looked out of the window, waiting for her bath to fill.

When Frank rang her bell at five minutes past seven she was ready to go out. Getting ready had kept her mind off Jeremy.

"You look good, Livy."

"*South Pacific*. If you can get tickets to *South Pacific* at Drury Lane I'll eat my hat."

"You don't have a hat."

"Then I'll have to eat someone else's."

PART VI

SEPTEMBER TO OCTOBER 1956 – "MISSING THE BOAT"

The exhibition, the first for a single artist, took place a month after Livy's thirtieth birthday. Jeanne Pétain had contacted each buyer asking them to loan their Livy Johnston paintings to the Nouvelle Galerie for a fortnight. The incentive for the people who had bought Livy's paintings was an increase in their value. Frank Brigandshaw had orchestrated the buzz, bringing Livy's name into the arts section of every London newspaper and magazine. Frank's bill to the Nouvelle Galerie was prohibitive but worth, according to James Coghlan, 'every damn penny'.

"It's not just Livy we are putting firmly on the map. It's our own gallery. She's the best artist we have. We have to use her. Frank says we can increase the value of every painting in the gallery by ten per cent at the end of this exhibition... He's invited the Lord Mayor of London. All the newspapers."

Every painting and piece of art that wasn't a Livy Johnston had been stored in the shed at the back of the gallery for the fortnight. Four of her latest canvases were to go on sale by auction at the end of the *Livy Johnston Exhibition*. Never in her life had Livy felt so popular.

On its own, different from the rest, was her portrait of *Princess*, the painting she had given to Josiah Makoni to hang in his room in Holland Park to remind him of his mother back home in the British Crown

Colony of Southern Rhodesia. The painting was a focal point, a message that the gallery approved of the swell in anti-colonialism that had built up in London among the liberal elite. In the world of the arts, according to Frank and his brother Dorian, it was good to be seen to be liberal.

She and Frank had long stopped sleeping with each other. They were now old friends, having banged the sex out of each other.

Wandering around, looking at paintings she had done long ago, she stopped at *The Big River* for a long moment remembering how happy she had been. Further down she found her painting of *The Funeral*. Like *Princess*, Livy's painting of Harry Brigandshaw's funeral had been given away. Now it was back on the gallery wall, the same look of loss echoing from the eyes of the man giving the eulogy. The tears. The sadness. The utter loss. She hoped the man himself enjoyed the painting, something she doubted. No one wished to be reminded of their better days.

"It's the most evocative painting you ever did," said Dorian Brigandshaw, standing next to her. "It's more than the look and everything in his mind behind those eyes. I would need a chapter to describe what you painted. It's all gone now, you know. Vic Bell's dead. Elephant Walk has been sold to Anglo-US Incorporated after Grandmother Brigandshaw died and Aunt Madge went to Cape Town to live with her daughter. A whole era. Appropriate for the end of the empire. I tried so hard to capture the life of Grandfather Brigandshaw. The old days of a white hunter. Didn't work. I'm much better writing modern trivia. That they read. You know, the publishers like rubbish, Livy. Doesn't make the reader think. Why my stuff sells. Why this painting of yours never sold. Looking at a man crying at a funeral makes them think of their own mortality. They want beautiful sunrises and sunsets... Anglo-US are using Dad's Mazoe Dam to irrigate his dream of a citrus estate. Ten thousand acres under orange trees all in perfect rows. When Jeremy drives into Salisbury he passes through the Mazoe Citrus Estate... Do you hear from him?"

"Not anymore."

"He's married, you know."

"I didn't. Who did he marry?"

"Your friend Carmen. They've got a kid. A boy I believe. They had to get married. Carmen was pregnant."

"These things happen."

"Yes they do. Happened to me. Only I didn't get married. Nancy is married. Her husband adopted Wendy. Wendy now has a father. All ended well."

"You sound sad."

"Of course I'm sad."

"Have you seen her?"

"They won't let me. I didn't have any money after Dad died. Everything got sold in the end to maintain my mother and that damn dog. Lives like Lady Muck in Mayfair while the rest of us get nothing. Auntie Madge got the house in Bishops Court in Cape Town to live in for the rest of her life. When she dies it goes back to the estate. Dad didn't make me a trustee. Said in the will I was too artistic."

"It's better to make your own money in life."

"I suppose so. I'm all right now. Books like mine sell well. The one I called *The Sweet Scent of Blossom* has done the best. Did you read it, Livy?"

"Not my kind of book, Dorian. Finish the one you started on Seb Brigandshaw and I'll read that. Especially if it makes me think."

"It's still in the drawer of my writing desk. If I publish something like that now, my readers will hate it... Is the Lord Mayor really coming?"

"Who knows? You can never be sure with Frank."

"I suppose not... Is the first day of a one-man exhibition the best?"

"I'm a woman, Dorian."

"You know what I mean... Don't turn round but he's coming over. The man who put the horns of a cuckold on the head of my father. What's he doing here?"

"He bought my first painting. *Pussy Cat* isn't my best but it has sentimental attachment for me."

As Dorian looked round the gallery, Livy turned to Barnaby St Clair.

"Thank you for lending us your painting."

"How much will I get for it after this exhibition?"

"You want to sell *Pussy Cat*?"

"You know the saying in the City, Livy. Never fall in love with your share certificate. A painting is just an instrument. When you see a good profit, sell. Why I bought the painting."

"I thought it reminded you of your cat. Didn't you have a ginger cat at home?"

"I can't remember. Where's Frank, Dorian? He's meant to be here."

"I am not my brother's keeper... Will you excuse me? My publisher has arrived."

Livy watched Dorian walk away.

"Rude bastard," said Barnaby, looking at Dorian's retreating back.

"Don't you think that might be an inappropriate word?"

"Have you read his books? Lot of trash if you ask me. They'll never make a film out of Dorian Brigandshaw. Not like Robert St Clair. They're making a movie out of my brother Robert's latest in America."

"What's it about?"

"I have no idea. I don't read fiction. Reading the financial papers takes up all my time. By the way, the funds I put you into have done rather well don't you think? Eleven per cent compound interest every year for three years. Come and see me after the auction if you want to invest. Or are you going to get yourself a bigger apartment?"

"My studio suits me. I can paint better in familiar surroundings... Why do some people always want something bigger?"

"Been in my house in Piccadilly for years."

"Then you bought Hastings Court."

"For Frank. His inheritance. Are you still seeing each other?"

"Not in the biblical sense. Frank's a bit like you, Barnaby. He likes young girls. I'm thirty. Far too old for Frank. I'll come and see you if the auction is a success. I like the freedom of money. Knowing whatever else happens I will always be able to paint without having to worry about money. The only point I can see in having a little money. If you want, I'll put *Pussy Cat* in the auction. The only way to find out what it's worth."

"What a good idea, Livy. Do I have to pay commission?"

"Auctioneer's fees and the usual forty per cent to the gallery."

"Exorbitant."

"Depends what they get for it. Don't you always tell me a profit is a profit?"

"Got to go. My new young lady doesn't like art exhibitions... Put it in the auction for me."

"Do you have a reserve price?"

"Two thousand pounds. You're famous Livy... Whatever happened to that Jeremy Crookshank you were going to marry?"

"Married a friend of mine."

"Lucky girl. Frank tells me he's doing well on his own farm. That the price of tobacco on the Salisbury auction floors has skyrocketed. He should get some of his money out of Rhodesia."

"How old is she, Barnaby?"

"About your age. If you hadn't gone out with Frank I would have asked you out to dinner." He was smiling at her, not meaning a word.

"Thank heaven for small mercies. Enjoy yourself. Which one is she?"

"The lady talking to the tall man with the bald head... Why do some chaps lose their hair before they are forty?... He's waving at me."

"Probably at me. I met him on one of my camping trips and put him on the gallery invitation list. He's in the City. Does rather well. You'd better go and get your young lady before it's too late."

"Say hello to Frank for me."

Surrounded by so many friends and feeling lonely, Livy went outside to look at the people walking up and down the Portobello Road.

"What's the matter, Livy?" asked Stan. "I love these exhibitions. Always good for business. The best thing ever happened is that gallery. Right next to my barrow. Winter and summer."

"Jeremy is married. Just found out."

"Can't keep them hanging forever."

"She got herself pregnant. A friend of mine. They do that when they see a man has money."

"You had your chance and blew it. Twice he came over to ask you to marry him. You chose your art... What do you think of this eighteenth-century French costume jewellery? Made in Hong Kong."

"Was I a fool, Stan?"

"We're all fools, Livy. Why don't you go inside and nick one of them bottles of wine with the cork out? Bring two glasses and have a drink with your Uncle Stan."

"Are you ever going to come inside the gallery?"

"Why should I? Miss a sale? Not likely. This is my world out here on the pavement. Looking at the people passing by. You can tell a lot from a person's expressions. Like that tall bloke with the bald head inside. Came in with that look of wistful hope written all over his face."

"What was he hoping for?"

"You tell me."

"Can't drink outside today, Stan. Much as I'd like to. I'm the star. They like to meet the artist... You think I'm dressed right for a painter?"

"Just right. That little black beret suits you."

"Jeanne's idea. French. Very Left Bank. You ever been to Paris, Stan?"

"Don't be daft. Furthest I ever been was to Brighton. Too old to join the army in the last war. Too young to go into the first one. My Dad went to France. The Huns got him. How I ended up working a barrow. No time for that education. Had to look after my Mum and my sisters. Not that I'm complaining. Had a good life."

"I hope I have one."

"Don't think of him. Good thing he's married. Now you don't have to make up your mind. Any young man would marry you, Livy. Take your pick of London. All that living in a foreign land gives me the shivers. Good old London. Pint or two on the way home. What more can a man want?"

"You have a wife and children."

"So will you, Livy. Now Jeremy has made up his mind you'll find yourself a bloke."

"He didn't tell me."

"By the sound of it your friend didn't tell him she was being careful."

"Maybe I'll get that bottle."

"That's my girl. Getting partial to French wine I am."

FRANK CAME in half an hour after Livy went to look for Stan's bottle of wine. Livy thought Frank looked more pleased with himself than usual. The moment she had stepped back into the gallery people had surrounded her, Livy's first taste of being a celebrity. Newspapermen and women were obsequious, deferring, wanting her opinions which they wrote down. From her years of anonymity when she was doing the work she was now worth talking to, Frank's PR blitz having made her name familiar to their editors... As she saw Frank, Livy caught the elbow of Ben Brown and asked him to take Stan a bottle of wine with her apologies. She was the centre of everyone's attention, no doubt about it. For preference she would have preferred a quiet glass of wine out on the pavement with Stan. What she had wished for had become a distasteful reality. They were feeding off her like predators, none of their nice words anything near being meaningful or true.

"It's all happening," said Frank. "Congratulations. Your old friend Walter Featherstone-Wallace from the *Tatler* is lapping it up. Saying he discovered you."

"Your father wants to sell *Pussy Cat* for two thousand pounds at the auction."

"Whatever for?"

"To make a profit."

"How is Walt from the *Tatler*?"

"He helped me when I needed it. Why do you look so smug?"

"Haven't you heard from Paul? Your old friend is in town. With a wife and a son. They've only been married five months. Jeremy says in Rhodesia they call it the only crop that never fails... What's the matter, Livy? You didn't want to marry him. Not with me around."

"It had nothing to do with you, Frank. I never had any intention of marrying you. Not that you asked... Your father was just here. Said to say hi. The girl with him was my age."

"What's wrong with that? Lucky Dad. Money is the best aphrodisiac for a woman. Even if they have to feign their orgasm. Most women I know want the man's money, not the man."

"You're crude."

"And honest. Never say never, Livy. Now you're famous you've become quite a catch. You should remember that. Why didn't he contact you?"

"I'm sure Carmen will want to see me."

"And gloat. Jeremy's making big money. He's the only one doing two tobacco crops a year, according to Paul. The weight isn't as good the second crop but he gets to use his curing barns twice. Smart lad. You see, it's all about money. My mother was asking about you. Read an article in her favourite magazine all about Livy Johnston. The magazine with all the pictures. She was most impressed."

"How's the damn dog?"

"Still got a flat face. We must go out to the theatre again. An opening night. Good for your image. From now on you need to keep your pretty face in front of the cameras. Nothing better than a celebrity with a pretty

face. We might have to give you a makeover. Keep you looking young...
Where are you going, Livy?"

"Outside to talk to Ben and Stan."

"I told Paul to tell Jeremy about your exhibition. He'll be impressed
when he finds out how far I have taken you."

"It's all you, Frank, isn't it?"

"Most of it. You can have the best product in the world but if it isn't
marketed properly it won't sell. People don't get known by chance.
Someone has to push them. That's my job... Who's the chap with the
bald head giving you sheep eyes?"

"Claud Gainsborough. I met him and his mother in Cumberland."

"Are you lovers?"

"Frank. Be careful. You'll screw up all your good work. They'll be
saying nasty things about me any moment in the newspapers."

"Any publicity is good publicity. Winston Churchill said that. What a
pity he handed over to Anthony Eden. Eden's handling of the Suez crisis
is a right muck-up. We're not an empire anymore. Can't throw our weight
around. The Americans don't like it. Anglo-Saxon power has moved to
Washington, for what that's worth. We've got to become like Switzerland.
Small and rich. The financial centre of the world. Not the policemen...
What did my father have to say for himself?"

"He thinks Jeremy should get his money out of Rhodesia."

"You see? You were right."

"Why was I right, Frank?"

"By not marrying Jeremy Crookshank. In the end all his money will
be worth bugger-all."

AT THE END of her interview with the *Tatler*, and being asked her opinion
of the great masters, something she knew absolutely nothing about, Livy
found herself looking directly into the sad, wistful eyes of Claud
Gainsborough. Livy suspected he had been trying to position himself for
a conversation ever since he had arrived at the gallery.

"Mother was asking about you on the phone just this morning. She
wanted to know if I had seen you. I'd told her about my invitation to this
wonderful exhibition. Thank you so much, Livy. It was so wonderful to
hear from you. What a splendid display. So much work. Among so much

genius we have a picture of my family's house hiding among the trees. I don't know how you do it. The girl I was talking to says you're expecting the Lord Mayor of London! My goodness. Next you'll be asked to meet the Queen. I always think meeting our monarch is more important than meeting the prime minister. Unless it was Churchill of course. Before all this I was plucking up my courage to invite you out. Now I can see it's out of the question. When I talk about knowing Livy Johnston in the office they are all so impressed. Did I tell you they've made me a director? In business I can always cut to the chase. It's when confronted by a lovely girl that I go all to pieces. Now a famous lovely girl. I still cherish the memory of our walk with Bo along the lake."

"I'm the same girl, Claud. I haven't changed. It's how people look at me that's changed. Come and meet my friend Stan outside. Nothing changes Stan's view of anything. With luck there'll be some wine left in the bottle. Get yourself a glass from the table. And one for me. All this talking to the newspapers as if I know what I'm talking about makes me wonder what life is really about. There's a little bench just outside. If Stan gets sight of a customer we have to leave him alone."

"You want me to come with you?"

"Of course."

"My happiness flows over. Who is Stan?"

"He sells fake antique jewellery off a barrow. I like talking to Stan. Never gives out all the bullshit. Walt from the *Tatler* was writing it all down as if what I said was gospel. Why any reader should want my opinion I have not the slightest idea."

"I'm sure you know much more about painting than most of them. There was a black man looking at your portrait of a black woman. I've never seen a black man so close before."

"The woman is his mother. We'll all hear more of Josiah Makoni. He's in politics. Lobbying the British government to break up the Federation of Rhodesia and Nyasaland. They all want their independence from Britain, not some new rule by a tiny white minority that call themselves Rhodesians."

"So you know something about politics?"

"Not a damn thing. What Josiah told me when he brought back the portrait of his mother for my exhibition. I think Josiah's a communist, whatever that means in Africa. No idea where he gets his money from. I gave him his mother's portrait. Didn't expect to see it again. Frank St Clair moves in so many circles. It was Frank who tracked down Josiah and asked him to loan us the painting of his mother."

"Are we really going to have a glass of wine together?"

"Of course we are. Don't be shy."

"Could we go out one day, Livy?"

"I don't see why not."

"I've never met a barrow boy before."

"Then it's two firsts in one day. A black man close up and now a barrow boy. England! How did we ever get through the centuries?"

"I don't know what you mean."

"That's the problem, Claud. We all live in different worlds."

2

*S*taying with his brother and sister-in-law in the Hammersmith flat Paul could no longer afford, Jeremy Crookshank wondered at how quickly a man's life could change. The grand piano had gone. Paul was left to play his clarinet. Neither of them drank or went out. No one came round to be entertained. The car had gone the way of the piano. Instead of Paul lending him money to pay for Livy Johnston's trip to Rhodesia it was Jeremy lending Paul money, a pleasure that Jeremy savoured. It was always pleasant to give back. To do the good deed in return. Kim Brigandshaw had called it karma, which he had learnt about while staying in a Buddhist monastery in Bhutan, before he had drifted out of Rhodesia, bored with farming, bored with standing all day in the lands overseeing the workers in the hot African sun.

They had left the women together in the flat, Jeremy catching the Tube with Paul to what was left of the Brigandshaw Limited office in Holborn. Katherine Marshbanks, Harry Brigandshaw's secretary at the Air Ministry, who had followed him after the war to Brigandshaw Limited, had been retired on full pension, a provision in Harry's will. Paul, as a trustee with Harry's nephew Tinus Oosthuizen, had found all the codicils in Harry's will looking after people had taken up most of the company income. With all the provisions the company was going broke. To Jeremy, as an outsider looking in, it was as if the stuffing had been knocked out of his once so enthusiastic brother. With Tinus living in New York, having bought out the Brigandshaw interest in the American company, Beth professing to know nothing about business, and the brothers-in-law, Dorian and Kim, more inclined to ask him what had happened to their money, Paul had no one to talk to. No one to build up his enthusiasm. With Harry dead, Katherine had grown more and more detached, putting nothing into the company, going through her last days at the office as if she were somewhere else. Paul had thought she was in love with Harry Brigandshaw. Now he was certain. The new girl in the office was a good typist. Good at answering the phone. She was polite and cooperative, came exactly on time and left when the clock said half past five. She was an employee with no interest Jeremy could see in the company. The major came in once a week, more to lift Paul's spirits than help the firm make money. Major Pilkington-Jones was seventy-seven years old and well past his prime. He had helped Paul start the antiques business of exporting from the stately homes of England, all financially in trouble after the war, to America, the last income producer for Brigandshaw Limited and the source of Paul's reduced salary.

"I don't know what to do, Jeremy. Beth and I now have two children. I have no written qualifications. What was left of the cash in the company went down the drain with Ridgeback cigarettes trying to fight the big tobacco companies before they put our brand out of business."

"You could come and join me and Carmen in Rhodesia."

"Beth won't hear of leaving England. She's an eternal optimist. Always thinks something will come along. Has great faith in me, bless her."

"You say the old families you do business with are running out of antiques to sell. That what they have left to sell the Americans don't want."

"The bigger furniture won't fit into American apartments. They don't want four-poster beds in Manhattan according to Tinus. We've drained the best out of the business. The old paintings. The nice chairs. Tapestries. The small stuff that looks good in apartments. They don't have anything left for us to sell."

"Are the families doing any better ten years after the war?"

"Worse, if anything. Farming in England doesn't make any money unless you have the capital to buy the new equipment. Giant combine harvesters. Efficient tractors. Cold rooms to keep the produce fresh. There's no infrastructure to get the produce to market in the cities from the farmland far into the country. I don't know much about it really. You'd know more than me. You're a farmer. My word, you are doing well. I can't believe what you're achieving."

"The first secret is learning how to farm. Roger Crumpshaw was a good teacher. He said the secret to making a profit was to do every job on the farm efficiently. He never lost a leaf of tobacco in the grading shed. Neither do I. You have to maximise your equipment. Have nothing lying idle. The barns are too damn expensive to build with the flues and all the steam piping. With one crop they get used two months of the year. Capital lying idle. They say I ranch tobacco. That my quality isn't as good as the chap who gets 'Grower of the Year'. Fact is, I cure more tobacco by planting the second late crop which together with the early crop adds up to a lot more money. Farming's a business these days. You make a profit or you go bust. All those aristocrats of yours don't know how to farm. Relied on tenants to pay the rent. Before socialism soaked them with taxes, they had money invested out of their estates. They're now inefficient farmers. Dinosaurs in a brave new world. Going extinct. How many estates do you do business with?"

"A couple of thousand."

"And you know all of them personally?"

"Most of them."

"And they trust you?"

"A gentleman's word is his bond, Jeremy. We had that drilled into us at school. All that honour, duty, loyalty and trust."

"So all they have left is a crumbling mansion with a roof that leaks they can't afford to fix and lots of land that isn't making enough profit."

"Sounds about right."

"Have you ever thought of going into the property business?"

"Other chaps do that."

"Other chaps don't have your contacts. You need to set up an estate agency that can sell parcels of their land."

"I know nothing about selling land."

"Then find someone who does."

Paul got up from behind his desk and stood with his back to Jeremy, looking out of the window.

"The tables really have turned, brother," said Paul, his voice small and lost.

"It looks that way... Don't give in, Paul. Think. You always have to think in this life."

"I'll have a chat with the major."

"Give him a ring. With luck he'll invite us both to lunch at the Cavalry Club. He's still a member, I presume?"

"One of their oldest members after Lachlan died. His friend Lachlan was a member of the Cavalry Club for seventy-eight years."

"There you go."

"If we sold a whole estate we'd make a lot of money."

"Why not to rich Americans? They'd become Lord of the Manor. From what I hear among all the republicans on the other side of the Atlantic there are a lot of closet monarchists who would pay anything for a title. Even the honorary title of Lord of the Manor which they would get when buying one of those old estates. Why don't you ask Tinus?"

"He's going out to Rhodesia at the end of the month to tie up all the loose ends at Elephant Walk. Beth's Aunt Madge was given two years by Anglo-US to vacate the family compound and sell the farm equipment."

"Bought some of it myself. There are ongoing problems with some of the old retainers who have to be looked after in the terms of Harry's will. Anglo only wanted the land and the water in the Mazoe Dam. Planting orange trees like crazy. Pass them on the road on my way into town from the farm... You'll have to register a real estate company. Shouldn't be too difficult. If Tinus finds you American buyers you can pay him some of your sales commission."

"No wonder you're making money in Rhodesia."

Paul turned round from looking unhappily out of the window. He was smiling.

"That's the stuff, Paul. Now you're thinking positively."

"Are you going to Livy's exhibition?"

"Carmen's not sure of her reception. I want to go. I mean, she wouldn't marry me, Paul. What's a man meant to do? Now I have a baby my life is just fine. Carmen gets bored on the farm. Probably drinks too much. Don't we all? Sundowners. A tradition in Rhodesia. We're all a bunch of alcoholics when it comes down to it. Give her half a dozen more kids. That'll keep her occupied. Has Livy got a boyfriend?"

"She was going out with Frank. Calls himself Frank St Clair... I'd better get hold of Frank and pass your idea across his mind. If anyone knows how to sell it's my brother-in-law Frank. Now there's a success story. Chap's coining it. Did you hear his father bought Hastings Court? To give Frank a true inheritance. The bastard turned out good. Life really is full of ironies. I like Frank. At least he's honest. Calls a spade a spade. Women! Goes through them by the dozen. All young and drop-dead beautiful. Beth says she disapproves but underneath she's rather chuffed with her half-brother. It's Kim she worries about. All the potential and just drifts around. Never sticks to anything. Lasted six months on Elephant Walk with his Aunt Madge and drifted off again. You know all that better than me living close to Elephant Walk. Kim's a drifter. His mother says he'll never amount to anything. Maybe she's right. Such a pity. Everyone likes Kim. He's so agreeable. Not a nasty bone in his body. People always want to do things for him, which is probably part of the problem. A likeable bum is my brother-in-law Kim. It takes all sorts to make a world. He's just got no ambition. One of these days he'll find a very rich girl, marry her and live off her money for the rest of her life. And the joke is it won't be intentional. Just happen. He won't even know what he's done. Lucky bastard if you ask me. Takes all the worry out of making a living with that attitude. When he has to he can live off the smell of an oil rag. Doesn't need money. Money doesn't impress him in the slightest. Maybe those Buddhists in Bhutan taught him something we don't understand properly. He once told me never to expect anything in life. That being content was more important than anything money could buy. Possessions, according to Kim, are an impediment. Get in the way... We shall see. Can you imagine what kind of a world it would be if we all had that attitude? Nothing would ever get done. Nothing would work. He's lucky if you ask me. I envy him. Doesn't have a care in the world."

"He'll have a problem if his charm wears thin."

"You think people will see through him?"

"They always do in the end. You can never rely on other people. You can only rely on yourself. Especially when it comes to money."

"I'll give the major a ring and invite ourselves to lunch. It was the major who first got me started. Got me out of being an insurance clerk. He was one of our valuers of antiques. How I got to know him. I was working in the claims department of Contingency Insurance soon after the war. I was just out of the army. Now that's a job I don't want to go back to. A dead end that didn't pay any money."

"What's the time in New York?"

"First lunch with the major by which time Tinus will be going into the office. The major never says no to a bit of company."

"I've a better idea. Why don't I take you all out to lunch at the Berkeley? Just down the road from the Cavalry Club as I remember. Let me buy you all lunch."

The lunch at the Berkeley down the road from the Cavalry Club in Piccadilly had gone better than the brothers had hoped. So had the phone call to New York. Both the major and Tinus Oosthuizen thought the idea of going into real estate was the company's salvation. From being positively negative, Paul had refound his enthusiasm. There was hope again in the Hammersmith flat. Beth had promised they would buy a grand piano for Paul to play his music when the first estate was sold. Tinus had come back the next day telling them he had two interested buyers provided the Lord of the Manor title went with the estate. One by one, Paul had been phoning his clients with the help of the new secretary telephonist who had taken the place of Katherine. All was going swimmingly again in Brigandshaw Limited with the major camped in the office vacated by Kenneth Grahame when Paul's old friend had had to look for a new job. When Paul phoned Kenneth with the new idea they had both laughed happily over the phone.

IN THE END they all went to Livy's exhibition at the Nouvelle Galerie working on Paul's principle of safety in numbers. After their first look at each other, Jeremy knew it was not a good idea. The way Livy looked at him stabbed his heart.

They had left the Hammersmith flat after Sunday lunch with the two youngest children in the same pram. Young Henry, Jeremy's nephew, almost four years old, walked behind. They got the pram into the taxi with Phillip in Carmen's arms. Deborah was held in her father's arms.

The kerfuffle outside the gallery caught Livy's attention. Phillip, Jeremy's son, was screaming his head off.

"This wasn't such a good idea," said Jeremy.

"Why don't I stay outside with the children?" said Carmen. "There's a bench I can sit on over there. When you've seen it all inside, Beth, you can take over."

"You're a coward, darling," said Jeremy, who had caught the first look of shock in Livy's eyes through the glass of the front window of the Nouvelle Galerie.

"Probably. If looks could kill I'd be dead."

Putting on a brave face, Jeremy pushed open the door to let Beth inside. Paul went in next, trying his best to smile. Up until that moment all four of them had been in the best of humour.

"How are you, Livy?" said Paul.

"Bloody awful if you want to know. Which one in that pram outside is Carmen's baby? Or did she have twins?"

"The girl is mine," said Beth.

"Why won't she come in?"

"The kid was screaming when we unloaded the pram from the taxi. At that age they don't like being woken from a sleep. You don't want a screaming child inside an art gallery. The boy making faces at the babies in the pram is mine. That one is Henry. Named after my great-grandfather Manderville whose family built Hastings Court. Just look at all these people. Frank was telling me what a success you were having. I'm so pleased for you. Is Frank here? I haven't seen my brother for a while."

"He came to the opening with his father. I haven't seen or heard from him since. We're not going out anymore."

"Oh. I heard Frank wanted to take you to the new show at the Strand... Have you forgotten Jeremy here? He's married now."

"I know, Beth... How are you, Jeremy? Why don't you and I go outside so you can introduce me to your son? How long have you two been married?"

"Three months, actually."

"My word. Whatever happened to being careful? You two have a look around. Come along, Jeremy... Carmen! How lovely to see you again. How is Mrs Wade? How is Mario Tuchi? I thought you two were going to get married. Don't say he married Candy?"

"Candy married a tobacco farmer."

"Good for Candy. Now, which one is your baby?"

"The one that looks like Jeremy. I saw Crispin Dane, the great lover, only last month when Jeremy and I had lunch at Meikles. He asked after you, Livy. He said he has fond memories of your voyage out from England on the *Carnarvon Castle*. He never married, you know. Just the same old Crispin. All the girls love Crispin Dane... Do you want to hold my baby? If he screams again just hand him back to me."

Watching them both being catty to each other, Jeremy held back. When he looked into the gallery Paul was talking animatedly to Jeanne Pétain, holding the hand of his small son. Beth was watching the interplay between her husband and Jeanne Pétain. She had the same look on her face as Carmen, the look of a woman threatened by the proximity of her husband to an old lover. It made him smile. They were all so much the same. Jeanne had not wanted to marry Paul when he thought he wanted to marry her after she had come over from America to help Paul with the antiques business. Jeremy seemed to remember they had first met in New York when Jeanne was a commercial artist living in Brooklyn and working for a firm of interior decorators. Coming to the Nouvelle Galerie had not been such a good idea for either of them. The kid was now screaming, much to Carmen's delight, and had set off his female cousin whose pram he was sharing until Livy had picked him up. Women! Why did Livy brush him off and then behave like this when he married Carmen? How did anyone know what was really in another person's head? Twice he had travelled back to England to ask Livy to marry him. Both times she had avoided the issue, not wanting to make up her mind. Carmen had been a fling out of physical frustration. Now they were married with a screaming kid. There was no logic to any of it and probably never would be, he consoled himself. In the end he would make the best of what life brought him.

"You'd better give him to me, Livy. For some reason I calm him down."

Taking the mite with the contorted face and the powerful lungs, Jeremy walked off down the street with his son, leaving the girls who had once been friends to come to terms with reality. The man tending the barrow selling jewellery gave him a sympathetic smile.

"It only gets better, my china," said the man in a cockney accent. "I can only guess you must be Jeremy."

Giving the man a surprised look, Jeremy said nothing. So often in life people knew more about him than he knew about himself. The cockney must know Livy. She must have talked about him. By now Phillip was gurgling, looking up into his eyes. The boy smiled, making Jeremy's heart flutter with intense happiness. He had a son.

When he walked back again to the gallery ten minutes later, enough time, he hoped, for the animosity between Carmen and Livy to calm down, his wife was sitting on the bench gently moving the pram backwards and forwards to soothe the child sleeping inside. With her on the bench was Beth. Inside Jeanne and Paul were still talking.

"Business," said Beth, following his look. "All about selling country estates to Americans. Jeanne worked with Paul before she started this gallery."

Carefully, Jeremy put his son back in the pram with his cousin, their toes almost touching.

"Later in life we can have some fun telling them they slept together in the same bed," said Carmen.

"Where's Livy?"

"Inside. Some newspaperman wanted to take her photograph next to one of her paintings. I'm so happy for her she's made it. In Rhodesia she told me how much she wanted to be a painter."

"Are you two all right?"

"We'll be good friends again. It will just take time. She had a choice, Jeremy. Her painting or you. She chose her painting. You have to live with your decisions in life."

3

A week later, when Jeremy Crookshank had taken his new family back to Rhodesia and the farm he had called World's View, Tinus Oosthuizen flew out of New York on the start of his journey to fulfil the last task given to him by his uncle, Harry Brigandshaw. The flight would take him to London and Johannesburg before finally arriving in Salisbury, Rhodesia. He had left Genevieve and his two children in their three-bedroomed flat in Manhattan a short distance from the offices of Oosthuizen Inc, a company he now owned one hundred per cent. With the pressure for money coming from Harry's wife Tina after his death, and his estate being largely cleaned out by death duties paid to the British exchequer, Tinus had leveraged his minor shareholding in the American company, previously controlled by Harry Brigandshaw, with the Rosenzweig Bank and paid out the proceeds to Harry's estate. There was a good chance the income from his hundred per cent shareholding in the company would be insufficient to pay his interest to the bank but it was the chance he had to take. He was on his way to Elephant Walk. Ironically, the money he owed was due to a bank owned by Rebecca Madgwick and her Rosenzweig brothers who had inherited the Rosenzweig Bank from their father, Sir Jacob Rosenzweig, moving Rebecca and her husband out of Rhodesia to live in New York. Before the considerable inheritance of his wife, Ralph

Madgwick had been the manager of Elephant Walk, his leaving precipitating the sale of the farm to Anglo-US Incorporated by Tinus's mother. It was one thing to talk on the phone with Paul Crookshank about selling British estates to rich Americans, another to get the cash coming in to pay the bills at Brigandshaw Limited.

As the plane took off from New York, Tinus could hear the words of Harry Brigandshaw playing in his mind.

"The family is only to sell the diamond as a last resort. I'm sure it will never be necessary in your lifetime, Tinus. Tell your son Barend where it is when you're an old man. No one else in the family knows. I found the diamond in South West Africa on the Skeleton Coast during a trip with your father at the end of the First World War, after I came out of the Royal Flying Corps. By the time I found it, Barend had gone off on his own. Your father was always looking for something else. I told Anthony where to find the diamond before he was shot down over Berlin. I trust you, Tinus. Why I have made you the chief executive of my estate."

Thinking of his Uncle Harry made him smile. The disaster in his life of his father being killed had been partly overcome by the kindness of the man who had taught him how to fly an aeroplane, the reason why Tinus hated being a passenger. He was not in control. When it came to aircraft Tinus liked to be in control. Being out of the cockpit made him sweat for the first half hour of a flight.

"Have you ever flown before?" asked the American girl sitting next to him. "I could hold your hand if you're frightened. Where are you from? You have a funny accent. Heard you talking to the flight attendant when we boarded the plane. I'm Mary-Jane."

"Tinus Oosthuizen. I grew up in Rhodesia. School in Cape Town, university in England."

"Never heard of Rhodesia."

"Most people haven't."

"Where's Cape Town?"

"In South Africa."

"My, you have been around. Why are you frightened of flying? There's nothing to it. Got a better chance of killing yourself in an automobile. First time I've been out of America. Going to tour Europe."

"Hope you have fun."

"Are you married? You don't wear a ring."

"Some married men don't wear a wedding ring. I'm one of them."

"Is she nice?"

"Chances are you know of her. I'm married to Genevieve, the mother of my two children. Did you see *Robin Hood and his Merry Men*? She starred in the film with Gregory L'Amour."

"You've got to be kidding me! What happened to her? Hasn't made a film in years."

"Looking after our children. Why I'm flying alone."

"Oh gosh, it's making sense now. I read about you. Weren't you a pilot in the British air force?"

"Why I hate flying when I'm not in control. My imagination runs riot. I know what can happen."

"Are you staying in London?"

"No. I'm going on to the farm where I grew up in Rhodesia."

"Wasn't her father a lord or something? She wrote a book. My mother read it three times."

"My Uncle Harry was married to Genevieve's Aunt Lucinda, before she was killed by the same man who killed my father. How I knew Genevieve. Before she was famous."

"Do you love her?"

"More than anything in the world. A happy marriage with children is all a person can want from life."

"Then I'd better not hold your hand."

"I appreciate the offer. Now we are up and away I feel better."

"When does the bar open?"

"Right now by the look of that trolley."

"Let's have a drink together. I want to hear all about your wife."

"You're not a reporter?"

"I'm just out of college looking for a husband."

The hours of flying were always better for Tinus when he had someone to talk to. Mary-Jane was a right royal chatterbox, making the rest of the flight quite painless. They said goodbye at London airport knowing it unlikely they would ever meet again. There were many strangers in his life he had talked to in depth. Strangers were easy to talk to. There were rarely any repercussions.

For six hours, Tinus wandered around the airport knowing he should have phoned Paul Crookshank, excited about his new idea for making money. Three of his cousins were in England not far away. Tinus still considered Frank his cousin regardless of whatever surname he now called himself. It was better to get the diamond in his hand, find out its true value, before getting the family excited. In forty-six years the only person who had looked at the diamond in its resting place was his Uncle Harry. Who knows, with no one living in the old house a bush fire could have burned it to the ground, the diamond found in the sands on the Skeleton Coast lost forever. If nothing else the trip would take him back to the place he thought of as home. The home on the section of Elephant Walk where his mother and father had lived and farmed, separate from the old homesteads in the family compound, had burned in a raging bushfire that had swept Elephant Walk in the dry season soon after his father was killed with his mother moving closer to hers in the family compound.

When the flight took off for Johannesburg the sweat broke out again on his brow. This time there was no Mary-Jane sitting next to him to distract him. He watched the flaps on the wing of the aircraft move as the plane climbed up into the clouds. In his experience during the war there was mostly a cloud base over England. Unlike Elephant Walk where Uncle Harry had taught him to fly. When the drinks trolley came Tinus took a small bottle of red wine. After drinking the wine he felt better, the excitement building now he was on his way back to Africa. The lights in the cabin were dimmed. Exhausted from the tension of travelling, Tinus fell asleep with a blanket pulled up under his chin. The inside of the plane had been cold.

He woke during the night, taking a glass of orange juice from the stewardess. She was pretty and smiled at him. Tinus thought of his family now far away in New York. Barend junior, ten years old, and Hayley who was eight. Genevieve's soft voice played through his mind, soothing him back towards sleep. When the kids grew up they would all take a trip together into the African bush – unless Genevieve went back into films, bored with an empty nest. Life had so many imponderables. The plane droned on as Tinus fell fast asleep into the jumbled world of his dreams.

When he woke it was daylight, the dawn breaking down below over the emptiness of Africa, the home of his Oosthiuzen ancestors for three hundred years. Peering down out of the window made Tinus feel deliriously happy. He had been away too long.

Having boarded another plane at Johannesburg, two hours later the Tannoy told him what he wanted to hear. They were about to land at Salisbury airport. He would again smell the bush of Africa when he stepped off the plane. He was almost home.

The managing director of Anglo-US Incorporated Rhodesia was waiting for him at the checkout point after Tinus went through immigration and customs with his luggage. There was no family left on Elephant Walk to meet him, everyone having gone down south to South Africa after Anglo purchased the family estate. It was rumoured Kim Brigandshaw was somewhere in the bush but no one in the family had been able to tell Tinus where.

"I've seen every one of your wife's films, Mr Oosthuizen." The man was like a schoolboy he was so excited.

"Please call me Tinus."

"What's she like, Genevieve?"

"A good mother and wife."

"I saw *Robin Hood* three times before the war. I was a kid. *Robin Hood and his Merry Men*. Amazing how something like that can catch a boy's attention and stay with him the rest of his life."

"Where are you from, Mr Dexter?"

"Johannesburg. I joined Anglo after Wits University. We're all pretty loyal to the company. Once you join Anglo-US and do the job properly they look after you for life. Loyalty works both ways. Do you want to drive straight to Elephant Walk or drop your bags at Meikles Hotel?"

"Straight to the farm. I'm sure you're a busy man. My main concern is the staff, the people who worked for us all those years."

"We've given those under fifty contracts of employment. Those over are your responsibility. They will be entitled to stay in the compound down by the river with their families for the rest of their lives. We will maintain the roads to the village. Keep the fire-break cut round the thatched houses. Tembo is the de facto chief of the village."

"He's important to our family. Did you know his son Josiah is living in London? My uncle put him through school and Fort Hare University. My uncle and Tembo were close friends. One of the few blacks of his generation who flew in an aeroplane. What happened to Uncle Harry's First World War plane that was stored in the shed?"

"It's still there, I believe. Most of the farm equipment had been sold. You won't recognise what we have done with the place. In the end we will be irrigating twenty-four thousand acres from the Mazoe Dam. Exporting fruit, juice and oil extracted from the skins across the world. We have great hopes for our citrus estate."

"Mining is still your main occupation?"

"Gold, manganese and chrome. The Great Dyke is a storehouse of wealth for centuries to come. Diamonds and gold are our main interests in South Africa. No one has found diamonds in Rhodesia. There are rumours of emeralds but no one can find the original seam. Some of the old-timer prospectors have brought back emeralds they found washed down in the rivers. They all live in hope of finding the mother lode."

"Are the houses still standing in the family compound?"

"Until the end of next month when the two-year lease to your family runs out. They are going to be bulldozed."

"Whatever for?"

"Orange trees."

"My uncle's grave!"

"That will always be preserved as a monument to Harry Brigandshaw and his father Sebastian, even though Sebastian Brigandshaw isn't buried on the farm. Pioneers of Rhodesia. Harry a hero and legendary pilot. Their names will last as long as Cecil John Rhodes. Did you know our original mining assets belonged to Rhodes? Why Rhodesia is so important to Anglo-US. For as long as Anglo-US own the Mazoe Citrus Estate, the graveyard will be tended with reverence. Give me your bags so I can put them in the boot of the car. I like to drive myself. We don't believe in status at Anglo so we don't have chauffeurs to drive us around. Keeps our feet on the ground. Our minds on the real things of business. After you and I have tied up the last of the Brigandshaw family details I'd like to take you to dinner at the Salisbury Club."

"Most kind of you. There's a son of my uncle's somewhere in Africa. Kim Brigandshaw, the youngest of the boys."

"The one with long hair down his back? He's into religion so I hear."

"Do you know where he is?"

"Somewhere in the Congo I believe. There's going to be trouble in the Belgian Congo. The communists want to take over when the Belgians get out. You did know Josiah Makoni is a communist? I heard he's being paid by the Russians to stir up trouble in England. The Russians want to kick the colonial powers out of Africa and take it over through proxies themselves. To control the minerals. There are more raw materials for the modern world in the Congo than most places on earth. All that copper in the Katanga. Where there's potential wealth there's always trouble. If a country has nothing no one is interested. What a lovely world we live in, Mr Oosthuizen. Everybody grabbing after something."

"What's Kim doing in the Congo?"

"Heaven knows."

TWO HOURS LATER, having satisfied himself of the future viability of the thatched hut village by the river, Tinus walked back for the last time to the family compound built by Sebastian Brigandshaw and his grandfather, General Tinus Oosthuizen of Paul Kruger's Boer Republic after whom he was named. There was so much family history around him that his voice choked talking to David Dexter, making Tinus go silent with his memories. The graves of Uncle Harry, his first wife Lucinda and their unborn child were well tended. Next to them was the newer grave of his grandmother Brigandshaw.

The two of them walked from one house in the compound to another, Tinus remembering the dead members of his family vividly. Most of the doors to the houses were open, inside the rooms were empty. Everything had been taken by his mother or given to Tembo to distribute in his African village down by the river. The houses were morbidly silent. In the lounge of the first house built by Sebastian, Tinus found what he wanted. Over the fireplace, embedded in the centre just below the mantelpiece, Tinus could see a piece of stone different to the rest. The stone was black with soot from the smoking fire from all the years in its resting place. There was no sparkle whatsoever, making Tinus think his journey was not going to help Paul Crookshank after all.

"Do you mind if I take that rock embedded above the fireplace? It has family history from our past. They first put up a house here before the country became Rhodesia. There was a stockade round the grounds at the time of the Shona rebellion that came down later. So much of our history has gone with our selling you Elephant Walk. Oh, well. None of Uncle Harry's boys wanted to come out and farm in Africa. Families change."

"You take what you want, old boy."

"Are you sure?"

"We bought the land and the water in the dam. This place is coming down. Be my guest."

"You're quite sure?"

"Of course I am."

"I need a hammer and chisel to get that rock out of the chimney."

"Passmore here can get you what you want up at the office. There are tools in the storeroom next to the estate office."

They stood chatting while Passmore went off to find a hammer and chisel. They had finished their business. To amuse the man who had been so helpful, Tinus talked of his wife's friends from her days in the film business, unashamedly dropping names. By the time the hammer and chisel arrived, David Dexter was enthralled.

"What makes the rock so interesting, Tinus?"

"I'll show you."

With four heavy blows around the black rock the cement used by his Uncle Harry to embed the stone came away. The rock with bits of the chimney attached was the size of his fist. The back of the stone looked like it must have done when his Uncle Harry found it in the washed sand of the Skeleton Coast. Tinus's stomach flipped with a rush of adrenaline.

"My word, old boy. What is it?"

"A diamond."

"They don't come that big. Not even an uncut diamond. I'd guess it is quartz crystal you've got in your hand, old boy."

"It's a diamond. My uncle would not have made that kind of mistake. This is our family insurance against the time when we ran out of money. After death duty the British government didn't leave his family a hell of a lot. The previous socialist government in Britain frowned on people inheriting money."

"Where did he find it?"

"In South West Africa just after the Great War."

"If that is a diamond it's worth a fortune."

"Let's just say it's worthless until I get it to the safety of Switzerland, away from government eyes. Swiss bankers don't ask questions."

"Let me have a look. I trained in Kimberley with De Beers, the diamond arm of Anglo-US."

David Dexter licked the cleaner side of the rock with his tongue and looked at the stone carefully taking it out into the light of the sun. The man had the look of awe written on his face as the diamond sparkled in the sunlight turning a lovely blue.

"It's ice-cold. It's a diamond all right. I'll be buggered."

"Not a word."

"My lips are sealed. Just after the First World War there were no diamond concessions in South West Africa. You can do what you like with it. How long's it been stuck above the fireplace?"

"Nearly forty years. It was so obvious no one thought it could have any value. My uncle said the best place to hide anything is right out in the open."

"We'll crack a bottle of French bubbly over dinner."

"What a good idea."

"Does anyone else know?"

"Not a soul."

"What an extraordinary man he must have been."

"Have you any idea what this stone might be worth?"

"In Switzerland, you'll have to find a cutter. Or take it to Antwerp. Only when the gems are cut out of the rough diamond will you know what it is really worth. But a piss pot full of money."

WHILE TINUS WAS in Antwerp with a diamond cutter who appraised the rough diamond to see the best way of cutting the most value out of the stone and restoring the fortune of the Brigandshaw family, Livy was attending the auction at the end of the exhibition the Nouvelle Galerie had thrown for her thirtieth birthday. The gallery was crowded. Facing them on a raised platform was the auctioneer from Sotheby's. The first one to go under the hammer was *Pussy Cat*, the last bid coming in at three thousand one hundred pounds. After that it was all downhill. Her paintings went for a total of eighteen thousand seven hundred and fifty pounds, making Livy Johnston the highest-selling female artist for her age in London. She wasn't just in favour anymore with the patrons of the arts. At that price they would make sure a Livy Johnston stayed in fashion. The buyers like Barnaby St Clair, who was now wondering if he had made a financial mistake by selling too soon, were investors who expected a return on their money and now had it in their interest to keep her name in the eye of the public. In art circles they had just made her famous. Whether she had won the game of life, Livy was not so sure. Waking at night, all she could think of was Carmen with Jeremy on the new farm he had dreamed about for them for so long. Carmen in his life was an accident of copulation. Not only should Livy have been the woman next to him, it should have been her child. All the new money and fame in the world would not make up for her missing the boat. She was thirty. The bells were tolling.

She had tried a show and dinner out with Claud Gainsborough, a nice enough man and a perfect gentleman. But he was boring. All the man wanted from life was a house on Wimbledon Common with a mortgage to pay off for the rest of his working life, with the occasional visit to Cumbria and his ancestral house by the lake. Claud, tall and thin, balding and pale, wanted a home with a family where he would happily spend his days. He liked going to the office. He even said over supper he liked cutting lawns, provided the lawn wasn't too big. Everything about the man was a complete contrast to the suntanned, broad-shouldered athletic Jeremy Crookshank now with his six thousand acres of farm.

"You must feel so pleased with yourself, Livy," said Tessa when the auctioneer stepped down from the dais.

"I'm going to the loo to be sick."

"Are you pregnant?"

"I wish I was. We were going to have a dozen kids."

"Oh, you're back to Jeremy."

"You don't get love out of money, Tessa."

"That may be true, but it lasts a lot longer if you have enough of it. With what you have made today you can go out and buy yourself a house, plonking down cash, not a financial worry for the rest of your life. Love is fickle. Comes and goes. Now you got it now you don't. That money you got today is real. Be thankful. Enjoy it. Forget about Jeremy. You know your trouble, Livy? It's the fact he married your friend. That Carmen has got what you didn't want. If he'd married a stranger he'd have drifted out of your mind. A fond memory of a happy time gone past. Don't dwell on it. Enjoy your success. My God, so few of us get it. Especially in the field of art... Frank's coming over. Smile. Walter Featherstone-Wallace is looking at you, beaming all over his face. Be happy. Forget Jeremy. He was yesterday's man. From now on you can take your pick of the best."

"I had the best."

"I give up. Nothing in life is perfect, Livy. Just some of its bits."

4

---

*A*t the same time Livy was helping to take down her paintings at the end of the two-week exhibition for return to their owners, Tinus, across the English Channel in Antwerp, was having his own problems, the words of David Dexter ringing the alarm bells in his head.

"Be careful who you do business with in the diamond trade, Tinus," David Dexter had said during their celebratory dinner at the Salisbury Club, a dinner as much to cement the final handover of Elephant Walk as it was to talk about the uncut diamond firmly in Tinus's pocket. "Don't let the rough diamond out of your sight, or the stones when the cutter turns your rock into gemstones. The value of a diamond varies tremendously on its colour, cut and size of the stones. More money is made taking the stone forward from its uncut state than selling the rough stone. De Beers controls eighty per cent of the rough diamonds in the world from our mines in Kimberley and South West Africa, together with our agreements with most of the independent mines in the world. You can either take that stone to the De Beers head office in Kimberley where you will receive a fair price for your rough stone, or you take it out of Africa to a cutter as you intend and sell the cut stones direct to the jewellery trade. You'll find they'll try to cut out one big stone with the rest falling in smaller pieces. You will find considerable interest in the big stone as a gemstone that size is so rare. Think of the Star of Africa in

the British Crown Jewels. Your job is to get the stone cut without the
cutter substituting inferior stones. You know nothing about diamonds so
be careful. They'll have big smiles on their faces when they see an
innocent with a stone like that. You've got to stay with your cutter while
he cuts out your stones. Then let the trade know what you have and sit
back in your Antwerp hotel and wait for the buyers. To control the flow
of gemstones to the market De Beers has what we call 'sights'. Usually
every two or three months in Antwerp depending on the market. Cecil
Rhodes, when he owned De Beers, knew the importance of a closed
market to regulate the price of diamonds on the market. Why he bought
out Barney Barnato and the rest of the diamond diggers in the Kimberley
mine to set up his monopoly. The Russians sell their diamonds outside
our consortium but they don't have enough to disturb the market. We
have huge stocks of diamonds in our vaults that if offered to the market
in one fell swoop would make most women's engagement rings
worthless. We have to live up to our advertising by controlling the flow of
gemstones to supply the manufacturing jewellers with what they need
and never more. At our 'sights' we try to offer them just what they need
in size and colour, never to flood the market. It's in all our interests. The
diamond miners. The cutters. The manufacturing jewellers. The retail
shops up and down Bond Street and Fifth Avenue. Remember our
slogan: 'A diamond is forever'."

"How do I let the market know I have a large stone that hasn't been
stolen?"

"Ask them to phone me if they have any doubts about your integrity.
The cutter will let the word out. The story of what you have in your
pocket will go round Antwerp like a wildfire, you mark my words. Before
you hand over the big stone get a bank-guaranteed cheque in your hand
and then take it to Switzerland. The Swiss won't ask any questions. It's
how they have built up their country."

"Isn't all this illegal?"

"How right is a majority government to pass a law taking eighty per
cent of Harry Brigandshaw's estate just because the few with so much
wealth are in such a minority? That's legalised theft however you look at
it, however morally right the socialists talk about the redistribution of
wealth. Governments, when they get other people's hard-earned money,
piss most of it up against the wall in a desperate effort to keep themselves

in power. Robin Hood had a nice idea of robbing the rich and giving it to the poor. I have no problem with helping the poor as much as possible. The trouble is, after too many robberies there aren't any people left with the knowledge and energy to make the money and we all go down the drain together. People with the ability to make wealth are much rarer than politicians. This is me talking, Tinus. Not my company. In business you do the best you can within the bounds of law. Put your money in a numbered account in Switzerland as the clever Jews did before the war. You've got to be smart to hold on to your money. Look what happened to the Jews who didn't get themselves and their money out of Nazi Germany! In the trade what you are doing is perfectly legal. You have a gemstone and wish to sell it. What you do with the money afterwards is none of their business. Or none of the business of the British government, if you want my opinion. I think Harry Brigandshaw knew exactly what he was doing when he hid that stone now resting safely in your pocket. If he hadn't, the British government would have taken most of it, laughing all the way to their bank. You have to think in this world to survive. To let your children survive. Didn't Charles Darwin call it the survival of the fittest? You've got a chance of legally going round the system. Good luck... Now, how about a cognac to end our evening? Talking about Genevieve to her husband has really made my day. *Robin Hood*! It was all so romantic. The reality of life is a lot more ugly."

WITH THE LAST of her paintings off the walls of the gallery, Frank asked Livy to go out to supper. The night, as he put it, was still young. Success, even Livy's success, made Frank horny.

"Why not, Frank? Everyone else is happy."

"Not my father. Says he sold short."

"Let's get off the subject of money."

"Money, my successful girl, is irrelevant when you have it. Just try running short so you don't have food or a roof over your head. What are you going to do with your money when you get what's left of it?"

"What do you mean?"

"The gallery takes forty per cent but that isn't the end of your woes. All that money earned in one year puts Livy Johnston into the highest tax bracket. You'll be paying supertax after tonight. At the very top, the

British government will be taking eighteen and six pence in the pound of your money."

"That's not fair. It's taken me years living in a one-roomed studio to get where I got tonight. Ten years of work. They can't consider what I get tonight income earned in one year."

"Oh yes they will. And there is no point in arguing. You can never argue with the government."

"So I can't finally buy myself a house?"

"We'll see how much is left. With what my father invested of your earlier sales you should have enough."

"All that work for the bloody government."

"Something like that. It's the same for all of us. Death and taxes. Paul Crookshank had a phone call from Cousin Tinus this afternoon. From Antwerp. Tinus says he's found the answer to Paul's problems in Harry Brigandshaw's old house on Elephant Walk. There was a diamond the size of a duck's egg embedded in the top of the fireplace in the lounge. Whatever next? Anyone but Tinus I'd say was talking bullshit. He's far too crafty. You know my luck, Livy. Now I'll get an income from the Brigandshaw estate by the sound of it. I've changed my name to St Clair but I'm still a beneficiary of the estate after mother's somewhat expensive needs are taken care of. One fifth of the income and when Mum dies one fifth of the estate. I get it both ways. Father has made me sole heir to his estate. He doesn't have anyone else to leave his money to. Frankly, with my PR company doing so well I don't need their money... Kim will be happy. So will Dorian. Those dreadful books of his can't go on selling forever. Paul will be able to buy back his piano. Afford himself a car."

"How much does your cousin expect the diamond to be worth?"

"In his own words, Livy, 'a piss pot full of money'. He flew over to Europe some days ago."

A WEEK later Tinus took himself to the cinema. He was lonely and missed his family. The sound of treble voices and happy children. The smile of Genevieve's face when she looked at him.

The film in English with French subtitles was his wife's second film with Gregory L'Amour, *Keeper of the Legend*, the story of her early ancestors in England written by her uncle, Robert St Clair. She was as he first remembered her when they met up again at Oxford for the first time. She had been with Gregory L'Amour. He could still see her in his mind's eye under the trees by the river, their eyes meeting, understanding each other. They both said now they knew then they were going to be together. Then the war had made Genevieve shy away from marrying a pilot and potentially finding herself a widow.

Settling back in his seat with a bar of good Belgian chocolate, Tinus prepared to enjoy himself. The cinema was only half-full for a film made nearly twenty years ago. Then she was there up on the screen, making the frustration of the previous week seep out of him and leaving only happiness.

The Belgium cutter had the eyes of a ferret. Tinus had never seen so much greed in a man's eyes when he produced the rock, black on one side from the fire and coated in old cement. The man only spoke broken English but that did not matter. They were talking diamonds, a language both of them understood. Ferret-eyes was the fifth cutter Tinus had been to see. The others all wanted to keep the rock so they could decide how to do the cutting. There was a great skill required in the cutting if the largest diamond with the largest number of carats was to be had from the rough stone. They all told Tinus how difficult it was in detail. The first man had asked him to come back again the next day with the stone, after he had made a phone call to David Dexter in Rhodesia. There was nothing open about the business of cutting diamonds. When the man wanted to keep the rock, Tinus left his office. There were many diamond cutters in Antwerp. The fifth man, the little man with the ferret eyes, had agreed to do the cutting in front of him, Tinus taking away the work-in-progress every evening and bringing it back the next morning. After the first call to Rhodesia, Tinus suspected the word had gone round the closed diamond industry that was Antwerp. In two more days, the man with the ferret eyes said he would have finished cutting the big stone, the smaller side pieces from the cutting of no interest to him. The man said it was the biggest diamond he had ever seen. Without putting the word out to anyone, buyers were calling on Tinus at his hotel. They would all be given a chance of looking at the cut diamond when it was finished, putting in their bid. Tinus was going to hold a one-day 'sight' for the single diamond on the Wednesday up in the room of his hotel. They had all been warned of the need for a bank-guaranteed cheque from a reputable bank. Tinus told them the work-in-progress was locked in the vault of Le Banque de l'Indochine, the French bank of Indo-China. In fact, Tinus kept all the pieces in his pocket, the door of his room locked at night.

As he ate the chocolate with one hand he could feel the big, almost-cut diamond in his trouser pocket right next to his balls. All three made him happy. The chocolate in his mouth, the diamond next to his balls and his wife's face up on the screen.

When he left to go back to his hotel, no one in the cinema any the wiser, he took a bottle of Scotch whisky up to his room. Tomorrow was another boring day watching the cutter. He would not have to think. A hangover wouldn't matter.

He was almost home. One more flight to Geneva to deposit the cheque from the highest bidder and across to London for the night before flying home across the pond to his family, once more Uncle Harry's fortune back where it belonged.

On the Wednesday morning, his brain sharp and free of any trace of alcohol, Tinus placed the fifty-nine carat white diamond on the coffee table in the room of his hotel and waited. He had said his 'sight' was open for business at nine o'clock in the morning. The diamond was exceptionally beautiful, something he would have liked to show Genevieve.

They came all morning, peering at and into the stone through the lens screwed into their right eyes. Each wrote down a price and placed it with their company's names and phone number in a sealed envelope. The pile grew through the day. At five, when the bidding closed, Tinus opened the envelopes. When the man who had bid two million three hundred and fifty thousand pounds came back with a cheque on the Union Bank of Switzerland, guaranteed by the bank, Tinus gave him the diamond. They shook hands. It was all over except for depositing the cheque.

At five-thirty, Tinus left for the airport, arriving in Geneva in time for a late supper at his hotel. The buyer had given him the name of the hotel. The buyer had seemed very pleased with himself.

In the morning, Tinus took a taxi to the offices of the Union Bank of

Switzerland where he opened a numbered account, depositing the cheque. It was all over in half an hour. There was no interest to be earned on the account. Just the security, and the anonymity from prying eyes. From the account he could send money anywhere in the world by making a phone call. He had to give them two words known only to himself and the bank and the number of the account.

"Only give the two words to the trustees, Mr Oosthuizen. Along with the number of the account now in the name of your uncle's estate. We will never divulge this information to anyone. Have a good flight back to America."

The two words were Elephant Walk. The farm that had originally belonged to the Brigandshaws and the Oosthuizens would live on in the name that controlled the money from the diamond left by Harry Brigandshaw embedded below the mantelpiece above the fire in the lounge. After making a call to Paul Crookshank from the bank manager's office, Tinus took a taxi to the airport.

At London airport, Paul Crookshank was waiting for him.

"You've saved our lives, Tinus."

"Not me, Paul. It was Beth's father who saved the family fortune. We have a lot to talk about before I fly back to New York. Now we have some capital, we can look properly at the estate business. Ridgeback cigarettes are over. We lost out on that one."

"How do we get the money to Brigandshaw Limited without anyone finding out where it came from?"

"We borrow our own money without paying interest. They know exactly how to handle it in Switzerland. Why the Swiss are so dominant in banking. You will know the code along with Uncle Harry's solicitors. The three trustees."

"They're all coming to dinner tonight. Dorian had come up from Cornwall. Frank wants all the details. Kim won't be there, of course. We don't know where he is... Beth wants to know if I can buy a company car?"

"Of course you can. And your salary goes back to what it was before you closed down Ridgeback Cigarettes."

"The major will be happy. Said he was bored doing nothing. All we needed was some capital to get ourselves off the ground."

"Always costs money to start a worthwhile business. Where are we going now?"

"To the office by train and Tube."

"Right. You do need a car."

"How are you, Tinus?"

"As you see me. On top of the world."

Livy came to the Brigandshaw family reunion with Frank, the new money bringing them all together. Everyone was full of smiles. Dorian, who wrote books, had the biggest smile of the lot of them. Frank thought it amusing. For some reason Paul seemed surprised to see her. She thought he deliberately kept his brother Jeremy out of the conversation. The whole evening was going to be about money and what they were going to do with it.

How a rock pulled from the sea could be worth so much money to mankind was beyond Livy's comprehension. There was far more in looking at a painting than looking at a diamond hung round some old bag's scrawny neck. The only time Livy had seen expensive diamonds was on old women, the wives of the patrons of the Nouvelle Galerie after their husbands had used the young female artists for more than their paintings. Why, she asked herself, if it wasn't out of guilt or to impress a young woman with how much money they had, did a man spend so much money on something so useless as a piece of jewellery? You couldn't eat it. It did not talk back like a good painting. It sat there looking rich... The human race never stopped amazing her. Most of the people she had met through her life were all about possessions. Like Frank. He used money to impress people. To show them how good he was in business. Jeremy had wanted his farm for the love of creating something. Making it bloom. She painted to capture a field or a tree, the face of a person. To create something from her vision of life that would communicate with other people. Neither her nor Jeremy's desires had had anything to do with wealth. She wanted to create her paintings. He wanted to create a flourishing farm out of the African soil. To make something out of his life. She hoped Carmen appreciated what he was doing. Not like her friend from the boat, now Mrs Pamela Crumpshaw, who Livy knew was more interested in her status married to a rich farmer than the farm. Pamela had wanted to bask in the glory of her husband. It was all about her and how clever she was to have found herself a wealthy husband.

Poor old Roger, she thought, as she sat down to dinner with the rest of them. There was always a price to pay for everything. Feeling out of it and not wishing to get in, Livy let them run on, talking to each other all about money. Then it was small talk. Watching Cousin Tinus, she suspected he was bored. Especially when Frank monopolised the conversation, telling them all how little he really needed the new money Cousin Tinus had just put back in the family. She watched them like a spectator. Smiling when she was meant to smile. Drinking her wine. Hoping Paul would talk about Jeremy. Knowing with certainty she had missed the boat. She was going to be a rich old maid painting pictures all by herself, growing old.

PART VII

DECEMBER 1957 – "WILL YOU MARRY ME?"

1

*C*armen Crookshank, who was Carmen Crossley when she lived with Mrs Wade and first met Livy, was bored out of her mind. Why, she asked herself, had she deliberately got herself pregnant the first time, let alone the second? All her romantic ideas of peacefully looking up at the African stars for the rest of her life was a reality she would gladly exchange for the roar of London's traffic. Even her mother had never warned her of the boredom of marriage. There was nothing wrong with Jeremy, except he was never there, going out into the lands with the rising sun, coming back when it set. Her problem was boredom. No one visited, the farms were too far apart. Once a month if she was lucky, she went into town in the truck, spending the day tearing around Salisbury doing the shopping, then fighting the dirt road with its loose sand for three hours to get back. In Carmen's life there was no longer any fun. No one to flirt with. No one to make her feel wanted. Often at night, Jeremy was too tired for sex, falling asleep the moment his head hit the pillow. So she stopped being careful and got herself pregnant.

There were seventeen working farms in the new tobacco block they called the Centenary, spread over fifty miles. There was talk of a sports club. Of a cricket field, tennis courts and a clubhouse. Just none of the farmers had time to start the buildings and stop most of the wives going out of their minds.

"Livy knew what she was doing staying in England," she said to the cat. "What the hell made me want to get married? I must have been out of my mind."

The cat didn't even look at her.

Phillip was out on the lawn under the shade of a tree, asleep in his pram, watched over by his nanny. Carmen had absolutely nothing to do.

"Where the hell is everybody?" she screamed. "I want a life." She listened to the grandfather clock strike the hour, counting the chimes while she looked out the window. It was beginning to rain. The nanny had got up from where she had been sitting on the grass. The old clock had belonged to Jeremy's father who had gone down with his sailboat off the coast of Dunkirk. Jeremy's mother had given them the clock as a wedding present. The chimes kept banging into her head until they reached eleven. She watched the nanny push Phillip in his pram out of the rain. The boy had not woken up.

Before the noonday chime her waters broke. It was still dropping big drops of scattered rain outside. The cat had not moved from the windowsill. The nanny was in the kitchen feeding Phillip. The girl came in from the kitchen and saw what had happened, shouting something in Shona to the gardener outside.

Carmen waited. Her contractions were far apart. If this one was anything like Phillip it would be hours in coming. There was still time if the gardener knew where Jeremy was working. The clock struck twelve and again she counted. The cat was looking at her. Sitting on the couch in the lounge, Carmen watched the big hand on the grandfather clock tick by the minutes, the hand jerking when it moved up a minute. She had no idea how far Jeremy was working from the house. She listened for the sound of the car's engine. When it came, her heart beat faster with relief. The contractions were still far apart. The truck was driving fast by the sound of the engine. Outside, the rain was coming down hard.

When Jeremy came into the house he was soaked to the skin, his wide-brimmed bush-hat dripping with rain.

"Into the truck with you, Carmen." Jeremy was smiling.

"What about the rain?"

"We'll get across the drifts. Driven in worse weather than this. My word, the farm needs the rain. How are you feeling?"

"What about Phillip?"

"I've asked the girl to look after him until I get back. They'll be all right. Come on, old girl. Time for number two. I'm going to back the truck up to the kitchen door and load a mattress."

"Why the hell did I ever leave London?"

"This is much more fun. Well before the sun goes down you'll be in the maternity ward of the Lady Chancellor."

When they got under way, Carmen could barely see thirty yards down the road. They travelled at thirty miles an hour.

THE TIME between her contractions shortened. A kudu ran down the road in front of them, the big horns held up high. The animal veered into the bush. Carmen could hear the pounding of the rain above the noise of the engine.

"It's a bit of a bugger. Never rained so hard before. We'll let the rain ease up and then go on. How are you feeling, Carmen?"

"Bloody frightened. Where are we?"

"Out of the Centenary block and into the Tribal Trust Lands."

"Is there anyone around?"

"The few villages are far off the road. They'll all be in their mud huts away from the rain."

"If the rain doesn't stop?"

"We'll get into the back of the truck. Why I put in the mattress. Rain goes in Africa as fast as it comes."

"Do we know what we're doing, Jeremy?"

"I hope so. Just keep yourself calm. Being all het up won't do the baby any good."

"Phillip's alone with that girl."

"She loves Phillip. In the bush we have to help each other. Do you want a cigarette?"

"I put a bottle of gin and a bottle of whisky in my overnight bag."

"Clever girl... Wow. Can it rain?"

"We won't get swept away?"

"Not up here. We're on the crest of the ridge. Are you still having contractions?"

"Of course I am. Get me the gin bottle."

Surprisingly, they both laughed. Carmen smoked her cigarette. They both drank from the neck of the bottle. Inside the truck they were dry.

"This is kind of fun," said Carmen. "Something to tell the little bugger when he grows up."

"That's the spirit. Life always goes on."

"The gin tastes good."

"So does the whisky. The gin will make you relax. If we can't get over that river down there we'll climb in the back of the truck. Cheers, old girl."

WHILE CARMEN WAS GIVING birth to her second son in the back of the truck sedated by the gin, Jeremy cutting the umbilical cord with his hunting knife, Kim Brigandshaw was watching the sun go down on the banks of the Chobe River, four hundred miles to the west. He was comfortably seated in a camping chair outside the tents, drinking his sundowner whisky. The American wildlife photographer had gone off with Tembo to look for an evening shot of animals coming down to the river to drink. The Bechuanaland bush around Kim was tinder-dry. Behind his chair a foraging elephant had pushed the small riverine tree on its side to forage the leaves at the top. There was a pack of baboons in the tree in front of him, the smallest of the monkeys making Kim smile as they peered briefly round the branches of the tree to look at him. Karen Sanderson, also American, had stayed in camp. She was twenty-four years old and a newspaper reporter. They were taking photographs and writing an article for *National Geographic* magazine. Kim had a .375 rifle next to his chair.

Behind them, Kim heard the American Parker Hirsch returning. The two African servants were lighting the fires. Within half an hour the darkness would fall. Karen was pretty, dressed in her khaki safari suit. The two Americans had flown in to the small bush airport ten miles from the Victoria Falls the previous day, Kim meeting them with the two Land Rovers loaded with camping equipment.

Not far down from the airport they had driven out of Southern Rhodesia into the British Protectorate of Bechuanaland, camping sixty miles from the falls where the wildlife was prolific.

"Get any good shots, old boy?"

Kim did not get up. One of the servants handed the American a glass of whisky. There was ice in the whisky from the Victoria Falls Hotel, Kim having filled up the ice box before going to the airport.

"Cheers, old boy."

"You English know how to live in the bush."

"Of course we do."

"Did your grandfather roam these parts?"

"Probably. There weren't colonial boundaries in 1887 when Grandfather first came to Africa."

"Lucky man. All this to himself."

Tembo had gone off on his own down to the river. There was a shot, followed by a second blast of the twelve-bore shotgun.

Tembo came back with two dead birds he had shot out of the tree down by the river where they had gone up to roost.

"Guinea fowl," said Kim.

"Are we going to eat those?" said Karen.

"Best bird flesh in the world, old girl. The chaps will pluck and roast them over the campfire. You'll see. Just pretend we bought them from the butcher. We only kill what we eat."

"How many copies of *White Hunter* has your brother Dorian sold?"

"Couple of million I was told by Cousin Tinus. What irony. His fortune was based on ivory, and then to be killed by the Great Elephant."

"It was a good book," said Karen. "I want to know everything about him for my article."

"Ask Tembo. Knows far more than me. He grew up with my father on Elephant Walk. His ancestor's village was destroyed by a Matabele impi. The Zulu raiding party had taken the cattle and young girls, killing the rest. My grandfather saved some of the young boys, Tembo's kin."

The colours of the sunset had turned a crimson red, reflected in the surface of the river. One of the servants gave Tembo a clay pot filled with white maize beer Tembo had brewed himself. At the second fire nearer the river Tembo sat down to drink his beer.

"Can you tell us about Sebastian Brigandshaw, Tembo?"

The black man looked round at Karen and pretended he did not understand. Kim smiled.

"Can you speak his language, Kim?"

"Of course not, I grew up in England... Let's have some more to drink while the birds are cooking."

"I wish I had written *White Hunter*," said Karen.

"Dorian had trouble writing the book. Why he wrote that other stuff. He first wrote the story of my grandfather as a novel. Didn't work, so he said. Dorian spent weeks with my grandmother getting the details down in his notebook before she died."

"Made your grandfather famous in America. So that man's family he saved from Lobengula's impi? My word. Now I really want to talk to him. I want to sell an article on Sebastian Brigandshaw to the *New York Times*. How do I get Tembo to talk?"

"He'll talk when he gets to know you, Karen. Speaks perfectly good English. Ask him about his son Josiah. A real firebrand is Josiah. Believes in independence for his fellow Africans from colonial rule."

"Good for him," said Parker Hirsch.

"He's a communist, Parker. They don't like Americans."

Tembo had looked round at the mention of his son.

"Colonialism isn't right whatever the colour of your politics," said Parker.

"You're probably right. Doesn't worry me. I'm only in Rhodesia at the request of my Cousin Tinus. Wanted to give me something to do. Why we set up the safari company after the book on my grandfather stirred up so much interest. I don't involve myself with politics. Learnt that trick with a lot of others in Bhutan when I was living in a Buddhist monastery. They believe in doing good deeds, not self-serving politics that often as not ends up hurting people. I'm sure Josiah's heart is in the right place. We all want to change the way of the world when we're young. Usually nothing changes except the people at the top."

"What's your profession?" asked Karen.

"I don't have one. I take life as it comes. Why I agreed to this job when Tinus found me in Zanzibar."

"What were you doing in Zanzibar?"

"Looking for a free berth on a boat back to England. Work my passage. Ran out of money up in the Congo hanging out with the drunks. There are white drunks in the bars all over Africa. They get away with it because they are English or Belgian. One was an American in Elizabethville. That's where there's all that copper in Katanga province.

There will be a fight over that from what I heard. Tinus said to phone him in New York when I got into trouble. I've been roaming the world on my own since I came out of the Royal Air Force. National Service. Only real job I've ever had, I suppose. Spent time on a ranch outside Milo in Kansas. Sheep farm in Australia. I'm a drifter, Karen."

"This isn't a bad place to drift to, if you ask me." She was looking down to the river between the trees. "Ever had a girlfriend?"

"There was a Chinese girl in Singapore. I can still see her face."

Instinctively, at the memory of the girl in the bar, Kim put his hand up to the right side of his face. After the plastic surgery the visible scar had mostly gone where the man had cut his face. Underneath the grafted skin the cut still throbbed when he thought about the girl.

"What's the matter with your face?"

"An old wound. Mental more than physical. I never saw her again. When I came back to the bar from the doctor who stitched up my face she was gone. Strange how a face can stay with you for so long. That fight in the bar was years ago... Drifting around the bars in the world has its dangers... Who wants another drink? Isn't that sunset over the river magnificent?"

"Drifters like you fascinate me," said Karen.

"Thank you. I'm glad I can be of interest."

"Living in an apartment between four walls and working as a journalist in an office is so different. You must have learnt so much."

"It's not a good idea to get too wise too young. You don't want to comprehend the imperfections of your fellow man far away from home, and drunk people have the bad habit of telling you the truth, about themselves and about you. Reality is often not very pretty."

"How long is this job going to last?"

"As long as I want it to, which usually isn't very long."

"Don't you want to settle down and have your own family?"

"Not really. Married with kids you have to conform. Do what society dictates. Do what your wife and kids want you to do. You can't be selfish anymore when you're married."

"You never met anyone you really fancied?"

"Only the Chinese girl."

"Are you serious? A girl in a bar?"

"It was the way she looked at me. Drowning in her own gaze."

"Did you talk to her?"

"I can't speak Mandarin or any Chinese dialect. You can bullshit with words. Tell people what they want to hear to get what you want. That look was genuine."

"How old were you?"

"Twenty-one."

"Before you became just a little cynical."

"Facing the truth isn't cynical, Karen... Tembo. Be a good chap and come and talk to the lady about my grandfather. She wants to write an article. You can bring over your pot of beer. You should both try Tembo's home brew. More like a soup if you ask me, but it's delicious. Something of an acquired taste. Gets you pissed as a newt."

BY THE TIME the guinea fowl had roasted it was pitch-dark. There was no moon, just layer after layer of stars in the heavens. Away from the light of the two fires Kim could see deep into the universe. He had left the Americans talking to Tembo and walked down to the water's edge. The stars in the heaven reflected in the slow-moving surface of the river. On both sides of Kim, animals were drinking at the river. All of them had their own business to do, taking no notice of each other. Kim had left his gun by the fire. It was important to look as though he was protecting the paying clients. Protecting himself did not matter. They were all animals drinking at the river.

They were talking quietly behind him, Parker having swapped his whisky for a bowl of beer. Tembo had refused the American's offer of a glass of whisky. Listening to Tembo's stories of his father and grandfather made Kim feel hollow. Elephant Walk had been sold. The Brigandshaws, father to son, no longer had a home in Africa. If his life had been different, Kim would have lived in Africa. Become part of the bush. His short while working on Elephant Walk, supervising the labour in the lands, had not caught his imagination as much as the bush. Being one with the animals... Maybe one day he would settle down far away from people to find peace with the world and himself.

Looking back, Kim could see the two servants crouched over the roasting fire by the soft light of the coals. The other fire was burning bright, showing him Karen's face. She was looking down in his direction.

They each had their own tents to sleep in. Kim wondered what was going to happen.

The plop of the fish out in the river brought him back to the present. When a lion roared over in the direction of Northern Rhodesia, Kim thought of his gun by the fire. He was hungry. He could smell the birds cooking. Night birds were calling from the riverine trees up and down both banks of the Chobe River. The trees took water from the river, not having to wait for the rains.

Kim slowly walked back to the fire. Karen smiled at him. She was very pretty. Bending down at the ice box, Kim filled his glass up with ice. Then he poured in the whisky. Right to the top. The lion roared again. Karen was writing in her notebook by the light of the fire. The khaki shirt was pressing on the nipple of her right breast, reminding Kim how long it had been since his last woman. He noticed Parker was also looking at her nipple. When their eyes met, Kim could see Parker thought he was competition. They were part of the animal kingdom in more ways than one.

Taking his drink, he walked up to the fire and raised his glass to Parker.

"Cheers, old boy."

"Was that a lion?" asked Karen.

"There are two of them," said Tembo. "A male and a female. The female hunts for the male. He was telling her to get his supper... I get the other rifle from the Land Rover," he said to Kim.

"Thank you, Tembo... What a perfect night. Just look up at all those stars."

IN THE MIDDLE of the night, Karen crept into his tent. They could both hear Parker snoring. Outside the animals were quiet, the fires burning. Only the owls were hooting. She had taken off her safari suit before getting into the tent. Without a word they made love. Without a word Karen left. Both of them were satisfied.

In the morning neither of them looked at each other to say they remembered. Tembo had caught bream from the river. The frying pans were on the fire cooking the fish.

"Everyone slept all right?" asked Kim.

"That beer of Tembo's knocked me out. I was going to get up with the dawn and take more photographs."

"There's plenty of time, Parker."

Kim took his first cup of morning coffee from one of the servants. He felt good. Relaxed. The old wound in his face was not throbbing. With the coffee he walked down to the river. The river was beautiful.

THE TRACK along the river turned south into the mopane forest. It was a slow drive. Among the trees there was water from the earlier rain, the rain flushing out holes in the dirt track, the surrounding bush tinder-dry. There were thunder clouds coming down from the direction of Angola as they drove through the trees. Kim thought it was going to rain. Both Land Rovers had a winch on the front. All the time they saw game. Kim was driving with Parker, Karen with Tembo. Parker had the camera with the long telephoto lens on his lap, his eyes searching the trees. The sun was hot. Above the vehicle the tsetse flies could be heard circling above the sound of the engine. It was important not to be bitten by the tsetse fly. The mosquitoes carried malaria, the tsetse sleeping sickness. For Kim it was all part of the challenge of Africa.

Soon after Karen had left to go back to her own tent, the lion had roared not far from their camp. In the morning Kim had found an area of crushed tall grass away from the fires that the servants kept burning all night. Kim had not told his guests an elephant had slept the night not a hundred yards from their tents. There wasn't any point in photographing a patch of crumpled grass. Tembo had found where the elephant slept and shown it to Kim.

Tembo spotted the leopard in the trees an hour after they had stopped for lunch. The animal had yellow eyes. Parker spent half an hour taking photographs while the animal looked at him. The leopard was resting high in the fork of a tree. The leopard only hunted at night, or so Tembo told them. Kim was not so sure. He rather thought the animal had eaten recently. During the day the lions slept in the long grass only bringing up their heads to look at the Land Rovers. Most often there were elephant and black rhinoceros in the small glades between the forests of mopane trees.

When Parker had taken enough photographs of the leopard they drove on. The leopard had not moved from the fork of the tree. The leopard was king.

That night they camped among the mopane trees. Tembo made the servants bring up large quantities of firewood. He wanted a bonfire all night among the trees. They cut the long elephant grass around the fire to stop the flames spreading into the bush. Tembo had swapped his shotgun for a rifle. Always the rifle was close.

The light went fast among the trees, shrinking their world to the campfire. Seven people, three tents and the Land Rovers. Tembo and the servants preferred sleeping under the stars. When Karen said she was safe from the animals inside her tent, Tembo looked amused. Tembo had shot a small buck when they stopped for lunch, before he had spotted the leopard. The servants had gutted and skinned the animal.

While they drank their sundowner whisky still with ice from the Victoria Falls Hotel, the venison roasted over the cooking fire, the coals fed by the servants from the bigger fire intended to keep off the predator animals. A hyena, Tembo explained, could bite through a man's leg... Tembo was enjoying himself. He had told Kim on a previous trip it was all part of the African experience for the white people who lived in the big cities, his son Josiah told him on his brief visits home. That night Karen kept to herself, Kim sleeping right through the night. They ate cold venison for breakfast with their coffee.

For three days Kim took the Americans through the Okavango swamps. They hired dugout canoes to go out into the swamps from a local fisherman.

On the fourth day they drove into Crocodile Camp, Kim's home base, ten miles out of Maun. Crocodile Camp was on the southernmost extremity of the swamps. The Americans had had enough of the bush, wanting a good shower. Neither of them had wanted to swim in the crystal-clear water of the swamps for fear of the crocodiles. All of them had been bitten by insects. They were happy, laughing, talking about their experience now it was over. In forty-eight hours they would be back in New York. There was a light aircraft field on the outskirts of Maun, the only village of any size near the swamps. Karen was looking at Kim now they were going to part. She looked quizzical. Slightly amused. Kim kept his eyes away from her. Parker, the paying customer, was jealous. The safari was almost over. Kim would be unlikely to reappear in her life, unlike Parker Hirsch. Kim wondered if Karen had used him to get Parker's attention. Parker was a famous photographer. Karen was an unknown writer who wrote the captions of Parker's photographs in the *National Geographic* magazine. Unless the article she was writing on his grandfather was published by the *New York Times*, giving her a byline and making her famous. Then she would not need Parker so much. Kim thought people not very different to the animals. Among all the animals in the kingdom there were predators wanting their own way.

Tembo went off to see his youngest wife who had come to Maun to live with him. Princess was the mother of Josiah. The three other wives had stayed in the village Harry Brigandshaw had left to them on the Mazoe Citrus Estate with the help of Tinus Oosthuizen. Seeing Tembo go off to his wife made Kim think of his family in England. He was going home for Christmas, to stay at Hastings Court with his half-brother Frank whose father now owned the estate. He would see Tinus, instead of talking on the phone. Then he would decide whether to come back to Africa. Kim was always looking for something new in his life. Rather like Karen, he smiled to himself. They had both satisfied each other, Kim thought, which was what life was all about. There was nothing permanent. Just moments in time.

"I'm coming on the plane with you to Johannesburg," he told them. "Did you get everything you wanted?"

"Yes, thank you," said Karen. "Everything. That trip was an experience. One I won't forget in a hurry. Africa is so wild. If I can't sell what I dug out of Tembo I'll eat my hat. What a life that man has lived, being part of both worlds... I wonder what will happen to Africa?"

"My father wasn't too sure there is going to be a happy ending. Clash of cultures. If you ask me, living by the side of an African river in a mud hut beats London any day. Or New York. In the cities we are so insular. So enclosed in our own prefabricated world. City life is artificial. The nearest Parker's readers will get to seeing an animal like that leopard is looking at his photographs. It can never be real to them. Those two worlds are too far apart."

"There are many compensations living in New York," said Karen. "A good restaurant. Good company. Theatre that makes you think. In the bush everything is what you see, never in your mind. I like to think the conscious mind of man has left the world of animals and become something apart. That there is a purpose for my life, not just day-to-day living ending with death. There has to be more otherwise what is the purpose in life?"

"Man's been trying to find the answer to that ever since he came down from the trees. Where all the religions came from. Don't you think we just might be kidding ourselves that our souls are somehow immortal?... My father loved Africa. He would have spent all his life here were it not for my mother... An hour before the flight, Tembo is coming back to drive us to the airfield. There's a bar in the camp overlooking the edge of the swamps. Three hours to spare. More characters came into that bar than I ever met in the Congo. And that's saying something. Not a New York restaurant, Karen, but we do our best. Let's go and enjoy ourselves. Your work is over. You can relax. Savour your trip. Take a long last look across the Okavango Delta where the Okavango River sinks below the African earth."

2

They both asked Livy to spend Christmas; Frank Brigandshaw with his family at Hastings Court, Claud Gainsborough with his mother by the lake in Cumberland. Her lover, and her friend. Frank's brother Kim was flying back from Africa for a Christmas family reunion. The question for Livy was which one to please – her occasional lover who satisfied her sexual needs, or her friend who satisfied her mind, a good listener with whom she could talk about her frustrations, about a painting that wouldn't work. Claud was her muse who loved art and literature, who lived in a business world most of the day, leaving it happily behind when he visited her studio two or three times a week after work. Once or twice she had asked him how was his day at work to be told it was fine, never a detail or an anecdote. He was doing well in a company that bought and sold produce around the world, taking something Claud once referred to as options. Apparently 'options' paid for the house he had bought himself in Surrey, some five miles from Hastings Court. Every day, Claud caught the eight-ten from Ashtead Station to Waterloo where he took the Underground to Bank. Often when he visited the studio in Chelsea they cooked each other dinner, Claud bringing a bottle of wine then catching the last train from Waterloo back to Ashtead. He was a man with a daily rhythm some would have called a rut, his only deviation his visits to Livy. Claud was thirty-four years old, tall, thin and bald, his financial life as solid as the man himself. If only he turned her on, she lamented to herself, when he left of an evening to go home to his empty home, a house Livy knew Claud wished to fill with a wife and children. He was a stubborn man, despite his upbringing by the lake on the family estate in Cumberland. Tessa said she was mad not to marry him. The perfect catch. Rich enough, slightly boring with an eye that would never deviate an inch from a wife.

"You want to see the way he looks at you when your eyes are turned, Livy. The poor man's like a faithful dog hoping for a spark of love. He looks so damn longing. No man ever looked at me that way. The longing isn't the same look they give me when they want to get in my pants. Claud wants all of you, Livy. Not just sex."

"I might as well have chanced my arm in Africa as bury myself in the suburbs."

"How's the stallion?"

"You mean Frank? Frank is good for me in short sharp doses. He keeps my sex drive under control."

"We all have our physical needs... Let me look at the painting. Jeanne Pétain sold one of my paintings, bless her heart. Enough to keep me going. I wish I was famous like you... Where are you spending Christmas?"

"With Frank and his family at Hastings Court. Claud is going up to his mother in Cumberland. He wanted me to go. Would have been the three of us by the lake with Bo."

"Who's Bo?"

"The dog. Hastings Court is going to be crowded with lots of exciting people according to Frank. I won't be bored."

"Poor old Claud. Be careful, Livy. Don't miss this boat. Frank will never marry you."

"Who ever said anything about marrying Frank?"

"People get into a habit and take the line of least resistance. Better the devil you know than the devil you don't."

"When are you getting married, Tessa, instead of lecturing me?"

"When I find a tall, thin man with a bald head and a house in Surrey who looks at me in that all-absorbing way."

"I'm too wrapped up in my painting. Now tell me, is it finished?"

"Probably. Show it to Jeanne and James Coghlan. They are far better critics than me. Whoever thought those two would make so much money out of an art gallery?"

WHEN FRANK CAME round late that evening he found Claud stretched out on the couch. They were playing Brahms's third symphony on the record player, neither of them speaking as they let the music flow over their minds. Frank was annoyed to find what he imagined was the competition looking as if he owned the studio.

"Whatever happened to Bill Haley and the Comets?" he said nastily. "What is that damn music?"

"Brahms, Frank. You wouldn't understand."

"Damn right I wouldn't. Isn't it time for your train, Claud?"

"Hello, Frank. I spoke on the phone to your father this morning. He wants to take a position in Brazilian coffee."

"How do you know my father?"

"Does business with my firm. Livy mentioned you had changed your name from Brigandshaw to St Clair by deed poll. I asked him if you two were by any chance related. Have you come to buy one of Livy's paintings?"

"No I haven't. If you don't run you'll miss your train."

"Yes, I will. Goodnight, Livy. Thank you for cooking my supper. I love the new painting. Have a good look at it again in the light of day tomorrow. The background colours may be a little too dark. I'm leaving for Cumberland tomorrow. Have a happy Christmas. You too, Frank. Your father said you are all having a big family reunion at Hastings Court. That was a good buy of your father's. In five years' time Hastings Court will be worth twice what he paid for it. Buy at the bottom, sell at the top."

"We are never selling the Court. And if you didn't know, Livy is spending Christmas with us."

"Got to fly... May I borrow your Somerset Maugham to read on the train, Livy? He's such a good writer. Have you read *The Razor's Edge*, Frank?"

"No I haven't. I don't read books."

"You should. Goodnight, both of you. I'll see myself out."

Livy and Frank watched Claud put on his coat and leave the studio.

"You don't usually come round this early, Frank."

"I want a drink. Bad day at the office. Some of my clients are idiots. What do you see in that man?"

"He thinks, Frank."

"Don't I think?"

"Not in his way."

"Did you see the way he looked at you?"

"Come here, Frank. Jealousy doesn't become you. We have a deal. Sex when we want it. It's only sex we have in common, don't you understand? Now tell me. Who are you expecting for Christmas?"

FRANK DROVE himself home at one o'clock leaving Livy to sleep in peace. She dreamed there were lions on the shore of the lake chased by a black and white dog. Two men were floating above the water of the lake in the mist. They were sinking. Livy woke herself up shouting to them. Her room was pitch-dark, her heart thumping. Quite soon she fell back into sleep.

In the morning she woke late to a wintry sun coming through a small slit in the curtain Claud Gainsborough had not drawn properly. The room was ice-cold. After five minutes Livy willed herself to get out of bed and light the gas stove. She had a jar of shillings next to the fire to feed the metre. Shivering, Livy drew the curtains to let in the watery sun and went into the small kitchen to put on the kettle. Then she looked at the painting on its easel in the big bay window and saw it was finished. Whether Frank was finished she was not so sure. She smiled to herself ruefully. Before the kettle boiled she jumped back into the double bed. The sheets were still warm. Living in one room was practical, everything close.

The kettle whistled, making her get up and make the tea, the reason she had fitted the whistle in the first place. Otherwise the kettle would boil itself dry, Livy warm back under the blankets... The studio was warming up.

She made the tea in a brown pot and got back into bed. Tea in bed was the perfect luxury. She had turned the easel towards the bed for another good look while she drank her tea. She was happy. She hoped

Frank and Claud were happy. Then she remembered her dream and the African lions bringing her mind full circle to Jeremy. She hoped they were happy. Paul had told her on the phone Carmen had had a second baby. Another boy. The news had not made her as dissatisfied as the first one. They must be happy, she thought, to have had a second baby.

After her third cup of tea Livy got out of bed. She took the finished painting off the easel and replaced it with a clean canvas... Then she began to paint. The painting was going to be surreal. Of lions roaming the shores of the lake in the mist with two heads floating out over the water, their lower bodies deep in the cloud. All day Livy painted. Hunger made her stop, her feet cold in her slippers, her dressing gown still keeping her body warm. One of the faces had a slight resemblance to Frank, the other to Jeremy. Frank never looked at her paintings so it didn't matter. Jeremy was far away.

She cooked herself sausage and bacon and made the toast. She was ravenously hungry as she cooked in the small kitchen off the studio. She looked at her watch when she finished the food, leaving the dirty dishes in the sink. The studio smelt of fried bacon. She was late. Tessa and the girls were meeting at seven in the pub down the road. She looked at her new painting.

"You're going to be all right."

Then she dressed for the first time in the day and went out. The street lights showed her the way. In the pub it was warm and full of her friends, all of them laughing. The gin and tonic tasted nearly as good as that first cup of tea. She was smiling.

EVERY ROOM in the old house was ablaze with light, the forecourt of the old mansion full of cars. Livy could see people in the lower rooms where the guests had congregated, all in their finery. It was Christmas Eve. Frank parked the car in a small space and turned off the engine an hour after they had driven away from Livy's Chelsea studio. Frank had played the radio all the way down from London not wanting to talk, his mind still full of the week's business. Livy had packed a small suitcase hoping, as she looked through the ground floor windows, she had enough clothes.

Frank had stopped after getting out of his car, looking up at the façade of the old building with its crenellated battlements.

"When I grew up here I thought Hastings Court was part of my ancestry. That my great-grandfather was Sir Henry Manderville. It will be mine to own in my father's will but it never feels the same as bloodline. I always imagined my ancestors smiling at me, me a part of them. There are portraits of them up the stairs from the hallway. In the Great Hall. It was part of my heritage. When I found out my mother had had me by another man I was bitter. Hated both her and the man they had told me was now my father. You never get over living with a lie. Oh, well. Here we are. It all looks the same. Mostly the same people. Half-brothers and -sisters nonetheless. It's Mother's first time at Hastings Court since she sold the estate to my father. She's only come down because of Father. Can you imagine loving the same man since you were a child? I should be lucky, I suppose. A true child of love. Come on."

"From a one-room studio to all this... Bully for Livy... Are you happy, Frank?"

"What a silly question... My goodness here comes my younger brother, Kim. With the light at the back of him I thought he was Anthony. My brother Anthony was shot down in the war by the Germans over Berlin. There's a memorial to him in the ancestral mausoleum where all the Mandervilles are buried. I used to be so proud of them as a young boy walking round the graves. Effigies of knights in chain mail holding their swords over their dead bodies. My real ancestors, buried at Purbeck Manor, don't feel the same."

"It's Christmas, Frank. Don't be morbid... Hello, Kim. Happy Christmas. You really have a good tan. Where've you been?"

"In the African bush. Bechuanaland. We've started a photographic safari business."

"When are you going back?"

"I'm not... Hello, Frank."

"Have you told Tinus?" asked Frank.

"Not yet. He's inside with his famous wife. Oh, I forgot. You and Genevieve are actually cousins. They bought the kids over from America."

"Everyone arrived?"

"You're the last."

"Working right up to the last moment. God, it's cold. Who left all the lights on?"

"Your father said 'Let there be light'. It's Christmas. Happy Christmas, Livy."

"Are you tight, Kim?"

"Of course I am. It's Christmas."

Livy entered the house she had painted for Barnaby St Clair to hang in his Piccadilly townhouse through the iron-studded doors only one of which was open. Inside it was surprisingly warm for a house with tall ceilings and so many rooms open to the central hall. There were people everywhere, most with a drink in their hands. There were fires burning high in every grate. Livy took off her coat and put it on the top of her suitcase.

"We're sharing a room," said Frank.

"How convenient."

"Leave your case. A servant will take it up to our room. We bring them in from the village when the house is full. Some chap has a business in Leatherhead providing staff for functions. Making a fortune. No one wants to be a full-time servant in this day and age. Smithers stayed at Father's Piccadilly townhouse. Doesn't like the countryside. Everything gets turned into a business these days. If they lose your suitcase it can only be in one of twenty-seven rooms."

"How rich is your father?"

"Very. And getting richer by the day. You know what they say, money makes money. People usually start off being a crook and then get the hang of making money. The final move after a house like this is buying a peerage. Father's just an honourable. Younger son of a baron. Oh, well. Let's get a drink. Is there anyone here you know? You'll excuse me if I introduce you as the famous Chelsea artist. Impresses people. Life is all about impressing people for some reason. The people have all got money. If we play our cards right they'll all be knocking down the door of your studio to buy a painting."

"Don't you ever stop doing business?"

"Not really. I have to think of Jeanne Pétain's commission and my own."

"And I thought you were just after my body."

"Of course I am... Tinus, old chap. How are you? How's the lovely

Genevieve? I'd like to introduce you to Livy Johnston, the famous artist. I'm sure you've heard her name. How are tricks in America? Is the rumour right you are going back into films, cousin? Is your father coming up for Christmas?"

"Hello, Frank. Happy Christmas to you both. Dad's staying in Dorset. He never gets out. My mother stays in her London flat. And yes. I am going back to do a film."

"One of these days they'll make a film about us and call it *Those Two Bastards*."

"What a lovely title."

"Is your Uncle Barnaby around?"

"Your father is in the lounge with your mother. It's so strange to be at Hastings Court without Uncle Harry. You know, I always thought of him as my uncle he was so good to me as a child. Why don't you two go off and have a men's talk while Livy and I have a chat? It's so nice to meet another person in the arts. Is there anything of yours I can look at?"

"I don't think so. Once you sell a painting it goes out of your life. As is someone has taken it away from you. What was once in my head becomes public property."

"Rather like making a film. You have the advantage, Livy. They don't know what you look like. Keep it that way. Keep your face from the television or you won't own your life."

"And you want to go back?"

"A painter paints. An actress acts. I never did it for the money. Or the fame. Tinus and I fell in love long before I was famous. When you're famous you wonder if it's you or your fame they are after. People in general, not just husbands looking for a trophy. Do you want a drink?"

"Love one... How old are your children?"

"Barend is eleven. Hayley is ten. I think they are old enough to let their mother go away for a while to make a film. Aeroplanes bring everyone within a few hours' flight of each other in America."

"Where are they?"

"Somewhere with the other kids. They grow up so quickly."

"Does Tinus mind you making another film?"

"It was his idea. Said I was getting bored sitting at home all day. He's away on business so much. The meat canning business has expanded. Now they're selling British real estate to wealthy Americans. The farm's in Virginia. It never stops. I'll enjoy making a film. Seeing old friends. You can't let yourself get into a rut."

Livy's eyes travelled away from Genevieve and the guests to the old paintings on the walls, some so dark it was difficult to see from a distance what they were. Frank had said many of them went back hundreds of years, the paintings long forgotten, along with their subjects.

"Why don't we both have a look?" said Genevieve, following the direction of her eyes.

Step by step, drinks in hand, they walked up the winding stairs with the dark wooden banisters that guarded the drop down into the hall where the Christmas tree rose thirty feet into the house topped with a fairy. The Christmas lights from the tree threw light on the paintings, all of them in need of restoring. They were mostly portraits of people. Looking closely, Livy could make out what some of them were wearing, costumes she had never seen before, not even in books. The eyes of the Manderville ancestors followed them up the stairs. At the top of the stairs there was a landing. They could look over the top of the Christmas tree to the tops of the people's heads, the guests below unaware. Livy smiled. It was odd seeing the hand movements of people talking without hearing them or seeing their faces. It was going to be some party.

"Can you imagine what they would look like restored?" said Livy, turning her back to the banisters and looking at the line of paintings on the wall that guarded the landing. She went forward and peered hard at each of them, looking for the signatures of the artists. Maybe, she thought, if the pictures were cleaned they would find the names of the long-dead painters.

"Your paintings lived forever," she said quietly, as much to herself.

"Do you think they are worth anything?"

"There's more to art than money. Downstairs they wouldn't agree with me. Most people when they meet me want to know how much I got for a painting. They could only judge from the money to decide if I'm any good."

"Films are the same. *Robin Hood and his Merry Men* is still taking in money. It wasn't a good film. Good escapism, I suppose. What they want. So who can judge? A really good film would have a small audience. They call them cult movies. A few good ones make money at the box office. Makes it all worthwhile... We'd better go down and mingle. I've been seen from down below. Before you go I'll show you the Witches Circle on Headley Heath if it isn't raining. It doesn't snow much these days my mother was saying. She's an alcoholic. Lives on her own. Kept company by a bottle of booze. She's happy. Isn't that strange? Over all those years my father, Lord St Clair, has cared for her as much for my sake as Mother's. I'm his only child. He never married. Now isn't that strange? My mother was the barmaid at the Running Horses not far from here. We can visit the Running Horses after we walk up to Headley Heath. Where I started, I suppose. We all have to start somewhere."

"Did they love each other?"

"Who knows? It was wartime. Father back from the trenches in France on leave not knowing if he'd survive the war. Nobody cared about class when the young men could be dead in a week. So many of them died. When mother was pregnant with me she married Corporal Ray Owen who died three weeks later when he went back to his regiment. My father only found out about me when I was seven. Oh, well. That's life. I'm lucky to have been given life. Life's all one big chance if you ask me. Getting through it happily is the tricky part. Poor Mother. Poor Father. What can you do?... Tinus is waving at us. We'd better go down."

"My drink's finished."

"So is mine... Are the eyes on the wall following you?"

"All the time. It's the sign of a good artist."

"This house brings back for me so many good memories. Tinus and I consummated our love in this house. With the help of Bruno Kannberg and the girl that became his wife I wrote my autobiography in this house, telling the world I was a bastard before the press found out my parents weren't married. There's a lot of publicity in the movie business. But you'd know all that, going out with Frank."

"We don't exactly go out. We both use each other."

"Frank was very bitter when he found out Harry Brigandshaw wasn't his father. More the fact that Uncle Harry didn't tell him."

"What's the point of the Witches Circle?"

"You make a wish. When my co-star Gregory L'Amour visited here at the start of the war, he found a rabbit's foot in the Manderville graveyard, had it silver-mounted on a chain and gave it to Tinus. Tinus never flew in combat without that chain. In 1944, Tinus sat in the Witches Circle and prayed to the gods. To come out of the war alive and marry me. There's a lot in superstition and luck. What do you want most in life, Livy?"

"To be happy."

"Have you been in love?"

"I'm not sure. I think so. I didn't want to live in Rhodesia after Harry Brigandshaw said the country had no future for the whites."

"If you weren't sure, you weren't in love. It doesn't come to everyone."

"Does it last?"

"Ours has so far."

"Do you expect it to go on?"

"I hope so... They are doing suckling pigs on spits in the inglenooks of the Great Hall. It's a tradition. My father has the same tradition at Purbeck Manor in Dorset... Why don't you marry him?"

"He married someone else. A friend of mine. She's just had a second kid."

"You'll find someone else."

"As you get older you become more choosey. You can see through people so much easier. You don't believe everything you're told... Here comes Frank."

"Don't you want to marry Frank?"

"Never in a million years."

They both laughed as they walked down and joined the rest of the Christmas guests. Genevieve was soon surrounded. Livy went off on her own to find another drink, Frank having been swallowed up with Genevieve.

'He wants to do her publicity,' she said to herself. 'Good old Frank. Never misses a trick.'

On her way past the base of the Christmas tree she stopped for a moment to look at the Christmas presents, most of them for the children. It made her sad. If she didn't find herself a man to marry soon she would be too old to have a family. The thought made her envy Carmen on the farm in Rhodesia. She wondered if they had a swimming pool like the one Jeremy had promised her.

"You look sad, Livy," said Kim Brigandshaw, who had moved away from the other guests to stand next to her without Livy noticing, her mind lost in her dreams.

"I was thinking of Africa."

"It does have a certain charm. Can I get you another drink? Frank's spouting off his mouth about how much money he is making."

"I'd love another drink. Are you jealous of Frank by any chance?" She was smiling up at Kim. He was good looking with the easy movements of a man who knew what he was doing, the rare example of a man comfortable in himself.

"I've never been jealous of anyone in my life. What's the point? If money makes Frank happy, good luck to him. Now we have the money in Father's estate from the diamond Tinus found at Elephant Walk we children all have a little money to live on. More than enough for me. Why make more money than you need? You can only sleep in one bed at a time. When you have eaten enough food you become full and don't want anymore. To me, using money to impress people is rather pointless for Frank."

"But it works."

"What a sad indictment of our fellow man and woman."

"Have you been to the Witches Circle?"

"Why do you ask? I went this morning. On my own. It was cold on Headley Heath, so I dressed up in a thick coat over three sweaters. The circle was still there. Cut logs of trees round the flat stone in perfect symmetry. No one ever knows who replaces the logs but they always look fresh, the wood never rotting. They surround the ancient flat stone where you sit to make your wish. They say the flat stone was as tall as a man when placed in that one same spot by the ancients. That all the sitting made it sink into the ground where it is now, only the smooth top visible above ground."

"How did they sit on it if it was the height of a man?"

"They climbed onto the top of the stone from their horses, I suppose. Or gave each other a leg up." Kim was smiling, his rich suntan reminding Livy of Jeremy.

"What did you wish for, Kim?"

"That I'd meet a girl like you and now here you are. They say you have to be in harmony with yourself and the world for your wish to come true."

"You're a charmer."

"That's not charm, Livy. It's what I wished for. You're an artist. I can relate to artists. They're not all after money like Frank."

"You are jealous."

"Maybe just a little. Come and follow me to the bar. Frank was on a roll surrounded by admirers."

"He usually is."

"Can we have a word, Kim?" said Tinus Oosthuizen, Kim's first cousin, when Livy and Kim reached the small bar the caterers had set up to one side of the entrance hall next to the Christmas tree.

"What's up, Tinus? Have you met Livy?"

"At Paul and Beth's flat when I returned to London after finding the diamond. Hello, Livy."

"Ah, the diamond," said Kim. "What a little blessing."

"And maybe a curse for you, cousin. Frank tells me you don't want to go back to Rhodesia. That you don't want the job running photographic safaris."

"I was going to tell you. So Frank spilled the beans."

"Where are you drifting to next?"

"The Great Hall for suckling pig... Don't look so unhappy. When you meet them again in New York I think you will find Parker and Karen were impressed with the service. Tembo knows all about the bush and the animals. He loves the job and living in Maun with Princess. There are plenty of eager young men in Salisbury just dying for my job. I have a list of them in my pocket with their phone numbers. Both vehicles are with Tembo in Maun. I've made my recommendation. Give Mario Tuchi a ring. He works for the Lusito Sugar Estate as their electrical engineer. Knows more about the bush than the rest of us put together. I said we'd give him a share in the business. Ask Livy here. She and Jeremy Crookshank went into the Zambezi Valley with Mario. He wants a change. Perfect man for the job isn't he, Livy?"

"If he wants the job he'd be perfect."

"Then that's settled."

"You're a rolling stone, Kim."

"I know I am, Tinus. The point is, unlike Frank, I have no wish to gather any moss... Did you come over for a drink?"

"At least you are responsible and found your replacement. I'm going to wait for a glass of wine at the table to enjoy with my suckling pig. Paul's going to play the piano. Frank's had the piano moved into the Great Hall."

"How lovely," said Livy, trying to calm the look of annoyance in Tinus's eyes. Kim turned to the man behind the table that stood in for a bar. Tinus shrugged. Livy smiled at him as if to say 'what can you do?'. The tension subsided.

"Oh, what the hell," said Tinus. "Make mine a Scotch."

"I love this house where I grew up," said Kim, turning back from the table with Livy's drink. "There was so much happiness. I went to look at the memorial cross in the graveyard Dad had put up for Anthony. 'Flight Lieutenant Anthony Brigandshaw, DFC. Died fighting for his country three days before his twenty-first birthday.' Dad was so proud of him."

"We all were," said Tinus.

"There were fresh flowers at the foot of the cross. Who put them there?"

"I did," said Tinus. "When I arrived at Hastings Court. On behalf of the family and the Royal Air Force. I was just lucky to come right through the war in the air without a scratch."

Tinus took his whisky from the barman and raised his glass.

"To your brother and my cousin, Anthony Brigandshaw. God bless him."

"God bless him," said Kim, raising his glass.

When Livy looked from one to the other she saw tears in their eyes. It made her sad. What a waste, she thought. To die so young. It made her wonder what Anthony would have been like.

In the silence, Genevieve joined them, not saying a word about Anthony. Livy thought Genevieve must have heard her husband's words when he raised his glass. They all stayed silent for a long moment remembering Anthony.

When the clock struck seven-thirty a gong was rung that stood next to the Christmas tree.

"Dinner is served in the Great Hall," said a tall man in tails and a white bowtie.

They all trooped away following the tall man who led the family and guests into the Great Hall, the big doors opened for them by two men who had been standing with their backs to the closed doors while the man in tails rang the gong.

"Who is he?" said Kim.

"I have no idea," said Tinus. "Frank arranged everything with some firm in the village. Come on. Bring your drinks. I'm hungry."

A waft of warm air and the smell of roasting pig had come at them as the doors to the dining hall were thrown open. Livy smiled. A feast if ever she saw one.

"My goodness," she said. "Just look at all that food."

A firm hand had taken hold of her arm. When she looked it was Frank. He was smiling.

"Dad's sitting at the end of the table as Lord of the Manor. You and I, Livy, sit opposite the Honourable at the other end of the table. The Lord of the Manor facing his heir. It's some kind of tradition. Let me carry your drink."

Inside on a raised dais under the minstrels' gallery above the head of the long oak table, Paul Crookshank, Jeremy's brother, was sitting on a stool at a long, black grand piano. He was playing softly as if to himself. Livy knew it was Chopin. In the big fireplace, which Frank called the inglenook, an affair big enough to stand up in with seats along both sides of the fire, Livy could see the suckling pigs roasting over the wood fire on two side by side spits. She had an urge to paint the room with its vaulted ceiling held up by tall pillars, crested shields high up towards the ceiling. She half-expected people to be dressed the way the people were in the portraits she had looked at with Genevieve up the stairs and along the landing. The room was medieval. Only the people sitting down to dinner in their fancy clothes looked modern.

"What a beautiful home you have," she said to Frank.

"One day I'll show you Purbeck Manor in Dorset. I went down there last weekend, not to the Manor but to see my grandfather in his railway cottage. I wanted him to come up to Hastings Court for Christmas. I thought going down to Dorset myself might persuade him. Old Pringle, as they call him, wouldn't come. Too content with Mrs Battle who looks after him now my grandmother is dead. Said he preferred the familiar. I just can't impress my Grandfather Pringle."

"Now him I would like to meet."

"He's a wonderful old man. Worked at the same railway station at Corfe Castle all his life."

"Does your mother visit him?"

"Sometimes... Oh good. Paul's stopped playing his classical music. This one is Gershwin. Much more my taste."

Absorbing every detail of the picture for later use, Livy sat back in her dining room chair to listen to the general conversation, most of it banter. With the increase in the alcohol level from the line of open wine bottles down the table, Livy doubted she would hear anything that might be construed intelligent. On the principle of keeping up with her drinking companions, she sipped at the red wine Frank had poured for her. Apparently the bartenders from the village were not there to pour the wine, just to bring in the refills. Everyone was helping themselves or topping up the glasses of the girls next to them.

Livy was seated on the right of Frank in the first chair in a line that stretched up her side of the table. On her immediate right Dorian Brigandshaw was flirting with a young girl next to him on the other side. Opposite Livy was Beth Crookshank, the chair next to her still empty while Paul played the piano. Everyone was asked to put paper hats on their heads. To Livy, they all looked slightly ridiculous. It was Christmas, she told herself, so what else could they do?

The wine was good, old and probably expensive, one of the advantages, Livy conceded, of having money. At the top of the table, some thirty people away, Frank's father Barnaby St Clair was sitting next to Frank's mother, Tina Brigandshaw. With the wine nicely swirling in her head, Livy wondered what her children and the other guests thought of the situation. Before he died it would have been Harry Brigandshaw sitting next to her as Lord of the Manor. Life was indeed complicated when it came to people's relationships, but whether it mattered or not Livy decided she didn't really care.

A bowl of soup was put in front of her which tasted good. Dorian was telling the girl next to him how many copies his publisher had sold of *White Hunter*, the book he had written about his grandfather Sebastian Brigandshaw who had been killed by the Great Elephant. Dorian was giving the girl the whole story. Livy had not read the book. She hoped Dorian would not ask her if she had enjoyed his book, making her lie. By the sound of it the book had sold a whole lot of copies.

Across the table Kim was smiling at her. He was getting tight by the look of him, but no worse than the pretty girl sitting next to him. Without knowing who she was, Livy decided she did not like the girl.

Where Frank found the girls for his two unmarried brothers Livy had no idea. It might just be a coincidence. Knowing Frank as well as she did, she doubted it. The girl was getting annoyed with Kim looking at her. She gave the girl a smile that wasn't returned. Livy smiled, this time to herself. Life never changed. There was always competition. With a nice income from the family, Kim was a catch. Maybe Tinus was right. Money could be a two-edged weapon.

"Why are you so quiet?" asked Frank.

"I was thinking you must have paid a fortune for the wine."

Frank smiled smugly. He liked to be complimented. It was all part of telling friends what they wanted to hear.

"Here come the suckling pigs, carved and ready. You just help yourself, Livy, from the silver salver. How they ate in medieval times. When they'd eaten and drunk too much they just slipped under the table and slept it off with the dogs... Hello, Paul. Thanks for playing us the piano. Everyone get stuck in."

The frenzy of feeding lasted half an hour. The young pigs ate well, Livy saw from the looks on people's faces, their mouths full of food. Covered dishes of roast potatoes and an assortment of vegetables had been placed down the long oak table alongside the suckling pigs. The table was so old there were deep ridges in the grain of the wood. The wood was black from age. There were no cloths on the table, just cutlery and the plates on mats. The cork mats stopped the plates of food sliding off the ancient oak, polished over the centuries by countless guests. One of the big paintings on the wall behind Frank was of guests like themselves sitting at what Livy suspected was the exact same table, the painting most likely a few hundred years old. Restored, Livy expected the faces of the people enjoying their food would look much the same as themselves, the faces of the Brigandshaw children, Beth, Dorian and Kim not much different to their Manderville ancestors.

"What's behind me that's so interesting?"

"A painting, Frank. A very old painting that needs restoring. Won't interest you."

"Would it be worth money restored?"

"Probably. Leave it as it is."

"I might talk to Jeanne Pétain. She'll know a restorer."

"Ask James Coghlan."

"I will."

"You might find out who did the painting."

"Oh, my goodness. The man could be famous."

Here we go again, thought Livy, turning back to the food on her plate. She cleaned her plate and sat back full.

"I couldn't eat another thing."

"They are bringing the pudding in an hour," said Frank. "Wait till you see what we've got. The Romans used feathers down their throats to make themselves sick. Outside, of course. Not over the food."

"How disgusting."

"They ate all night, slept awhile and then had an orgy."

"Who are the girls for your brothers?"

"Friends of mine. There's an art to entertaining. Have a look up at the minstrels' gallery. We have a chap with a guitar. Brought him down from London. They say he's good. When the carcases are cleared away he'll start playing. Modern music in an ancient hall."

"It's all modern when it first happens. Even Mozart."

"I hate Mozart."

"I know you do."

"You want some more wine?"

"Why not?"

Half an hour later, when the last suckling pig from the spit was put in front of them, the crackling rich yellow-brown, Livy found herself taking pieces of crackling from the silver salver and putting them on her empty plate. Next to the crackling she dolloped a large spoonful of sweet apple sauce. Mouthful by mouthful, covered in applesauce, she fed the rich crackling into her mouth, letting the sauce mingled with fat drip down the side of her face. With all the expensive wine she had drunk she did not care what anyone thought. The food was delicious, the word piggery coming to her mind, not appropriate, she told herself, when eating pork. Frank was doing the same, feeding his face. When Livy looked around she could see others doing much the same, the time for etiquette past. There was no knowing when any of them would again eat suckling pig spit-roasted over a wood fire in a walk-in fireplace at the end of a baronial hall. She winked at Frank, wiping the sides of her face with the tip of her index finger. She put the finger in her mouth, sucking as she pulled it out slowly looking straight at Frank. He leaned towards her, putting his hand on her knee under her dress. His hand slid up inside her thigh. They were both tight as ticks, laughter spilling out of their eyes.

"Later, Frank," she whispered hoarsely pulling away his hand.

Kim was looking at them across the table. The girl next to him watched them while she drank from her glass of wine. The guitar player began playing, the notes drifting down over the babble of the guests. A waiter was replenishing the wine, bringing fresh opened bottles and removing the many empties from the centre of the table. Tinus was laughing with Genevieve halfway up the table looking so happy.

"What have they done with the kids?" said Livy to Frank.

"We feed them in separate rooms. Gives the parents a chance to let down their hair. Are you enjoying that crackling?"

"I'm so full and I can't stop eating."

"The party is going well don't you think?"

"He can play the guitar."

"Wait until he sings... Will you marry me, Livy?"

"You're drunk, Frank."

"Will you marry me, Livy?"

"Absolutely not."

"You're drunk, Livy. Say yes and hold me to it."

"No, Frank. I don't wish to marry you."

"I'm rich."

"I wouldn't marry you studded in diamonds. Keep it as it is, Frank. We're good this way. Don't spoil it... Pour me another glass of your expensive French wine."

"You're being silly again, Livy. You want kids. You told me so."

"But not with you."

Quietly, deliberately, she fed a piece of her crackling into his open mouth and shut his mouth gently with the tip of her finger placed under his chin.

"That's better," she said. "Now you can't talk."

Chewing very slowly, Frank watched her eyes. Then he swallowed and picked up his glass of wine, tossing it back. Then he smiled at her.

"You'll change your mind, you know. Here's to us. You'll be lady of this manor one of these days. You can do what you like with the Manderville paintings. Clean them. Sell them. Do what you like. You can paint all day if you want while I'm up in town. There'll be servants to look after our kids. You can entertain your arty friends. Think about it, Livy. In the end life is all about money whatever you might want to think to the contrary. All that crap about living on fresh air and love is just that. Crap. You need a good home. A nice nest for your kids. Think about it."

"I could have had that with Jeremy."

"No you couldn't. Rhodesia won't last. The blacks will take over and take away his farm. They call it democracy in the modern era."

"Won't the socialists take away your money?"

"You've got to hide it. Like Tinus hid the diamond money in Switzerland. You have to out-think the bastards to hold on to your money. Politicians on average are stupid. They always leave gaps... Have some more of that golden crackling. With me there will always be more. Cheers, my love."

"You don't love, Frank. Only in bed. I'd be your possession like this place."

"The house isn't complaining the way we look after it. We'd better stop talking. My father has hit his empty glass with a spoon. I rather think he's going to make a speech."

"Saved by the gong."

They both laughed and the moment was gone, neither of them sure if the other one had been serious. Livy picked up a last piece of pork from the tray with her fingers and put it straight in her mouth. When she looked across, Kim was looking at her. His eyebrows were raised. At the head of the table the Lord of the Manor got to his feet. All conversation died. Barnaby St Clair lifted his glass.

"Happy Christmas," said Barnaby into the silence. "That's all I've got to say. Raise your glasses with me. A happy Christmas to all of you."

As if one, the guests got to their feet, scraping back their chairs and lifting their glasses.

"Happy Christmas," they chorused.

Then they kissed each other and all sat down.

From her chair Genevieve got up and walked to the stairs at the side of the minstrels' gallery and walked slowly up the wooden steps to join the guitar player, whispering in his ear. Everyone was watching her. The guitar player plucked the first chords of 'Greensleeves' and Genevieve began to sing the old ballad, the same song Livy had watched her sing as

Maid Marian in *Robin Hood and his Merry Men*. When Genevieve finished, the entire room got to its feet applauding. Barnaby blew her a kiss. Then she walked all the way back to her place while some of the guests thumped on the old oak table. She kissed Tinus on the mouth before sitting down.

"She can sing," whispered Livy to Frank.

"My cousin can do anything... Did you know Henry the Eighth wrote that song? Or so says the legend. The same Henry who founded the Royal Navy making us Britons the most influential people to stride this earth. Henry was the start of the empire. It seems his song may well last longer than the empire."

"It's art, Frank. That's the part of me you don't understand. The reason why I won't marry you. You are condescending when you talk about my painting, only impressed when it turns into money. You have absolutely no idea what I'm doing. What I am... So sad. Keep it in bed, Frank. Where we can be of use to each other. When painting I go into another world. I disappear. A far better world than politicians and people wanting to steal people's money. The real world is too real for me. Your world. You know how to live in it. I don't. I have to escape, which I can through my painting. For long, beautiful hours at a time. I'm probably selfish. I don't care what people think of my painting. I just love standing at my easel painting, my only world the picture in front of me."

"But you need them to buy it to live. You're a hypocrite, Livy. But don't let's argue."

"Do you love me?"

"What on earth does that hackneyed word mean? I want to marry you. Isn't that enough? For you to be part of my life. I want kids to pass all this on to when I'm dead. Love? There isn't such a thing. You have to be comfortable with each other, that's what matters. You're a romantic, Livy. To be successful in life you have to be practical."

"I like being a romantic. It makes life with all its heartbreaks worth the living."

"Have we just got sober?"

"Being proposed to can sober up a girl."

"Have some more wine."

"Maybe I should so we can go back where we were under the table."

"Live for the moment and to hell with the future. What say you, Livy?

I want both. I'm also selfish. Just a little more practical. You'll come around. I never take no for an answer when I want something. You know that. Why my public relations business is so successful."

"You come across hundreds of girls."

"None of them are famous painters. None of them keep my interest in bed."

"Please, Frank. Let's just stay as lovers when the need takes us."

"Someone else will grab you. That Claud Gainsborough is besotted with you. My brother Kim has that look in his eye. Right now from across the table but don't look. With a wedding ring on your finger you'll be mine."

"Wedding vows don't mean much these days."

"But they will to you. You're a romantic. You said so yourself."

"Oh, Frank. You just don't get it do you? Pour me some more wine. I want to be drunk again."

"Just look at them."

"Who?"

"My mother and father at the end of the table. She's been watching us. Mothers can be jealous of their sons. Thank God she didn't bring that damn dog. Dad said the Alsatians would have eaten it. She's left Mabel Sayers in her Mayfair flat to spend Christmas with Chin-Chin. It's not even a dog with those bulging eyes. If Mabel has any sense she'll strangle the thing."

"Are they going to marry?"

"Who knows? They've known each other since they were children."

"They look happy."

"Do you think so? Or are you saying that to please me?"

"Maybe they love each other. Always have done. The perfect soul mates from different sides of the railway track. There's love up there, Frank. Between your parents. Even if they don't admit it to each other and get themselves married. If it isn't love why is she here?"

"They do look rather comfortable sitting next to each other. She orders us kids around left, right and centre. She's plain rude to poor Kim for not getting what she calls a proper job. She's a little less abrasive with Dorian now his book is selling. She criticises Beth constantly for the way Beth is bringing up her children. But when it comes to my father she's a pussy cat. She treats him like he can never do wrong. Poor Harry. He really did his best. When I thought he was my father I felt sorry for him. Strange for a kid. Maybe even then I sensed there was something wrong."

"And you, Frank? How did she treat you?"

"Different to the others. Maybe not Anthony. She loved Anthony. Should a parent love one child more than the others?"

"You don't believe in love, Frank, don't forget."

"That word love has too many meanings."

"So it does exist?"

"We interpret the word differently. It's a word difficult to communicate. We all see it in our own selfish way."

"Do you love your mother and father?"

"To be honest, who knows? We all say we love someone when we want something even if we don't admit the truth to ourselves. We think we love our mothers when we are children as we need them to survive. Life's pretty basic if you ask me. My poor mother. She hasn't had an easy life. I was often horrible to her."

"All you have to do is say you love her."

PART VIII

JULY 1960 – "GO WELL, MY DARLING"

1

*J*eremy Crookshank, proud father of two sons, was having a good day: the bulk sheds were full of the year's second crop of dried tobacco, the roofs had gone on six new curing barns and he had just scored sixty-two runs for Centenary in their match against Macheke, the side he had played for when he worked at Ashford Park for the Maples. It gave Jeremy wry satisfaction that his old club, a club that had put up with him as a lowly learner-assistant, was being soundly beaten.

By the time he had removed his pads and found his wife, Carmen, in the bar surrounded by admirers, the game was over, Sandy West having scored the winning runs. By the look of her, Carmen was well on the way to getting tight. The two boys were somewhere with the nanny and the rest of the young children. Next to Carmen at the bar was Pamela Crumpshaw, her eyes as bright as Carmen's. Around them in a solid phalanx were men, among them Jeremy's brother Paul. With Paul was Mario Tuchi, the general manager at Photographic Safaris, who Jeremy knew had once been his wife's lover when they all camped on the banks of the Zambezi River when Livy Johnston had been Jeremy's companion. Jeremy, looking at so many attentive men, hoped none of them were his wife's lover though he could never be sure. Carmen had her own car and went on her way round the block during the day while

Jeremy worked in the lands. The girl was bored. There was nothing for her to do on the farm. Not knowing what she was up to was part of the price he paid for having a bored, good-looking wife who craved distraction. Carmen had two vices so far as Jeremy knew: drink and men.

"How many did you get?" asked Paul, moving out of the circle.

"Sixty-two. Sandy just scored the winning run. Beat them by eight wickets. Where's Beth and the kids?"

"Round the pool. Doesn't like drinking too early."

"How is she today?" Paul said quietly to his brother.

"I just don't know where she puts them all. By my count she's had half a bottle of gin."

"She's enjoying herself. That's something."

"Pamela was saying she came out on the boat to marry Roger Crumpshaw with Livy. She and Livy shared a cabin. She's been with Carmen in the bar all day."

"They both have the same problem... It's so nice to beat Macheke. We might as well collect up the kids and head for home."

"You'll have trouble convincing Carmen."

"Oh, well. We'd better have a drink, if you can't beat them, join them. We're selling tomorrow so I don't want to get too tight... Mario. How are you? Hope the cricket hasn't bored you. What do they play in Italy?"

"Never bored with your charming wife's company. Or the company of the ravishing Pamela. Did you have to run up and down sixty-two times? Heard you tell Paul you had scored sixty-two runs."

"I scored some boundaries."

"To an Italian, cricket will always be a mystery. What a lovely club. Tennis I play. Next time I bring a tennis racket when your brother makes a visit. We have done all our business at a table over there before joining the ladies. No more talk of Photographic Safaris."

"Can I buy you a drink, Jeremy?" said Paul as Mario turned his attention back to the ladies.

Jeremy smiled at Carmen. So long as she was happy that was all that mattered. She had given him two beautiful sons. A man needed a wife in the middle of the African bush. A family.

He looked around while Paul ordered the drinks. The two African barmen were busy. The Macheke team, having come off the field, were finding their way to the bar. The level of noise increased. The wives by the pool joined their husbands at the bar.

The Macheke captain, Roger Crumpshaw, ordered a round of drinks for everyone in the bar. It was how it was done. The head barman was a wizard at remembering everyone's drinks. Some of the girls had been playing tennis. Their short white skirts showed off their knees. There were bursts of loud laughter. Most of the men's conversation centred around tobacco except for those surrounding Carmen and Pamela. There it was all banter, the girls joshing the men. Two of the farmers' wives joined Carmen and Pamela to gaze at Mario. He was very good-looking.

Paul gave Jeremy the drink that had been paid for by Roger Crumpshaw and took his brother's arm. They went outside to the long veranda. The sun was still hot. The cricket field was empty. They could hear the treble voices of children playing in the swimming pool away to the left. The mountains behind the gum trees behind the sight screen were a hazy blue. From where they stood all they could see was the rolling African bush.

"That was the first time you mentioned Livy, Paul. How is she?"

"Do you want to know?"

"Of course I do. I heard she married Frank."

"And divorced him."

"That I didn't know. What happened?"

"When Frank owns something he treats it badly. She walked out. She told me she never should have married him in the first place. They have the one daughter who's living with Livy, in her new studio down the road from the old one. It's the sixties, Jeremy. Marriage isn't forever anymore."

"Did she get anything from Frank?"

"Not a penny. Didn't want it. He pays for the girl. Livy hopes one day they will be friends again for the sake of the little girl. The children pay for the sins of their parents. Thank God I married Beth. It never was a violent love affair but we're stable. Respect each other. Like each other. Getting on together day after day is more important than all the passion. Passion fades in a marriage. Friendship grows."

"Is Photographic Safaris making money? It was easier for Mario to come to World's End than you go to Maun. We'd have lost days together."

"Thank you for arranging his visit. He's driving back tonight as far as

Salisbury. His figures look good. He's honest. I like him. So do the girls. With Dorian Brigandshaw as editor we're starting a magazine for distribution in England and America. *African Safaris*. All the new spots to go to. Mario likes the idea. He'll have to take on new staff to cope with the increase of tourists. What business is all about. The magazine was Frank's idea... How are your figures this year?"

"I want you to get some of the profits out of Rhodesia for me. I never forget what Harry Brigandshaw said before he died about the white man's future in Africa. The Federation won't last much longer. The likes of Josiah Makoni are agitating for independence from Britain for Rhodesia and Nyasaland. We've got a few more good years. The price of tobacco is high. I want some of my assets safely out of the country. Can you help?"

"Of course. Cheers, old boy. The old times. Good to see you."

"How's business in England?"

"Never been better. England's on the up again after the dark years of the war. You're right to take precautions with your money. Ghana's been independent three years and it hasn't done them much good. They scream at the world for aid. Consider themselves a victim. For God's sake, who built their roads and their railways? We did. Left it all behind without so much as a thank you from Nkrumah... There are some good companies quoted on the London stock exchange to invest in. I'll have a word with Barnaby St Clair, Frank's father. He's made himself another fortune investing in the market. I was going to ask you what you were doing with your money. The girls don't like us talking about business. Beth says I have enough of it in the office. It's difficult in two days to appreciate how much you have done with World's View."

"If the political threat of losing control wasn't hanging over my head I'd invest every penny of the surplus back into the farm. Water's the problem. We farmers spend a lot of nervous moments looking up at the sky once we've planted out the tobacco from the seed beds. I want to build dams along the rivers. There are three small ones running through the farm that dry up by this time of the year. In the rains they form a single raging torrent that runs off eventually to the Zambezi and down to Beira and into the sea. We want to keep enough of that water to irrigate every acre of World's View. Cost a fortune of course. But stop us worrying about the weather. I've been lucky so far planting two crops. The rains have come from November and stayed with us until the end of March. Sometimes we only get three months of intermittent rain. A few cycles of irrigated water would save the crops. Water, Paul. Farming in Africa is all about water and knowing what you are doing. The government has been superb. They have research stations across the country and send out extension officers to the farms. New and better types of seeds. Better ways to fertilise the lands without wasting fertiliser. Farming is now a science. You have to think. No longer are the days of planting a seed in virgin soil and waiting for the crop to grow. Or moving the cattle to find new grazing. You have to conserve the top soil by planting grass after the tobacco crop. Leaving the land fallow for another three years with good contours so the rains don't wash away the soil. The days of small farming are over in Africa. Too many people. Organised commercial farming is the only way to go. And that takes knowledge and money to maximise the return from the soil. Farming in Africa isn't easy. This year I'm reverting to one crop of tobacco like the rest of them. You can chance your arm just so far... A good portfolio of shares in England will make me less nervous. Harold Macmillan talked of a 'wind of change' blowing through Africa when he addressed the South African parliament in Cape Town earlier in the year. And the British prime minister is right. The trouble is that wind is going to do a lot of damage to everyone, black and white. You have to have honest governance for a country to prosper. People trained who know what they are doing. Not politicians with big mouths and bigger promises they will never be able to fulfil as they shout their way to power. Harry Brigandshaw was right. In the end, Africa is going to be one big mess. And with the surge in the population half of them are going to be starving... Come on. We'd better get her out of the bar. We farmers all go to bed at eight o'clock to rise before the sun. Let's go and first find our kids. Mine are better at getting their mother out of the bar than I am. It really is wonderful having you here, Paul. Pity it's so short a visit."

"You have to keep your hands on a business."

"Don't tell me."

"This country is so damned beautiful."

"Isn't it?"

"What a pity it will be for everyone if Harry Brigandshaw was right."

"That's the trouble with life. Once they see someone making money they want to steal it. No one ever lived in the Centenary before we opened up the block to farming. It was just bush left to nature. Maybe we should have left it to the animals instead of inciting people's envy. Who knows what is the right thing to do? I wanted to fulfil a dream. World's View was that dream. We all have to dream. Isn't it strange standing here on the boundary? Typically English, we build a house and then a cricket field."

JEREMY'S CHEVROLET IMPALA sent a cloud of dust behind them a hundred yards long. They were driving into the setting sun. Jeremy and Carmen were in the front whilst their two small children sat in the back seat with their nanny. The top of the Chevrolet was down, open to the late sun, the wind blowing through Carmen's hair. Paul, Beth and their children followed a little behind in Carmen's car. They had said goodbye to Mario Tuchi in the parking lot. One of the girls who had been to the cricket needed a lift home to Salisbury, Mario's first stop on his journey back to Bechuanaland and Maun. He looked happy. The girl was pretty. Jeremy wondered who she had come with.

Ten minutes later Jeremy drove onto his property through the avenue of Australian gum trees he had planted along the drive up to the house. The house sat on a rise with an unrestricted view all round. The low thatched bungalow stretched along the ridge with well-cut lawns in front going away down the slope. The gum trees finished at the low fence with its gate that led into the two acres of English garden. The rose bushes were in full bloom. Msasa trees, twice the height of a man and flat-topped, were sprinkled through the garden each surrounded by a flowerbed. The canopies of the msasa trees were alive with birds. A gardener with a long net was scooping leaves from the swimming pool next to a wood fire burning inside a grill-topped metal stand. A long table had been laid next to the *braai*. On the table were bowls of salad each covered with a lace net. Silverware sparkled in the evening sun next to a small pile of white plates.

The four children piled out of the cars as soon as they stopped, running to the pool. They were still in their swimming costumes from their day round the pool at the club. They ran through the gate in the ring fence that surrounded the pool, the elder three screaming and jumping in, the youngest a little hesitant. The gardener had opened the gate.

The adults followed and walked through to the pool. Carmen was smiling. Next to the long table was a smaller drinks table with a full bottle of gin. The ice bucket was dripping water down the outside from the cold of the ice, the long drops cutting lines in the frosty surface of the silver bucket.

A servant took Jeremy's cricket bag out of the boot of the car and walked away with it up towards the veranda and into the house. There was a blush of colour beginning to paint the evening sky. The birds were calling to each other from the trees. From the pool, looking away from the setting sun, were the mountains now tinged with a pastel red. There was not a breath of wind. The air was soaked with the perfume of flowers.

"I've never seen anything like this," said Paul, gazing far out to the distant mountains.

"Neither had I. Why I called it World's View. It's like being on top of the world up here. The perfect setting for a house. As far as you can see and not one sign of man."

"Anyone for a drink?" called Carmen.

The kids were splashing in the pool, excited with each other, the smaller boys in the shallow end, Henry and Deborah swimming up and down.

"No wonder my father loved Africa," said Beth.

"They say once the bug of Africa has bitten you there is no living anywhere else," said Jeremy. Where the sun had gone behind the mountains it was getting dark in the shadows.

Carmen had poured herself a gin and was drinking. Jeremy helped his brother to a cold beer from a white foam cooler box. Beth said she had had enough to drink in the club and walked closer to the children.

Quickly the sun went down, flaming the sky with red. Jeremy took the chops and steaks from under the doily on the serving plate and put them on the grill over the fire. He gave Paul a pair of tongs to turn his meat.

"We all like meat cooked our special way. What makes a *braai*." They both had cold beers, drinking from the bottles.

By the time the meat was cooked it was pitch-dark, only a tinge of red in the distant horizon. Their world came down to the fire and the two gas lights at the ends of the long table the gardener had lit before going on his way back to his hut in the native compound.

When they ate, Carmen said she wasn't hungry and poured herself another gin. The children were fed and taken to bed by the nanny. The nanny was the gardener's wife. The night came down.

"What are all those noises?" asked Paul.

"Cicadas in the long grass outside the garden and up in our trees. Animals some of them. That call was a baboon. July is the best time of the year. Can't you feel it's getting cold now the sun is down? No mosquitoes. October is suicide month, it's so humid and hot. Then the rains break if we're lucky and life is good again."

"You have a perfect life."

"We think so don't we, Carmen? Don't you want to put the kids to bed?"

"They're fine, Jeremy. Stop worrying. What a lovely day in the club. So many interesting people. Who was that damn girl Mario went off with?"

There was a small silence as the two brothers kept on piling the cooked meat on the serving plates, putting each on the table when it was full. Then they sat down, helping themselves to the meat and the salads.

When the food was eaten Jeremy was tired. He had been up since five in the morning. His eyes would not stay open.

"Sorry, folks. I have to go to bed. Work in the morning. We can go into the lands together, Paul. Give the girls a chance to natter all day in peace."

"You always go to bed when the party's just starting."

"I have to work, Carmen."

"Paul and Beth can keep me company... Beth, have a drink."

"All right. Just one."

"Be a devil, Paul, have another beer. We can sit out here all night."

Carmen was giggling. Jeremy walked across the lawn into his house, too tired to worry. Her drinking was becoming a habit.

2
_____

*T*he morning was cold before the sun came up. To Jeremy's surprise his brother appeared fully clothed. They could hear the gong being beaten in the compound calling the labour force to work. Outside they could see the first blush of dawn. There was still no colour in the sky. Jeremy was wearing khaki shorts and shirt, his bush hat resting on the dining table, the lounge and dining room forming one big space with a fireplace at one end. The fire had been lit the previous night and the smell of woodsmoke still lingered.

Jeremy was drinking a cup of tea, holding the big cup in both hands.

"Aren't you freezing?" said Paul.

"Morning, old boy. In an hour it will be hot. Have some tea. There's some on the trolley. Do you have a hat?"

"Afraid not."

"I'll lend you one of my bush hats. Can't have you getting sunstroke if you're coming with me into the lands. Silas will bring us breakfast down to the lands at nine o'clock. How did you sleep?"

"Pretty well when I finally got to bed. We sat by the fire keeping your wife company. I went to bed at ten leaving her with Beth. They likely won't be up for a while."

"So, are you ready?" He was smiling at his brother, enjoying the company. "I use the motorcycle to get around the farm. The gang come down to work from the compound behind the tractor sitting on the trailer. You'll hear them singing in a few minutes.

"What was that clanging noise?"

"The gong. An old plough disc the gang boss hits with a spanner. Gets them out of bed. They have the morning shift until twelve when the tractor driver takes them back to the compound for two hours to be fed. They each have an area of bush to clear each day. If they are finished they don't come back after lunch... You'll need a sweater on the back of the bike."

"There's nothing like the first cup of tea in the morning."

"You can say that again."

"Everything's so quiet."

"The birds will start singing as the sun comes up... There goes one of them. In a minute you'll hear a full chorus."

"Sounds like an orchestra tuning up before the conductor hits the rail with his baton to start the symphony."

"Are you still playing jazz in Benjie Appleton's jazz club in Oxford Street?"

"Haven't been for years... The kids are still asleep. Not a squeak from them."

"Let's go before they wake."

"My tea's hot... I'm so glad we came out to see you. Mario and *African Safaris* was a bit of an excuse. To be able to offset the trip against the tax man as a deductible expense."

"I'm glad you came. I miss you and Mum. She won't come out. Won't get into an aeroplane. Something about Dad's boat being sunk by a German dive bomber."

"To her, Africa is so far. She's afraid."

"Tell her to come by boat."

"Not on her own. She prefers it when you come home... How much money are you going to send back to England?"

"Depends on the price of tobacco on the auction floors. Last year I averaged five shillings a pound. All the tobacco goes to England. Without the British buyers we wouldn't have a business, and Rhodesia wouldn't have an economy."

"Why don't you buy a house with some of the proceeds? I can manage a tenant and pick up the rent."

"Good idea... Swallow your tea. I like to get to where we are stumping before the gang arrives. Lead from the front. What we were taught in the Royal Navy."

THE LAND BEING CLEARED WAS a slope that went down to a river. In the river there were pools of water, the river having stopped flowing. The trees were taller along the banks of the river and provided shade. Jeremy parked the motorbike under a tree. They could hear the gang singing while they sat on the flatbed trailer being pulled by the tractor. Jeremy had driven past them on the motorcycle. The sun was coming up showering forks of light into the morning sky, the new day greeted by the singing birds. A male kudu was drinking from a pool in the middle of the riverbed, taking no notice of Jeremy and Paul.

The path they had driven had been cut through the bush the previous week to give Jeremy access to the new land he was preparing that sloped down to the river. When the tractor stopped thirty men piled off onto the ground. Everyone carried a machete and a Dutch hoe. Jeremy gave them each an area to clear by cutting down the msasa trees and digging to get out the roots so the tractor could come back later and deep plough. Some of the holes from the previous day's work were big enough for a man to stand in showing only his shoulders. Cords of wood stood next to the holes waiting to be transported back to the sheds where they would next year go into the fires that burned at the base of the barns, sending heat up the flues of the tall buildings to cure the Virginia tobacco by drying out the leaves, turning them a mahogany brown. The sound of chopping wood began. Jeremy moved from one man to another suggesting the easiest way to take out all the roots of the trees. When he had finished he walked back to Paul standing under the tree next to the motorcycle up on its metal stand. The kudu had moved to a place under a tree on the other side of the river, its hide blending perfectly with the dappled sun beginning to play through the trees. The kudu appeared almost invisible.

"You got to get all the roots out or it buggers up the plough. We put a big sack of sand on the plough to keep it down to dig deep. The tobacco roots go two feet into the ground. When we top the tobacco before it flowers the plants are head-high, the leaves longer than your arm. When the leaves are ripe we take them to the barns for curing on the trailers. Reaping is the heavy time for work on the farm. A ripe leaf waits for no one. The trick is to pick them just right and dry them carefully in the barns, slowly upping the temperature. You need just the right amount of fertiliser close to each plant which we grow in seed beds before planting them out in the lands."

"You've lost me, Jeremy."

"The biggest problem on the farm is communication. Half the gang don't speak the other half's language. There's a shortage of labour in Southern Rhodesia so they come from Nyasaland and Mozambique to fill the jobs. We've created a common language called Fanagalo. Bits of Shona. Bits of Zulu. Even bits of Portuguese and Afrikaans. They speak it down the mines in South Africa. It's all right for simple conversation but you can't explain anything technical. There are no words in Shona or Zulu for an aeroplane so far as I know. Or the crankshaft of a tractor. The only way is to teach everyone English but it's going to take time. I'm putting in a school. If the tractor driver understands English and what I explain to him, it will cut my repair bill in half. Noises in the engine you and I would pick up and fix before the engine blew up are foreign to them. Without the words I can't make them understand. You can't teach the kids maths or any kind of science before they first understand English. It was the same in India. All over the empire... There's so much work to be done. Clearing the lands like this is only the very beginning."

At nine o'clock, riding a bicycle, Silas delivered their breakfast along with a flask of hot tea. Both of them were hungry. The work was progressing, the sun getting hot. Silas pedalled off to go back to the house. They sat under the tree next to the motorcycle. The kudu had gone.

At twelve o'clock the tractor driver took the gang back to the compound for their two-hour lunch break, giving the ones without wives enough time to cook their food. All but three of the men had finished their quotas for the day.

"I want to walk you down to the river. Show you where I want to build weirs. Then we'll go back for lunch and see the girls. I've lots to do in the workshop. I do most of my own repairs. Costs too much to transport a tractor to Salisbury for servicing. We have to be self-sufficient so as not to waste money. You can call it a jack of all trades but it's how it works. Successful farming's a cross between being a farmer, a mechanic and a businessman. The difficult part in this game is making the money by keeping down the costs and maximising the amount and quality of the crop. Being a farmer in Africa wasn't what I thought it was when I first heard about it in England... Come on. Let's walk along the river. If I can hold back the river during the rains and use that water on these lands if the rains don't come, half my problems will be over. You need water, Paul. And pipes and pumps to take it to the crops. Expensive. And you have to know what you're doing. I'll have to add dam building to my learning curve. Along with water engineering. Anyway, it's fun... Just watch the buffalo grass near the water. If it gets on your skin the dry seed from the grass itches like hell. Drives you mad."

"Which is the buffalo grass?"

"That one right next to you. Welcome to Africa."

They laughed, wending their way through the bush, Paul following the path of his brother. The sun was hot beating down on their heads. Without knowing his way back along the river, Jeremy knew he could easily get lost. Beside the river the bush was dense. When he found a spot where the river turned its course through hillocks on either side where the water had cut into the earth showing Jeremy rocks on either side, he stopped.

"A thick, curved concrete wall six feet wide will hold back the water if it's anchored onto those rocks at both ends. A perfect spot don't you think, Paul?"

"Frankly, I have no idea. Tell me something. What the hell are two Englishmen doing here? Is there anywhere in the world further away from anything?"

"I told you. Growing tobacco. So everyone who wants to in England can smoke."

"It's a bad habit."

"Anything's a bad habit if it's overdone. Fifteen fags a day won't hurt you to smoke with a couple of pints down the local of an evening. Three packs a day will stuff up your lungs... This is a perfect spot for a weir. What I need is an aerial photograph so I can map out where I'm going. On the ground there are too many trees blocking the view to get the big picture. There's a chap in Salisbury who will photograph the farm. I'll get him up here in his aeroplane."

"How do you read an aerial photograph when you are looking down on top of everything?"

"I'll have to find out. They give you two photographs of the same piece of land and a pair of spectacles that stand over the photographs. When you juggle the photographs the picture leaps up at you in three dimensions so you can see what is going on. What he said, Paul. If it works, I'll be able to plan an irrigation system right across my six thousand-acre farm and never have to worry about the rains not coming on time again. Later, I want to diversify my crops. Plant wheat in the dry season when there's nothing for the gang and the tractors to do on the farm. Double our productivity. They say Southern Rhodesia is the breadbasket of central Africa. You must never wait. A lot of the other farmers have similar ideas. You must never stop thinking to be successful in life. We can turn this part of the world into an economic paradise to match its natural beauty... We'd better get back. That breakfast has long gone down. I'm starving again. Just watch that buffalo grass. If it gets under your shorts onto your balls you'll be scratching all night."

*A*n hour later the brothers climbed back onto the motorcycle, Paul putting his arms around Jeremy so he would not be thrown off going over the bumps. The new path was rough, not helped by the ruts made by the wheels of the tractor.

At the house, Jeremy stopped next to the swimming pool where he parked. There was no one around. Laughing, they stripped off their clothes and jumped in the pool. The cool water took away the heat and the dust.

"Like when we were kids on the Isle of Wight," said Paul. "Skinny-dipping in the sea. Makes me feel so damn young and free again. I must come out for a visit more often. They say you achieve more after a holiday in a day than you would have done in a week if you had stayed at work."

"I enjoy the company. Old friends and family are so important."

"Will you ever come back to England?"

"Who knows? That depends on Josiah Makoni and his friends. People don't like being colonised and ordered around by strangers. It hurts their pride. Impinges on their dignity. A man's pride is as important to him as his physical wellbeing. The politicians are good at playing on that emotion. The politicians are after their own physical comforts of course. Appealing to the people's pride supports their agenda, which is rarely anything other than their thirst for power. Everyone is after something. How the world goes round... Carmen gets lonely for her friends in Salisbury and her family in England. Who knows where we all end up? Before the war, when you and I went swimming in the sea, we had never heard of Africa except as a dark continent full of dangerous savages. The idea of going there had never entered my head. I'd never been as far as France. Never crossed the English Channel. All I knew about Africa came from boys' adventure books I read with a torch under the blankets when Mum turned out the lights to make us go to sleep. Didn't you read under the blankets?"

"Of course I did. There was only reading in those days. We had to entertain ourselves... Do you think Josiah wants the whites out of the country?"

"They'd be much wiser learning from us. Picking our brains... Making a living in the bush without any mechanical help is all nice and romantic but damned hard work. They all lived short lives even if they got through infancy. Most of the people in this country owe their very existence to us British. When there's something wrong with them I take them to the hospital in the truck. The women don't have their babies in the bushes on this farm or any of the other white-owned farms in the block. Some of the people in the TTLs come to us for help despite the government putting in clinics for them"

"What are TTLs?"

"Tribal trust lands. For some of them I'm closer than the clinic. Nothing's too far when you have a truck. Just try walking when you're sick."

"Walking back up the river in that heat was enough for me."

"We all need each other hereabouts. People forget that... Where I end up with my family, we'll just have to see. In the end it's all in the lap of the gods... Aren't you hungry?"

"Lead the way, brother."

"Maybe a cold beer."

"Now you're talking."

"I don't usually open the bar until the evening. You're a visitor so we have an excuse."

"Does your wife drink at lunchtime?"

"Always. She worries me, Paul. Carmen's drinking too much to compensate for her boredom. It's becoming a habit."

"Give her another kid to think about."

"She doesn't want one."

"It all looks a great life to me. Beats four walls in an English winter when you can't go outside."

"But when you do go out there's so much to do close at hand. There are people all around you. That's what she misses. Alone for days with only each other for company we get on each other's nerves. The kids are always demanding attention. In London people say they want to get away from the rat race. Here there are no rats. Just ourselves... There they are. Hello, darling. Are you having a good day?"

"It's so wonderful having someone to talk to... Did we see you skinny-dipping in the pool? That's naughty. We've opened the bar. Have a drink. Silas is bringing a cold lunch down to the pool."

"I was suggesting a cold beer to Paul. Walked him downriver. My brother's thirsty... What a lovely day."

"Isn't it just?" said Carmen, beaming all over her face.

Jeremy laughed, trying to avoid what to the others must have been obvious. Carmen was drunk. Beth, standing a few feet behind Carmen, had a pained look on her face. It was half past one in the afternoon. Today, Jeremy knew the nightmare had started earlier than usual.

They all gathered round the pool while Silas laid out the lunch. When Paul finished his beer, having turned down another one saying it would put him to sleep, he helped himself to the cold chicken and salads. Carmen didn't want to eat. The kids arrived with the two older ones jumping in the pool before getting out to eat by helping themselves to lunch from the table. Jeremy helped his boys, four-year-old Phillip and the two-and-a half-year-old Randall. Randall sat on the grass under a flowering tree with the plate between his fat legs and stuffed food in his face using his podgy hands. Carmen took no notice. She was telling Beth a story of a night she had had with her friend Candy at Bretts.

"You'd like Bretts, Paul. Great jazz pianist. Hennie Bekker. Why don't we all go into Salisbury and spend the night at Meikles? The nanny can look after the kids. Hennie will be happy to meet another piano player. Let you sit in with the band. The way Jeremy says you sat in with the Benjie Appleton band in London. It'll be fun. Get us off the farm."

"I have to work tomorrow, Carmen," said Jeremy.

"There's never any fun. Paul and Beth are going home on Saturday. I have another idea. We can go to Bretts after we take them to the airport. Stay the night in Salisbury."

"Won't be as much fun just the two of us," said Jeremy, imagining a night drinking and talking to strangers.

"Then we can go now. You never take a day off from boring work."

"A three-hour drive to a nightclub sounds heavy," said Paul. "The farm here is so new for us and the children. The kids are having fun."

"They can have fun on their own."

"I wouldn't want to leave mine alone, Carmen," said Beth uncomfortably. "They'd get into mischief. Paul likes the family to stay together."

Seeing she wasn't making any headway, Carmen walked over to the drinks table and poured herself another drink. Paul winced at the amount of gin she poured into her glass.

"Cheers everybody," said Carmen, turning round with the refilled drink in her hand. "Down the hatch."

"Don't you want some lunch?" asked Beth.

"Not really."

Leaving the girls sitting round the pool watching their children playing in the water, Jeremy went back to work. There was always work to do on the farm.

"If I don't watch everything something always goes wrong," he said to Paul.

Neither of them mentioned Carmen as they got back on the motorcycle. The talk of Bretts had reminded Jeremy of Livy, giving him a jolt, making him sad. He hoped she was all right alone with her kid. As a younger man he had had no idea how difficult a marriage could be. He had thought people married, had kids and looked after each other for the rest of their lives. In harmony. In an atmosphere of peace. Not a perpetual undercurrent of tension with everyone pulling their separate ways. It had never been like that with his parents.

"I never heard Mum and Dad ever once have an argument," he said to Paul when they stopped at the brickworks near the three big anthills where a gang were using the contents from inside, the clay covered in the saliva from millions of ants, to make bricks in small wooden boxes by leaving them out in the sun to harden before stacking them inside the kiln.

"They argued all right. Just never in front of us. In those days you never argued in front of your children... So this is how you make bricks?"

"You see that tunnel into the kiln? We burn wood in there and leave it burning for a couple of weeks all closed up. Good as any bricks you'll find in the world. The residue from the ants' saliva binds the bricks like cement. You saw the sheds and the barns. They're good. The timber comes off the farm which we cut and treat by soaking the planks and beams in creosote. Stops the white ants eating the rafters of the buildings. We have to bring cement and that kind of thing from Salisbury. My biggest job was teaching the gang on the farm how to lay the bricks. How to build. How to do everything. Why I don't get any time to take Carmen into Salisbury. A game of cricket at the club is the sum total of our social life. Poor Carmen. I don't think she knew what she was doing by getting herself pregnant so that we had to get married."

"Was it deliberate?"

"Both times."

Having checked each worker was putting the right amount of raw clay in the brick-sized wooden moulds, Jeremy drove on. There were four tractors out ploughing. When they stopped, Jeremy turned off the engine of the motorcycle to listen to the engine of the tractor.

"Sometimes I can pick up an engine problem before it becomes serious. This land grew last year's tobacco. Now we deep plough and later plant maize. The maize plant draws up any leftover nitrogen fertiliser from the tobacco. Fertiliser is expensive. So is maize for the gang if we don't grow it ourselves. The surplus goes to the Grain Marketing Board. We get forty bags of maize to the acre. The TTLs get one or two bags if they're lucky. Scratch-and-plant-a-seed farming doesn't work anymore. Too many mouths to feed. Not long ago they were largely hunters and gatherers. A few crops round the huts. A few cows and goats tended by herd boys. There w fish in the rivers. What more did a man want? We buggered all that up by showing them our way of life and stopping them dying in infancy and from Africa's wealth of adult diseases. Progress, I suppose. We all think we want a better way of life. Why I came out here. Trouble is, you solve one problem and create another. Inherently, man is never satisfied. Come on. Three more tractors to check. It's easier to plough the second time. Ploughing virgin land after stumping is the bugger. Broken more ploughs that way than you can imagine... So what do you think of it all, Paul?"

"Damned hard work. For everyone."

Towards evening, with the wind gone down to nothing, Jeremy drove them to the site of his seedbeds. There were neat rows of heaped seedbeds with paths in between. Heaped on top of the beds was brushwood a foot high. Four black men were waiting on their hoes for Jeremy. With his cigarette lighter, Jeremy lit the tinder-dry brushwood sending flames high into the evening sky. Smoke rose straight up. Not a trace of wind.

"If the wind's blowing you can start a brush fire and all hell breaks loose."

"What are you doing?"

"Scorching the earth of bugs so they won't eat my tobacco seedlings. You can fumigate the beds by covering them with plastic and pumping in a fumigant. That's expensive. The small branches from the stumping that don't go into the fires at the bottom of the barns go on the seedbeds. Costs nothing. Low growing costs and high tobacco yield. How to make a profit."

"The principle is the same for every business."

"Of course it is. We'll wait until the fires have died down. You've got to watch everything. Then we'll go back to where we were stumping this morning. Those three chaps should have finished. Here I have my first irrigation system from the dam that feeds the house and the native compound. They have taps with running water in the compound. For the first time in their lives the women don't have to hump buckets of water. If the brush on the beds gets out of hand we can start the pump and turn on the sprinklers. Never happened yet. Later, when we water the seeds onto the beds in watering cans, we have water to irrigate the beds so the plants are ready to go out into the lands when the rains break. Gets us two months ahead in the growing season."

"I never thought you needed brains for farming."

"You need brains for everything. Why people who think in this world get on and the ones who don't go short. I think through every job on the farm before going ahead the best way. Don't you remember Dad always telling us to think before we did anything?"

"I still miss him."

"So do I."

When they got back to the house the sun was going down. Beth met them before they climbed off the motorcycle. They were both smiling, happy with their day.

"Carmen's gone somewhere leaving the children with the nanny."

"What do you mean, Beth?" said Paul.

"After you went off on the bike I went to our room to have an afternoon nap. God knows what time it was when we eventually got to bed last night. I was too tired to look at my watch. Just before I dozed off I heard her car go out. She hasn't come back. She really shouldn't drive a car in that state."

"She's probably driven to the club."

"I feel bad. She wanted me to stay round the pool and drink with her. I was too exhausted. Two drinks are usually my lot. The kids have gone off to look at the cows that have come from the fields to the milking shed. Silas told them what was happening and they all ran off. All except Randall. The nanny had put him down for the night. Little mite was exhausted, trying all day to keep up with the older children."

Going inside the house, Jeremy picked up the phone. There was no one on the party line, the same one everyone used in the block. He wound the handle on the box next to the phone, making two short rings followed by a long one they would hear in the club. Then he waited. Everyone had a different combination of rings, their minds only registering when it was theirs, ignoring the rest. An African answered the phone.

"Is my wife in the club, Noah? This is Jeremy Crookshank."

"No, boss. Last time she here was for the cricket."

"Thank you." Jeremy put down the phone. Outside the sun was sinking fast, the night coming down.

One by one he phoned the neighbours. No one had seen his wife.

"You don't think she's driven into Salisbury?" said Paul.

"She did it once before and frightened the hell out of me. She didn't so much as pack a bag. Stayed with her friend Candy who still isn't married. Candy says she's having too much fun in a town where there are three men for every single woman. I'll try and phone Mrs Wade. They all stayed with Mrs Wade. Carmen, Candy and Livy. How I first met

Carmen. Getting through to Salisbury at this time of day is a pain. The operator has to get the number. If Carmen's not there I'll phone Meikles Hotel. Then Bretts and ask for Hennie. If she's gone to Bretts she'll say hello to Hennie."

"She was too drunk to drive all the way to Salisbury," said Beth.

"Amazing what we can do when we want something. My wife is an alcoholic though neither of us will admit it. She's a social alcoholic at this stage. Hates drinking on her own. Once she gets going she doesn't want to stop. My bet is she's gone looking for someone to drink with."

"Shouldn't we go and look for her?" said Paul.

"Where do we start? It's just bush out there with a web of roads connecting each of the farms. One main road to Salisbury. Hopefully, she stopped somewhere and fell asleep. We'd never find her in the dark. She could be anywhere in the block."

"Let's try, Jeremy. I have a feeling this is all my fault. If I'd said I wanted to go into Salisbury tonight you would have agreed. I was trying to make it easier for you."

"I'll make the call to Mrs Wade. Chances are she'll be home before the call comes through. Usually takes an hour to put through a call."

"I'll help the nanny to put Phillip to bed when he comes back from watching them milk the cows," said Beth. "I always thought they milked cows in the morning."

"Where the hell is she?" said Jeremy, making the single long ring on the phone box to call the operator.

While they waited for the call to be put through to Mrs Wade in Salisbury they sat on the veranda protected by a long wire-mesh screen against mosquitoes and bugs attracted by the single gas light. Outside it was pitch-dark. Not a trace of the moon. None of them wanted a drink. The children were being fed in the dining room by the nanny, Randall already in bed fast asleep, exhausted by his day. Phillip did not seem to notice his mother was not in the house, having spent most of his day with the nanny.

Shortly after the children were put to bed, Beth making a fuss of them, Jeremy and Paul went outside and walked to the edge of the lawn, straining their ears out into the bush for the sound of Carmen's car engine. There were three layers of stars in the heavens giving just enough light for them to see where they were going. They stood next to each other in silence, both of them hoping they would hear the car's engine. All they heard was the screech of the cicadas. From the native compound there was silence, everyone gone to bed. There was no electricity in the compound, only a generator for the house and the workshop. Jeremy had not turned on the generator so he could listen to the sounds coming from the night.

"She'll be all right," said Paul.

"Of course she will. God looks after drunks. When they fall down they never break a bone. She'll have passed out somewhere on the side of a road, parked under a tree, sleeping it off. My poor Carmen."

"Shall we go and look for her?"

"We'll wait for the call to Mrs Wade. I feel so damn impotent. Where do we start? Just look at it out there. It's all so vast. She'll be safe inside the car. Wild animals won't be able to hurt her."

When the call came through to Mrs Wade Jeremy drew a blank. The call he had booked to Meikles and Bretts drew the same. No one had seen Carmen.

"You stay and look after the children," Paul said to Beth. "We're going out to have a look."

All night the brothers drove round the bush in the truck, finding no trace of Carmen or her car. When the sun came up they drove home. All through the night they had stopped, shouting her name above the screech of the cicadas.

"She must be somewhere," said Jeremy.

"Of course she is."

4

For three days everyone in the Centenary went out in their trucks looking for Carmen. The police had been called in across the country.

"I'm not going home until we find her," said Paul on the Friday. "Do you think that chap's aerial photographs will turn up anything? The bush is so dense in parts it would swallow a car without a trace. I'm sorry, Jeremy. You've got to face facts. Carmen has vanished without a trace."

"*Can* you stay a little longer?"

"Of course we can. The kids are not due back in school until the end of August."

"It's my damn fault for not controlling her drinking. I should have stopped having booze on the farm. It just made her seem a little happier in the evenings. Rudy Gordon, a friend of Carmen and Livy's, has found an ex-RAF photographic interpreter he has asked to scan the aerial photographs. They can pick up a car more easily looking down between the trees where our view from the ground would be obstructed. Rudy says he's good. Young chap. Did his National Service in the RAF where he helped plan the bombing of Egypt's airfields during the Suez crisis. I feel so damn impotent. What do I tell the children? Phillip keeps asking for his mother and Randall won't stop crying."

"We have to be patient."

"I'm not good at being patient, Paul. Not right now."

"I'm sorry. I'm so damn sorry. If we hadn't come out for a visit, none of this would have happened."

The main job on the farm, grading and baling the tobacco, continued despite the crisis. The daily life of the farm went on. Jeremy spent most of his time supervising in the grading shed, trying not to think of Carmen. Paul stayed with him. They talked of everything they could think of except Carmen. Beth sat by the phone in the house.

On the Monday, Jeremy had a sale. He and Paul drove early into Salisbury leaving Beth on the farm with the children. They had told the children Carmen had gone to visit friends. Believing their father, Phillip stopped asking for his mother and Randall stopped crying. All day they played happily by the pool, watched over by the nanny. Jeremy's first sale was at eleven o'clock in the morning. Paul had extended his visit by phone. In Salisbury, the travel agent booked him a flight with his family back to England for the following Wednesday.

"Tinus Oosthuizen, who owns our American operation, more our agent now, is flying in on the Friday. I have to be home for that meeting, Jeremy."

"You've been wonderful, Paul. I know you still have your own life."

They were sitting in the restaurant of the auction floor eating a free breakfast on Tobacco Sales, a custom for any farmer who had a sale. They had been to the police in Salisbury. No one had heard of Carmen or seen her car. Rudy Gordon had taken off that morning with a photographer to sweep the Centenary and the area surrounding the road into Salisbury. The ex-RAF chap had agreed to study the photographs for any sign of Carmen's car.

At the auction people came up to Jeremy offering their sympathy. It was a small community among the whites of Rhodesia. One woman, trying to be kind or catty – Jeremy wasn't sure – suggested Carmen had left the country.

"Marriages break up, Jeremy. She'll be all right. Instead of arguing she upped and left you. Happens all the time in Rhodesia."

Both Jeremy and Paul looked at her, saying nothing.

When the sale was over, they drove again to the police station.

"We had our people check the airports and the border posts to see if your wife had left the country. No one with the name of Carmen

Crookshank, or Carmen Crossley, your wife's maiden name, has left Rhodesia since you reported her missing. I'm sorry, Jeremy. We're still searching."

"She's lying dead somewhere isn't she, Joe?"

"It's been ten days. We're doing our best."

"Thanks. I know you are."

They got back to World's View after dark. Rudy Gordon had landed, handing the photographs to the local chemist for developing.

"Take a couple of days, Jeremy. We took a lot of photographs. The moment Damon Chesson finds something we'll be on the phone. How are you doing?"

"Bloody awful. I've told the kids she's visiting friends. Thanks for your help. I'll pay you, of course."

"You don't owe me anything."

They had been silent all the way back in the car. In the house, Beth had heard nothing. They ate supper mostly in silence before going to bed, Jeremy lying awake, the side of the bed next to him empty.

"Where are you, my love?" he kept asking.

When he slept his dreams were tormented. In the morning he was more tired than when he went to bed. Phillip asked when his mother was coming home.

In the afternoon, Paul put through a call to New York to tell Tinus Oosthuizen what was happening. He had earlier called his London office to tell them he was delayed. The meeting with Tinus in London was to talk about Mario Tuchi and Photographic Safaris, where they were going with their marketing in the States, and for Tinus to talk to Dorian Brigandshaw about *African Safaris* magazine. They had not seen each other face to face for a while.

"If she's gone offroad you may never find her, Paul. I know that part of the country. Uncle Harry and I went up from Elephant Walk on horses. My grandfather rode all over that bush. It's wild. Nobody lives there. She could easily become disoriented and not know which direction she was driving. I'll cancel my trip. You stay with your brother as long as you have to. When you get back to England why don't you fly out to the States? There are travel agents we can go and see. With you just back from Africa it will make a better sell. They like to meet the

Lady Come Home

executives of the companies with whom they are doing business. Your poor brother. Those kids."

"What about his wife, Tinus?" asked Paul, the line to America surprisingly good.

"I hate to be negative but if she's been on her own in the bush that long she'll be dead of starvation or thirst. There'd be no one to help her. You have to know the bush to survive. I know, I grew up in the African bush. Carmen was a girl from London. What a tragedy. Give him my best. You stay with him, Paul. Your brother needs you. What's he going to do with those two young kids. My God. You can't run a six-thousand acre farm and bring up two children at the same time. You need a wife. The nanny will only do what she's told."

"My kids go back to school at the end of next month. From where I'm standing in the lounge of Jeremy's house everything seems so far away."

"The pleasures of living in the bush. When the pressure gets to me in New York I tell Genevieve we're packing up and going back to the simple life of Africa."

"Has she ever lived in Africa?"

"Of course not. She's English. She's making a new film. In the early days it was all about being good-looking. The camera liking her face. She's a damn good actress, my wife. She's enjoying herself. Your poor brother. I don't know what I would do if anything happened to Genevieve. I'd be completely lost. I appreciate the call. Letting me know. You stay right where you are."

After days of being told nothing, Jeremy couldn't wait any longer. The grading was going well on its own, the black bossman making sure the grades were correct, the bales of tobacco exactly two hundred pounds.

"I can't stand all this waiting, Paul. We have to go into Salisbury. Visit Damon Chesson. I want to look at those photographs with my own eyes. The kids will be fine with Beth if she doesn't mind another day on her own."

"Of course I don't, Jeremy. What family is all about."

They drove in again in the truck, Paul driving, Jeremy searching the bush on the sides of the road. He was silent all the way into Salisbury.

"The police station first," said Jeremy. "To see Joe Kemp. Damon Chesson has a flat in Baker Avenue, the block of flats not far from Mrs Wade where Livy stayed."

The police had no news. Joe Kemp was busier than he had appeared on their previous visit. There was more than one crisis in the headquarters of the British South Africa Police. A young man answered the door to the flat in Baker Avenue.

"Come in. You must be Jeremy Crookshank. When I phoned, a lady said you were on your way into Salisbury to see me... I've set it all up in the spare bedroom. No good news, I'm afraid. Not a trace. The two wrecks I picked up are old. I checked with the Centenary police. Spoke to the Member in Charge. Old accidents, both of them. Come and have a look. I've set up a complete photographic mosaic of the Centenary on a makeshift clapboard table. I've scrutinised every inch of the ground. Those glasses standing on my writing table over the two photographs create a three-dimensional image. They're a pair of 3D glasses that you stand over the photographs instead of wearing them on your face. How we did it in the RAF. The chap that trained me was a navigator during the war. Seventy-eight operations over Germany. They gave him the DFC and bar. You have to be meticulous with aerial photography. I was doing my National Service. Never thought my knowledge would be any use out here. I work at the Standard Bank. Boring, really. Not much money. Better than England. The booze and fags in Rhodesia are cheap. Have a look through the glasses. You must be Paul, Jeremy's brother. Had a long chat with your wife. What a terrible tragedy."

On the makeshift table in the room was the aerial photograph of the entire Centenary made up of photographs. Each, twice the size of a book, neatly locked together by drawing pins. There was a smaller writing table in front with a chair where Damon Chesson had been sitting. The rest of the room was bare.

"You have to bring two photographs of the same piece of ground together to bring up the three-dimensional picture. Before placing them together on the big board I inspected every inch of the ground sitting at my writing desk. The bank gave me a couple of days off... Rudy Gordon made five photographic sweeps of the area in an exact pattern. The same way we planned the bombing of Egypt after Nasser nationalised the Suez Canal in '56. The Americans told us to get out. Took us twenty-four hours to retake the canal. We and the French built that canal. Without British and French engineering they'd still have an isthmus separating the Med and the

Indian Ocean. You can't just confiscate someone else's hard work and money, someone else's property, whoever you think you are. The Egyptians got a royalty for using their land. What was their problem? The Americans will regret siding with Colonel Nasser. The Middle East is a nest of vipers. Nasser won't do the Egyptians any good. Neither will the Americans. Mark my word. I was at the Joint Air Reconnaissance Intelligence Centre just outside Oxford. I could tell you a lot more about the British–American argument were it not for the Official Secrets Act. A flaming bloody row. We were right. The Americans were wrong. You can't side with a thief."

"Not a trace of her?"

"Not a trace, Jeremy. I'm not sure whether to be happy or sad. If she isn't there among all that bush she has to be somewhere else. She could still be alive. Look, you can see your own farm. Even the swimming pool next to the house. When you look down from the heavens the msasa trees don't look so dense. You can see through the canopy. All the contours of the land stand out which I've marked on the big picture. By the way, you chaps are drilling boreholes for water in all the wrong places."

"You can see the boreholes?"

"Every one of them."

"Most of them are dry."

"I'm not surprised. The contours lead you to underground water."

"You've done so much work. Thank you."

"Glad to try and help."

"Rudy won't take any money."

"Neither will I. Just tell the farmers I now know the best spots to drill for borehole water, so they have drinking water when the rivers stop flowing in the dry season."

"They'll pay for that... Where is she, Damon?"

"I have no idea. I'm so sorry."

Jeremy sat down at the desk and peered through what looked like a pair of inverted spectacles on a metal stand, Damon Chesson leaning over his shoulder slightly moving the two overlapping photographs of the same sweep of brush. Suddenly the trees and hills came up to meet him, the picture he was seeing leaping up alive. A metal cylinder three feet high with a metal cap had caught the reflection of the sun. Around the cylinder the bush had been flattened by the drilling rig, leaving a small opening among the trees.

"I can see where someone drilled for water."

"They're on the wrong end of the contour. Never find water there unless they drill a thousand feet and that's too damned expensive if you ask me. They only go down two hundred drilling for underground water. Even a piece of metal that big sticks out of the bush like a sore thumb when you're seeing it in three dimensions. A car crashing through those trees would have left a path. On one of the photographs at the edge of the Centenary you can see where an elephant has walked through the trees. Boughs have been broken. The disturbance is obvious to a trained eye. If your wife had gone off the road in a car she would have left some evidence for me to see, even if the car itself had been hidden from view which I doubt. The Centenary is a mix of savannah and trees, the msasa trees dispersed between the shoulder-high elephant grass giving an impenetrable view from the road. I told the Member in Charge he'd have to look outside the Centenary to find that car."

"I'm glad I came to see you. I understand aerial photography better. You've done so much work."

"Tell them in the club if they want to find water without drilling a string of dry wells, come to Damon Chesson. We now have the photographs. If I could make a business out of this it would be better than sitting in a bank."

"You could sell the farmers a mosaic of photographs covering their own farms," said Paul, trying to help.

On the way back down Baker Avenue they passed Mrs Wade's house, Jeremy not stopping. There were no cars parked outside the house.

"That's where it all began," said Jeremy. "I rented Livy a room for a month when she came out by boat to see me after I met her at your party. Carmen and Candy were staying with Mrs Wade. We all went to Chirundu and into the Zambezi Valley where we met Mario Tuchi. If I had booked Livy a room in another boarding house I would never have met Carmen."

"They say the whole human race is linked together a few people away. Some call it fate."

"People are being so kind. Rudy Gordon and Damon Chesson have spent hours of their time. Neither want any money."

"Not everyone is on the take. They understand what you are going through and want to help. What do we do now?"

"Go home, I suppose. I feel so damn powerless. When Dad went down at Dunkirk we knew he was gone. There were witnesses in the other ships. If we don't find Carmen I'll always think she's out there. Somewhere. That somehow she'll come home. That all this will never be over."

Paul put his hand on his brother's shoulder as Paul turned the car into Second Street and the start of the journey home. For three more hours Jeremy searched the sides of the road for any sign of a car having left a passage into the bush. Neither of them talked until they reached World's View.

"I'll just have to bring them up on my own," said Jeremy finally. "What else can I do? I'm going to have to tell them their mother has gone to heaven. Phillip may understand. Randall won't. They're very young. Years from now they won't even remember her except as a vague memory. Someone in a photograph. Carmen will just be someone smiling at them from a photograph, the smile never changing."

"Life goes on, Jeremy."

"Of course it does. Which is why you must take your family home. You can't do any more for me. Either of you. I'm now on my own with the kids. They love their nanny. I think she loves them. That's something, don't you think?"

Beth was waiting for them on the veranda. It was exactly fourteen days since Beth had heard Carmen drive off in her drunken state while Beth was trying to take a nap. The neighbours had stopped coming round having given up the search.

"I've just got to face reality," Jeremy said as much to himself. "She's dead."

"Do you want me to tell the children?" said Beth.

"Would you? I'd just break down and make it worse, if that's possible. What do children that age do without a mother?"

"I'll tell them she's not coming home. They won't understand death or their mother going to heaven."

The kids were playing next to the pool in their swimming costumes, watched over by the nanny. Their treble voices echoed happily through the trees. Jeremy heard a splash and laughter and turned away. Inside he went into the bedroom he had shared for so long with Carmen, throwing himself face down onto the bed. Only then did he cry, sobbing his heart out.

TWO DAYS before Paul Crookshank and his family were due to fly out of Salisbury on their rescheduled flight back to London, a police van drove into World's View and parked among the barns and farm buildings. The place was busy. The tractor and trailer were loading cans of fresh milk for the native compound and the children of all the workers on the farm, it being Jeremy's regimen to give each of them a pint of milk every day when they arrived at the improvised school where a teacher employed by the farm was starting to give them the first rudiments of an education. Bales of tobacco were being loaded into an RMS truck, the road motor service of Rhodesia railways, the truck and its trailerload of tobacco to be taken to the auction floor in Salisbury for sale on the Monday. The grading shed door was wide open, men and women, many with babies strapped on their backs with lengths of wide cotton linen, standing at the rows of trellis tables grading the leaves of tobacco.

Jeremy had his back to the door, the noise inside of a hundred people talking as they worked at the tables having drowned out the noise of the police vehicle. When Jeremy turned round Clay Barry, the Member in Charge for Centenary, was standing behind him. For a long moment they stared at each other, neither of them saying a word.

"We've found Carmen's car fifty miles north of the Centenary at the top of the Zambezi escarpment. There's an old road that goes down into the valley, originally a trail used by the elephant hunters hunting for ivory in the last century. It's sometimes used by our Land Rovers to patrol down into the valley. One of our chaps was on his way down to Mana Pools on the Zambezi River. You can get through to the new Kariba dam that's slowly flooding the valley with water. We're having a tremendous problem with animals stranded on ever-decreasing islands as the water level of the dam rises. She wasn't in the car, Jeremy. The driver's door was open. There was a game tracker in the Land Rover who followed her spoor. The car had run out of petrol. She likely had no idea where she was. Ten miles back down the trail – she must have been following the spoor of her own vehicle – the tracker found bits of clothing you'll have to identify. That's lion country up there. The car is still where we found it. This is terrible what I'm going to say. We found body parts. The bigger bones, the skull, the face eaten away. The tracker says a pride of lions killed your wife. Afterwards the wild dogs and the hyenas ate what the lions had left. He says your wife would have died instantly in the first attack. Probably a female lion hunting for her family. The male lions are lazy and wait for the lioness to make the kill. We could hunt down the pride of lions and kill them if you want."

"What for, Clay?... My poor Carmen. She must have been terrified."

"She would likely have died of thirst anyway up there on the escarpment. There's not much water away from the river. The tracker says the lions were a mercy."

"Can someone show me where she died?"

"Do you want to do that, Jeremy?"

"I want to bury her bones. Build a cross. Say a prayer to God. I want to bring peace to the place where she died. My brother will come with me. He'll help me put up a cross."

"The tracker is in the truck. His name is Wilson. I don't know his Shona name. I'll leave him with you on the farm. He can stay in your compound until you and Paul are ready to go. I'm so sorry."

"Thank you for finding her, Clay. Somehow it's better to know what happened. We'll fashion a wooden cross in the workshop and then we'll go."

"Will you identify the clothing? I have it in the truck. Official stuff, I'm afraid."

"Of course."

"Are you all right?"

"I'm not going to be right for a very long time, Clay."

Immaculate in his uniform with khaki shorts to his knees, polished leather puttees protecting his legs, hat square on his head, Clay Barry walked to the back of the truck followed by Jeremy. Paul, left standing at the door of the shed, watched his brother from a distance. Jeremy gave out a loud sob when the policeman showed him the remnants of Carmen's clothes, the same clothes she had been wearing at the pool when Paul and Jeremy had returned from the lands for lunch on the day she went missing. A black man in uniform got out of the passenger side of the truck and stood waiting in the shade of a row of brick barns. The

truck drove off. Jeremy was sobbing, trying to control himself. Two black
men who worked for him tried not to look as they passed: The police had
taken away the remnants of the clothing. Paul walked across and stood
next to his brother.

"I don't want to bring the bones of their mother back to the farm,"
said Jeremy. "If the kids saw something like that they'd be traumatised
for the rest of their lives. Will you help me? I've told Wilson to go to the
kitchen for Silas to give him some tea. Later, Silas can give him lunch
before we go. There's timber in the workshop for us to make a cross. We
can burn an inscription into the wood by heating a piece of metal with
the blowtorch... Africa is going to get all of us one day, Paul."

When they drove off with Wilson sitting in the back of the open truck
next to the large wooden cross, two empty grain sacks and three cans of
petrol, it was half past twelve in the afternoon. Neither of them had
wanted any lunch. Beth had watched them drive away, holding the hands
of Jeremy's children. Jeremy knew the old track, barely a road, that led
through and out of the back of the Centenary.

They found Carmen's car two hours later. The driver's door was still
open. Jeremy took the cans of petrol from the back of the truck and filled
the car's tank through a funnel. The keys were still in the ignition. The
car started when Jeremy attached jump leads from the truck, the battery
having gone flat. They left Carmen's car and got back into the truck.
There was no lion spoor around the car.

Wilson sat in front, squeezed between Jeremy and Paul, and showed
them where to go.

They first put her bones in the one sack that, when Paul lifted it,
weighed no more than five pounds. Carmen's face had been eaten away
and was unrecognisable. Ants had cleaned the bones of any flesh. Apart
from the remains of the skull they were bones like any other bones
Jeremy had found in the bush.

"It's not Carmen," said Jeremy. "Just bones. She's somewhere else. Far
away. What we have in that sack has nothing to do with her."

With the two shovels that had gone in the back of the truck with the
cross and the cans of petrol, Paul and Jeremy dug Carmen's grave, deep
enough to prevent wild animals finding her bones. The longer job was
sinking the heavy wooden cross in the ground. They had chosen a place
looking down from the top of the escarpment, down into the Zambezi

Valley. To the right of the grave and the cross was a thin waterfall, as the river that ran out of the Centenary fell over the escarpment. Before the water hit the trees far down below it was mist. The place was beautiful. A gentle wind played over them as they stood by the graveside. Jeremy took the prayer book he had carried with him since his schooldays in England and read a prayer. They stood looking down into the vast silence of the valley hundreds of feet below. They could see the Zambezi River far away in the heat haze of the day, the water shimmering. An African fish eagle circled on the thermal out in front of them, the big eyes of the predator bird watching. As it turned, its great wings spread, the bird cried out.

Burned onto the cross were the words:

GO WELL, MY DARLING

Paul said he would drive Carmen's car. They drove away, leaving the remains of Carmen at the foot of the big cross looking out over the African valley.

"WHEN THE KIDS are big enough I'll take them to their mother's grave," said Jeremy when they reached the house.

The sun had gone down leaving a red blaze in the sunset, the same sunset Livy had painted what seemed to Jeremy so long ago. He sighed, going inside. A part of his life was over. Beth was feeding the children before putting them to bed.

"They don't understand do they?" said Jeremy quietly to Beth.

"Not really. It's a blessing they're both so young."

TWO DAYS LATER, when Jeremy returned to the farm after seeing his brother off at Salisbury airport, he had never felt more lonely in his life. The children were down by the pool with the nanny.

"Now what the hell do I do?" he said, shaking his head.

He walked across to the pool. The children ran to him, both of them crying. Beth had been wrong. They understood. Jeremy put his arms round his boys and cried with them. The nanny had left them alone, waiting in the shade of a tree. She too was crying. When Jeremy looked at her she tried to smile. It was going to be a long day for all of them, he thought, standing up. Holding each son by the hand, Jeremy walked his family back to the house.

"We can all have some lemonade," he said.

"Is Uncle Paul never coming back?" said Phillip.

"He wants us to go to England. Would you like to fly in an aeroplane?"

"What's England?" asked Randall.

"The place where Uncle Paul and I were born."

"Will Mummy be there?"

"No, Randall. Your Mummy has gone to heaven."

"Where's heaven?"

"Far up in the sky."

"Can she see us?"

"Of course she can."

PART IX

AUGUST TO NOVEMBER 1961 – "THE SILENT BITE"

1

They buried Old Pringle in the shadow of Corfe Castle, a year after his granddaughter Beth and her family returned from their stay in Rhodesia leaving Jeremy alone on the farm with his two children. Through the year Paul had written to his brother suggesting Jeremy sell World's View and return with the kids to England. The 1960 Rhodesian tobacco crop had been particularly good in weight and price, Jeremy sending his brother twenty-one thousand pounds to invest, the Rhodesian pound and the British pound being fully interchangeable, both countries part of the sterling block. With Britain still short of American dollars, the competition for Rhodesian tobacco, payable in sterling, had driven the average price on the auction floors to an all-time high. The problem for Jeremy was Phillip, five years old and without a school to go to unless he was sent to a boarding school in Salisbury. Jeremy had written that the trauma of losing his mother and then being taken away from his father would be too much for the boy. With no one to control them during the day, when Jeremy was out working on the farm, the boys were running riot, the nanny having lost control of them. The nanny was just nineteen years old and never so much as shouted at them, let alone smacked them when the children went off the rails, waiting for the boss to come home in the evening to take control.

Reading Jeremy's letters, Beth understood the problem better than Paul: the boys needed a mother.

All four of Pringle's English grandchildren, Beth, Frank, Dorian and Kim, were at the funeral, none of the South African or Australian grandchildren responding to Tina Brigandshaw's cables. Her brother Bert in South Africa and sister Maggie in Australia had died some years earlier, severing the grandchildren's ties to a grandfather they had never met. Barnaby St Clair had driven down with Tina to her father's funeral from London, the whole family staying with his brother Merlin at Purbeck Manor, the first time in her life Tina had gone through the front door of the St Clair manor house, since as a child she had never ventured further than the tradesman's entrance into the kitchen. The shackles of class that separated the St Clairs and the Pringles for centuries had finally broken.

Frank, the most upset at the graveside, had brought down his latest girlfriend to the funeral. Kim and Dorian, in a more appropriate vein, had come alone. Henry and Deborah, Beth's children, had been left in London with friends. Merlin, the eighteenth Baron St Clair of Purbeck, was to preside at the wake having himself attended the funeral of a man he had lived ten miles from for most of his life and barely knew, the irony not lost on old Mrs Battle who had looked after Old Pringle in the railway cottage the last years of his life. She had decided not to go back to the manor house with the family, preferring to go home to where she was now living with her daughter in the village of Corfe Castle.

So THERE IT WAS, thought Frank, the old man's dead, let's have a drink. What was a man's life all about? He doubted if any of them had thought that without Old Pringle none of them would be alive.

"You lot go back. I'm going for a walk," Frank said.

"What about Bambi?" asked Kim.

"She'll be all right. Give her a drink. I'll find my own way back to Purbeck Manor."

"It's miles."

"So what, Kim? The least I can do is think about him. I was the only one to get to know the old man."

"How old is she, for God's sake?"

"Why don't you ask her? You had your eye on Livy I seem to remember."

"Do you see your daughter?" said Kim, deliberately changing the subject.

"Not really. Much like I never saw my real father when I was growing up... I've never seen our mother dressed from head to foot in black before. At your father's funeral in Rhodesia she wore a floral dress and a big hat like the rest of the colonials."

"Where are you going to walk?"

"Up to the ruins of the castle. It kind of beckons to me. Where I came from. Up there on the hill down here in a railway cottage. The rich and the poor. Grandfather Pringle would understand. We talked about it. I talked more sense with that old man than all my school teachers put together. You know Oliver Cromwell knocked it down? Blew the walls to pieces with gunpowder. My family went out for the king, for the Cavaliers against the Roundheads. The Commonwealth didn't last long. Revolutions never do. People like that are best at knocking things down."

Frank walked away. He had brought Bambi down to Dorset more to show off to the family than because he liked her. After Livy had walked out on him he had quickly grown bored with a string of women, all of them after his money. He was going to sleep with Bambi for the first time that night. Now he was not so sure. The funeral had put him off. He had been a fool to force Livy to marry him. They had had the perfect relationship, ruined by marriage. The very sight of her big belly when she was pregnant had put him off. Sent him off looking for other women and Livy had walked out. Poor little Donna. She'd have a life just like her father's, never quite knowing where she belonged.

Looking back at his family getting into the cars, Kim in deep conversation with Bambi, Frank turned and took the path away from the church towards the hill that straddled the Purbeck Hills.

It took Frank half an hour to climb up to the ruins on top of the hill, looking back over the village to Purbeck Manor far away in the distance.

"What's it all about?" he said to the ruins. "What's life all about? We build it all up and knock it all down."

Frank began to laugh. Gently at first until he couldn't control himself and ran down the hill towards the village. At the bottom he walked on down the road and into the parlour of the Greyhound Inn. Many of the villagers who had been at his grandfather's funeral were in the bar.

"This round's on me," he said to the barman. Everyone stopped talking to look at him.

"To my grandfather," said Frank, lifting a glass of beer the publican had pushed across the bar to him. "He had a good life."

The conversations picked up again, leaving him alone at the bar. Frank left ten pounds behind with the publican and walked out, nobody noticing.

WHEN FRANK GOT BACK to Purbeck Manor in a taxi he had found at the railway station, the wake had fizzled out. In the lounge the remnants of the food were still on the tables. He could see Kim through the window, sitting on a wooden bench under an elm tree with Bambi. He watched them only mildly annoyed. The rest of the family were nowhere to be seen. He poured himself a drink and sat with his back to the window. He was lonely. In a house full of family he was lonely. The idea of seeing his daughter made him stand up and look out of the big bay window. Bambi and Kim were walking away from the bench into the woods.

He had done what he had come to do and paid his respects to his grandfather.

Going upstairs, he retrieved his overnight bag from the bedroom. His car was still in the driveway where he had left it, having driven to the funeral in his father's car with his mother and father. There was no one around to see him go. The pigeons were calling to each other from the trees. Opening the car door and throwing the bag in the back, he got in the driver's seat and sat for a moment looking down the driveway through the long avenue of old trees. He turned the key in the ignition and gunned the engine before letting in the clutch. Nobody came out of the house. Nobody had noticed. He was going back to London to see his daughter. Bambi and Kim wouldn't mind. He doubted if anyone would mind. Particularly his mother, engrossed as she was with his father; staying in the house she had had her eye on from a child, her dream come true.

· · ·

Tina Brigandshaw watched the car go away from her second floor bedroom window. She had taken off the black dress and lain on the bed, hoping to have an afternoon sleep. They had stood in the lounge after they came back in convoy from the funeral, none of them knowing what to say. Now Frank had gone off without a word to anyone. The old manor house of the St Clairs she had once so envied wasn't so important anymore. She questioned in her mind whether the father she had just buried had done any worse in his life in the small railway cottage, all of them crammed as kids in the bedrooms into bunks, one for the girls and one for the boys, all of them dead but her. They had laughed. She had been happy as a girl. Happy with Barnaby who came so often to call, the thought now crossing her mind that the railway cottage was more fun than the old manor house with all the corridors and so many rooms, servants at Barnaby's every beck and call. They had each wanted the life of the other. Her father had been happy through his life, of that she was sure. He had loved her mother, brought home enough money to give them all food. Her mother had made a home that was warm and welcoming, the smell of cooking permeating the cottage. They had never been rich. Never dressed posh. Never owned anything much in their lives. They had never gone wanting for homemade food and the comfort of family. The manor house was cold. The corridors and stairways so big. The ceilings so high. The bed behind her so small in such a big room. Had Barnaby's father been any more happy than the old man she had just put to rest in the churchyard next to his wife and the rest of the Pringle family? She doubted it. All her life she had wanted to appear as someone, not just the daughter of a common railway worker. Now she was not so sure as she watched her son's fancy car disappear down the long avenue of trees. Maybe life wasn't all about possessions after all.

"I wonder where he's going," she said to herself before climbing back into bed to stare up at the ceiling.

Strangely content, she quickly fell into a trouble-free sleep, only waking when Barnaby knocked on her door.

"Want to go for a walk, old girl? Thought we'd take the old paths again. Sleep well? Frank's gone. Probably back to London. Not a word to anyone. The rest of them are either taking a nap or have gone for a walk. It's a beautiful summer's evening. The birds are singing. Reminds me of how it was when you and I were children. Come on. We're going for a good tramp through the woods. It was a nice funeral if there is such a thing. If you ask me the vicar meant every word he said at the graveside about your father."

"They had known each other all of their lives. Everyone loved my father. Thank you for helping me, Barnaby."

"It was the least I could do. For you and Frank. He's not happy, you know. He's probably got business to attend to in London. Trouble with making so much money. He's always on the go. You can never relax when you've got money."

"Would it have been any different if we had married each other when we were young?"

"Probably not. Life has a habit of never being quite what you want."

"You remember Johannesburg? You arriving at my twenty-first birthday party out of the blue? I was so happy to see you. Salisbury? We were the best pair of con artists in the business. You'd flash your title and I'd flash my boobs. Not only did the marks pay for the dinner, they lent you money... Did you ever repay any of them when you got rich?"

"One or two. I never paid back my army colonel though I tried to. Colonel Hugh Parson paid back the fifty pounds I had borrowed from the officers' mess funds instead of having me cashiered out of the army in disgrace. Harry Brigandshaw said I'd find someone else to repay the colonel's good deed one day."

"It was all in good fun. We were good, you and I. Memories. That's what life is all about. You'll find someone to repay. We all get in those kind of binds when we're young."

Pulling back the bedclothes, Tina got up from the bed, crossed the room in her underwear and gave Barnaby a kiss on the cheek.

"What was that for?"

"Those lovely memories of youth. Come on then. Let's take a walk back into our past."

Quickly putting on a top, a pair of slacks and sandals, she took his hand and walked with him out of the bedroom.

There was no one around when they strolled down the path and into the woods where they took the path along the river back in the direction of the old railway cottage where Tina had lived as a child.

"Just like old times," said Barnaby.

"Isn't it?"

They were still holding hands. As they had always done as children. They were happy, two old people walking the same old path by the river.

KIM AND BAMBI had found a grassy bank below the bridle path that led from the manor house along the river. Further down was the Pringle railway cottage halfway to the village of Corfe Castle. Looking back they could see the brown chimney pots of the old St Clair house above the trees. They heard voices. Along the road above the bridle path Kim saw his mother walking hand in hand with Barnaby St Clair. The two were talking and smiling at each other, giving Kim a flash of annoyance that flooded his mind. She was being disloyal to his father walking hand in hand with another man, especially Frank's father. Kim stared in silence, expecting his mother to feel his annoyance and turn round. The two old people walked on, oblivious to everything around them. They were talking of old times they had spent together, Kim trying not to listen. Both of them kept bursting into giggles. In silence, Kim and Bambi listened to the voices go on up the road, fading into the distance, the gurgling sounds of the small river in front of them coming back. Kim gave Bambi a wry smile and shrugged his shoulders. His father was dead, his mother alive. Kim could not remember seeing his mother and father look so happy together.

"What do you do for a living, Kim? You don't think Frank will mind us going for a walk?"

"Are you two lovers?"

"Of course not. He's far too old for me. Frank's well into his thirties. I'm hoping he's going to offer me a job in his PR firm. I only finished school last month."

"My goodness. Didn't realise you were so young."

"Eighteen. Frank said he only employs good-looking girls. Says they are better at getting what he wants for his customers. I may go to university. It all depends if I get into Cambridge. Meanwhile I need a job. My parents aren't wealthy like yours. All that old money. Frank's promised to take me to Hastings Court, your father's old home. I know all about him finding out he wasn't really a Brigandshaw. What a dreadful thing to find out. I don't blame you glaring at them just now. Frank said they both grew up here as children. They looked happy. You must be glad for your mother she looked so happy... Don't you think we should walk back? Frank must have got back to the house by now. It's such a lovely place here by the river. There is nothing more beautiful than the English countryside on a perfect summer's evening. I can see a stickleback in the shallow water just in front of my foot... You didn't tell me what you do. Come on. You can tell me all about it as we walk back to the house."

"I'm a drifter, Bambi. I don't have a job. Maybe next month... There's more scandal hereabouts. Not just my mother and the Honourable Barnaby St Clair, who is the brother of my father's first wife who was killed by a gunman."

"How terrible."

"The man was trying to shoot my father. If he'd succeeded I wouldn't have come into this world. The man who shot Lucinda, Barnaby's sister, was my father's CO in the Royal Flying Corps when Dad was fighting in France in the First World War. Dad said all the killing in the air war had driven Colonel Braithwaite mad. That he couldn't stop killing. There was a girl involved but that bit was never explained to us kids. Dad's buried next to Lucinda and her unborn child on Elephant Walk in Rhodesia. We don't own the farm anymore. Belongs to the Anglo-US Incorporated. My brother Dorian wrote a book about the Brigandshaws in Rhodesia. *White Hunter* was a bestseller. But that's not the scandal I was talking about. Lord St Clair, your host, is the father of Genevieve the actress, by a barmaid he met during the First World War."

"I've seen her films. The one I liked best was *Keeper of the Legend*. Gregory L'Amour played the hero. He's gorgeous."

"That movie was about Genevieve's ancestors, the St Clairs. Merlin St Clair never married the barmaid."

"So the famous Genevieve is a bastard!"

"And married to my cousin, Tinus Oosthuizen. They are coming back to England now their girl is old enough to go to boarding school. Her brother's been at Charterhouse for a couple of years. Genevieve is going back on the West End stage. Tinus will commute across the pond. He has a successful business in New York. Genevieve thinks she has got me a job as an assistant stage manager, which will give me something to do. My father left me an income enough to drift but not enough to settle down with a wife and kids and become responsible. I like the idea of being part of the theatre. With luck I'll get myself the odd walk-on part. I find people in the arts more interesting than people in business. People in business only talk about money. Be careful of my half-brother Frank. He'll be after your body. It's how he works. Money and women. Often they go together."

"I'm far too young for him."

"Don't you believe it. Come on. I'm hungry. They should be having supper back at the house round about now. Are you hungry, Bambi?"

"Starving... What lovely stories. I could listen to you all night. What does an assistant stage manager actually do?"

"Paints scenery and moves the furniture and props between scenes. Pretty ordinary. What's exciting is being a part of the theatre. You have to start somewhere. Who knows what it will bring? If Genevieve doesn't get me the job I was thinking of going back out east. I lived in a Buddhist monastery in Bhutan. I like the mysticism of the east. They're much more civilised than we are. We Europeans are savages. Look at the way we've turned on each other in the last fifty years."

"Where else have you been?"

"Australia, on a sheep station. America, on a ranch in Kansas. Africa. I ran a photographic safari operation for a while, until I got bored. The first few lions are interesting to photograph. Made the adrenaline pump. After a while they are just big pussycats."

"I hope I have as interesting a life."

Kim, conscious of trying to impress the young girl, gave her a smile, asking himself why men always tried to boast to an attractive woman.

"Sometimes life is more interesting in the telling," he said.

"I hope you enjoy the theatre."

"So do I."

When they reached the old house half an hour later the family were out on the terrace with its six-foot drop overlooking the gardens. A long table had been covered with a white tablecloth where an old servant was putting out food. They walked up the steps onto the terrace, Kim looking for his mother and Barnaby.

There was no sign of them.

"Our mother's still out walking and Frank's gone home by the look of it," said Dorian. "Didn't you pass them on the road? Come and have a drink. Frank just took off, not a word to anyone."

"How am I going to get home?" said Bambi.

"I'm sure Kim will take you up to London on the train in the morning. Leatherhead is on the Waterloo line. Or you can drive back with Beth and Paul. Don't worry. You're in good hands. Come and have a look at the food. Looks wonderful. I hate funerals. When I know I'm dying I'm going to be like a cat and go into the bushes to die on my own."

"Didn't you love your grandfather?" asked Bambi.

"Didn't really know him."

"That's awful."

"Not really. Didn't know my great-grandfather or all the grandfathers before them. We're all just a link in the chain. All part of the process of evolution."

"Do you have any children, Dorian?"

"That's a sore point," said Kim.

"Have I stepped on somebody's toes?"

"In a manner of speaking. Her name is Wendy. She was adopted. How old is she now, Dorian?"

"Eleven."

"Do you see her?"

"Of course not."

"Do you think of her?"

"Sometimes. I'm going to write the story of me and Nancy into a book, so if the kid finds out she's adopted she'll understand. It was a one-night stand. I was a private in the army. What was I meant to do?"

"You're quite a family... Can I have a drink? So Frank just drove off. So much for the job. Can I have a gin and orange?"

The two brothers looked at each other and shook their heads. Then Kim went off to pour Bambi a drink. She was a pretty girl. Kim hoped she would go through her life without so many complications.

"There you go," he said, handing her the drink. "I slipped a bit with the gin bottle. Here's to your health and here's to your wealth. May you have a good life, Bambi. I enjoyed our walk by the river."

"So do I."

"Can you do me a favour?"

"What's that?"

"Don't grow up too quickly."

Bambi sipped her drink, looking into his eyes over the rim of the cocktail glass, mischief bubbling in her smile.

Half an hour later, Dorian watched his mother and Barnaby St Clair come in from their walk. They were unconsciously holding each other's hands like two young children. Dorian, always looking for a plot line, wondered if the love between two children could last a lifetime, filing the picture in the back of his mind. It was how he wrote books. He was back to writing the sweet books some of the critics called trivia. *White Hunter*, the true story of his grandfather Sebastian Brigandshaw and his only book of value, had stopped selling in England and America. He was always searching for storylines. Childhood sweethearts growing old together was everyone's dream, the kind of story his publisher encouraged him to write. 'Light and fluffy, Dorian,' Alex Wimpleton always told him. 'Never make the reader think. Tell them what they want to hear. Light and fluffy. That's what sells. What makes money. *White Hunter* is a good book. May even make you famous. But it will never sell more copies than *The Sweet Scent of Blossom*, and that's what it's all about. The reader wants to live in a perfect world because the one he lives in is horrible. Take them away to somewhere nice where they can hide.'

Kim's mention of Wendy was still niggling Dorian's mind when they all sat down to dinner. No one mentioned the absence of Frank.

"So, what are you writing these days?" asked Beth from across the supper table. "You looked miles away. Was the new story writing itself in your head?"

"Something like that, sis. Are you driving back tomorrow?"

"First thing in the morning."

"Bambi needs a lift."

"Good old Frank. Never changes. Always thinking of himself. There's plenty of room in the car."

"Can I drive up with you?" asked Kim. "Save me the train fare. I'm trying to get myself a job in the theatre."

"That's new," said Beth.

"Give me something to do... Here's to Grandfather," he said, standing up and holding his glass to the family. "May his soul rest in peace."

The room went quiet. The family stood up. Tina was crying.

"Old Pringle," they all said, lifting their glasses.

2

*N*ot trusting the vagaries of the stock market or the value of the British pound with his brother's money, Paul Crookshank had looked at buying a block of flats. The snag was twenty-one thousand pounds not being enough to cover the twenty per cent of the small block he had looked at in Chelsea within walking distance of the Thames. Paul had found the flats by accident when he and Beth had driven the car to Chelsea and gone for a walk by the river. They had passed the 'For Sale' sign after parking the car in a side street at the end of autumn when the trees were losing their leaves. That morning, Paul had received another letter from Jeremy in Rhodesia asking what he had done with the money Jeremy had been sent a week before Old Pringle's funeral.

"That looks a nice investment," Beth had said, triggering the idea in his mind.

After their long walk by the river in the autumn sun, the children having been dropped off at a Sunday birthday party for one of Henry's school friends, Paul had written down the name of the estate agent and gone to see them the next day. The Brigandshaw Limited business of selling old English mansions to Americans had made Paul savvy with the property market, the value rising steadily each year.

"How much do you want for it?" he asked Netherby and Saint when he called at their office in Knightsbridge.

"One hundred and eighty thousand pounds, Mr Crookshank. I know of your company, of course. You have an associate in New York which gives you the advantage or we'd have had a go at selling country estates ourselves. You, of course, have contact with so many of the old aristocracy from selling their antiques. Such a pity to see them going broke after so many centuries. It's the new taxes of course. One man's bad luck is another man's fortune."

"I want to buy the block of flats for my brother."

"Oh, I see. Well that's another kettle of fish as they say. Does your brother have that kind of money? What does he do?"

"He's a tobacco farmer in Rhodesia."

"Goodness. That is a long way away. How is Rhodesia? I had a cousin who trained to fly in Rhodesia during the war. RAF Thornhill I seem to remember. Outside a town called Gwelo. I could be wrong. He was shot down over Normandy."

"I'm sorry... We don't have the full one hundred and eighty thousand pounds."

"You could get a mortgage on the building and use the income from the flats to pay the interest if your brother doesn't need a private income."

"He sent me twenty-one thousand pounds."

"Not quite enough, I'm afraid. You require twenty per cent of the purchase price. Thirty-six thousand pounds. You could put in some of your own money. Bring in some of your friends. Form an investment property company. With your good name in Brigandshaw Limited, Mr Crookshank, I'm sure the loan would be approved by the bank."

"Could you arrange such a loan?"

"Of course. It's part of our business. Of the twenty-eight flats, twenty-seven are let. The block of flats was built on a bomb site after the war. The leases are all for five years at a fixed rental."

"Can you fix the interest rate for five years?"

"That can be arranged."

"May I have an option, Mr Netherby?"

"I'll require your cheque for five thousand pounds for a thirty-day option. If you fail to complete the transaction you will forfeit ten per cent of your deposit. I'm sure you understand."

"I will give you my cheque. You are welcome to phone my bank manager. My brother's money is in a deposit account on twenty-four hour call only requiring my signature."

"The word of a gentleman is quite sufficient, Mr Crookshank. I'll have the option agreement drawn up straight away. Shall we say three o'clock this afternoon to sign the agreement?"

Wondering where he was going to find fifteen thousand pounds in the next thirty days, Paul drove from Knightsbridge to Chelsea to have another good look at the block of flats and talk to the caretaker.

"Mr Netherby is right, Mr Crookshank. Just one of our flats is vacant. Mr Netherby increased the rent substantially after the previous tenant left, I'm afraid."

"By how much?"

"Thirty per cent, I believe. The original rental was set five years ago without an escalation clause."

"Are you going to get that kind of increase?"

"We can only try. Only went on the market last week. Netherby and Saint are also the letting agents. Are you wishing to rent the flat yourself?"

"No. I'm wishing to buy your block of flats."

The man went pale. Paul smiled.

"I'm sure you'll keep your job, Mr?"

"Sanderson. We have a small apartment, my wife and I in the basement. Can I show you round?"

"That would be kind."

"I have a key to all the flats if the tenant is not at home."

"I'm sure you do… I'm buying the flats for my brother in Rhodesia."

"Isn't that somewhere in Africa?"

"I believe so."

"Mrs Penrose. I'm so sorry to disturb you. As you know, this block of flats is on the market. The gentleman is a prospective buyer. May we come in?"

"The place is in a bit of a mess. Come in. You're not going to put up the rent I hope. We have another year to go on our lease. I've heard the vacant flat is much more expensive."

"Sitting tenants will receive preferential treatment if they wish to renew their five-year leases," said Paul. "Do you have any problems with your flat, Mrs Penrose?"

"None at all. Whoever built this block of flats built it properly. Would you like a cup of tea?"

"I never say no to a cup of tea, Mrs Penrose," said the caretaker. "If Mr Crookshank here has the time. He's buying the block for his brother in Rhodesia."

At three o'clock Paul was back at the offices of Netherby and Saint with a cheque drawn on his brother's account for five thousand pounds, the cheque dated the following day. The option agreement had been completed which Paul read through before signing. He had a month to find the fifteen thousand pounds or he had thrown away five hundred pounds of his brother's money.

"Why don't you go and see Livy?" Beth said that night over supper in Paul's Hammersmith flat where the grand piano had been restored following the resurgence of Brigandshaw Limited.

"Has she got that kind of money?"

"Frank's father invested her money. You don't think my brother would have married a pauper?"

"Then why did he divorce her?"

"She divorced him. For adultery."

"Are you scheming, my love?"

"Of course I am. There's your brother in Rhodesia with two children and no mother and Livy with one and no father. You know Frank went to see them after grandfather Pringle's funeral. Hasn't been back since. My niece needs a full-time father and your nephews need a mother. If you tie Livy and Jeremy financially together in a block of flats, who knows what can come?"

"Her money's invested."

"She can sign guarantor for the fifteen thousand pounds while she's liquidating some other assets."

"Is she that rich?"

"Oh, yes. And getting richer. She has another exhibition at the Nouvelle Galerie on Guy Fawkes night."

"Come on then. Let's go and see her."

"Right now?"

"No time like the present."

BY THE TIME England was exploding with fireworks on the fifth of November, Paul had finalised the purchase of the Chelsea block of flats with the mortgage and equity split between his brother and Livy in equal proportion to their invested money. The twenty-eighth flat had been let by Mr Netherby for the thirty per cent increase in rent. Provided twenty-five of the tenants paid their rent on time there was sufficient income to cover the mortgage repayment to the Abbey National Building Society with whom Mr Netherby had arranged the mortgage earning himself a good commission. With a small rental increase as the five-year leases came due for renewal, Jeremy and Livy would be, in Barnaby St Clair's words, 'laughing'. Before the purchase was completed, Barnaby, as Livy's long-time financial advisor, had gone through every detail of the transaction.

Three days after Livy's successful exhibition at the Nouvelle Galerie, Paul phoned his brother in Rhodesia on a fixed-time call.

"You've done what, Paul?"

"Bought you a block of twenty-eight flats in Chelsea."

"With twenty-one thousand pounds!"

"You have two partners. The Abbey National Building Society, who hold an eighty per cent mortgage, and Livy. You put in your twenty-one thousand and Livy fifteen."

"Why, Paul?"

"Because it's a good investment. The block of flats is close to her studio. Beth wants to know how are the kids?"

"The kids are running riot and we haven't had any rain. The storm clouds build up every evening but nothing happens. It's as hot as hell. On Sunday I got a duck and Centenary lost the game... How is Livy?"

"You know her daughter is almost three? Donna is five weeks younger than your Randall."

"Is she now?"

"Livy had an exhibition of her latest paintings on Guy Fawkes Night. Sold five of the paintings. Now you are business partners, Beth suggested Livy might visit you for Christmas. We're having a terrible beginning of winter in England."

"Are you now?"

"Beth thinks a trip to the sun for little Donna would do her good. Beth is very fond of her niece. Or you could bring the kids to England for Christmas. Mum would love to see them."

"December is the height of the tobacco season, if we get some damn rain we should be reaping by the middle of December. There's no way I can get off the farm at this time of the year. Last weekend was my last game of cricket. The kids won't get off the farm for weeks."

"Livy could help you with the children. She can bring her paints. Frank's being a pain in the arse as usual. Hasn't visited his daughter in months. He won't be a problem if the kid wants to spend a few months with her mother on the farm."

"Sounds like you and Beth have thought out all the angles. Whose idea was the block of flats?"

"Mine, Jeremy. We were going for a walk by the Thames and saw the 'For Sale' sign."

"And Livy?"

"That was Beth's idea. We worry about you on the farm all by yourself. Livy can paint. She always said she wanted to paint all those wonderful Rhodesian wild animals. She especially wants to paint a giraffe."

"You haven't suggested this to Livy have you, Paul?"

"Not yet. We thought it might be nice if you phoned and invited her."

"She never wanted to live in Rhodesia."

"It's a holiday for goodness sake. If Livy and Donna don't like it they can fly back home. I'm sending you all the details of the flats. I've signed the purchase agreement under your power of attorney. Barnaby, Frank's father, checked everything with a fine-tooth comb."

"He's been good for Livy financially. What went wrong with the marriage?"

"Frank went off with other women when Livy fell pregnant. Doesn't like the look of pregnant women. Turns him off."

"The bastard. I hope Livy sued him for half his money."

"Didn't want a penny. Instead she has full custody of Donna."

"Does she now?... Is my money safe?"

"Safe as houses. Twenty-eight of them. Can I give you Livy's phone number?"

"Might as well."

"What the hell was that?"

"Thunder. Thank goodness. At last we're going to get some rain... Got to go. The kids are hollering."

"You will phone her? It's Pimlico 121. Can you remember that?"

"Of course I can. Say hello to Beth for me."

"Good luck with the rain."

Smiling, Paul put down the receiver onto the phone stand in the lounge of his Hammersmith flat.

"Did it work?" said Beth, who had been listening to the one side of the conversation.

"I think so."

"Should I tell Livy he's going to phone?"

"You can take a horse to water but you can't make it drink. The rest is now up to them. Having put in place so much subterfuge I need a drink. If nothing else comes of it that block of flats is a damn good long-term investment. Barnaby says there is talk of something called sectional title some time down the road. People will be able to buy their own flats the way they buy houses instead of paying rent for the rest of their lives. Give people a leg up into the property market."

"I'm not interested in the money, Paul."

"I know you're not. You're matchmaking."

"I'm thinking of the children. Why can't your brother sell that farm in Rhodesia and bring his money back to England instead of worrying about all the political arguments? The *Telegraph* said today the British government are going to break up the Federation of Central Africa at the end of its ten-year trial period in just over a year. They're going to be giving Nyasaland and Northern Rhodesia independence on the basis of one man one vote. The whites in Southern Rhodesia want their own independence from Britain with a qualified voting system that will keep the whites in power. They quoted Josiah Makoni as saying if Southern Rhodesia isn't allowed the same one man one vote there will be a war backed by the communists in Russia and China. He has a lobby in the British parliament that agree with him."

"The British government is tired of all the colonial squabbling. They want the blacks to get on with it. Wash their hands of all those small African colonies that cost more than they produce for Britain."

"We can't just walk away, can we?"

"Watch them. When there's no money in a bad deal that's just what they do. Walk away. If Livy gets a phone call from Jeremy and agrees to go out to Rhodesia, you two should have a talk... To build up that farm and end up in a war zone isn't worth it. You're right. My brother should get out with his money while Rhodesia is still in the sterling block and his money is freely transferable... Woman to woman stuff. Jeremy can find something to do in England. Especially if he has some capital. And it will solve Jeremy's problem as to where the kids go to school. Mother would be so happy with all her grandchildren in England. The British Empire is over. People have to accept it. Even the white Rhodesians. The whites with roots in South Africa can go back to the Union. South Africa has had its independence from Britain since 1910. They all have to face the reality of the modern world, including my brother. What a shame. All those wonderful ideas of having a farm so big he couldn't see the smoke of his neighbour's chimney. A place that was truly his own."

"It looked too good to be true, six thousand acres."

"It was, Beth. Your father warned him. Why Livy got cold feet and came back to England. If your father with deep roots in Rhodesia thought there wasn't any future for the white man in Africa, there isn't one. Anyway, the Americans want the British Empire to come to an end, according to Tinus. The Americans want the British markets open to their trade. It's all about money."

"I hope your brother phones Livy."

"So do I."

WHEN LIVY GOT the call from Jeremy the next day she was not sure whether to be sad or excited. Old flames that had gone out had the bad habit of staying cold. Going backwards in life was usually a failure.

When Livy answered the door to her studio on the Wednesday to find Beth, she was somehow not surprised.

"How's my niece, Livy? I was just passing. Can I come in? It's freezing cold. They say it's going to be another terrible winter like 1947 with all that snow and ice."

"Is this about Jeremy? He phoned on Monday. You'd better come in. I have a nice bottle of South African sherry. Did you come by car? I mean you didn't walk from Hammersmith to Chelsea in this weather?"

"I took a taxi."

"So you weren't actually passing."

"We want you to go out to Rhodesia and persuade my brother-in-law to sell his farm and bring those poor children back to England. Did he ask you to go out for Christmas?"

"You know he did."

"Are you going?"

"I'm thinking about it. I might just call you a conniving bitch."

"But you're not going to. Instead you and I are going to drink that bottle of sherry together. As luck has it, I have another one in my shopping bag. Spanish, I'm afraid, though it was Spain who invented sherry. The medium dry I remember you like... Hello, Donna. Has your Mum told you, you are going to Africa for Christmas where the sun is shining?"

"Are we going to Africa, Mummy?"

To Beth's delight, as Livy shut the door to the studio, Donna began to dance round the big room with excitement shouting 'Africa' at the top of her piping voice.

"That's done it," said Livy.

"Show me what you've been painting," said Beth, doing her best not to smile. "Look, Donna. Aunty Beth has brought you a box of your favourite chocolates."

"When are we going to Africa, Mummy? Are we going in an aeroplane? Can I tell Daddy when he comes to see me?"

"You can when he comes, my little darling."

Beth looked away, pretending to look at the half-finished painting on the easel in the big bay window. Tears had come to Livy's eyes at the mention of Frank.

"Do you still love him?"

"Of course not. It's Donna. He only comes round to see her on a whim. Last time was when he drove back after his grandfather's funeral. Three months ago."

"Then go and see Jeremy. His kids also need help."

"I suppose they do."

"It's so nice and warm in your studio."

"All the paraffin heaters."

"Why don't you get a bigger place? Something more modern with central heating."

"I can paint in this studio. A sterile, modern home might sap my urge to paint. This has all been so familiar for so long... Can you stay for supper?"

"I told Paul to feed the kids. There's a casserole for them in the oven. Paul just happened to pass the block of flats. That bit was serendipity... What's the painting going to be?"

"I don't know. First time I've tried something abstract. Probably throw it in the bin... Wildlife. That will be fun."

"So you're going?"

"She wants to go, don't you, darling?"

The child looked at her mother, her mouth full of chocolate and smiled.

"The poor little darling. She doesn't have much fun... Did I tell you Claud Gainsborough wants to marry me? What a hoot. Livy Gainsborough on all my paintings. He's very good to Donna. She loves him, don't you, darling."

"Why don't you?"

"He's the sweetest, nicest, kindest man I have ever known. And he's as dull as ditch water. I just can't imagine him sexually and that wouldn't be fair to him. You can't go on pretending you like it for the rest of your life. Do you still enjoy it with Paul?"

"Not every time. Once a week or so when the lights are out. I'm an old married woman. Henry is nine years old. But I wouldn't swop Paul for anyone. He's kind and always thinks of me and the children. Don't poo poo that sweet and kind."

"Frank was so different. I should never have agreed to marry him. What we had before was perfect. When the urge got to us we sated it on each other. Destroyed the little monster. Oh, well. You can't have everything... I suppose we had better fly out to Rhodesia. An almost three-year-old on a boat trip would be asking for trouble... What's going to become of Frank?"

"Much the same as his father. Eternal rich bachelors with a string of young girls until that little monster, as you put it, gets off their back. Barnaby has reached that stage in his life by the look of it. He and my mother see a lot of each other. Old friends enjoying their memories together. I'm glad for her. We all are. With Barnaby in the background my mother isn't such a pain. Do you know, he's persuaded her to get rid of that damn dog. The companion's going to be the next to go. Mother and Barnaby look so comfortable together. Content with life after a long struggle."

"I could never be comfortable with Frank, except in bed. No matter how old we get."

"Time will tell. At the moment you and Jeremy need each other, if for nothing else than for the sake of the kids."

"It's been a long time. Poor Carmen. We were such good friends when we were all staying with Mrs Wade in Salisbury. Me, Carmen and Candy. What a naughty combination. It was so much fun being irresponsible and young... Sometimes I feel so old... No. That painting is definitely going in the bin downstairs. I never did see the point of abstract painting. Just colours and weird shapes trying to look like something to fool the gullible public. People like to be seen to be one with the arts. Most of the time they have no idea what they're looking at. Or what they're paying for. They do what other people tell them to do. Why there's so much crap in the art world like that half-finished painting up there on my easel... Now that's enough about me. Tell me what's happening in your life."

"Not much really. There's Paul and the kids. That's about all. It's enough, I hope. What else can there be for anyone in life? A family. A comfortable living. A comfortable home. Paul is so happy now we bought another grand piano. It was sad having to sell the first one when we nearly went broke... Can you imagine living without money? You take it all for granted when you have it. Why Jeremy would be such a fool to lose the farm in Rhodesia and come back to England with so little and have to start to make money all over again."

"I'll do my best to talk sense into him this time."

"Why don't you go and visit Josiah Makoni before you go? You know my father put Josiah through school and varsity. I have his phone number somewhere. He'll tell you what's going to happen in Rhodesia. He owes the Brigandshaw family honesty if nothing else. He organised that rally in Trafalgar Square demanding one man one vote for Southern Rhodesia that was in all the newspapers. You've met him before in the

Nouvelle Galerie. If anyone can tell you what's going on, it's Josiah. They say he wants to be prime minister of an independent Rhodesia they are going to call Zimbabwe. He'll talk to you off the record. Then you can tell Jeremy. Give him a chance to make a rational decision on whether to get out of Rhodesia with his money while he still can."

"What would he do in England? He wouldn't want to farm. Farming in England is a whole lot different to running a plantation in Rhodesia with all those workers. In England he'd have to do the work himself. Drive the tractor. The harvester. That sort of thing. Rhodesia is more like the old-style gentleman farming."

"Ask him. Talk about it. There's always something of interest to do in life, even in suburban England. Paul enjoys what he does."

"I've finished the chocolates, Aunty Beth."

"You'll be sick, darling."

"No I won't... Is Daddy coming with us to Africa?"

"She needs a father," whispered Beth in Livy's ear.

"I suppose so. I'm just being selfish. I'm too comfortable as I am. A comfortable rut. How long does it take to fly to Salisbury these days? Oh, well. We can give my little tiger over there a sedative so she sleeps all the way. Africa. The word has such a lovely ring to it. Do you think the locals would know how to grow tobacco without the likes of Jeremy?"

"Of course they would. Just takes time. One of Josiah's slogans on the plaques people carried at the Trafalgar Square rally was 'Give us back our land'."

"According to Jeremy the white farms that now flourish were just bush when he and his friends found them. Had no value to anyone. Bush and wild animals. Not an African village anywhere to be seen."

"Maybe that's the problem. Now the farms have a commercial value, everyone wants them. What Paul said when he had read the article on the rally in the *Telegraph*. People have the instinctive urge to covet their neighbour's property. Been going on since the dawn of man. Paul says the most difficult thing in life is not making the money but holding on to it."

3

When Livy finally tracked down Josiah Makoni in a rundown building in Soho where the smell of Indian cooking was pervasive, the man she had first met in the Nouvelle Galerie looking at the painting of his mother that Livy had painted after seeing Tembo and Princess at the funeral of Harry Brigandshaw, was evasive. To Livy, Josiah looked much older than his thirty years. He was thin and looked worried. Uncomfortable with his surroundings.

"You know what is going to happen in Rhodesia? That depends on the British government. The whites have self-government but the British parliament are the final authority. Queen Elizabeth is Queen of Rhodesia. All us Rhodesians, black and white, are meant to be subjects of the Queen of England."

"Are you going to throw out the whites if you get your one man one vote?"

"That depends. What can I say, Mrs St Clair? In politics you have to be careful what you say to everyone or it may come back to haunt you."

"You owe something to the Brigandshaws."

"They owed more to my people. They stole our land. When are you going out to Rhodesia?"

"Next week. With my three-year-old daughter. For a holiday."

"If you happen by chance to see my mother and father tell them I miss them. That I miss what one day we will call Zimbabwe. My father works for your sister-in-law's husband, Mrs St Clair. For Photographic Safaris out of Maun in what soon will be called Botswana. Africa is changing, that much I can tell you."

"Are you happy, Josiah?"

"Who ever is happy in life? There's a struggle to be won. That's all that is important. Being happy doesn't change anyone."

"You don't need to change when you're happy. Thank you for your valuable time. I appreciate it. And please call me Livy."

Outside in the cold street, a thin sun was shining in Greek Street. The smell of Indian curry was enticing. Despite her thick overcoat, Livy shivered as she walked back to Piccadilly Circus. The poor man was so miserable. Like a fish out of water. He had told her more than enough. Jeremy Crookshank, Livy concluded as she looked at the Shaftesbury Memorial in the centre of Piccadilly Circus, would be a fool not to take his money out of Rhodesia as soon as possible.

On the way walking home from the Tube station, Livy had another look at the block of flats she owned with Jeremy. She smiled. Paul and Beth were right. The flats were a good investment.

She collected Donna from the crèche and went to her studio where she stood in the big bay window for the rest of the afternoon while she painted, the winter sun streaming through the glass of the window giving her perfect light.

"You're wrong, Josiah. It's all about happiness, not about possessions. They can all have my money if they leave me to paint."

When she looked round at the end of the day, Donna was watching her from where she had been colouring her book with different coloured crayons. They smiled at each other, mother and daughter. Both of them were happy and that was what really mattered to Livy.

"I wonder what made him so bitter?" she said to herself, thinking again of Josiah.

Then she went into the small kitchen to make them both supper where she first poured herself a large glass of sherry.

"Cheers, everyone," she said, lifting her glass to the ceiling. "Here's to happiness. To being content. To hell with the struggle."

She took a good sip and savoured the rich wine as it went slowly down her throat, warming the cockles of her heart.

When Claud Gainsborough came round later on one of his frequent visits she told him she was going out to Rhodesia for Christmas.

"This time are you going to marry Jeremy, Livy?"

"I'm going for a holiday, Claud. For some sun."

"And you won't marry me."

"Please, we're good friends. I'm not very good at marriages remember."

"All a man can do is hope. Just give me hope."

"How's your mother and the lake?" She put her hand on Claud's shoulder. He looked so sad.

"She's getting old. The lake is just the same. Why do you always avoid the subject?"

"What's wrong with just being friends? There are a lot less problems with friendship."

"I want to make love to you."

"Don't forget Donna has ears."

"She's asleep in her bed. I kissed her brow while she was sleeping and she didn't wake up."

"We can stay as we are or you'll ruin everything, Claud... Do you like my new painting?"

"Of course I do. I like everything about you, Livy... I have to go. Early meeting with a client tomorrow morning."

"How's business?"

"Never been better. I've all this money and no one to give it to. No one to enjoy it with."

"Aren't you lucky? The man I saw this afternoon wants money and power. He was miserable. I have a feeling that when he gets his power and money it won't make him happy... Enjoy what you have. Who you are. Don't wish for what you can't have and forget the rest of your life in the process."

"I'm not miserable. I'm just in love with a girl who isn't in love with me. Have been for years. It's eating me away. You and I could be so happy. Try me, Livy. I'll be so good to you."

"London is full of nice girls who want to get married."

Deciding that saying nothing more was better than any words, Livy kept her mouth shut. How could she tell a friend he was barking up the wrong tree when he wouldn't listen? A long trip to Rhodesia would give them a break, give Claud a chance to meet someone else.

When she went to bed feeling bad about Claud, she turned out the bedside light and tried to go to sleep. A moon was playing light onto her easel through the big bay window. She got up and closed the curtains.

"Are you going to marry Uncle Claud, Mummy? I like Uncle Claud. He's nice to me. We could have a big house and a dog. I do like cats but I want a dog."

"So you weren't asleep?"

"Not even when he kissed me. I just kept my eyes shut. Goodnight, Mummy."

"Goodnight, precious. Sleep tight."

"Are you going to marry him?" came a small voice from the darkness five minutes later.

"Go to sleep."

Livy heard what she thought was a faint giggle. She could hear the distant sound of London's traffic. For a long while she lay awake thinking about why no one ever seemed satisfied with what they had. Not even her happy little daughter who now wanted a dog. Livy could feel the warmth of the cat next to her face on the pillow. The cat was purring.

"At least someone is content," she said to herself before falling asleep.

IN THE MORNING Livy woke with the feeling of something having gone wrong. She looked at her daughter in the next bed sleeping like an angel, a smile on the child's face. Then she remembered the look of sadness on the face of Claud Gainsborough as he looked back into the warmth of her studio before going out into the cold, her door closing shut behind him. She got out of bed, put on her dressing gown and opened the curtains to look at her painting in progress on her easel in the light of the morning. Getting dressed in a hurry and putting on her smock, Livy began to paint in the silence of the day. Donna was still fast asleep. As she painted, the feeling of disquiet seeped out of her. She was somewhere else, cut off from the outside world, her mind and soul deep inside the picture she was painting.

Later in the day, after a walk along the river with Donna, she put a fixed-time call through to Jeremy in Rhodesia to tell him she was coming.

"That's the only good news I've had since Carmen was killed by the lions. My kids will be so excited."

"You do have dogs?"

"Of course. We have a small pack of them on World's View. How long are you staying? It's the busy time of the year so we won't get off the farm except to go to the club. Anyway, the Zambezi Valley is too damn hot at this time of year down there in the Lowveld. The mosquitoes would eat us alive after all the rain we've been having. How's our block of flats?"

"Still standing."

"The crop looks good. Finished building two more curing barns. I'm putting in a big dam for more irrigation after we sell the crop. Rhodesia is flourishing. The Federation has been so good for everyone. They are calling Southern Rhodesia the breadbasket of Africa. It's the commercial farms doing it. Northern Rhodesia has the copper. Nyasaland had the surplus labour as there aren't any jobs for them at home and they're coming down here to work on the farms. Not having to worry about where the next meal is coming from for their families is a blessing. Welensky says with another influx of whites with their money and skills, he'll make the Federation as prosperous as Canada. We've never had it so good... Wonderful news. I'll give Candy a ring and tell her you're coming. I'm sure she'll come out to the farm for a visit."

"Phone Salisbury airport before you come into town to make sure our flight is on time... I saw Josiah Makoni the other day."

"What did he have to say?" said Jeremy, changing his tone.

"He wants independence and one man one vote."

"All that money Harry Brigandshaw put into his education. You don't get much thanks in this life. You have to know what you're doing to run a modern economy."

"I'll tell you more when we get to the farm."

"You're bringing your paints?"

"I can't live without painting."

"Say hi to Paul and Beth for me. Got to go. We're cleaning the tobacco lands of weeds at the moment. The women do that job but I like to watch them so they don't damage the tobacco plants. You have to watch everything on a farm if you want to make a profit. Can't wait to see you, Livy."

"Why do you always sounds so enthusiastic, Jeremy?"

"Because I am. Tell Donna I'm looking forward to seeing her. So are the boys."

"How are they?"

"Missing their mother."

When Livy went back to her painting it didn't work. Her mind was elsewhere. The bad premonition kept coming back to her and wouldn't go away. Getting Jeremy to pack up and leave Rhodesia was going to be a lot more difficult than she had imagined. What looked so obvious from London would not look the same under the African sun.

"They've all got their heads in the sand," she said, putting down her paintbrush and going into her small kitchen where she put the kettle on to make herself a cup of tea. She was thinking how completely differently two people could see the same problem.

"Let's go to the Nouvelle Galerie and see Aunty Jeanne," she said to Donna who was fidgeting with nothing to do.

"Are you going to drink sherry with Aunty Jeanne and Uncle Ben?"

"Probably, darling. Are you looking forward to meeting Randall and Phillip?"

"How many dogs have they got?"

"A whole pack of them. Put your coat on, little girl. We're going out."

IT WAS six o'clock when Livy got to the gallery; what Jeremy would call sundowner time. Donna had had a good sleep in the afternoon so she wasn't tired. Stan was outside on the pavement trying to sell the passers-by in the Portobello Road his fake antique jewellery that was made in Hong Kong.

"You two look pleased with yourselves."

"How's business, Stan?"

"Could be better. Ben and Jeanne are inside the gallery. Not a visitor all day. It's the weather. They don't come out in the winter. I'm packing up my barrow and going home. Wife's got kippers for tea. My favourite."

"Enjoy your supper. We're going out to Rhodesia for Christmas."

"All that nice sun. You're lucky you are."

"I hope so."

Inside the gallery Livy found Jeanne Pétain in the storeroom. Ben Brown was nowhere to be seen. The Nouvelle Galerie was empty of people. Livy had smiled at one of her paintings on the wall as she passed looking for Ben and Jeanne.

"Can I ask you a favour, Jeanne? Donna and I are going to fly out to Rhodesia. We may stay a few months. I'm going to paint all those wild animals I promised myself. Frank's at home. I phoned him to say I was coming round before I left my studio."

"You want me to look after Donna. No problem. How are you, Livy?"

"Harassed. I'm going out to persuade Jeremy to sell his farm and come back to England. I want to tell Frank face to face. I'll be gone an hour. I need his signature to have Donna added to my passport."

"Good luck. We'll be just fine together, won't we, Donna? Uncle Ben's somewhere around. He might have slipped out the back door to go to the pub. In my life I've found trying to tell men anything they don't want to hear is a waste of time."

When Livy parked her car outside the row of townhouses in Lennox Gardens where she had gone to live in Frank's new house after they were married, it was the first time she had been back since their divorce.

"To what do I owe this pleasure? Where's our daughter?"

"With Jeanne Pétain and Ben at the Nouvelle Galerie. I need your signature on a piece of paper. We're going out to Rhodesia for a holiday and Donna has to be added to my passport. I'm not running off with our daughter to the other end of the earth. Despite the fact it wouldn't make any difference to you, Frank. Why don't you come and visit her? You have no idea how many times that child says to me 'When's Daddy coming to visit?'"

"I've been terribly busy. Come in. It's freezing out there."

"That's what they all say. She's our daughter. Nothing in the world can change that. You of all people should understand."

"Beth tells me you and Jeremy are in partnership in a block of flats. Bully for you. No one ever lost money investing in property."

"Except in Rhodesia. Paul wants to persuade his brother to sell up and come back to England."

"How convenient. You get the man you want in the country you want to live in. So you two are going out to World's View."

"His kids are the same age as our daughter."

"How nice of you. Give me the piece of paper. You don't want a drink I suppose?"

"Of course I do. How are you, Frank?"

"How's our daughter?"

"She misses not having a daddy."

"Sounds like my sister getting involved. First the flats and now you're going out to Rhodesia to see Jeremy and his kids who don't have a mother."

"I have another favour."

"This is interesting."

Frank was smiling at her. The same old smile that sent the same old shockwave right through her body down to her groin. What she and Frank had called the silent bite.

"Will you look after the cat?"

Frank burst out into laughter.

"That damn cat. Does it still sleep on the pillow?"

"I'm afraid so."

"Of course I'll look after the cat."

"How's your love life?"

"The same as usual. They come and they go. And yours?"

"In a one-roomed studio with our daughter, what can you expect?"

"She's not here now. We're not married. What's stopping us?"

"You're serious aren't you!"

"It's what worked in the past. I can't wait to tap all that pent-up frustration. We don't have to get involved. Just every now and again when the mood takes you. Just how it used to be before I forced you to marry me. You've still got the same look in your eyes. There's no one else in the house. Kicked them all out when you phoned to say you were coming over."

"On one condition. You don't ever again ignore our daughter."

"I can live with that. All three of us can. The perfect relationship again. Come along, my Livy. You and I are going to bed. Then we'll have a drink to celebrate."

"You're not jealous of me going to stay with Jeremy?"

"Why should I be? If you're coming back and we have our old relationship, it doesn't matter what you get up to with Jeremy Crookshank. Life's to be lived. To have fun. And the one fun thing you and I have always had together is in bed."

"I must be mad."

"Aren't we all, darling? It's what makes life so exciting."

PART X

DECEMBER 1961 – "STORM IN THE NIGHT"

1

*D*onna slept curled up on her seat leaving Livy to her thoughts. When the BOAC Comet landed at Nairobi airport Donna was still half asleep. The passengers were told they could stretch their legs to the transit lounge in the small airport building. It was Livy's first reminder of the strange smell of Africa, an interesting mixture of sunshine on dry earth. After the wet drabness of England the sunshine and the slight smell of musk lifted her spirits.

"You know they've let that Kenyatta out of British custody for the first time in seven years. They're going to give them independence. Of course the country will go to the dogs."

Livy smiled at her fellow passenger, a man in his sixties with a military moustache. 'Welcome to Africa,' Livy thought.

"Thank you," she said to the old man.

"Why thank me? After building the colony into something that looks like a civilised country, it will all go backwards."

"You just confirmed what I already know."

"Are you getting off?"

"Going through to Rhodesia."

"Southern I hope. They'll be all right. They are a self-governing colony in charge of their own police and army. If the British government breaks up the Central African Federation, the Southern Rhodesians can go their own way. There's no financial support from Britain."

"Are you getting off?"

"I have a tea plantation in the white highlands though I don't know for how long. Communism. That's the root cause of our trouble. And American meddling. They want to see the end of the British Empire and the rise of American hegemony."

"What's hegemony? Not a word in my vocabulary, I'm afraid."

"Power. Control. Economic stranglehold."

"Sounds a bit like the British Empire." Livy was smiling to herself as they walked side by side towards the airport buildings, the sun burning her face.

"I go through that entrance. You, good lady, go through that one into the transit lounge. Wish I was going to Rhodesia. Is your husband farming?"

"We're divorced."

Livy smiled at the look of disapproval on the man's face.

"Divorced! I'm afraid that's a word that isn't in my vocabulary. Good day to you, madam."

After an hour waiting in the cool of the transit lounge while the plane was refuelled, they all trooped back to the plane which was shimmering in the heat on the tarmac. As they boarded, Livy was more convinced than ever that Jeremy selling up and going back to England was the right thing to do.

"Who was that man you spoke to, Mummy?"

"I have absolutely no idea."

"I don't like him. He was nasty. I'm going back to sleep."

Curling up on the seat of the aircraft, Donna closed her eyes and went back to sleep. Livy rested her hand gently on her daughter's bare leg. The excitement was building up, mixed with trepidation. After so many years apart, she was not sure what they would now think when they looked at each other. She was thirty-five years old, Jeremy thirty-three. A lot of water had passed under the bridge since last they were lovers. She could still hear the sadness in the old man's voice at the thought of losing his tea plantation mixed in with the bravado. She wondered if she and Jeremy had changed as much as Africa.

.   .   .

AT SALISBURY AIRPORT, getting off the plane, it was just as hot as it had been in Nairobi, a shock to Livy's system coming out of the cold of a typical English winter. Slowly, with the rest, Livy went through immigration and customs.

Jeremy was standing at the rail with two small children, one on either side of him. His tan was darker than Livy remembered. Donna, going shy, hid behind her skirts with her thumb in her mouth, looking with big eyes at Jeremy's two small boys. A porter had their luggage on a trolley, Jeremy giving him a coin for his trouble.

"How are you, Livy? Wonderful to see you. This one on my right is Randall and this one Phillip. Say hello to Aunty Livy and Donna, boys."

"Did you know my mother?" said Randall looking up at Livy with wide-open eyes, wanting the comfort of his dead mother.

"We lived in Mrs Wade's house in Baker Avenue when I first came out to Rhodesia to see your father eleven years ago. She was my best friend. It was through me your father met your mother. She was a very lovely person. Full of fun."

"Will you tell us about her?" said Phillip.

"Of course I will. I brought you some photographs. I've also made a big painting of your mother."

"How did you do a painting?" said Randall. They both looked so lost Livy wanted to pick them up.

"I'm a painter, Randall. I paint pictures."

"Can we see the painting of my mother?"

"It's carefully packed in that big suitcase. I want to have it framed first and then I'll show you."

"We're all going to have lunch at Meikles and stay the night in the hotel. There's more than one picture framer in town. Candy wants to see you. So does Pamela Crumpshaw. They're all waiting at the hotel with Mario Tuchi."

"Quite like old times. I thought you had to go straight back to the farm?"

"I have some good news. The moment you booked your plane ticket, I employed a learner assistant. Should have done it last year. The workload on the farm is too much for one person. He's straight out from England. Eighteen years old. They don't have to do their National Service in the army anymore. Got him through Rhodesia House in the

Strand where they go to apply for Rhodesian residence. The chap who was going to employ him sold his farm and Bobby Preston was stuck without a job to come to. Went to Wellington. Top-rate young chap. There was nothing for him in England. Father doesn't have enough money to send him to university so he's come out to the colonies. It was that or starting at the bottom in an office. He's my eyes when I'm not on the farm."

"Does he know what he's doing?"

"Not really."

"How long has he been on the farm?"

"A week."

"And you left him on the farm all on his own!"

"Didn't turn a hair when I told him I was staying in town. He's got a gun. Chap's a damn good shot with a twelve bore shotgun. He'll be fine. I'm going to phone him from Meikles. We'll all drive back together tomorrow. Candy's going to stay with us for a few days with Mario. They have a thing together, I think. Known each other for years. I came to town in the Chevy Impala not the truck. Plenty of room for all of us. One of those big Yank tanks. Doesn't like the corrugations on the road but if I drive fast enough it flies over the top of the ruts. You look just the same, Livy. Just as beautiful."

They grinned at each other, the shock of both of them seeing a completely different person to the one that had stayed in their minds only registering in their eyes.

She was glad Candy and Mario were coming back with them to the farm, giving them time to get to know each other again.

"Paul and Beth send you their best."

"How's our block of flats?"

"Still standing. How's the crop?"

"Looks all right at the moment. We'll see what it looks like when it comes out of the barns."

"You look good wheeling a trolley."

"Just my kind of job. How was the flight?"

"Long and boring. Met an old tea planter getting off in Nairobi. I'll tell you all about him."

"Did they give you lunch on the plane?"

"Breakfast. I'm starving."

"That's my Livy... There she is. The top's down. What do you think of my Yank tank?"

"Looks very exotic doesn't, it Donna? We don't have cars that big on the streets of London. Why don't you run off ahead and let the boys show you that lovely car?"

Shouting excitedly, the three children ran off through the parked cars that surrounded the single entrance to the airport.

"I've got something to give you, Jeremy."

Before he could do anything Livy gave him a wet kiss on the mouth.

"Bring back memories, darling?" she said, smiling at him.

"We'll need some time, Livy."

"Of course we will. We'll be starting all over again. Right from the beginning. The kids look happy together. That's something."

MARIO TUCHI LOOKED MUCH the same, the only one who hadn't aged. Pamela Crumpshaw, the girl with whom Livy had shared a cabin on the *Carnarvon Castle*, was a complete replica of Flossy Maple, right down to the stuck-up daughter. So far as Livy could see, looking round the lounge of Meikles Hotel, nothing much in Rhodesia had changed. The waiters still wore the same beaming smiles on their black faces, the whites of their eyes startlingly prominent.

They all drank tea as was expected at half past ten in the morning. The Impala was parked outside the hotel, Livy's luggage in the cavernous boot, Jeremy having given the attendant a shilling to look after it.

"Well, this is all such a wonderful surprise," said Livy. "Do you have any children, Candy?"

"I never got married. Pamela's brother Andrew proposed a few times. While I was trying to make up my mind he married someone else. They have four children. You know that old saying in Rhodesia: 'the crop that never fails'. I was having too good a time. Mario never married, did you, darling? Sadly Mario lives in Maun from where he operates Photographic Safaris for Jeremy's brother in London and Tinus Oosthuizen in New York. The company's a joint British–American venture. You're lucky to see him, Livy. He brought a group of British tourists to the airport this morning. They're flying back to England on the Comet that brought you from London. Jeremy suggested we came up to the farm so we can all have a good natter about old times. Pamela is in town to do her monthly shopping. When Jennifer's school were told an old friend of her mother's was in town they gave her the morning off classes. They do that sort of thing for the farmers who have to send their young kids to boarding school. To give the children a few hours with their parents during the school term."

"This all reminds me of such happy times. When we were all in the Zambezi Valley with Carmen. Your mother caught a big fish in the river, Randall, and Mario cooked it over the fire. We were all so happy, weren't we, Jeremy? Youth goes so quickly... So, anyway, how are tricks? How many kids have you got, Pamela?"

"Just the one."

The awkward silence was finally broken by Mario.

"Why don't we all have a drink?" he said, brightening up. "To celebrate Livy back with us again. How long you stay, Livy?" To Livy's amusement, Mario's Italian accent was as strong as ever, his English still fractured.

"Depends on Jeremy," she said.

"Why don't you and I, Livy, leave the kids with Pamela and Candy and get that picture out of your suitcase and have it framed? We'll have that celebratory drink when we come back, Mario. Ateliers is only just round the corner. We can walk. Back in twenty minutes. How does that sound to everyone?"

"We'll be one drink up on you, Jeremy," said Pamela, looking pleased with the idea, the girl who on the boat coming out, Livy remembered, didn't drink.

"I'm definitely back in Rhodesia," said Livy.

"What else is there to do in Africa?" said Pamela, making Livy give the woman a second glance. The girl was unhappy. Livy wondered why. Like everything else that didn't work with her friends' lives, she knew she would soon find out. 'Poor Pamela,' Livy thought. 'The start of her marriage to Roger Crumpshaw looked so idyllic.'

"MRS WADE TOOK THE PHOTOGRAPHS," said Livy as they walked away from the hotel, the painting of Carmen rolled up in its cardboard tube under Livy's arm. "I've never owned a camera. When I want to remember something for later I make a sketch. This time I used Mrs Wade's photographs she had given me. Carmen was a very pretty girl. You must miss her so much, Jeremy."

"She was a drunk. The day she got herself lost in the bush she was drunk. Mario had gone off earlier with a girl from the club. You know they'd had an affair?"

"Mario loves all women, Jeremy. You shouldn't be upset... He's Italian."

"It was the children that suffered. Anyway, it was probably all my fault dumping a girl like Carmen in the middle of the African bush. She liked the Centenary Club. There, she was in her element, poor girl. Surrounded by men. I think her pregnancies were deliberate. Here we are. I said Ateliers were just down the street."

Jeremy opened the door to the shop, letting Livy walk in first. It looked to Livy as if the place doubled as a photographic studio, picture framing only a part of the business. There were half a dozen other customers in the shop.

"Can I have a look at what you have done?"

"Better to let them frame it first... Hello. I have a painting I would like you to frame. Can you show me what you've got? Something plain. I don't want the frame to distract from the beauty of my subject."

"Are you the artist?"

"As a matter of fact, I am. I couldn't frame the portrait in London or I wouldn't have got it on the plane... There's a snag I'm afraid. Can you do it by this afternoon? We're driving back to the farm."

"May I have a look?" said the man.

"Of course."

"I may have a ready-made frame that will fit... My goodness. That is so good. We don't get many amateurs in here with something as good as this."

"She's not an amateur," said Jeremy, looking over the man's shoulder at the opened canvas he had pulled out of the tube. "In London, Livy Johnston is famous."

"I'm so sorry. I'm a photographer myself."

"Can you do it by closing time?"

"I'll do this one myself. The girl is so beautiful. So sad. All that yearning. Who is she, may I ask? People will pay a lot of money for something as good as this."

"My late wife. She was killed by lions. We're staying the night at Meikles. Could you get one of your people to bring it to the hotel when it's finished? I'll pay you now if that's all right. Please wrap it for us. I don't want my children to look at a portrait of their mother until we get back to the farm tomorrow."

All the way back to Meikles Hotel Jeremy was silent. There were tears in his eyes. Livy wanted to take his hand.

"Can we walk around the block? I don't want to face all those people at the moment. My poor kids. It's always the kids that suffer. After my father went down on the *Seagull* off Dunkirk my life was never the same. Ever since, I've wanted to talk to him. For him to tell me what went on in his life. To find out if he had been through all the same bruises. I wanted to get to know him. The war stopped all that. I was twelve when Dad went down. Too young to have had a good talk."

"Maybe the portrait wasn't such a good idea. In a few years your children will only remember photographs of their mother. Photographs and my portrait hanging on the wall. I'll take it back to London."

"You'll do nothing of the sort. She was beautiful. That will be comfort for the boys. Photographs won't give them an insight into their mother like that painting. You've painted who she was, not just what she looked like."

"That's the point of being a painter. I try to get behind the face. Behind the surface of whatever I paint. To give the feeling behind the picture. Without that, painting would be just another job to make money... We've got lots of time to talk together. It's an old cliché but life goes on, Jeremy. Otherwise none of us would be here. Remember the good parts of Carmen. You must have been happy together. All of us drink too much at times... Don't you think Pamela has turned into a second Flossy Maple? Does Roger have an assistant that has to buy his vegetables from the farm the way she made you pay for your greens? What happened to Flossy and Bertie Maple and their little bitch of a daughter? What happened to Petronella?"

"She's done rather well for herself. She was a stuck-up little prig as a thirteen-year-old but she did have brains. She went back to England. Attended Manchester University. She's going to be one of those do-gooders that tell us what we're all doing wrong in Africa. She's a friend of Josiah Makoni. Wouldn't be surprised if she isn't a communist. The complete opposite of her mother. Bertie and Flossy are still on Ashford Park. Flossy is still very much the Lady of the Manor... Thank you, Livy. For talking me out of my morbs. I can face the others now. You haven't told me. What happened to your marriage?"

"Frank went off screwing other women when I was pregnant."

"Charming... Why are you smiling, Livy?"

"That was just the way Frank is. I should never have agreed to marry him. We were doing fine as we were."

"How were you?"

"Lovers when we needed to screw."

"Was that all we had?"

"No, Jeremy. There was more to you and me. Come on. I could do with that drink. Nothing's permanent in life. That much I have found out. That man in Ateliers was quite charming."

"They say if he went to England or America he'd be a famous photographer."

"That good?"

"So they say... It's lovely to see you again, Livy. Thank you so much for coming. It's been lonely on my own. You can't explain your feelings to your children."

"They're adorable."

"Aren't they? They took to Donna quite quickly."

"Kids flirt at that age, didn't you know? The town is booming."

"The price of tobacco has been sky-high these last few years. We keep our fingers crossed each season. Does Donna see her father?"

"No, Jeremy, she doesn't."

"Sorry. I'm treading on toes."

"Frank has only thought of himself his entire life."

"Then why did you marry him? You had your own money. Your own successful career."

"We don't want to go into that."

They completed the block and walked back into the hotel.

In the lounge the drinks were flowing, the children stuffing their faces with cream buns. With the start of drink time the noise of voices in the hotel lounge had increased. The place had filled up with farmers and their wives in town to do their shopping. Jeremy smiled and waved at the people sitting round two of the tables, getting smiles and waves in return.

"Our big happy family, Rhodesia," said Jeremy as they made their way through the tables to the children.

"On the surface."

"Everything is on the surface, Livy. Just as well. If we all knew what everyone was really up to we'd want to cry. There's more promiscuity among the young farmers and their wives than any place on earth, so I'm told."

"I don't believe you."

"Neither do I. Everyone is solidly British."

"Are you British or Rhodesian?"

"That's a good question."

"What you having?" said Mario standing up as they got back to their table. "We're on the second round."

Three drinks later they all trooped through into the dining room that led off from the lounge. There were more waves and smiles. The punkahs were going round and round above them, stirring up the air. Livy was perspiring.

"I want some of that Rhodesian beef I can't afford in England."

"Not surprising," said Jeremy. "Our beef is the best in the world. None of that stall feeding. Runs free in the bush. We get the highest prices on the Smithfield Market in London every time. Not that I'm a cattle farmer. That's more down by Bulawayo in Matabeleland. Sixty thousand-acre ranches. You need twenty acres for every cow. How about a T-bone steak?"

"Now you're talking."

"Are you sure Scottish beef isn't the best in the world?"

"I'm quite certain."

They were all a bit tight, Livy thought, sitting down at the big table. The head waiter, a black man of huge proportions, had put cushions on the chairs for the children. Livy doubted if they would eat anything after all the buns. With everything so new and exciting the children were behaving themselves. Jeremy had sat himself between his boys, with Livy between Randall and Donna. Jeremy winked at her. Pamela Crumpshaw suggested they ordered a bottle of wine, making Jennifer give her mother a look of disapproval.

When the T-bone steak was put in front of Livy it was the size of her plate.

"Wow. I'd forgotten the size."

"Tuck in, Livy. Welcome back to Rhodesia, the best damn place in the world. After lunch I've got some jobs to do in the industrial sites. You can go up to your room for a nap."

"What about the kids? Donna slept most of the way from London."

"I'll take the kids. Give them time to get to know each other. No thanks, Pamela, I won't have any wine. How's Roger? Haven't seen him since the last cricket season. I think we're down to go to Macheke for a game at the end of February? He must be busy on the farm."

"My husband is always busy."

"And your two brothers, Andrew and Colin Lavington?"

"Since they married we don't see them. I don't like their wives."

"Are they happy?"

"I imagine so. They never stop breeding."

"I'd love to see Colin and Andrew," said Livy, sensing the strain in the conversation. "We all had a fun weekend at Pembringham Estate. I think you had to go back to Ashford Park straight after the cricket, Jeremy."

"Dear old Flossy Maple. She really wanted her pound of flesh from a lowly learner assistant. Well, isn't this all so much fun? Just like old times. When are you driving back to Maun, Mario?"

"After lunch. I take Candy back to Christian Bank where she works and down to Bulawayo. New clients coming Maun, Wednesday. Very good business."

"Are there any girls?"

"There are always girls, Jeremy. But none so beautiful as Candy."

"We were lucky to catch you between clients. My brother Paul and Tinus Oosthuizen must be happy sending you so much business. Those people are lucky to take their photographs. The African bush won't be around forever the way the world population is exploding. Isn't that Crispin Dane over there having lunch, Livy?"

"I rather think it is."

"Why doesn't he come over?"

"He's a happily married man," said Pamela Crumpshaw. "Another one you missed your chance with, Livy."

There was no doubt about it, Livy said to herself. Pamela

Crumpshaw, who had been Pamela Lavington when Livy had shared a
cabin with her while having an affair with Crispin Dane on the
Carnarvon Castle, had turned into a second Flossy Maple, a sad, bitter,
dominating bitch. A trifle miffed that Crispin Dane had not bothered to
recognise her, Livy went back to eating her steak. Maybe, she thought, it
wasn't quite like old times.

"I hope you've brought plenty of canvases and paint," said Jeremy.
"How's your steak, Livy?"

"Perfect. Just perfect. Like everything else. We could always drive
straight to the farm after lunch."

"Could we? The jobs I have to do in the industrial sites can wait."

"We can call on that nice man at Ateliers and collect the painting, or
pick it up next time if he hasn't finished the frame."

They were comfortable with each other. At least that hadn't changed.
For a moment, Livy thought her trip to Africa would be a big mistake,
that leaving the comfort zone of her studio in pursuit of another of her
dreams was going to leave her feeling miserable far away from home.

"Where's Roger today, Pamela?" she asked.

"Don't ask me."

She had proved her point. Marriage, even to a rich tobacco farmer,
was not all it was set out to be. Livy felt a shiver race through her body, as
if someone had walked over her grave.

"What's the matter, Mummy?"

"Nothing, darling."

"Randall's going to take me swimming in a pool."

"Uncle Jeremy and Mummy will teach you to swim while we're
staying on the farm."

"Are we going now?"

"Right after lunch."

For three days Jeremy took Livy round World's View showing her what he had done to turn six thousand acres of wild bush into a working farm. Young Bobby Preston was left to watch over the gang. It was the prelude to the reaping season. The calm before the storm. When the crop began to ripen from the bottom leaves up, the gang worked from sunup to sundown to bring in the tobacco; sometimes, according to Jeremy, filling up the last barn with wet green leaves by the headlights of the truck, the ripening leaves on the head-high plants waiting for no one. Bobby was bewildered straight out of England, not understanding one word the labourers said to him.

"You just stand there, Bobby. That'll be enough. I tell them what to do in Fanagalo. There's a chap in Vumba with one glass eye. When he goes into town he takes out the glass eye and puts it on a high rock to watch over them. Says it works like a charm."

"You're kidding me, Mr Crookshank."

"Actually, I'm not. If you'd never seen a man with a glass eye before you'd also wonder how he took out one of his eyes and put it on a bloody great rock to watch you. Bit like religion. God's watching you."

"But we're not God, Mr Crookshank."

"That's why I have you, Bobby. All flesh and blood with two good eyes."

"He couldn't go into town with one eye missing."

"He covers the hole with a patch like Long John Silver. I've brought a small book for you from Salisbury that will teach you Fanagalo. The word means 'something like this'. In six months you'll be able to have a conversation with them."

"I'm going to learn Shona."

"You can. But the gentlemen we employ from Nyasaland and over the border won't understand a word. Why we teach ourselves Fanagalo, the lingua franca of Southern Africa, so we can all make some sense to each other. It's what the different tribes use to speak to each other in the compound, when the local Shonas speak to the Nyasas and the Mozambicans."

When Livy got into the truck to visit the new site for the earth dam Jeremy was preparing, she was still smiling.

"Still a bit wet behind the ears," said Jeremy.

"Why does he call you Mr Crookshank?"

"Went to Wellington. Thinks of me as his housemaster most likely. All part of training the boys for the British pecking order. I'm lucky he doesn't call me 'sir'."

"That girl who looks after the boys is so good with them."

"Don't know what I would have done without her. Primrose is a real treasure. She has two of her own kids. I've encouraged her to bring them up to the house while she's working. The boys are picking up Shona without realising it. Fanagalo is all right for giving orders but it doesn't lend itself to any kind of conversation. Shona, an unwritten language, is incredibly descriptive. If we're going to get on with these people in the future we have to understand their language fluently. Write it down for them. Picking up a second language is easy at the boys' age. Especially with playmates. Primrose's boy and girl swim with them in the pool, I've given them costumes. The first time they jumped in naked."

"What happens when they grow up? That was Frank's mother's problem. She came from the lower classes, his father from the aristocracy. When they grew up, never the twain were allowed to meet."

"Who knows what the world will be like when the boys grow up? People don't like the class system in England. Bloody stupid if you ask me... From here we're going to build an earth wall twenty feet high and thirty feet wide right across that shallow ravine and push the water back over a mile. Then we'll have some water. We start building after the rains, when the river stops flowing. It's a small tributary of a tributary that flows into the Ruia River which flows into the Zambezi just north of Beira. What do you think?"

"Who taught you to build a dam?"

"The extension officer helped. The trick is knowing where to put it. I paid a chap for an aerial photograph of the farm in which he had marked out all the contours so we know where to stop the water. I've spent a year thinking about it. This and five more dams in the right places will give me enough water and enable me to reach every acre of the farm with overhead irrigation. Damon Chesson's aerial photography opened my eyes to the possibilities. In a few years' time I won't be worrying so much about drought, the scourge of Africa. We're slowly turning Rhodesia into the Garden of Eden with modern technology. No one in Africa will have to starve again when the cycle of drought withers the dry land crops. What's the point of all that raging water going over the Victoria Falls at the height of the short main rains and down the Zambezi where it spews out into the Indian Ocean above Beira? We need to stop what rain we get right here on the highveld. What the Kariba Dam is all about. Water and hydroelectricity so we have the power to pump water on the crops in the cool of the dry season. There's an old story among us farmers in the Centenary. The land is so fertile that if you put a steel pin in the ground at the start of a good rainy season you'll get a ten foot steel pole at the end of it. Water. Always water."

"Don't tell that one to Bobby. He's got enough problems with your man from the Vumba with the devil's glass eye."

"He'll learn. In five years when he applies for his own Crown Land farm he'll be telling that joke against himself in the club. Five years of apprenticeship. We'll turn him into a farmer. Now I want to show you my experimental grove of mango trees. It's a new strain they've developed for the overseas market. Stringless. The same beautiful taste without getting string stuck in between your teeth. When I first came to Rhodesia I used to eat mangoes in the bath, chewing away with the juice all over my hands and face."

"You've done so much on the farm. It would be heartbreaking to lose it."

"We're not going to lose Rhodesia, Livy, whatever the likes of Josiah

Makoni have to say. We all have so much more to gain working together under a stable government that isn't corrupt. Slowly, the educated blacks will get the vote so that in the end the colour of your skin won't matter. Josiah and his cronies just want control of the economy for their own benefit. They say it's all for the people what they are shouting about. But don't you believe it. They want to make themselves powerful and rich. A simple man is easily fooled when it comes to putting his cross on a ballot. Come on. You're not tired are you?"

"Where do you get all the energy?"

"There's nothing more exciting than building something. There's just so much to do. After showing you my mangoes I must get back to the gang repairing the contours where the last big rain ran through them in a couple of places. You have to keep on top of everything. Bobby can keep them working for me when I'm not there but he doesn't yet have the knowledge to make sure they are doing it right. Cecil Rhodes said it. 'So much to do. So little time to do it.' Developing this farm to its full potential is going to take me the rest of my life. It's not so much money. It's time. Knowledge. I'm always learning. Like these aerial photographs that showed me the right places for the dams."

Getting back into the passenger side of the truck, Livy sighed inwardly. What she had come all the way from England to say would have to wait. It was a pity Jeremy had not heard Josiah Makoni speak at the rally in Trafalgar Square when five thousand people roared their approval of his 'one man one vote'. Jeremy, and the rest of them, had their heads buried in the utopian sand, far away from political reality.

"What was that sigh for, Livy?"

"The human race."

"I don't think I want to go down that route. You didn't just come out here for a holiday."

"We've got lots of time, Jeremy."

"All the time in the world I suppose... Did I tell you how wonderful it is to see you?"

"Just a couple of times."

They both laughed as Jeremy drove the car on their way to see the mango trees.

"I've never eaten a mango."

"The perfect tropical fruit. There are spots on the farm among the rocky outcrops where we can't cut out a land big enough to plant tobacco. Where I'm putting fruit trees. It won't be just mangos, of course. Oranges, and certain types of apples that grow in the highveld. I may have a go at grapes. Can you imagine our own wine? Now look back and see that valley and visualise my dam. All that lovely water. We're going to introduce bream into the dam so the locals can fish for their dinner. Fish is good for them. A sailboat like the one we had on the Isle of Wight when Paul and I were children. There'll be enough water to tool up and down. Fishing competitions is another of my ideas... I'm not boring you am I, Livy?"

"Don't be silly. People with so much enthusiasm never bore me."

"It's so nice to tell someone."

"You must have talked so much about it to Carmen."

"Not really. She found the farm boring. All she wanted was to get off it and go into town. Use the farm profits to go to Europe in the off season. Her only interest in the farm was how much money it was making."

"I'm sorry."

"I should never have brought a town girl like that out to a farm. It was my fault she drank. I was selfish. Wanted a woman. I killed her, Livy."

"Don't be so ridiculous."

"All she did was read those dreadful romantic novels and drink. That way she could live in another world. Her real world with me on the farm she hated. You have to grow up on a farm to appreciate the peace and beauty."

"You didn't grow up on a farm, Jeremy."

"Would you like to live on a farm, Livy?"

"We won't go down that route."

They both laughed, Livy hoping her own laugh had not sounded hollow.

At the grove of immature mango trees they got out of the car, Livy making all the right noises of appreciation. To Livy they were just trees. Poor Carmen. Life never turned out quite right. All that image of a wealthy farmer came down to appreciating his trees. Candy was right. Despite still not being married she was living in a town with people, not stuck out on a farm with servants for companions who didn't speak your language. And a husband who was out in the lands all day. What did a girl talk about at the dinner table at the end of her day to a husband with his eyes half-closed, whose only thought was going to bed to sleep?

When they got back to the house, before Jeremy drove back to the lands to check his broken contours, all five of the children were splashing each other in the pool, squealing with delight. Donna was shouting the loudest. Away from the pool, doves and pigeons were calling, the pure sound mingling with the happy sound of playing children. Over towards the distant range of hills, storm clouds were building.

Going into the house, Livy brought out her paints and a clean big canvas. Her first day on the farm, Jeremy had knocked up an easel for her in the workshop. She took the easel into the shade of a msasa tree where she set up the empty canvas. Forgetting her problems, Livy began to paint the landscape from the commanding heights of the ridge where Jeremy had built his long, thatched bungalow. Slowly, magically, Livy went into her world, oblivious of time or place.

"MR CROOKSHANK SAID YOU WERE A PAINTER."

"Bobby! You frightened me."

"I'm sorry. Primrose is getting the children's supper. Mr Crookshank tells me you sell your paintings in London. I want to be a writer. Why I came to Rhodesia. There's so much to write about."

"A whole lot more if you stay, Bobby. Why don't you call him Jeremy? I hate being called Mrs St Clair. He'd much prefer you to call him Jeremy."

"I couldn't do that. He's so much my senior... Father wanted me to go to Sandhurst. Wellington, where I went, is a military school. Father is a brigadier. Mother's family have the money. They are in textiles. Made a packet during the war making uniforms for the army. How they had the money to send me to Wellington. There's not much money in the army. You need a private income. My father's family have been career officers in the army for five generations. A chap at school has an uncle in Rhodesia which gave me the idea of working on a farm. Went to Rhodesia House and put my name down. I'm going to write novels."

"Good luck to you... Would you carry my easel back to the house for me? Once the concentration is broken it's difficult to go back to painting."

"I'm so sorry, Mrs St Clair. I had no idea."

"Call me Livy. What time is it?"

"Half past five. Dark in half an hour."

"Goodness. I've been painting for two hours without any realisation of time. I go into my own world when I'm painting."

"Did you do the painting of Mrs Crookshank in the lounge?"

"Yes, I did."

"It's beautiful. Those poor children. I like to have supper with them. Mr Crookshank eats at half past seven after his sundowners. He likes to be on his own. I'm so tired by then I'm happy to go to bed."

"I hope I haven't put your nose out of joint."

"Not at all. We're building a small cottage on the end of the ridge so I'll have a place to myself. I have a gramophone, you see. All the records from the London shows. I like musicals. Better that way. When you're a junior you can't exactly live with the prefects. Makes everyone uncomfortable. My father says there's a right place for everything, Mrs St Clair. Carrying your easel will be a privilege. Here comes Mr Crookshank."

"Sundowner time, Livy. How did the painting go? Easel, all right?"

"How are the contours?"

"Just fine. We've properly packed earth into the breaches, haven't we, Bobby?"

"Yes, Mr Crookshank. I had a look at the cottage. Be ready in a week, according to the builder."

"The cottage is one room, a kitchen and a bathroom. We started it the moment Bobby accepted my offer of a job."

"Shades of Flossy Maple and Ashford Park."

"A man needs his own space, don't they, Bobby? Part of the job offer they explained to you at Rhodesia House."

"You're not going to make the poor boy buy his own vegetables! Bobby says he wants to write. Wants to be a novelist."

"Where do you want me to put the easel, Mrs St Clair?"

"I'm trying to persuade him to call us by our Christian names. Doesn't seem to work... Put it on the veranda. I want to paint again first thing in the morning. The colours are so delicate in the mornings, especially if it has rained during the night... Isn't that thunder?"

The rumbling was far away behind the range of mountains, a low, menacing growl that made the dogs run up the lawn and into the house, their tails between their legs.

"Why do dogs hate thunder?" said Jeremy. "The cats take no notice."

They watched Bobby stride away, carrying the easel into the house.

"He'll be more settled when he has his own house. Everything is new to him. Silas has put the drink tray on the veranda. The rain's an hour or so away. Bobby says the thunder and rain wake him up... Cold beef and salads for our supper on the veranda after I've had a drink. I start looking forward to a drink at about three o'clock. We all do. Part of what we are as Rhodesians."

"What does Bobby do in his spare time?"

"Tomorrow he'll stay in his room reading most of the day. He wants to read right through my library. Bit of a mixture, really. The stuff I read, which is mainly factual, and all those romance novels of Carmen's. If he wants to write, I hope they are not being a bad influence. He goes through two of them in a day."

"Are there any other eighteen-year-olds straight out of England in the block?"

"Not really. I'm going to buy him a motorcycle so he can get off the farm."

"Drive a motorcycle to Salisbury!"

"Probably not during the rains. There's always a price to pay for everything, Livy."

"Doesn't he miss his mother?"

"Never asked him. He's always asking me questions. About Africa. About the characters that have passed through the block. Did you know the Duke of Tewkesbury has bought a farm in Concession? Mau Mau chased him out of Kenya."

"What happened to that son of his?"

"No idea. What was his name? We met them in Dar es Salaam on our way back to England on the *Esquilino* in 1950."

"His name was Cecil. So Happy Valley wasn't so happy after all. Do people sell their farms in the Centenary or is it cheaper to wait for a Crown Land farm?"

"Oh, goodness no. We've worked it out that by the time you've stumped out the trees, put in roads, built the barns and grading shed and put in the dams with a workable water system for the house and the native compound, it's the most expensive agricultural land in the world. But that's not the point. It's the sense of achievement, turning a six thousand-acre tract of worthless bush into a productive estate."

"What would you get for this place, Jeremy?"

"Never thought of it. Fifty, sixty thousand pounds, I suppose."

"Is Donna having her supper?"

"She's fine with the boys and Primrose. Relax, Livy. Come and have that drink with me. The light will be going quite soon. I like to be seated on the veranda with a glass in my hand when the light goes. With the fly screens shut against the bugs. To relax. We can really relax tonight. Tomorrow is Sunday. The farm shuts down. Everyone has a holiday. My word, that thunder is loud tonight. We'll be able to see the lightning flashes better from the veranda."

"Let me have a look at Donna, change from shorts into a dress and I'll meet you on the veranda."

"Mind if I get one in first?"

"You go ahead."

Putting the canvas next to the easel with her paints just inside the veranda, Livy went to the bedroom she shared with Jeremy to change, smiling at the memory of the uncomfortable moment of their first evening when they got back to the farm after lunch in Meikles with Pamela, Candy and Mario Tuchi, the conversation playing back through her mind.

"Are you all right sharing a bedroom, Livy?"

"Don't see why not. I haven't changed. Have you?"

"It will be the first time after Carmen, Livy."

"We don't have to make love, Jeremy."

"You're so understanding."

"I hope so. Let's just take our time. Not rush into anything. Give me another kiss."

"The children look all right together."

"That's what I mean. We'll just take it easy. Go with the flow I think is how they say it these days."

With the smile no longer on her face, Livy changed into a dress and looked at herself in the dressing-table mirror. It was all a bit odd, sleeping in Carmen's bed, even if nothing had happened. The presence of her dead friend was always at her back, looking over her shoulder.

She could hear the children shouting as they ran to the small room with the low chairs and tables with the pictures of Donald Duck and his friends on the walls. A room, Livy had no doubt, decorated by Carmen for her boys. By the sound of the sudden silence, the hungry children were now eating.

When she went into the room, all five were sitting at the table eating their supper, not saying a word as they shovelled in the food. Primrose was sitting in an upright chair watching them. Livy and Primrose smiled at each other, the smile of two mothers content to watch their happy children eating their supper. Livy slipped away. Later, she would tuck Donna into bed, after Primrose had taken her two children back to the compound where she lived with her husband, Jeremy's gardener.

When she reached the veranda it was getting dark. Jeremy handed her a gin and tonic, tapped the side of her glass with his and gave her the obligatory 'cheers'. The paraffin lamp had been lit; the fly screens were firmly in place over the open windows, shutting out the bugs. Far away, Livy could see the forked lightning streaking down from the heavens, a momentary flash of light among the turbulence of the boiling clouds. The food was laid out for them on a table. All the servants had gone back to their thatched huts in the compound. They were alone. She smiled at him, her mind thinking of sixty thousand pounds, more than enough to set Jeremy up for life in England when added to his share in their block of flats.

They stood together looking out at Africa as the last light faded from the sky. They were comfortable together. Enjoying each other's company. The storm was still a long way behind the distant range of mountains that intermittently appeared out of the night in the flashes of lightning.

"We've known each other a long time, Jeremy."

"I know we have."

"It's so menacing at night."

"We're safe in the house. Has Primrose gone home?"

"Probably by now. I'll go and kiss Donna goodnight. Did you tuck in the boys?"

"Carmen did that."

"Then I'll go do it for her. You can sneak in another drink while I'm gone."

"Take one with you."

She could hear Bobby Preston playing the record of the musical *Salad Days* from his room, the music mingling strangely with the distant rumbling of the thunder. It was a plaintive sound of a life far, far away that to Livy did not belong in the prelude to an African thunderstorm. It made her shiver despite the oppressive heat still building up with the storm, making her take a swig of her gin. Donna was in a small bed alongside the boys, all of them sound asleep. The room was pitch-dark, intermittently lit by the flashes of lightning. All three of the dogs were awake under the children's beds, their eyes coming into brief focus with the lightning. Outside the open window, screened with gauze against mosquitoes, the cicadas were screeching, and frogs were calling to their mates. To Livy, the mating calls of the frogs sounded like 'fuck me, thank you, fuck me, thank you' which took her mind off the menace of the storm. There was no wind. Just the oppressive heat. Like Jeremy with the boys, Livy had trained Donna not to sleep with the light on to prevent her being frightened of the dark. The children's bedroom was next to Jeremy's bedroom with a connecting door.

Carrying her empty glass, Livy walked down the long corridor back to the veranda and the hissing sound of the gas light, the singing from the London musical faintly in the background.

"You have the sexiest frogs in the world, Jeremy. If you listen you can hear them call 'fuck me, thank you, fuck me, thank you'."

"Have another drink. Are you hungry?" They listened for a while together. "You're right," said Jeremy smiling. "Dirty buggers."

"Not yet, I just swallowed the last one. The kids are fast asleep, Bobby playing his records. Must be odd for him so far from his roots."

"It is for all of us at times."

"Doesn't a storm damage the young tobacco?"

"Only if it hails. We have hail insurance. The hailstones can be as big as golf balls. Rips the big leaves of tobacco to shreds."

"Sixty thousand pounds is a lot of money, Jeremy," said Livy into the quiet.

"Yes it is... Would you ever think again of living in Africa?"

"No, I don't think so."

"Well, that is a shame. We could make a life together. Does it really matter where you live? It's who we are that counts. Who we are inside. Africa has got into my blood. It does that to you."

"Politics, Jeremy. It's not Africa. The blacks want their country back."

"They'll never build a modern economy. Eliminate poverty. Give themselves a better and longer life."

"Probably not. Let's change the subject. It's none of my business what you do unless you decide to come back to England. With my money and yours we could live well in the country. Buy ourselves a small farm in Devonshire. Or a place on the Isle of Wight where you grew up. Have a sailboat and a future not worrying about politics. The kids would be happy together. We might have one of our own. The window's still open to get your money out but if the government of Southern Rhodesia argue with the British government over white-controlled independence that window of opportunity will slam in your face. Forever. You could lose everything at an age when you won't have the energy to start all over again. Especially without enough capital. Think about it, Jeremy. We never get everything we want from life. There's always a compromise."

"You've been talking to Paul and Beth. I have the block of flats. I'll send Paul more money at the end of the season. You can leave your money in England. They'd never take away what you put on canvas. To them it would have no value. I love the space of Africa. England is so claustrophobic, even on a small farm. It wouldn't be the same to me. This is all so new. A real life's achievement. Not buying someone else's place just for somewhere to live. I'm creating something the way you create pictures on your canvases."

"So you won't consider selling the farm and coming back to England?"

"Nothing's ever final in life, Livy. I'd be a fool to say it was. But no, not in the foreseeable future. A man needs a place that is truly his own. World's View is mine. I've built everything that's here and there's still so much to do. A lifetime of work."

"Not according to Josiah Makoni. He says you stole his land."

"Bollocks. There was nothing here. They'd done nothing with the land since time immemorial. How can he say I stole his bloody land? Everything on this farm I've made myself. Brick by brick."

"Paul thinks that's your problem. When it was bush and had no value nobody cared. Now you've built it into something of value they want it back."

"You mean by being successful I've screwed myself?"

"People only covet their neighbours' properly when it's worth coveting. They get jealous seeing someone with more than themselves. That's basic human nature. Now you've got something they want. Get out while the going's good. Bring the product of your hard-earned work back to England where they won't run off with it quite so easily."

"Do you want some supper?"

"I want another drink. We both do. Tonight we're going to get tight together and forget the damn world and all its lovely bickering people."

It was pitch-black outside. Moths incinerated themselves in the fire of the gas light. The music from Bobby's record had stopped. The frogs kept up their sexy calling.

"Cheers again."

"Cheers again, Livy. It's a long way from where we met on my holiday in England."

"Yes it is. Back then, I fantasised about living on a farm in Rhodesia. Why I came out and met Carmen and Candy and old Mrs Wade, and Pamela Lavington as she was then on the boat. I'm not the flighty artist I once was. Responsibility comes with children. You should think of that, Jeremy. Think of your kids. You make lifelong business contacts going through school which are often as important as a good education. They call it the old boy network. It's all about trust. Someone you've known all your life. They'd lose all that. With another sixty thousand quid behind you they could go to a good school. Go on to university. Have a real chance in life. A good education is something no one can take away. A good English public school education is the best start in the world, no matter what they say about the wrongness of class. England's moving forward after the war. Europe beckons instead of the crumbling colonies. We're going to become more like Switzerland on our island set in Shakespeare's silver sea. We have so much history. We have roots, all of us, that go back hundreds of years. That's where you belong, Jeremy. For an Englishmen, which you are, however much you now like to call yourself a Rhodesian, you will never put down solid roots in Africa because the blacks won't let you. There's too much disparity. Too much difference in wealth and culture. Europeans and Africans are too far apart to live in the same country without envy and animosity."

"I'm going to check the kids."

"Don't run away from me. They are all right. They have the dogs under the beds. I left their door ajar. I'll change the subject. Why haven't we had sex?"

"You're a guest in my house. I was waiting for you to make the first move. Taking advantage of a woman who has nowhere to run is wrong."

"Oh, was that it?"

"And Carmen. She now watches me from that painting of yours in the lounge. Her eyes follow me around the room."

"You'll have to move on sometime."

"Let's just see what happens... My. That was a big one. Lit up the whole sky. We're going to have one hell of a storm later. There's something about an African storm that is so exciting."

"Or so frightening to us Londoners."

"I'll hold you if it gets too bad."

"You promise? I'll hold you to that. Like your dogs, I'm frightened of thunder. Have been ever since I was a kid."

"Do you want a bottle of wine with the cold meat and salads?"

"Why not?"

"Good. I'll pull the cork... By the time-lag between that flash of lightning and the roll of thunder I'd say the storm is still twenty miles away... Further back is the Zambezi escarpment. Where we buried Carmen... I put up a wooden cross with the words 'Go well, my darling' burned into the wood. Just her skull and a few bones... What else could I do? Take a handful of bones and a skull all the way to a church in Salisbury for a religious ceremony? She's better where she is. One day I'll show the kids her grave."

Livy waited while Jeremy went into the lounge to find his bottle of wine and the corkscrew.

"You see, we do have roots in Rhodesia," he said coming back with the open bottle. "We're just putting them down. Most of us in England came from somewhere else back in history. The Vikings. The Danes. The Saxons. They say the whole human race started in Kenya and spread out of Africa into Europe. Some of us are coming back."

"You are trying to make it sound romantic when it was all about finding yourself a tract of land."

"Maybe. We all rationalise. Justify what we do. Even to ourselves. It's rarely all right or all wrong, Livy. It's mostly a matter of opinion. One man like Josiah Makoni with his political motive will say we're stealing their land. Another with the best interest of the ordinary man in mind will say we're providing investment and skills that create hundreds of jobs."

Watching them from the windowsill at the far end of the veranda was a green pair of eyes. Livy watched the cat while Jeremy poured from the bottle of wine. The lightning flashed again, the cat's eyes seeming to grow bigger. They waited for the thunder. When it came, Livy thought it closer, the time between flash and bang a moment or so shorter.

They sat down at the table on the veranda with their glasses of wine. She helped him to a plate of cold meat and salads. The cat kept watching. They smiled at each other.

"The wine is delicious," said Livy. "Red wine with red meat. I like that."

"I bought it for you specially."

"Do you miss her?"

"The children miss her. I miss the woman I hoped she was going to be. You see, we all want what *we* want, not what the other person wants. I was selfish only thinking of myself and the farm, thinking that as the breadwinner I was the most important person. I never took time to think what Carmen was feeling, cut off from her friends in Salisbury and her family in England."

"Was she in contact with them?"

"Not really. I wrote to them, of course. Received a short letter from her mother. And that was it."

"Aren't they interested in the children?"

"Never saw them after we went to England when Phillip was a few weeks old. We English never show our emotions. Especially in letters to virtual strangers. What do I say to them sometime in the future: these are your grandchildren; that one's Phillip, that one's Randall."

"I'm surprised they didn't come out."

"What could they do? Someone said we are all just a link in a never-ending chain in the long process of evolution."

"If you came back to England they would get a chance to know their grandchildren. With your family in England it would give the kids a sense of belonging."

"You can go round and round a circle, Livy. World's View is our home. It's where we belong."

"Does that cat ever move from the windowsill?"

"Not very often."

"I left my cat with Frank."

Frank, like the mention of selling the farm and going back to England, brought a break in their conversation. They both tucked into their plates of food. There was no sound from the rest of the house. From the outside, someone started to play the drums, a constant, even beat. Livy listened to it as she kept her head down eating her food.

"We have a beer hall in the compound that is open on Saturday night," said Jeremy. "A tanker comes up from Salisbury with the local white beer that's brewed from maize. Once my builder has a few drinks in him, he plays the drums all night. They come from the surrounding farms to World's View on Saturdays. The beer is sold to them at what it costs me to buy from the tanker that pumps the beer into big containers with taps. The tanker calls at half a dozen farms in the block. Saturday night is one long party."

"What about the storm?"

"Who cares about getting wet when you're drunk? They dance in the rain. It's cooler. For hours, some of them, mesmerised by the constant beat of the drum."

"Sounds fun."

"Makes me feel a bit out of it at times up here on my own... Want some more of this wine? All the way from France. Silly, really. You get just as drunk on maize beer at a hundredth of the price."

"I'd like some more of your expensive wine. Doesn't that drum wake the children?"

"They've heard it all their lives. To them it's comforting. Familiar. A normal part of their lives. One day, when I'm old, the boys will take over farming World's View. Nothing will change. Africa will be just the same."

"I hope so. For your sake. And the sake of the kids. But think about it. That sixty thousand pounds is an awful lot of money. You'd have just as good a life, all of you, in England. Just different. With family. We may fight with each other at times but family is still important. In the days without cars and aeroplanes, extended English families lived within twenty miles of each other. Everyone in the village was related to each other. One big happy family."

"Do you still see him?"

"Who, Jeremy?"

"Frank. You said you dropped off the cat."

"Yes, I did. We're divorced. He's a womaniser. Only thinks of Donna when it suits him."

"He hasn't remarried?"

"Not Frank."

"Are you still sleeping with him?"

"Is this an inquisition?" said Livy, putting down her knife and fork.

"Sorry. None of my business."

In the silence, Jeremy went to the end of the table to pump the base of the paraffin lamp to bring up the light. As he pumped, Livy watched the rest of the cat on its windowsill come out of the dark, the mantle at the top of the paraffin lamp glowing white hot. Away from the light she could now make out the wire mesh that covered the long open side of the veranda with the brick wall and its small window at the far end. In the corner, below the cat's window, was a cricket bat propped up against the wall. More moths flew at the top of the light, instantly incinerating themselves.

"Doesn't he get tired playing that drum?"

"It's not the builder, the man who's building Bobby's house. There are three of them in the compound who play the drums. When they change over they don't miss a beat."

"At least we have music. Don't you ever get frightened all on your own? A thin sprinkling of Englishmen each surrounded by hundreds of blacks."

"Not really. We both need each other. It takes weeks to brew their own beer. Much easier to buy it off a tanker with the money I give them. We have a water tap in the compound with running water. The women don't have to balance containers of water on their heads and walk from the river. We've made their lives easier. No one on the farm has to think about where their next meal is coming from. They work for me and I provide. There's not a trace of animosity between the races on the farm."

"Aren't the likes of Josiah going to stir up trouble for all of you? Change all that?"

"Probably. For the moment I feel quite safe. I didn't feel safe in England at night during the war. The German's bombed Southampton just across the Solent from our house night after night. I take life as it comes. World's View is peaceful."

"Long may it last for you, Jeremy. Give me another slosh of that wine. I'm getting tight."

"So am I. Let's all enjoy ourselves while we can. You, me and everyone in the compound."

"Who sells them the beer?"

"I have a shopkeeper with a small shop next to the grading shed. On Saturday night he sells the beer for a ten per cent profit or the whole thing would get out of control. What I meant was, I don't make a profit out of the beer hall. In the week, he sells them the bits and pieces they need that don't come with the maize meal, sugar, dried beans and meat rations that every worker gets with his pay once a month... I'm going to open another bottle of wine when we've finished this one."

"You'll have to carry me to bed."

"That's the whole idea."

The crash of thunder made Livy jump in her seat. They could now hear heavy drops of rain on the corrugated iron roof of the veranda just above their heads.

"The rain will cool the air down."

"I nearly jumped out of my skin."

"This is your first African thunderstorm. When you came out on the boat ten years ago it was the dry season. You'll get used to it."

"I hate thunder. I'm frightened, Jeremy."

"I'll bring my chair round and sit next to you. I always like to drink wine sitting up at the dining-room table. Force of habit."

"Can we hold hands?"

"Of course we can. When it bangs again I'll hold you."

"You're enjoying this!"

"I rather think I am."

"The bloody cat doesn't turn a hair. Sits there like Lady Muck with its paws tucked in under its furry little chest. There's another flash of lightning. It's coming. Why don't we go to the settee so I can sit on your lap? Bring the bottle. I'd better go see Donna."

"They'll shout if they're frightened. The boys will look after her."

"Those damn drums haven't missed a beat. Am I wrong, or aren't there now two of them?"

"Sounds like it. Someone else must have brought a drum."

"It's getting faster. The beat."

The crash of the thunder made Livy run to the settee and curl herself up in the corner nearest the hissing gas light.

"How long does it last?" she whispered.

"Sometimes half an hour, sometimes longer. This one sounds as if it's going to be a good one."

Her eyes pleading, Livy waited for Jeremy to sit down next to her. When he did, he brought with him two glasses of wine. Both glasses were full.

"You can sit up, Livy. We have very effective lightning conductors high on the house and the farm buildings."

"I could never get used to it. Is it going to get worse?"

"It looks like the storm is coming our way. It'll pass right over the house. Listen to that lovely rain."

"It's getting so loud I can barely hear you."

"Drink your wine. Drunks never worry about anything."

"Are you sure?"

Coming out of her foetal position and sitting up, Livy took back her glass of wine. Jeremy sat down on the settee next to her. In four good gulps, Livy emptied her glass of red wine just as another clap of thunder shook the tin roof on the house, sending the cat off the windowsill to sit under the table where it disappeared from sight into the dark. With Jeremy's help she climbed onto his lap. The cat had turned round to look at them, showing its green eyes. The thunder banged again right over their heads.

"Take me to bed. I want to hide under the blankets."

"In this heat?"

"Please, Jeremy!"

In his arms, Livy clutched Jeremy round the neck as he walked from the veranda into the lounge. The long corridor was dark, the light from the single gas light no longer penetrating into the house. In the bedroom, where the connecting door was open, Livy could hear the dogs whimpering. There was no sound from the children. Jeremy put her down on the bed and started to take off her dress. It was pitch-dark in their bedroom. She heard Jeremy close the connecting door, cutting out the sounds of the frightened dogs. The thunder crashed again making

her shiver despite the heat. The springs in the bed moved with the
weight of Jeremy as he got into bed. The last full glass of wine had gone
to her head. She felt his arms go round her. The thunder crashed again.
The lightning showed her Jeremy, his look of lust making her open her
legs, fear and survival becoming one with the storm. As they made love
she forgot the storm and everything, absorbed by the need to procreate.
As the storm banged, Jeremy thrust into her time and again making her
scream.

"It's all right, Livy. It's all right, my love. I'm here. It's all right. You're
wonderful. So wonderful."

"Please don't stop!"

Livy woke to the chirp of the birds, the early sun streaming in through
the bedroom window. It was cool, the night's storm having washed away
the heat. The connecting door to the children's room was closed. From
outside down by the pool she could hear them calling and splashing in
the water, most of the words not even in English. Primrose, she thought,
must have come up from the compound with her two children. The dogs
began to bark at them. Relaxed, calm and at peace with herself Livy lay
back on the bed. She was naked. Their bedroom door was open to the
corridor. Silas, the house servant, Jeremy had said, stayed in the
compound on Sundays from where the drums were still playing though
not so fast.

"How's your head?" said Jeremy, coming in with the morning tray of
tea. "We punished the red wine."

"The dreaded red... Are the kids all right? They're still playing those
drums in the compound."

"They stop when the beer runs out."

"Quite a storm."

"In more ways than one."

They smiled at each other, their ten years of separation blown away
with the storm.

"If you get bored this week while I'm working there's nothing to stop
you taking the truck into Salisbury to visit your friends."

"You think I'll get bored after last night? That storm did something
to me."

"You can say that again. The hills look so beautiful this morning."

"When does Primrose get a day off?"

"That's a problem. Her kids like the pool. It works both ways."

"Everything is so calm. So peaceful. There's nothing better than that first cup of tea in the morning. What are we going to do today?"

"As little as possible. Just the two of us. You want a swim after the tea?"

"The kids sound so happy. So are the dogs this morning. Listen to all that yapping."

"You still think I should sell up and go back to England?"

"It's beautiful," said Livy, getting out of bed and standing naked looking out of the bedroom window at the garden and the view to the distant hills that shimmered pinks and gold with the rising sun. "Tomorrow, I'm going to paint all day. If only there wasn't another world beyond those hills. With people. All those squabbling people. Why do people always want to destroy the beauty of life?... I don't believe it, the drums have stopped! They must have run out of beer. Or fallen over from exhaustion. Now, it all looks so damned peaceful. Last night in that storm I thought I was going to die. That God in his heaven was going to punish me. Instead, he gave me this beautiful day. A perfect day."

"It grows on you until you can't leave. I could never leave this place."

"I suppose not. So that's the decision. To stay or not to stay?"

"Drink your tea and we'll join the children."

"Why is life so bloody complicated?"

"I never asked last night but did you use any protection?"

"I'm not that stupid. Don't worry, Jeremy, I thought ahead. I'm not going to do a Carmen on you. At this moment my heart may be ruling my head, but I've learnt the hard way to separate them. Sometimes you want something so much you are blinded from reality. A bit like Rhodesia. Nothing has changed from yesterday. The British Empire is finished. There's no way a quarter of a million English men and women are going to control this part of Africa all on their own surrounded by two million Africans, however much you all want it. We've lost our power. Sapped by two devastating wars. Many of the best gone and most of the treasure. We have to face reality. Both of us. To be able in the future to look back on World's View as a beautiful memory instead of some dreadful disaster. I may be an artist but I do read the papers. A good cross section of them... The tea is just perfect."

"So are you, Livy. You haven't changed one bit."

"I'm going to have a lovely holiday. Enjoy myself. Paint a giraffe. Let the kids get to know each other. You'll see what's the right thing to do. We have a whole life ahead of us. Look at the next stage as another adventure."

"I don't want to lose you again."

"Hand me my bathing costume. Let's go for a swim. Then I want breakfast. Bacon and eggs. Sausage. Tomatoes. And lots of toast with lashings of coffee. Spend the rest of the day in the shade of the trees by the pool."

"There are raindrops on the trees. Sparkling in the sun. Like a million jewels."

"I'll paint them. We'll take them away with us. Have them forever. That way they'll never be lost."

PART XI

MARCH TO JUNE 1962 – "SUMMER SOLSTICE"

1
_____

$\mathcal{L}$ ivy came home with Donna at the end of March. The daffodils and crocuses were in bloom among the melting snow on the grass bank in front of her studio. Donna had turned four in January, ready for kindergarten. Paul had met them at London airport.

"Is he coming home?"

"I don't think so, Paul. World's View, he says, is his home. Donna has to go to kindergarten. There wasn't one in the Rhodesian bush. I can't be selfish. I have to think of Donna's future. As far as I can see, there isn't one in Rhodesia. They're all in a time warp. Living in the days of the Raj. I was beginning to believe it could go on forever myself. So here I am. A single mother... Can you take us first to Frank's townhouse in Knightsbridge to pick up the cat? With her cat in the studio Donna won't miss the boys and the animals on the farm so much."

"Did you do any painting?"

"You won't believe it. Shipped the canvases home separately by air freight there were so many of them. I want an African exhibition at the Nouvelle Galerie."

"Beth sends her love. She was hoping you would come back with Jeremy."

"So was I."

Looking out of the big bay window at the daffodils and crocuses down below on the winter-green bank, Livy felt perfectly miserable. The cat was ignoring both of them. The studio looked the same and felt different. So that was it, she told herself. Back where she began.

A WEEK LATER, the wooden crate with its twenty-three paintings framed by Jeremy was delivered to the studio by the air freight division of BOAC, the cat still ignoring her for having gone away. With a small tyre lever, Livy opened the crate, pulling out her works one by one. The one of World's View with the sparkling raindrops on the trees made her cry, her whole body aching. Donna was away, her third morning at kindergarten.

One by one she propped the paintings against the studio wall, each one making her want to rush back to Africa. The giraffe was smiling at her. The Volkswagen Kombi, that had been in the garage on blocks, was standing outside, ready to take the paintings to the Nouvelle Galerie for her friends to tell her if they were any good.

At the gallery, Jeanne Pétain kissed her on both cheeks.

"So lovely to see you again, Livy. We've missed you. Where is Jeremy?"

"On his farm in Rhodesia."

"When's he coming home?"

"He's not. He's sending Phillip to boarding school in Umvukwes, the poor little mite. Weekly boarding. Comes home at the weekends. They have some mad idea that if the British won't give Southern Rhodesia full independence when the Federation breaks up, they are going to declare themselves independent unilaterally."

"My poor Livy. Ben and James will be so excited to see you. Did you say hello to Stan outside? Had a new shipment of fakes from Hong Kong this morning. Isn't it nice to be home?"

"Yes and no. That damn African bush grows on you. Come and help me unload the Kombi and you'll see what I mean. I brought Africa back with me. Can you give me an African exhibition?"

"Do you love him?"

"We're comfortable with each other. At my age that's just as important. We'd have a good life together if I didn't feel so insecure. You never know what all those black people are thinking. Their eyes are inscrutable behind those white-teeth smiles. Even menacing. Their eyes follow you. No people want a bunch of foreigners telling them what to do. If Jeremy really wants to marry me he must sell the farm and come back to England."

"Will he?"

"He's married to that damn farm. He can't see the wood for the trees. My God, if there ever was a truer saying."

"Have you seen Frank?"

"He was at the office when we picked up the cat. I used my old key. How are tricks?"

"Bloody awful winter."

"What's new? I'm going to miss all that sunshine. They say if you spend more than two years in Rhodesia you never come back. Why I got out. Before it was too late."

AT THE END OF APRIL, when Livy had been back a month, the rally for African freedom to take place in Trafalgar Square at the weekend was splashed all over the newspapers. Paul Crookshank phoned her the news.

"Do you want to go to the rally?" Paul asked her on the phone. "You can leave Donna with Beth and the kids. Have Sunday lunch with us. The rally is at eleven o'clock. You can write Jeremy a first-hand report. Someone has to knock some sense into him. I'll pick you up at the studio at ten o'clock. When's your African exhibition?"

"You'll get a formal invitation. Frank's doing the public relations. He's been so nice since we got back."

"Nothing like competition."

"I'll be ready at ten."

"Josiah Makoni will be giving a speech, if you can call rabble-rousing a speech. All the newspapers and television crews will be in the square. Kaunda from Northern Rhodesia and Banda from Nyasaland will be there. Banda's some medical doctor turned politician. It's going to be big."

"Any white Rhodesians?"

"Just the usual left-wing writers and priests. They use this kind of thing as a platform for their own careers. Probably don't give a damn about the indigenous blacks. Beth's going to roast a chicken."

. . .

WHEN THEY DROPPED Donna at Paul's Hammersmith flat, Beth said she was coming with them.

"Mary's daughter is going to babysit the children. We Brigandshaws have a strong Rhodesian connection. I want to see what's going on."

"Who's Mary?"

"Neighbour four doors away. Her daughter is always looking for pocket money. I've put the chicken in the oven on a low gas. Come on. Political rallies can be fun. Something to do. London gets boring, stuck in the flat all day. How's my little niece finding school?"

Paul parked half a mile from Trafalgar Square in a side street, letting them walk the rest of the way. The square was packed with people, some of them holding placards. The rain had held off and the sun was shining. Finding a place on the steps below Nelson's Column, Livy looked around.

"It's a mob," said Beth. "Isn't that Harry Wakefield next to the BBC television cameras? Jeremy will get an eyeful of this."

"They don't have television in Rhodesia."

"No wonder they're out of touch. Harry was named after my father. Let's go and talk to him. He'll know what's happening."

"He's seen you, Beth," said Paul. "He's coming over. Having found this vantage point we're better to stay where we are. My goodness. I had no idea Rhodesia was so important."

"Beth! Paul! How are you? Who's your lovely friend? Hello, I'm Harry Wakefield of the *Mirror*. My dad's with the *Daily Mail*. We're always arguing. If it wasn't for Beth's dad I wouldn't be here. Father got himself abducted by the Nazis before the war. He was writing articles on the rise of Nazi Germany. Harry Brigandshaw, my namesake, got him out of Germany with the help of Klaus von Lieberman otherwise I wouldn't have been born. Your father shot down von Lieberman in the First World War. Landed and picked him out from his burning aircraft. So, what do you think? Lots of people. The Labour Party are using the Rhodesian crisis as a way to win votes. All those one liners on the activists' placards read so well in a tabloid newspaper. You don't want the public to have to read too much. Or think. Sock them with a slogan, I say. Dad says it isn't even journalism but who cares? Sells newspapers. That's what my editor wants. So what brings you lot here?"

"This is Livy St Clair, Beth's one-time sister-in-law. She's just back from an extended visit to Rhodesia."

"Are you the painter? I've heard of you. We've all heard of Frank, of course. Frank St Clair and Partners, Public Relations. Has his office in Fleet Street close to where I work. He must be here somewhere. His firm are managing the PR for Makoni. Dear old Frank. Never misses a good opportunity to get his firm in the limelight. Or his client... Look. Josiah Makoni is about to give his speech. They have microphones and loudspeakers rigged up. This is prime-time television. What I really want is an interview with Makoni but I can't get anywhere near him, Frank manages him so tight. When Frank does you a favour he wants free advertising for his client. My opposition newspapers are right up his bottom."

Livy smiled to herself: the young man was on fire with enthusiasm.

"If you can get us through the crowd after his speech, I'll introduce you to Josiah. On a trip to Rhodesia ten years ago I painted his mother. I gave him the painting. He's made prints of *Princess*. You may have seen a reprint in the newspapers."

"Was *Princess* one of yours, Livy?"

"Yes it was. Artists are often less famous than their paintings." She was smiling.

"Can you really introduce me?"

"We can but try."

At the end of Josiah Makoni's fiery speech it began to rain, a brief, sharp April shower that sent water streaming down Livy's face. The crowd in front of the speaker didn't seem to care as they carried Josiah away on their shoulders, people chanting his name. The second speech by Kenneth Kaunda, equally fiery, picked up on the same theme of kicking the British out of Africa. 'One man one vote' was shouted in unison, Kaunda punching the air with his fist. Next to her, Harry Wakefield was smiling.

"My dad says it will be 'one man one vote once'. When men like that get the taste of power, they don't want to give it up. Hitler could bring a whole stadium to its feet with popular slogans. My godfather, William

Smythe the columnist, quotes Churchill who said democracy is the worst form of government there is except for all the others."

"I've got a chicken slow roasting in the oven," said Beth. "Why don't you join us for Sunday lunch? We're trying to persuade Paul's brother Jeremy to sell his farm and get his money out of Rhodesia. Livy's been living with Jeremy on the farm and wants him to come home."

"I'll give you all the ammunition you want when you get me near Makoni."

Feeling sick in the stomach for Jeremy, Livy listened to another diatribe being blasted over the loudspeakers. Among the crowd was a good sprinkling of Africans, all of them well-dressed. Frank had called twice to see Donna after receiving the note she had left him when she picked up the cat. She could see him among the knot of people surrounding Josiah. As young Harry Wakefield pushed a way for them through the crowd, Frank turned, his face lighting up.

"Hello, Livy, sis. Where's our daughter?"

"At home," said Beth. "With my babysitter. Do you want to come to lunch, Frank? I'm roasting a chicken. Harry Wakefield here wants to interview Josiah."

"Sunday lunch with my sister. Wouldn't miss it for anything. Josiah's finished giving interviews for today. I can give Harry a copy of his speech. How are you, Harry?"

"I'm also coming to lunch."

"Josiah! It's Livy. Do you still have my painting of your mother? Both your mother and father are well. I saw Mario Tuchi and asked after them for you. Sent them your love and said how well you were looking. This is Harry Wakefield of the *Daily Mirror*."

"Is it true, Mr Makoni, you have recently returned from a visit to Moscow?"

"Don't know what you are talking about. Thank you for getting a message to my parents, Mrs St Clair. Excuse me. I have to go."

Josiah looked past Livy, avoiding her eyes. Then he looked back.

"I still have the original painting. My mother smiles at me every day from the wall of my room."

Only then did their eyes meet. His eyes were dark and angry. Livy felt sad for him.

"Why don't you bring Josiah to lunch, Frank?" she said.

"Neither of us will be able to come. I'll see you later. Busy day. And Harry, please don't ask my client questions without checking your facts."

"I did. Every detail."

"What a lot of rot. My client believes in democracy. One man one vote."

"The communists in Russia and China are training Africans in guerrilla warfare. From the British and Portuguese colonies. Ask him."

"My client knows nothing about such nonsense."

"Then what was he doing in Moscow?"

"Please, Harry. You're beginning to annoy me."

"I'll have to take a rain check on that chicken, Beth. More interviews, I'm afraid. Nice talking to you, Frank. You'll read the article on African Nationalism being financed by the communists in my father's article tomorrow in the *Daily Mail*. My report will be brief in the *Mirror*. 'Cold war spreads to Africa' is my headline... My goodness, I do believe it's raining again."

"Let's go back to the car and get out of the rain," said Paul. "I can smell that chicken."

"So can I," said Beth.

When Livy looked round, Frank had left without saying goodbye. Harry Wakefield had disappeared into the crowd.

"What a mess," said Livy. "What a bloody mess."

THAT NIGHT the cat slept on Livy's pillow for the first time, Livy lying awake. Donna was fast asleep in the small bed next to her. The argument in Trafalgar Square was still playing through Livy's mind. Frank and Harry Wakefield not joining them for lunch had left a shadow over the table. All three were thinking of Jeremy. All Livy saw in her mind was Josiah Makoni's eyes telling her more than the man was prepared to say. In another part of her mind she saw Jeremy with the boys on the farm. She began to cry. Silently. Feeling her life slip away. Wanting to be with them so much.

For the rest of the night as she lay awake, she told herself she was going back to Rhodesia. To hell with politics and all the damn politicians. She had a man she now thought she loved who needed her. Two boys who needed her. Out there in the bush she had a family. In the dark of the night she convinced herself the country might survive, that people with mutual interests didn't self-destruct but worked together for the common good. Outside the closed windows Livy could hear the rumble of London's traffic, a safe world, a world that had stayed the same for hundreds of years. Frank came in flashes, mocking her. Frank in all his selfishness from whom she had run away. There was never to be any peace in a life with Frank. On World's View, away from the whole damn world and its nastiness, there was peace and mutual love.

Donna made a noise in her sleep, putting Livy's mind back into turmoil. The studio was too small for both of them. A flat had become vacant in the block she owned with Jeremy. A three-bedroom flat. The cat put its one paw across her face. The cat was purring. She could still keep the studio to paint if she could only make up her mind once and for all what she was going to do. Donna needed her own bedroom. If Jeremy came back to England the flat was perfect for them. The big double room for herself and Jeremy. A room for the boys. A room for Donna. There would never again be a threat in their lives. Jeremy would come home to where he belonged. Josiah would go back to where he came from. The logic was clear.

'To hell with it' she said to herself, and got out of bed. She went to the small kitchen and closed the door. With the light on, she looked in the cupboard and found a half-open bottle of red wine. When the bottle was finished she found the bottle of sherry she used for cooking.

The kitchen door opened, light flooding back into the studio.

"What are you doing, Mummy?"

"Trying to make up my mind."

"Are we going back to Africa? Pussycat is all right but she isn't as fun as the dogs."

"We can't go back, Donna."

"Is Uncle Jeremy coming to England?"

"I hope so, I so really hope so."

"But we won't have the farm and the dogs."

"But we'd have each other."

"Can I have a glass of milk?"

"Come and sit on Mummy's lap."

"Why are you sad?"

"Do you want a piece of buttered toast? I saw Daddy today. I think he's coming to see you tomorrow. If you went to Africa you wouldn't see Daddy."

"I'm going to ask him to take me to the zoo."

"You do that, darling."

"My feet are cold."

"So are mine."

"Can I get into your bed?"

"Don't you want any milk?"

"Not if I can climb into your bed."

Within minutes, with Donna's cold feet between her warm legs, they were both fast asleep in the double bed.

2

―――――

The exhibition took place in June. Frank had been responsible for the publicity. Among the guests, to Livy's surprise, was Harry Wakefield. Josiah Makoni had also been invited to the African Exhibition. Livy was radiant, so many people complimenting her work. All the paintings were up for sale except *World's View*. By three o'clock in the afternoon, four of her canvases had sold, bringing smiles to Jeanne Pétain and James Coghlan's faces.

"Where did you find the giraffe?" said Harry Wakefield. "Did you read my article?"

"And your father's. If what you say is true, the white man in Africa is doomed."

"So is Africa, Livy."

"They won't kick the white man out of South Africa."

"They will in the end. Either by war or attrition."

"After the last barn of tobacco was cured we went back to the Zambezi Valley where it began ten years ago. Where I saw that giraffe browsing the top of a tree close to where we camped. The giraffe took no more notice of the kids than it did of the rest of the animals. There weren't any lions. Only lions scare away the giraffes. I sketched him for over an hour before he ambled off into the bush away from the river.

There were three of them. They watch you from up there with those big eyes as they chew the leaves off the top of the trees."

"He's very handsome."

"Isn't he?"

"You must miss Africa."

"More than you can imagine."

"My father's organising a big write-up for you in the *Daily Mail*. Frank calls it free advertising. He's over there. Frank invited both of us."

"Are you two talking? Last time you and Frank were having an argument."

"Makoni admitted his trips to Moscow when the *Mail* showed him the proof. Said he has friends in Moscow chased out of Rhodesia by the federal government... What a lovely summer's day. We get so few of them in England."

"Do you believe he was visiting friends?"

"Of course not. Unless his friends were undergoing military training."

"I have so many friends in Rhodesia."

"Do them a favour. Tell them to get out. That hill's not going to be worth the climb."

"Jeremy won't sell his farm. He doesn't believe anything bad will happen."

"We all believe what we want to believe. Convince ourselves."

"Do you think black rule is a good idea in Rhodesia?"

"The Americans want it. So do the Russians. They are fighting over who will control those black governments and all the minerals under the ground in Africa. They don't give a damn about the people. They want control of those raw materials. Rhodesia has chrome. There are only two places on earth with meaningful deposits of chrome: Russia and Southern Rhodesia. The mineral is highly strategic in a modern economy. If the Russians can gain a monopoly, the Americans will lose out. What the fight is all about. The likes of Josiah Makoni are pawns according to my father. They are being used by the two world powers fighting for world control. The Russians and Americans don't give a damn who gets hurt in the crossfire. When it all goes pear-shaped they'll blame someone else. Probably the likes of Josiah Makoni."

"Can't we British do something about it?"

"After the Americans made us get out of the Suez we don't have much say anymore. We do what the Yanks tell us to do whether we like it or not. We still haven't paid them back the money we owe them from the First World War, let alone the Second. We'll have to do what we're told. Which is why Southern Rhodesia will not be given independence without everyone in the country having the vote, the way they are offering independence to Northern Rhodesia and Nyasaland. The British mistake was giving the Southern Rhodesians self-rule in 1923. The other two countries in the Central African Federation are protectorates. Southern Rhodesia is a self-governing Crown Colony. That's the snag. That's the bugger up."

"Can we British force the Southern Rhodesian government to have a free election and hand over control?"

"Not physically. Brother fighting against brother won't wash with the British electorate. Financially, with the help of the United Nations, they can force them out of power through sanctions. It'll just take a long time and bring one of the best economies in Africa to its knees."

"Jeremy doesn't get involved in politics. Says he's a farmer."

"Then he should."

"His brother Paul wants to go out to the farm and talk some sense into him."

"Paul should go before it's too late... Come over and meet my father. He's been a newspaper reporter far longer than me. He's head of the Foreign and Commonwealth desk at the *Mail*. Never made editor. He's been out to Rhodesia twice interviewing Sir Roy Welensky, the Federal Prime Minister. Welensky isn't the problem. There's a chap called Ian Smith in the Southern Rhodesian government who's going to cause trouble when the Federation breaks up."

"Poor Jeremy and the boys."

"He's got children? Even more reason for getting out. Those boys will never have a future in Africa. Ask my dad... You're having a splendid exhibition, Livy. Just look at all these people."

DOING THE ROUNDS, a job James Coghlan told Livy was as important as painting pictures, she put away her personal life and concentrated on selling the paintings. For some reason Livy had never understood, the potential buyers were often more interested in her than they were in the paintings. Frank had said it was the 'I know the artist syndrome' giving bored, rich people something to talk about. Having to chat up people she barely knew was a part of her art she loathed. Most of it was all about money, all about whether a 'Livy Johnston' would go up in value making her art a good investment. If nothing else, she owed it to Jeanne and James whose livelihood came largely from selling other artists' work. On the way she found Kim Brigandshaw, the youngest of the Brigandshaw clan and Donna's uncle.

"Hello, Livy. You look agitated. This is Bambi Tate. Frank invited us."

"I'll bet he did, Kim. Is it true you are now on the stage?"

"Sort of. I paint scenery. You don't need talent to paint scenery, just connections. Genevieve has the lead. Have you seen my brother Dorian?"

"Not yet."

"Wonderful exhibition. Hugely successful. Frank is so good at promotions. How's my little niece? Mother and Frank's father were just asking after her. They are over by the drinks table. Mother says art exhibitions bore her, I'm afraid. She thought Donna's mother might need some support. How are they all doing in Rhodesia?"

"Never better. Mario Tuchi has taken your Photographic Safaris to new heights. He's seeing a friend of mine. Jeremy Crookshank has the best crop he's ever grown. Tobacco prices on the auction floors are sky-high."

"A little bird told me you two were getting married."

"Don't listen to little birds, Kim. I presume Beth told you?"

"Might have been. Good luck. You deserve it after Frank. We would love to come and see you both at your studio, wouldn't we, Bambi? Bambi and I are living together. It's the sixties. Bambi wants to be an actress. Given up getting into Cambridge. All that education is boring, isn't it. darling? I'm so glad this is going so well for you, Livy. Have you met Genevieve? She's as much a sensation on the West End stage as she was in Hollywood. But of course you must have met her. She's Frank's cousin, making her Donna's first cousin once removed."

"Help yourselves to drinks. James only buys in the best wines for the

gallery exhibitions. Will you both excuse me? Another old friend of mine
has arrived. So glad you could come. Good luck with the job."

"You'd better say hello to Mother."

Annoyed for some reason she couldn't put her finger on, Livy walked
across to meet Claud Gainsborough, passing Frank on the way.

"Was that one of yours, Frank?"

"Who, my lovely Livy?"

"The bimbo with Kim."

"Her name's Bambi."

"How old is she, for God's sake?"

"Nineteen, I think. She was eighteen when I met her."

"You're incorrigible."

"Can we have supper when this closes?"

"Why not, Frank?"

"What's the matter, Livy?"

"My life's one big bloody mess."

CLAUD GAINSBOROUGH KNEW he was a love-sick fool coming to the
gallery. Tall, thin, pale, bald and turning forty he had made the mistake
of looking in one of the full length mirrors that gave the gallery the
appearance of being much fuller than it was. He had looked at and
appreciated every one of Livy's new paintings, fearing the presence of
Jeremy Crookshank in every one of them. Watching her chat amicably
with her ex-husband had not helped his state of mind, the
consummation of his love for Livy as far away as ever. His dream of home
and family taking him through the life he craved was the same lonely,
distant hope. She was still so beautiful, walking towards him across the
room. All the money he had made lay in the bank with no one to share it
with. His mind's eye could still see Livy on the lake the morning he had
taken Bo for a walk, finding the girl camped in her Kombi on his
mother's land.

"Hello, Claud. How are you? Lovely you could come. What do you
think of my new paintings?"

"They are beautiful, Livy. Every one of them. I could feel the heat and
sense the heartbeat of the animals."

"You always were a flatterer. But thank you. I've been back a while and you didn't come round. Donna was asking after you."

"How is Donna?"

"Growing up. She goes to kindergarten. She's at home in the studio with the babysitter. Four years old. The studio's getting too small."

"There's always my house in Ashtead," said Claud, wanting to kick himself the moment the words were out of his mouth. Her expression immediately changed. Livy went on the defensive as she did whenever he tried to make their friendship more than it was to her.

"Is it nice, Claud? One of these days I'll take Donna and the Kombi into the Surrey countryside and see where you live."

"You do that, Livy. I've got to go. Dinner with a client, I'm afraid. How was Frank?"

"As evasive as ever except when it comes to business."

"When I'm in Chelsea one of these days I'll pop in and see Donna. That tan you got in Africa hasn't faded. Suits you... Well, I'll be off. How many have you sold?"

"Four so far. James is working on another potential client. They have to be convinced they are not wasting their money. So nice of you to pop in, Claud. Good to see you."

"Good to see you, Livy."

"Enjoy your dinner."

"I hope so. Most importantly I hope it will be profitable. There's a surplus of natural rubber in Malaya with all this synthetic stuff the tyre companies are buying. Chap's in a bit of a bind. He'll have to take a thumping loss if he wants me to unload his future options. In my business you can make as much money with the market going down by selling short. Fun and games. Boring. Wish I'd been an artist or a writer. Something worthwhile to show for my life's work. How's Jeremy's farm?"

"That's the trouble. It's too damn beautiful."

"He'd be well advised to get out of Africa from what I read in the newspapers. There's going to be trouble out there. His life may be in danger. Hasn't he got a couple of young boys?... Enjoy the rest of your exhibition."

They looked at each other for a long moment.

"I'm sorry, Claud."

"So am I."

Outside on the pavement of the Portobello Road, Claud stopped to gather himself. There wasn't any dinner with a client. He had sold half a million pounds' worth of natural rubber short first thing in the morning after a meeting with one of his clients.

"You feeling all right, old cock? Why don't you buy your wife a nice antique brooch?"

"It's Claud Gainsborough, Stan. Livy's friend."

"Bugger me. Then you know what's on my barrow is fakes. You should marry that girl. Been in the dumps ever since she got back from her trip to Rhodesia. You on your way home? Just look at it. Place is packed. Exhibition like this and Stan makes a bob or two out here on the pavement. All about feet, so they say. The more feet, the more Stan sells."

"Six-ten from Waterloo. I'll be home in an hour. All on my bloody own."

"Sorry, cock. Women! Once they get over thirty they can never make up their minds. You stick around, Claud. Catch her on the rebound's my advice if you love her. I love my missus. When I met her it was just sex. Now it's something much more permanent. Cheer up. Put on a smile. Best foot forward."

"Thanks, Stan. Now I feel better. Have they sent you out your bottle of wine?"

"Not yet."

"There's Ben Brown through the window. Wave to him."

"They've been good company, me on the pavement all them years. Like my second family."

Leaving Stan looking nostalgically through the closed window into the exhibition, Claud went on his weary way.

KIM BRIGANDSHAW WATCHED them through the window, still not sure what he was doing with his life. He had seen the interplay between Livy and Claud Gainsborough, the pain of rejection in the man's eyes. There had been a time when he too had looked at Livy. He was a drifter, the life of an artist appealing, their ability to make money on the move. Whether Livy was any good he had no idea, his only yardstick the amount of money they paid for her paintings. She sells, she must be good, registering in his mind. By an audience's spontaneous reaction it was easier to judge an actress like Genevieve. Or a pretty girl like Bambi. Living with a teenager was more about his ego than about her. She would move on like the rest of them. For a while they liked his private income, the image left by his father's wealth. Whether the monthly income from the sale of the diamond had done him any good he was never quite sure. It had made him lazy, taking the need to make money clean out of his life. He had enough. He would always have enough. What was the point of making any more? Looking at Claud Gainsborough through the gallery window it didn't look as though money had done Claud any good. Or his brother Frank over there. Frank, with his string of women. Or Dorian with his bestselling books, his only child adopted by some other man. Maybe there was a curse on the Brigandshaw men? It made him sad. Beth and Paul were happy, he hoped. He could see them smiling and laughing, talking to Livy's friend Tessa, the girl Livy had once shared a studio with. At thirty-three, Kim had the nagging feeling life had passed him by.

"Can we go now, Kim? This is boring. Let's go to a jazz club."

"You want to go, I want to go, Bambi. That's what life's all about. Doing something, never being bored."

"Does she really sell these paintings for so much money?"

"Oh, yes. She's famous. Going to be more famous, according to Frank."

"I'll go and say goodbye to Livy for both of us."

"You do that, Bambi."

"What's the matter, Kim?"

"Sometimes life isn't quite what it's meant to be."

"I don't understand."

"Neither do I."

He watched her go, vaguely watching the movement of her bottom through the silk of her dress. It was Sunday night and the theatre was closed. Where he was going to find a jazz club open he had no idea. He just found it easier to agree with people. Maybe they would end up in an Indian restaurant in Soho. To Kim, it was all much the same.

"Livy says the jazz clubs are closed. I forgot it was Sunday."

"Have another of James Coghlan's glasses of French wine. Later, we can wander down to Soho and find ourselves a restaurant. It's not as though either of us have to go to work tomorrow morning."

"Do you think I should get a job?"

"That's for you to decide, Bambi."

"You're so good to me, Kim. When are we going to get married?"

Tina Brigandshaw, the mother of Kim, watched her son from a distance: Kim was tall, good-looking, his blue eyes the colour of cornflower.

"Do you think he's happy, Barnaby? Frank's happy, that's as plain as daylight. Kim, like Frank, picks them young. Do you think she'll go back to Rhodesia? Donna is your only grandchild. Why are art exhibitions so boring? I can't see what they're all about. I would never have come on my own. I mean, if she goes back to Rhodesia we'll only see Donna once in a blue moon. I don't like Africa. Never have done. All those blacks make me feel uncomfortable. There are so many of them. I never did see what Harry saw in Africa... Isn't that Harry Wakefield over there? He was named after Harry. Some story during the war. Where's Dorian? He said he was coming. They never come round to the flat you know. Children! You were lucky just to have Frank. And that wasn't exactly planned. Oh, Barnaby. It's so good to be with you again. I feel like a new woman. To hell with the kids."

"If she goes back to Rhodesia it's her own business."

"Don't you care about Donna?"

"Just a link in the chain, Tina. All we are. It's not as though she's going to inherit the family title. They all have their own lives to lead. Grandparents don't have much say in the matter. Grandchildren are only interested in their grandparents if the grandparents give them money. She'd be a fool to go back to Rhodesia. The place is about to blow up. Powder keg if you ask me, with the Russians supplying the explosive. We're better off without an empire. The colonies are more trouble than they're worth. London will always be the financial capital of the world whatever the Yanks say about New York. So long as the country is making money, the rest doesn't matter... Dorian's arrived. He's outside on the pavement talking to the man with the barrow. I've been watching. That man's making money. All of it's cash. Bet he doesn't pay any taxes. Bit cold out there I suppose in the winter. There's usually a snag in everything if you ask me... Are you going down to Hastings Court next weekend? Frank's organised a weekend party. Didn't you do that in the old days when Harry owned the Court? Or we can go down to Purbeck

Manor and walk along the river. Merlin gets lonely. There's just him and Smithers, Smithers having finally decided to join his master. Merlin says Smithers is the only friend he ever had. Like some old married couple if you ask me. Genevieve has been down a couple of times to see her father but now the show's running she can't get away long enough to drive down. Can't get there and back on a Sunday. What with my brother Robert and his family back in America, the place is empty. His son Richard will inherit the title, which won't do him any good living in America. Can't even use the title. Like the empire, titles aren't worth anything these days."

"We can go down. I love bringing back all our lovely memories of when we were kids."

"So do I."

"Oh, Barnaby, I'm so happy."

"So it's settled. We'll leave Frank to his house party and drive down to Dorset. The countryside is beautiful at this time of year. Give old Merlin the surprise of his life. Arrive unannounced."

"That will be a giggle. Want another glass of wine? Stay just where you are and let Tina fetch you one. Do you remember those picnics as kids? Just the two of us down by the river, you with your fishing rod."

"Don't remember catching anything."

"It didn't matter. We were just happy to be together... Who's that woman with Dorian?"

DORIAN BRIGANDSHAW, never one to miss out on a free drink or the opportunity to impress his publisher, watched his mother walk to the drinks table and receive two glasses of wine from the barman.

"We'd better go in, Alex, and face my family. They're all there. The whole bang shoot of them. Nice talking to you, Stan. Good luck for the rest of the evening. You should do all right when they come out with a few drinks in them. Booze makes people generous. Jeanne has the habit of inviting all the up-and-coming Chelsea artists to her parties. Especially if they're young and pretty. She mingles them with the rich patrons. Frank says the bored rich come for the girls as much as for the paintings. Then they show off by buying a painting for some exorbitant price. They'll buy your jewellery if they come out with one of the girls. Don't you just love Jeanne's French beret, Alex? Jeanne's French though she lived in New York where she met Paul, my brother-in-law. Paul wanted to marry Jeanne. Just shows how it all works out. At one time Jeanne was having an affair with Ben Brown the street artist. They're all so bohemian. You'll love them. How's the publicity going for my new book? *The Prodigal Daughter*. Don't you just love my title?... Hello, Harry. How are you, old boy? This is Alex Wimpleton. Alex, meet Harry Wakefield of the *Daily Mirror*. Why don't you tell Harry all about my new book while I get us a drink and talk to my mother?... Hello, Frank. If you want my publisher's account you should come and talk to Alex... Livy. Lovely to see you. Another big success. Good God, is Kim still with Bambi? I don't believe it... Mother, dear. How are you?"

"Who's that woman you brought?"

"Calm down, Mother. She's my publisher. I haven't started dating women your age."

"How are you, Dorian?"

"I'm just fine. Never been better. Started a new book. *The Prodigal Daughter* will be in bookshops for Christmas."

"What's it all about?"

"A young girl who never knew who her father was until she grew up. Light and fluffy. Alex likes them light and fluffy. Housewives buy them to live with the characters and escape from their boredom. Are you going down to Hastings Court this weekend?"

"No. We're going to Purbeck Manor. Just the two of us."

"I'm happy for you."

"Come and say hello to Barnaby."

"Do you ever miss my father?"

"Of course I do. How old is she?"

"Fifty, Mother, but you wouldn't say so."

"I would. You should find yourself a nice young girl and settle down. I don't know what's happened to the new generation. They just fool around. Look at Kim. That girl's almost young enough to be his daughter."

Collecting his glass of wine with a gin for Alex, Dorian pondered the irony of life. His mother hadn't done badly fooling around producing Frank. Then his eye travelled to Bambi. 'You're a lucky bastard, you old dog' he said to himself, and walked across the room to collect Alex and take her across to his mother.

"Alex, may I introduce you to my mother and an old friend of my family? The Honourable Barnaby St Clair. His elder brother is the current Baron St Clair of Purbeck. The eighteenth Baron, I believe. Very old title. My publisher, Alex Wimpleton."

"How are you, Dorian?" said Barnaby, giving him a stare.

"Just fine... Just fine."

AT THE END of the evening, with six paintings sold, Livy watched Ben Brown water the flower box outside on the pavement before locking the gallery down.

"It's always sad when everyone has gone."

"Aren't you dining out with Frank?"

"You know Frank. Mind like a butterfly... Thanks for everything."

"Have you made up your mind?"

"Of course not. I'm a woman. Goodnight, Ben."

Feeling flat with everything over, Livy drove home. In the studio, Donna and the babysitter were fast asleep.

"You can go home now, Sammy," Livy whispered in the girl's ear.

"What time is it? I must have fallen asleep."

"Half past eight. I've put your money in the envelope."

Drawing the curtains in the bay window, yesterday's canvas still on the easel, Livy followed Sammy out of the studio, gently closing the front door. She smiled at Sammy downstairs when they parted. Donna had been fast asleep, her face angelic. Livy had kissed her brow.

Walking to the river in the twilight, Livy found her favourite wooden bench facing the river and sat down. The light was beginning the long, slow slide into night. It was the summer solstice, the longest day of the year. On the river, a crew of four rowers were powering upstream, the long sleek boat running swiftly through the still water. Everything was long and thin – the boat, the oars and the young men. Children, a few years older than Donna, were playing down by the water, their voices echoing in the still of evening. There was not a breath of wind.

'He won't go out to Rhodesia,' Livy told herself, thinking of Paul. 'Even if he does, he won't change Jeremy's mind. Rhodesia is Jeremy's home. The farm his life. And who knows if we would work anyway? Face reality, Livy Johnston. You're on your own with Donna.'

A few minutes later, with the boat and its crew out of sight, the tears came. Tears of self-pity she couldn't stop. Chasing off halfway around the world just hadn't worked, wherever she had to take herself. Running away never helped. She had her friends. Good friends. She had her painting. A beautiful daughter. What more could she expect out of life?

Count your blessings, Livy she said to herself. Jeremy's boys would survive. If Rhodesia turned into another Congo he would have to come home with only his memories of the farm. Maybe living in the bush wasn't all it was cracked up to be. Carmen had gone on the bottle. Candy had avoided marrying one of the farmers however rich they appeared to be. She would always be able to paint wherever she lived. That was something. Most probably everything. Her art was her true escape from the day-to-day upsets that flowed through her life. Then there was Claud, poor man. Nothing there she could do for him except hope he would find another girl. Frank, the butterfly flitting from one girl to the next, had the answer to life, never staying with one long enough to make himself miserable. She was who she was, not what others could make her. There was still so much. No one she had ever known stayed happy all of the time. The ups and downs were part of it. Part of a life. So when the up was high it was more appreciated.

A boatload of trippers passed downstream, lights flooding the deck in the gloaming, loud, happy voices echoing to Livy from across the water, the booze making them happy. Livy shivered for no particular reason. Part of her mind wanted to shout, 'To hell with it, I'll go back to Africa. Take my chances. Hope life will be better with Jeremy!' Then she thought of the angel asleep in bed and changed her mind.

'You can't have everything. Just bits of it.'

When the booze cruise was out of sight and sound, she got up and walked along the path by the river. A bargeman waved to her. Livy waved back. Then she went home.

The studio with the curtains drawn was dark. Quietly, Livy climbed into the big double bed, drawing the sheets up to her chin. There were chinks of light through the curtains where she hadn't drawn them properly.

"Can I get into your bed, Mummy?"

"I thought you were asleep."

"Has Sammy gone home?"

Pulling back the sheets, Livy let her daughter climb into her bed. Soon after, the cat got onto the pillow next to her face. The cat was purring. Donna snuggled up into the crook of her arm. She was blessed. Her life was perfect. With sweet thoughts in her mind, Livy fell asleep.

~

THE BEST OF TIMES (BOOK NINE)

CONTINUE YOUR JOURNEY WITH THE BRIGANDSHAWS

They chanted. 'Release Mandela'. But for three young individuals, their motives are their own...

During a London Anti-Apartheid march, the *Daily Mirror* reporter Harry meets the impassioned Petronella, a communist activist. Alongside her is Josiah Makoni, a man spearheading his own cause to free his people from colonial Rhodesia. A country threatening to declare unilateral independence from Britain...

Enamoured after his brief encounter, Harry wants more. Why is this woman so intriguing when her political agenda is in direct contrast to her family background? The granddaughter of an English magnate and daughter of a privileged white Rhodesian farmer. Playing with Harry, it becomes clear that Petronella and Josiah are lovers, driving Harry ever more to win her over.

But for Josiah, his desire and passion are for his land. To break free of white oppression. To recruit freedom fighters and take back the power of his country, Zimbabwe. No matter the unthinkable...

The Best of Times is the ninth episode in the Brigandshaw Chronicles. It's the best of times for some, but the start of a bitter war to come.

PRINCIPAL CHARACTERS

~

The Brigandshaws
Harry — Central character of *Treason If You Lose*
Tina — Harry's wife, formerly Tina Pringle
Anthony — Harry and Tina's eldest son, killed in the Second World War
Beth — Harry and Tina's only daughter
Frank — Central character of *Horns of Dilemma* and Tina's illegitimate
son but recognised as Harry's
Dorian — Harry and Tina's second eldest son
Kim — Harry and Tina's youngest son
Emily — Harry's mother who lives on Elephant Walk

The Crookshanks
Paul — Works for Brigandshaw Limited
Beth — Paul's wife and Harry and Tina's daughter
Henry and Deborah — Paul and Beth's children
Jeremy — Paul's younger brother and farmer in Rhodesia
Phillip and Randall — Jeremy's sons

The Oosthuizens

Tinus — Harry's much-loved nephew
Genevieve — Tinus's wife and Merlin St Clair's illegitimate daughter
Barend and Hayley — Tinus and Genevieve's children

The St Clairs
Merlin — Eighteenth Baron of Purbeck, Lord St Clair
Robert — Merlin's younger brother
Barnaby — Youngest son of Lord and Lady St Clair and father of Frank Brigandshaw
Freya — Robert's American wife
Richard and Chuck (Charles) — Robert and Freya's children

Other Principal Characters
Bambi Tate — Kim's girlfriend
Ben Brown — Jeanne's neighbour in Chelsea
Bertie Maple — Jeremy's boss who owns Ashford Park in Rhodesia
Bobby Preston — Learner Assistant on World's End
Candy — A young English girl who is a lodger at Mrs Wade's and Livy's friend
Carmen Crossley — English girl who lodges at Mrs Wade's and Livy's friend
Claud Gainsborough — A businessman who is in love with Livy
Clay Barry — Rhodesian policeman
Colin and Andrew Lavington — Pamela's brothers and Rhodesian farmers
Crispin Dane — Rhodesian farmer onboard the Carnarvon Castle with Livy
Damon Chesson — Photographic interpreter
Flossy Maple — Bertie's arrogant wife
Harry Wakefield — A journalist and son of Horatio Wakefield
James Coghlan — A sculptor who lives in Chelsea
Jeanne Pétain — Owner of the Nouvelle Galerie
Jennifer Crumpshaw — Pamela and Roger's daughter
Josiah Makoni — The only son of Tembo and Princess on Elephant Walk
Livy (Olivia) Johnston — Artist and central character of *Lady Come Home*
Mario Tuchi — Engineer with Lusito Sugars
Mrs Wade — Livy's Rhodesian landlady
Pamela Lavington — Livy's cabinmate on the *Carnarvon Castle*

Petronella Maple — Bertie and Flossy's precocious daughter
Primrose — Nursemaid to Jeremy's children
Roger Crumpshaw — A farmer in Marendallas and Pamela's fiancé
Silas — Jeremy's African house servant
Tessa Handson — Artist and Livy's friend in England

DEAR READER

～

Reviews are the most powerful tools in our kitty when it comes to getting attention for Peter's books. This is where you can come in, as by providing an honest review you will help bring them to the attention of other readers.

If you enjoyed reading *Lady Come Home* and have five minutes to spare, we would really appreciate a review (it can be as short as you like). Your help in spreading the word and keeping Peter's work alive is gratefully received.

Please post your review on the retailer site where you purchased this book.

Thank you so much.
Heather Stretch (Peter's daughter)

ACKNOWLEDGMENTS

~

With grateful thanks to our *VIP First Readers* for reading *Lady Come Home* prior to its official launch date. They have been fabulous in picking up errors and typos helping us to ensure that your own reading experience of *Lady Come Home* has been the best possible. Their time and commitment is particularly appreciated.

Hilary Jenkins (South Africa)
Derek Tippell (Portugal)
Marcellé Archer (South Africa)

Thank you.
Kamba Publishing

Made in the USA
Columbia, SC
30 March 2024

33839486R00271